PATH OF
THE SUN

PATH OF THE SUN

AL DEMPSEY

A Tom Doherty Associates Book
New York

This is a work of fiction. All the characters and events portrayed in this book are fictitious, and any resemblance to real people or events is purely coincidental.

PATH OF THE SUN

DEC 1 '92

Copyright © 1993 by Al Dempsey

All rights reserved, including the right to reproduce this book, or portions thereof, in any form.

This book is printed on acid-free paper.

A Tor Book
Published by Tom Doherty Associates, Inc.
175 Fifth Avenue
New York, N.Y. 10010

Tor® is a registered trademark of Tom Doherty Associates, Inc.

Library of Congress Cataloging-in-Publication Data

Dempsey, Al.
    Path of the sun / Al Dempsey.
        p.   cm.
    ISBN 0-312-85403-X
    1. Hill, James Jerome, 1838–1916—Fiction. 2. Great Northern Railway (U.S.)—History—Fiction. I. Title.
PS3554.E493P38   1993
813'.54—dc20   92-28384
                                                                          CIP

First edition: January 1993

Dedicated to
Nancy and Harold Enebo

What Europe is to Asia, what England is to the rest of Europe, what America is to Europe and England, that the Western States and Territories are to the Atlantic States. The heat and pressure and hurry of life, always growing, is that following the path of the sun.

—From a speech before Congress, 15 February 1889
by Congressman Samuel Sullivan Cox
New York City, New York

►◆◆◆◆◆◄

PROLOGUE

It was just after noon on June 10, 1775. Thomas Jefferson had spent most of the morning trying to convince a dozen men to stay with the revolt against King George III. Many in the colonies were beginning to weaken in their resolve, and many in Delaware in particular. Thus Jefferson had come to the Dover home of merchant George Read and had used his considerable skills in speech to state his case. The battle against the British was going well: in March, there had been a spirited convention in Virginia where Patrick Henry had delivered his "Give me liberty or give me death!"; in April, the Minutemen of Massachusetts had effected a stunning victory at Lexington; in May, Ethan Allen had captured Fort Ticonderoga; and Colonel George Washington had begun mustering and training a considerable force in New York. But Jefferson's pleas this morning had been resisted. Nine had left the meeting before lunch, saying they would only continue down the avenue of rebellion if the king transgressed more directly against the interests of Delaware.

Only George Read, Caesar Rodney, and Thomas Mac-Kean remained strongly for the cause.

Elisa Read had lived up to her reputation of setting an excellent table; the mutton was well prepared, the fresh vegetables from her garden especially tasty. "Let's talk of something else," George Read offered. "As your host, I feel there is too much tension at our table."

Jefferson realized that Read was embarrassed. "George is right!" Turning to the man on his right, he said, "MacKean, what do your hear from your people?"

Tom MacKean was a lumber dealer in Delaware City who had been fostering a plan to dig a canal from the Delaware River to the Elk River at the northern tip of the Chesapeake Bay, in an effort to help commerce with Maryland and Virginia. Jefferson had supported the idea and had invested his political support and his money. For the next several minutes, the conversation took a temper of excitement; all of those in Read's house were infected with the vast potential of the colonies. As Mrs. Read was seeing to the serving of a magnificent rhubarb pie, Caesar Rodney, who had a minor interest in the canal project, observed, "If this canal works out, Mister Jefferson, maybe you will join us in the Western Adventure."

Jefferson eyed the slice of pie in front of him. "The canal is going to work, Mister Rodney. Of course I am committed to the Western Adventure. I will become involved very soon."

The Western Adventure! Expansion into the vast land beyond the frontier. Colonel Washington had been to the edge of the wilderness as a surveyor; he had shared his experiences with Jefferson several times at their estates in Virginia. Jefferson made no secrets of his two dreams: to launch the colonies on the path to self-government, and to see that government expand the holdings of land and riches. The term *Manifest Destiny* had found an indelible niche in his mind.

Jefferson had taken the first, bitter bite of the pie. "Mrs. Read, I must beg you to write up your cook's recipe for me to take back to Monticello."

Elisa Read graciously agreed. Jefferson then said to the others, "Once our people can see the treasures out to the west, they will give us a mandate to acquire what we can; I intend to see that the will of the people shall be followed."

Thomas MacKean offered, "One of my wood buyers has just arrived back from the Kentucky Territory, and he claims there's Indians who talk of water running all the way from the Pacific into the Mississippi River."

Jefferson smiled. "I've heard those same reports. What a splendid discovery that would be, eh?"

Read questioned, "Where would the water be coming from to fill a river like the Mississippi?"

"There's no telling," Jefferson admitted. "But, my friend, I intend to find out, somehow, someday."

To the west lay a gigantic land, but no one knew the size. Four years earlier, Vitus Bering had discovered the land called Alaska. Each new trip of exploration was revealing an image greater than the last. But there were problems with any dream of westward expansion. The French had lost Canada to the British in 1763, during the French and Indian War, but the French still claimed title to the vast swath of unmeasured land called Louisiana, which reached from the western Gulf of Mexico past the Mississippi River, northwest to the Pacific Ocean. The southwest, from what would come to be called Texas to northern California, was ruled by the King of Spain.

As Jefferson washed down the last bite of pie with a glass of cool milk, he repeated, "I intend to find out."

It would not be until Jefferson became president of the United States in 1801 that he would be able to bring his dynamic personality to bear on the search for a way to the Pacific. In 1803, he dispatched James Monroe to France to deal with Napoleon, to try to buy New Orleans and the western tip of the Florida panhandle. The price Jefferson was willing to pay was set at ten million dollars. When France offered the whole of the Louisiana Territory for eleven million dollars, Jefferson accepted gleefully. Even before the transfer of title was formally completed, Jefferson sent his friend Captain Meriwether Lewis, along with William Clark, on an expedition that would justify Jefferson's faith in the greatness of the West. Lewis and Clark traveled west, inventoried the assets, and found a route to the Pacific. It was not a navigable water route they found, but they had confirmed Jefferson's belief; travel to the Pacific was possible.

Before Jefferson left office in 1809, he had set in motion a multitude of programs that, by their sheer weight, could never, would never be halted. The man who dreamed of breaking through the frontier lived to see citizens of the United States living in the Oregon Territory, raising families in the land of the Great Northwest.

▶◆◀

Spring showed its presence on the afternoon of May 10, 1869; at least she showed up well in Promontory, Utah Territory. The day was warm; a slight breeze made the sunlight less burdensome. There was an hour and a half to go before the ceremony would begin; tens of thousands of spectators had been making their way up to the rugged point where the Union Pacific Railroad, which had constructed 1,086 miles of track from Omaha, would be wedded to the Central Pacific Railroad, which had built 690 miles of railroad from Sacramento.

Wu Chuang stood in front of an oak table, on which rested a velvet-lined box holding the Golden Spike. "It is a fitting symbol," he said.

Fu Hsun, standing next to Chuang, replied, "It is good." He paused, then repeated, "It is good."

Both men were wearing long black coats over black silk jackets and loose white trousers, white socks, and shining black slippers. Chuang wore a brown derby hat. Hsun was bareheaded.

Gruffly, they were told, "Only a couple of minutes now, boys, you know that."

The speaker was a uniformed Pinkerton guard who stood off to the side of the table. Chuang looked up, offered a polite smile, and nodded.

"You Chinks know how to talk English?" the guard asked, then added, "You know: You fella talkee Engrish?"

Chuang held his smile, nodded, and replied, "We talkee okay, you bet. We just be a few minutes."

The guard laughed.

Chuang moved slightly, brushed his shoulder against Hsun to remind his companion, Say nothing.

Chuang was worried; Hsun had been with the forward division work crew for only three weeks, and that was not long enough for most Chinese workers to learn to control their tempers. Chuang had worked on the construction job for a year and a half; he knew how to handle arrogant white bosses, and the Pinkerton guard was an insignificant toad who presented less difficulty.

Chuang looked back down at the Golden Spike.

For the previous month, conversation among most of the Central Pacific Railroad workers had centered on the spike. Chuang had heard many jokes told about how best to steal the spike as soon as the ceremonies were over; he hoped they had been only jokes. The spike weighed a mere nine ounces, less than a hundred dollars in bullion value, and Chuang had taken up a collection from his fellow Chinese workers, amassing a $120 fund to pay the white workers not to steal the spike once it had been driven. He had been filled with anxiety by the appearance of fifteen white workers stating their willingness to take the money in exchange for not stealing the spike; each of the whites wanted the whole $120. Chuang had a difficult time understanding the humor and irreverence demonstrated by the white workers in the forward division construction crew.

He concentrated on the spike.

To Wu Chuang, the soft yellow glow of the metal was a warm monument to friends who were no longer suffering the trials of living away from China: the hundreds who had died from accidents, disease, or loneliness. Work on the Central Pacific construction had been demanding; many had been lost, too many. Much had happened since the construction began in January of 1863; Chuang had been told tales of the days before he had arrived. Some of the stories were near impossible to believe, but the elders, the ones who first worked for the Central

Pacific, those men were truthful. There were five Chinese laborers left from the initial fifty who were hired. Chuang was always elated when he was told how Charles Crocker began using Chinese workers. Crocker had been a successful drygoods merchant when he formed a partnership with wholesale grocer Leland Stanford and two hardware-store owners, Mark Hopkins and Collis Huntington. All were situated in Sacramento; all had been beguiled by Theodore Dehone Judah's dream of a transcontinental railroad. Crocker, a burly 250-pounder who assumed responsibility for supervising the initial construction, first hired several hundred peons from Mexico. When that venture did not work, he employed fifty Chinese laborers left over from the Gold Rush of 1849. The coolies swiftly proved their mettle and, before construction was completed, more than fourteen hundred had worked at laying ties and rails as well as building roadbeds and drilling tunnels. Wu Chuang felt a great pride in them; the Golden Spike in front of him was a fitting symbol.

The guard said, "You Chinks done?"

Fu Hsun spoke a grotesque obscenity in Cantonese dialect. The guard demanded, "What the hell'd he say?"

Chuang, softly, asked, "You do not understand?"

"I ain't no Chink lover, boy."

"His words were merely an expression of truth. Words of his own that paint a fine picture, a picture I wish I could describe to you, Mister Guard."

"Ain't that a crock. You two had better git."

Chuang smiled. "Ah, you are so right, sir; it is a crock."

The guard grunted, annoyed that the Chinaman did not even know when he was being insulted. "Now, you two just git. You've been here long enough."

"But, sir, we were told we had a full ten minutes; it has been less than five."

The guard pulled out his billy club and took a step toward Chuang.

Chuang reached out to hold Fu Hsun from charging at the guard. A voice spoke from behind them: "You let them be."

Chuang knew the source but could not turn away from the threat of the billy club. The voice spoke again. "These men have the right to be here; it is with my authority."

The man speaking was General Grenville M. Dodge, the man who had directed the westward building of the Union Pacific. General Dodge came forward. "Mister, you put that nightstick of yours away, and you get the hell out of here until these men are done with their visit."

"They might steal the spike; I'm paid to protect it."

"I'm doing the paying. Now, get out of here."

For an instant, the guard balked. He knew the face of General Dodge, but the guard had been assigned by his Pinkerton boss; he was tempted to challenge Dodge. Seeing the glare in Dodge's eyes, the guard yielded and walked to the front of the tent.

To Chuang, General Dodge said, "Take your time, Mister Chuang."

Chuang smiled his thanks. Then Dodge asked, "Who is your friend? I haven't seen him before."

Chuang made a polite bow and announced, "This is Fu Hsun, newly come to the honorable work crew of the Central Pacific Railroad Company. He is also a cousin of my wife; coming with me to view this treasure will make him very important man with the rest of the workers."

Face. Dodge smiled at the thought; the Chinese were so involved with that thing they called face. "Well, you take your time. That guard will not bother you again." Dodge paused for a moment. His Union Pacific crews had been a diverse collection of European immigrants, mostly Irishmen. The Chinese workers of the Central Pacific had consistently outdistanced the Irish, and that had cost Dodge some bonus dollars. He had a great respect for the Central Pacific crews; like Chuang, few of the men weighed over 110 pounds, but they were strong in muscle and will.

"You take your time, Chuang." With that, Dodge left.

Fu Hsun demanded, "Who was that?"

Chuang explained, then added, "I had the honor to speak

with him two weeks ago. When I was taken to The Meeting."

Fu Hsun did not have to have that explained; The Meeting had become famous. Chuang had gone representing the forward division construction crew; he had been allowed to say little at The Meeting, but his presence there gave great pride to the Chinese labor faction.

The Meeting had taken place in Salt Lake City, its purpose to establish where the Union Pacific would join up with the Central Pacific. The original mandate from Congress had vested the Union Pacific with building west from Nebraska to the California state line; the Central Pacific was to build east from Sacramento to the same place. But the Central Pacific construction had sped forward much faster than anyone had anticipated, so the Central Pacific was allowed to continue building eastward. There was a great deal of money at stake. The Congress had authorized varying payments for construction costs, ranging from sixteen thousand dollars per mile to forty-eight thousand dollars per mile, with the added bonus of alternating sections of land (a section being 640 acres defined in one-square-mile blocks) up to ten miles on each side of the right-of-way. The more each railroad built, the more it received. The problem was, no one had had the foresight to tell the competing crews where to join up the two lines. In early April, the crews had approached each other; one swung north, the other swung south, and they overlapped the lines by four miles.

The Meeting was held in order to settle the question. After long debate, a spot six miles east of Promontory, Utah Territory, was agreed upon. Chuang and the others at The Meeting felt that they had been part of the negotiations, but the real compromise had been worked out in the cloakrooms of the Senate and House of Representatives in Washington; the monies involved were too vast to be delegated to the people who did the job. It was during a recess that General Dodge had met and talked with Chuang; the introduction had been made by Charles Crocker. It was Crocker who had groomed Chuang as a work leader, coming to rely on his skills; the Chinese worker's abilities had led in part to the Central Pacific gaining an additional 423 miles of grant money and land.

Chuang pointed to the Golden Spike and said to Fu Hsun, "You must relish this moment, cousin. It will become a memory which you will be expected to relate in great detail to your generations."

Outside the tent, General Dodge had walked thirty feet to where the delegation from the Union Pacific construction crews waited for their allotted visit; Dodge kept a sharp eye on the guard to ensure that Chuang was not disturbed again.

The Union Pacific delegates numbered eight. The majority of the group, five Irishmen who served as section bosses, knew better than to complain about having to wait for the Chinese. But one of the Norwegians said, "By golly, dem Chinks is in dere a long time. That's the truth."

Dodge's withering glance silenced him.

Mallory, the chief foreman, asked mischievously, "Will you be needing a couple of me boys to be doing the hitting, General?"

"No, Sean, the honors are going to Mister Stanford and Mister Durant."

"I hope Durant whacks the hell out of that spike."

The other Irishmen laughed. They had put wagers on who would hit the spike first; none of the workers had much faith in the ability of the company bigwigs to do any actual work. The fact was that most of the workers for the Union Pacific had little faith in any of the management, excepting General Dodge, and with good reason. The management had caused a scandal that had nearly caused the nation to give up the idea of a transcontinental railroad.

The Union Pacific directors had established a separate corporation, named Credit Mobilier, to purchase supplies and subcontract work for the Union Pacific to friendly businesses. The directors also made themselves shareholders in Credit Mobilier. The mess came to light when a Union Pacific manager quit in protest: the estimated cost for the first hundred miles of construction was thirty thousand dollars, while the actual final costs were doubled. The manager also exposed the process by which equipment and supplies were purchased at exorbitantly inflated prices by the dummy corporation. What followed was the first real financial scandal to rock the nation.

The Central Pacific owners had their own financial device for milking the corporation of congressional monies; it was called the Contract and Finance Company, based in Sacramento. Crocker, Stanford, Huntington, and Hopkins were more discreet, or more devious, because their skimming never drew wide criticism; each eventually left an estate in the tens of millions of dollars.

But General Dodge, even though he was close to the Credit Mobilier operations, had managed to keep an untarnished image; he was the man who got the job done, and his construction crews loved him.

"Yes, boys, it'll be for the bigwigs to do the spike driving today." There was laughter. Dodge added, "But I want a couple of you to stay handy with your spike drivers; the bigwigs might need some help."

At that moment Wu Chuang and Fu Hsun came out of the tent; the pair approached General Dodge and the Union Pacific delegation cautiously. Over the past couple of weeks, when the crews had been passing each other in the rush for added construction miles, there had been active, dangerous harassment. Boulders rolled in one direction, dynamite was tossed in the other direction. There had even been a few shootings; miraculously, only mild injuries had resulted.

"Thank you, General."

"You earned it, Wu."

"We will go get the final rail, if that is proper."

"You bet, Wu."

As soon as the two Chinamen were out of earshot, Mallory asked, "Would you mind telling me what all that is about, General?"

"Not at all, my friend. We are letting the Central Pacific crew set the last tie in place." The sparks of tension were immediate.

Quickly, he told them, "The thing the Chinamen don't know is that YOU boys are going to set the last *rail* in place. How about that, now?"

The Union Pacific men knew that the last rail was going to have to be placed on the Central Pacific side of the juncture; the Union Pacific rail was already in place. The fact that they would be trespassing onto Central Pacific property carried with it a wicked form of gratification. Smiles appeared. Before the mood could turn brittle again, General Dodge said, "Now, you boys get on over there and take a look at the spike."

Mallory looked at his chums. "The general knows how to take care of us, fellows."

Dodge said, "Don't you go telling them Chinks about the last rail. That's our secret."

At that moment, the Central Pacific's 4-4-0, *Reno,* was pulling out of the town of Promontory, six miles to the west. On her cowcatcher was a carefully varnished railroad tie carved from a log of clear laurel. The transcontinental railroad was coming to completion.

At precisely 1:15, the ceremonies began. The commemorative tie had been set in place, the final rail laid and spiked except for the final Golden Spike. It is doubtful if even 10 percent of the thousands attending saw or heard much of what was done and said. Speeches were the order of the day, and the speeches were many, all praising the workers and managers of the two railroads.

The Union Pacific's 4-4-0, *Number 119,* was brought into position just eleven feet from the Central Pacific's *Reno.* Workmen climbed onto every available space on the locomotives, bottles of champagne and whiskey were waved, and Central Pacific President Leland Stanford picked up his spike driver. Union Pacific's vice president, Thomas Durant, took his in hand, and the two men assumed the appropriate positions. If not many in the crowd could see the event, the whole nation was tied to the event with telegraph lines attached to the rail, waiting for the moment when the blows would be transmitted. Predictably, Stanford and Durant both missed on their first strikes, but they finally hit. The cheers of the vast crowd shattered the air. America was connected by rail.

◆◆◆◆◆

CHAPTER 1

Zachary Horton climbed down from the cab before the horse had completely stopped moving.

The cabbie snapped, "Hell, man, wait till I stop!"

Zack laughed. "How much, cabbie?"

The horse was fully reined in. "You gave me a scare, sir."

"How much?"

"Seventy-five cents."

Zack handed up a dollar as he accepted his small valise. The cabbie said, "I could take you the whole way, mister. It's pretty hot to be walking, very hot for May."

"I like walking."

Zack stepped up onto the sidewalk as the cabbie, shaking his head at the way the younger generation was acting in this year of grace 1888, swung his hansom cab into a U-turn on Old York Road, heading the horse back toward downtown Philadelphia.

Traffic on Old York Road was busier than Zack remembered. Wagons were heading back north to the dairy and truck farms of Montgomery County after their morning market deliveries downtown. From the other direction rumbled goods vans loaded with building materials for the countless housing and commercial projects of the city.

Zack watched the cab merge easily into the traffic, then began walking the half block to home.

Home. It was a part of his daily thoughts, yet he had not come here in over a year, even for the Christmas holidays. He was walking the last few yards partly as a penance, partly to retune his thoughts to the place where his personality and attitudes had been formed.

The mansion was a splendid-looking building: three stories tall, granite walls, intricate dormer windows, and the delicate gingerbread trim that was the mark of Victorian architecture. The Boynton Mansion sat on two acres of landscaped, manicured gardens. Spring had produced its annual splash of color in the flowers; Zack smiled, recalling the hours he had spent with the gardeners who tended the beds of petunias, crocuses, tulips, and roses. The roses. He could hear Grandfather Boynton's voice: *Remember, Zack, wild roses are beautiful in their power to survive, but these, our garden roses, are beautiful for their beauty*. "Oh, Grandpa, I wish you were still here."

Zack had startled himself with the thoughts and his voiced words. A year later, and it was still hard to acknowledge that Grandfather Boynton was gone.

He turned into the curved driveway, walking up the slight incline to the front entrance. Back behind the house, he saw Grandmother Boynton, clipping furiously at the purple lilac bush to the south of the carriage house.

He paused and smiled. She was so small: only five feet tall, weighing barely over ninety pounds. He never remembered her hair color being anything other than the white that now showed under the wide brim of a straw hat. She wore a simple calico dress—He smiled thinking the dress probably cost her fifteen dollars or more at Strawbridges—and a white apron. Her white calf work gloves matched her white calf, high-button shoes. Grandmother Boynton was the strict standard by which Zack had come to judge the way women dressed; many young ladies who did not meet the mark had wondered why the handsome man had not bothered to call again. But then, they did not know about Grandmother Boynton.

He lowered the valise to the gravel of the driveway. "Grandma Letta. I'm home."

"Come give me a hand."

He grinned, then laughed. No syrupy fuss from this woman! It was her way of letting him know that he had never really been away, never been far from her thoughts.

He approached, making no effort to hug her or even touch her hand in greeting; affection, to her, came through the mind.

"Pull that branch down, Zachary."

He knew which branch: the one that had had the audacity to strike out from the gentle shape of the bush. Ever since he had grown taller than she, one of his duties had been to aid her in quelling branches and blooms that tried to exert their independence. Of his twenty-five years of life, fourteen had been spent tugging things within the range of her pruning shears and clippers, he thought now, grinning. How much time, how very much time he had spent in this magnificent garden.

"You were not due until this evening, Zachary." She snipped, and the branch ended its rebellion.

"I was able to get away early."

"How could *la Madame de Pompadour* allow you to deny her the extra moments of joy?" Not waiting for a reply, she pointed upward and ordered, "Grab that fellow."

Another errant branch was to be made to conform.

Four months before, on January 25, Grandmother Boynton had come to Zack's apartment in New York City. It was the forty-seventh anniversary of her marriage to Clifford Boynton, and she did not want to be alone in their home, not on that day. It happened that Zack's paramour at that time was the estranged wife of the French general consul in New York; Grandmother Boynton had killed the affair. The most telling wound had come when, during a luncheon at Luchow's, Grandmother Boynton had observed, *Zack always has had a penchant for older women,*

Pauline. Smiles, from that moment onward, had been only marginally civil.

"She's gone from the picture, Grandma Letta. Gone for good."

Loretta Boynton never gloated over such trivial victories; she walked a few steps back to study her handiwork.

Zack laughed silently. He knew she was glad to hear that he had abandoned the Frenchwoman; he guessed she would be elated to know that there was no current involvement in his life. He wanted to please his grandmother, needed to make her happy, as happy as she had made him during his early years. She was, at sixty-five, still a beautiful woman. He had been told she had had golden hair in her youth, just the same blondness his own hair showed. He had inherited her grey eyes, just as he had been told that his mother had grey eyes. He had never known his mother or his father. James Horton had been killed in 1862 during the battle at Shiloh. Zack's mother, Mildred Boynton Horton, had died three months later giving birth to Zack who had been raised by Clifford and Loretta Boynton.

"Enough pruning for today," Grandmother Boynton announced.

They left the pile of clippings on the ground, to be removed within minutes by the yardman who was assigned to keep an eye on the mistress but not to interfere with her work. The head gardener had learned as a youth that the Boyntons were outstanding employers but did not appreciate hired hands who presumed to do all of the manual labor; the Boynton family liked working in their gardens.

Zack retrieved his valise as his grandmother headed across the back lawn toward the far side of the mansion, past the large fountain and fish pond. Zack knew what was next: a refreshing encounter with tangy, chilled lemonade. It was good to be home.

In the shaded comfort of the north porch, the crystal pitcher showed yellow from a half-dozen lemons, two tall glasses waited, and a plate of sugar cookies was in place. Nothing had changed: his favorite snack, instantly baked and ready for him.

He should have known better than to sit down. "Zachary, you might think about going to your room, dressing more comfortably, and saying hello to cook, before you settle yourself." Another smile came to his tanned face. As long as he could remember, Grandmother Boynton had couched her orders in the form of contemplative suggestions.

His room was the one just above the north porch. When he had begun to experience the challenge of exploration—at about age eleven—Grandfather Boynton had installed a heavy lattice near his window with the alleged purpose of cultivating a climbing plant, but the plant was never planted and the lattice provided a convenient and safe way for him to slip out on a dark night to wade in the fish pond.

"It is not wise even to think about that, Zachary."

He had been eyeing the shortcut up to his room. He savored her talent for being able to anticipate nearly anything that came to his mind. He took his bag and went through the house to the kitchen where he was hugged by Yutta, the rotund German woman who had been the Boynton cook for all of his memory. She gave him a small plate of cookies, "to keep in your room for tonight," and he went up to his bedroom.

So many memories. There was the small, silver Tiffany frame containing miniature oil portraits of his father and mother. It stood on the yellowing runner on the chest of drawers; the runner had been crocheted by his mother. There was the framed medal awarded to his father for gallantry, the athletic trophy Zack had won in high school, and the gold watch his grandfather had given him upon his graduation from Villanova; the watch had not been wound since Zack put it on the chest of drawers on the day Grandfather Boynton had been buried.

Zack undressed, tossing his traveling clothes onto various pieces of furniture—Gwendoline, the upstairs maid, would not be pleased if Zack was tidy. In the bathroom—the Boynton Mansion was one of the first in Philadelphia to have bathrooms designed into the plan of the house—he doused himself with water, wiped away the grime of the railroad ride from New York, gave a quick pass of the brush through his hair, and dressed in a pair of soft canvas trousers, workmen's pants, really, but very comfortable, and a fresh, bleached white cotton shirt.

After a quick glance in the mirror showed that he looked presentable, he was ready. Out the window, onto the shingles of the porch roof, then down the lattice, to end up on the polished wood of the porch railing.

"You had to do that, didn't you, Zachary?"

"You knew I would."

"I knew you would." There was her smile. Warm and loving. "Come," she said, "you might like some of this." And she poured him a glass of lemonade.

He slouched on the soft cushion of a white wicker armchair and tasted the drink. The memories kept spilling into his mind. Times with his grandparents, times with his friends, even his first kiss, which had been stolen from a third cousin, Joyce, on the afternoon of his fourteenth birthday. So many incidents in his life pivoted around this porch and the taste of lemonade. But, as fond as the recollections were, they were, it seemed, in a distant past, at a time no longer to be lived, or even desired. New York had been exhilarating; his developing knowledge, skills, and feelings for high finance were making him respected. But New York was to fade in his life soon, joining home in fond memory, and he was pleased.

"Did cook give you cookies to take to your room?"

"Yes."

"Oh dear. We have been having trouble with ants upstairs."

"I ate them."

"That is good."

"I mean, I ate the ants," he teased. "They were delicious."

She chuckled. "It is nice you enjoyed them."

He took a long drink of lemonade, then accepted a refill. As she placed the pitcher on the table, she said, "Zachary, I'm pleased at your attitude about leaving New York; I know your activities mean a great deal to you. When I wrote to you, it was one of the more difficult things I've ever had to do. Lord, I wrote that letter in three or four different ways; nothing seemed to set forward what I wanted without making it sound as if you had some sort of . . ." She reached for a word. ". . . some sort of obligation. I didn't want you to accommodate me out of a sense of obligation."

He nodded his understanding. "Actually, I'm looking forward to seeing just what the other side of the business world's all about. My investments are doing well. It's time I learned about how businesses operate, not just how they make money."

"The activities of business are what make the money, Zachary; there's no income without activity."

He told her, "I bought some shares in a brass and bronze foundry in Connecticut, and the owner asked me to come up and see his factory; it was fascinating."

"Your grandfather started out his working life in a foundry."

"I know; but," he added with some regret, "I never saw that. I've a better idea now."

She looked at her grandson with fondness. "I'm very proud of what you've done while living in New York."

He waited.

"Grandfather Boynton was also pleased, Zachary."

"I always felt I'd disappointed him."

"Disappointed? Yes. But he was pleased. He wished for you to work more closely with him, but he knew that you had to get out on your own; he knew that, Zachary."

At age seventeen, Clifford Boynton had gotten out on his own and had gone to work in the wheel foundry of the Baldwin Locomotive Works on Spring Garden Street in Philadelphia. His job had been menial, the cleaning of casting molds, but he had caught the attention of Matthias Baldwin. In only a few years Clifford Boynton had moved up through the engineering section of the company into the sales division. He was friendly and curious, a natural for selling. By the time Zack graduated from college, Clifford Boynton had left the Baldwin Company for his own ventures. Although an opening was there for him, Zack had no interest in joining the Boynton enterprises. Instead, Zack had taken his five-thousand-dollar inheritance from his parents and, in one year, expanded its value to twenty thousand dollars; that had pleased his grandfather. The old gentleman had repeatedly invited Zack to join him; Zack had rejected each proposal politely. Zack was enjoying the challenge of the financial mecca of the nation. The dramatic success of his first year as an investor was not repeated, but he was doing well. Then Clifford Boynton had been accidentally killed while supervising the installation of the electric trolley-car system in Richmond, Virginia. The death had had an emotionally devastating effect on Zack; only the strong will and gentle wisdom of Grandmother Boynton had kept Zack going. She had recognized that Zack had felt guilty about not being more attentive, about not yielding to his grandfather's wishes.

She said now, "If your grandfather were still alive, he'd be elated about your agreeing to consider giving some help to Mister Hill. Delbert really does not wish to leave at this time."

The Mister Hill she referred to was railroad mogul James Jerome Hill of Saint Paul, Minnesota; Delbert was Delbert Cummins, the manager of the Boynton family railroad, the Dakota and Western.

She added, "As I told you in the letter, our Delbert has decided to join the ranks of matrimony." She let a hint of a grin slip onto her lips.

"That was great news. I never thought it could happen. Who's the lady? You didn't mention that."

"I don't know all that much about her. Actually, I first heard about it from Mister Hill. That was one of the reasons Delbert gave for not wanting to take on an obligation other than the Dakota and Western."

Zack ran an impatient hand through his hair. "That devil! What's her name? . . . Where's she live?"

She cut him off; she was now wearing a pleased smile. "Be patient. I know little or nothing about the details. Delbert must have guessed that Mister Hill was going to spill the beans. A letter arrived a few days ago. . . ."

"I'm kind of looking forward to seeing Del out in the Wild West." Zack mimicked what he took to be a cowboy accent.

"You'll be seeing Del right here, tonight. The train from Washington is due in an hour. He's come back so that we can have a talk together about this Hill matter. I want to make sure that it's the best for you." She paused. She wanted desperately not to act in a way that would become oppressive for Zack, but she could not help wanting to protect him. "Let's wait and listen to what Delbert has to say."

Del's visit was good news to Zack. Zack had never gone out to see the Dakota and Western, which had been built by his grandfather and which was both lucrative and easily managed. Its 262 miles of line ran south in Dakota Territory from Dickinson to Buffalo, then west to Ashland in Montana Territory. Freight was the main revenue producer: wheat and cattle, mainly. The passenger traffic was mostly connected with farming or ranching.

The Dakota and Western was, for all practical purposes, a feeder line to the Northern Pacific Railroad, but Clifford Boynton had remained fiercely independent of Northern Pacific influence and had refused to involve himself in the rate fixing and gouging that had been carried on by other railroads. His customers trusted him because they paid a fair price for good service.

Zack's grandmother poured herself another portion of lemonade; she drank, put down her glass, walked over to him, and placed her hands on his shoulders. "This'll be good for you, young man. I wish your grandfather was here to see this; it was a thing he really wanted. He wanted you involved in all of the Boynton enterprises."

Zack laughed. "That, I don't think I could handle, Grandma."

The coquette showed on her face again. "We'll see about that, my boy; we will see about that." She returned to her seat. "Delbert's been in Washington on some matter concerning Congress setting rates." She finished off her glass of lemonade, then stood. "Before he arrives, I'll finish my yard work." She reached for her gloves. "Didn't Delbert write anything to you about his romance? I'd have thought he'd have confided in you."

"Not a word. I'd have told you."

"I know. It is strange."

"The only thing I've heard from Del was about the Storm."

She pulled on her gloves. "The Storm was a horror."

The Storm was the Great Blizzard of 1888 in which over four hundred souls went to their reward, mostly from the bitter cold but many from being caught in heavy snows. The entire nation had been crippled for five days.

"Well," Grandmother Boynton said, "we'll hear more in a little while. You have an adventure in front of you."

Zack looked out over the gardens. Absently, he said, "Maybe I'll drop in on some of the neighbors."

She laughed. "Dot Martz still lives at home. I think she'll pine for you forever."

"Quit kidding me, Grandma."

"Seriously. I believe that pretty young thing will become a spinster if you don't marry her."

"There is no marriage for Dot and me."

"She claims you promised her."

"Gawd, Grandma! We were eight years old."

His grandmother grinned, picked up her bonnet from the chair, and went back into her garden.

Casual dress was allowed at Grandmother Boynton's dinner table when guests were absent. Zack had bathed and changed into a seersucker suit; his grandmother wore a summery shantung dress. Del Cummins had arrived in a dark business suit but had doffed the coat and tie; his sleeves were rolled up for comfort in the warmth of the evening.

The meal had been light: cold sliced lamb with fresh garden vegetables. The dessert they were enjoying was a tangy sherbet made in accordance with a secret family recipe. Del Cummins had, years before, been able to get the formula, but Zack, no matter how he tried, had not been made privy to the secret. "I keep telling you, my dear grandson, when you settle down with a wife and home of your own, then you will be granted several of my culinary treasures."

Zack looked across the white linen tablecloth at Del Cummins. "Would you share the secret with me?"

Del shook his head.

"Don't try that," his grandmother scolded. "You embarrass Del, and you challenge loyalty in the extreme, Zachary."

"I really should have it, as a tie with home."

Grandmother Boynton enjoyed a final spoonful of the sherbet. "Nonsense."

Zack looked across at Cummins, a tall, sturdy Irishman. "You'll give it to me, won't you, Del?"

Cummins raised a large, gnarled hand to his face—the hand of a man once used to physical labor. There was a slight sound as he rubbed his chin; his red beard was as tough and curly as his sparse hair and dense eyebrows. The face had a few small scars from fights and accidents, but it was his eyes that made him a man people trusted; they announced a gentle soul within. "You want me to give it to you?"

"Will you?"

"You bet."

Zack looked at his grandmother. She showed no dismay at the apparent treachery. Cummins added, "I'll have it engraved on a silver plate for your wedding present."

Grandmother Boynton grinned. She made sure Zack and Del had had their fill, folded her napkin, and stood. "We can have our coffee in the library."

The library was one of those rooms in Victorian houses that could be a success or a failure. The thing that made the Boynton library a success was that the volumes on the shelves were there for enjoyment, not decoration. Zack once calculated he had read about six hundred of the thousand books; casual reading was not a universal pastime in the era, but in this house literary exploration had been encouraged.

The room was rich in dark colors: deeply stained wall paneling, bold emerald drapes and carpets, and darkly tanned leather furniture. The evening sun picked up color accents from the bindings of the books, and a painting over the fireplace showed a pastoral scene with a railway train barely discernible on the distant horizon as it puffed through autumn twilight. Grandfather Boynton's deep, soft armchair was left vacant. Zack sat on a mahogany bench by the window, and Del and Grandmother Boynton were seated on the sofa in front of the heavy, carved-oak coffee table. She poured as she said, "Delbert, we must now hear about the mysterious lady who has entered your life."

He smiled at her.

"We've a right to know," she declared with the hint of laughter in her voice.

Zack asked. "Del, are you afraid we'll tell her the truth about you?"

Mrs. Boynton dispensed the appropriate amounts of sugar and milk to the coffee.

Del gave a sheepish look as he accepted his cup. "It started during the Storm, Loretta. I got hit by a rough storm and a wonderful lady, both at the same time."

Zack said, "You wrote me about the blizzard, but you didn't mention the romance."

"I thought it could wait till we were together."

"There's no need for apology, Delbert."

"It's not really an apology, Loretta, it's more like needing to tell you in person."

"I understand." She handed a cup to Zack.

"Well," Del began, "the snow began on Saturday afternoon. About two or three o'clock."

"It hit New York early Sunday night," Zack said.

Del continued. "We're used to spring storms out there; not unusual for a dump of snow on Easter. But about eleven o'clock, the night manager sent a boy to my house; there'd been a message from the station in Buffalo that the evening train was snowed in, trapped on the bridge on the west bank of the Little Missouri, right at Camp Crook."

Zack nodded. "When the storm got to us, Del, trains in and out of New York were halted. The Astor House turned away three hundred people who were stuck in the city; four friends who live in Westport had to stay with me overnight."

Grandmother Boynton offered, "I read where a woman froze to death at Broadway and Fulton Street."

Zack said, "They call it the busiest intersection in the world, but she was simply buried under six feet of snow. They didn't find her until three days later, frozen."

Del sipped his coffee. "It was bad all over; we lost a few folks, too. The wind was clocked out there at seventy-five miles an hour. Drifts were the worst thing; that's how the train got trapped."

The memory of that March night was frozen in his mind's eye, just as clear as his memory of hearing that President Lincoln had been shot to death; everyone remembered where he was when he heard the news. Del wanted to share the experience with these two friends. He had dressed quickly and gone to the railroad main offices with the messenger boy; he had not wanted the child out alone again because the Dakota and Western headquarters town of Dickinson was being blasted with the killer storm. When Del arrived at the office, the men on duty told him that there were two cars loaded with cattle and one passenger car with eighteen people, plus the train crew of eight. The men had taken the initiative and set in motion the steps needed to get the rescue train ready. By midnight, the rescue was on its way, Del riding in the locomotive cab. The going was slow, seldom more than twenty-five or thirty miles per hour, because the wind was whipping piles of snow onto the tracks; drifts were building dangerously fast. It was dawn when they arrived at the bridge; in minutes the work crew was out, across the icy span as they planned how to dig out the trapped train. It was treacherous even getting across the bridge; they nearly lost one man, who was blown off balance but managed to hold onto the railing until two other men pulled him back onto the walkway. The problem was obvious: the snow had to be dug out of the way. The crews set to the task, and Del went to see how his customers were faring in the passenger car.

"That was when I met Felicity."

"Felicity. What a splendid name, Delbert."

Del grinned. "A splendid woman, too, Loretta."

He finished his cup of coffee and placed it on the table. While she refilled it, he continued. "There was so much confusion, so much danger with those people on our train; I was really concerned. The temperature was reading eighteen degrees below, unusual for a storm with heavy snow, and the snow was still coming down by the ton."

Zack accepted a refill of coffee from his grandmother. "That storm was a mystery to everyone. High winds, heavy snow, deep-cold temperatures; and it hit the whole country."

Grandmother Boynton added, "It hit the whole world, from what I've read of it; Europe was also devastated. Several hundred killed there, too."

Del smiled proudly, "Well, we didn't lose anyone on our train . . . thanks to Felicity." The look on his face pleased his audience; he was obviously enraptured. "Talk about a woman who can take charge. While the crew was doing what they could to free the train, she realized they might be stuck for a long time. She made her way to the baggage and freight car and found some tinned meat and a case of tea that was being shipped to a store in Ashland. She hauled some back to the passenger car, then sent one of the men to the caboose to get a kettle and some pots. By the time we arrived to save them, everyone was in pretty good shape. Felicity had not only organized warm food and drink, she had worked out a schedule for the male passengers' digging. She really helped out the Dakota and Western."

Zack teased, "Sounds like she did more than that by getting you thinking about marriage and all."

Grandmother Boynton beamed. "Why, Delbert Cummins, you have finally fallen in love."

Cummins was blushing. He rubbed his hand over his face and said, "I do guess you could call it that; but I sort of think that word is for young people."

"Nonsense, Delbert Cummins, sheer nonsense."

Zack asked, "Who is she? Where does this wonder come from?"

"She's a widow living in Bismarck; her husband was killed in a machine accident a while back. I had met him. Nice man."

Grandmother Boynton said, "That poor woman. I know what she's gone through. Does she have children, Delbert?"

"No, Loretta, no kids. She's only twenty-four; her husband was an engineer and salesman for McCormick Harvester. He shipped with us; a good customer. But I'd never met her until the Storm." Then, he said to Zack, "Her name's Felicity Patterson."

Mrs. Boynton said, "Felicity Cummins . . . has a nice ring to it."

Del said, "That's why I don't want to leave Dakota Territory. She and I have hit it off and she's become a real Dakotan. Even though she's from right here."

Grandmother Boynton asked, "Oh? What's her family name?"

"Clark. They're from Willow Grove."

"From Willow Grove! Good heavens, I've met her mother. I had no idea she had a daughter out in Dakota Territory."

Del smiled. "I don't really know if her mother talks that much about Felicity; marrying a plough dealer was not what her mother had in mind when she sent her daughter to Swarthmore."

"Stuffy types, I gather," Zack said.

"I guess so. I've never met them."

Grandmother Boynton said, "Well, never you mind. You marry this young lady and we'll not be stuffy."

"When?" Zack asked.

"Soon," Del said. "We'll be married out there." He added, "It's sort of become home to me . . . to us."

Grandmother Boynton announced, "That then puts an end to Mister Hill's other request."

Zack asked, "What was that?"

"Loretta, didn't you have a chance to tell Zack about the other development?"

"No." She paused. "Zachary, this is the situation. You

know that Mr. Hill asked for Del to take some time away from the railroad and help him on the statehood issue. Del felt he could not be away and Mr. Hill came back asking for you, and you know I'd like to see you do it. You'd be returning an old favor Mr. Hill once did for your grandfather. But now something new has come up: James Hill has made us an offer on the Dakota and Western."

Zack was surprised. He had never thought of selling the Dakota and Western. As an heir to his grandfather, he had inherited a 20 percent block of stock. Earlier, Grandfather Boynton had given Del Cummins 10 percent; the remainder was owned by his grandmother. He asked both of them, "Is there a reason we should want to sell?"

"Not any pressing reason," she said, "but Mister Hill says he has a reason to want to buy. I believe it's really just his desire to control as much railroad property as possible."

Del interjected, "Hill has a dream, Zack, and it's not a bad dream: to own all of the railroads in the Northwest."

Sitting back, with her coffee cup held on her lap, Grandmother Boynton said, "Unless you gentlemen have some other desire, I think the Hill offer should be rejected. Del wants to make his home out there, and he is the best person to run the railroad."

Zack went to the coffee table and waited while his grandmother refilled his cup, then walked back to the window and looked out into the darkening shadows cast by the setting sun. "I don't understand." He turned back to face the room. "If Hill is so god-awful intent on being the railroad monarch, and he has so much power, why the devil does he need somebody like me to help him out? I don't understand."

She nodded. "It'd be understandable if Hill *was* the railroad king, but he's not. Besides, there's more to it than that. Come, sit down."

Zack sat in the comfortable rocking chair that was normally hers. "Zachary, the major wish your grandfather had for you was that you would join the enterprises he had built. If he'd not been taken from us, he'd be conducting this conversation. He felt proud of the way you went off to New York to make a mark all your own. But he always hoped that you would find your way back to work with him, to learn the reality of business. He spoke of this dozens of times to me. More coffee?" Zack shook his head.

She looked at Del. Del accepted. "You learned to drink a lot of coffee out west."

After she had poured for Del and herself, she gave a warm grin. "Now don't go getting all serious on me, child."

Zack forced a smile.

"I'd be willing to sell the Dakota and Western to Mister Hill; that's not the problem. What I'd originally wanted was for you to take on the responsibility of managing that operation. Now that has changed; Delbert has the right to benefit from the work he's done by being out where he and Felicity want to begin their life together. I believe you learned a great deal from Grandfather Boynton. I desperately wanted to see you extending his skills into your life." She hesitated, and it seemed as if she might begin to cry, but she pulled herself back under control. "The whole thing was a selfish desire on my part. I wanted to see you doing what your grandfather wanted you to be doing. That would've made me a very happy person." She paused and looked at the men. "It would seem as if Grandfather Boynton did nearly all he intended to do in his life. Seeing you in the family businesses is the only task he didn't accomplish." She added, "We were blessed, in a way. After your mother was born, I was told that there'd be no more children. Then we were blessed with the responsibility of loving and caring for you. You became another child for us, and you became the son that I was never able to give to Grandfather Boynton."

These were not new thoughts to Zack Horton; each one had come to his mind at some time or another.

She sipped the last of her coffee. "There's one other aspect of this whole thing." She watched to make sure he was paying attention. "I do not want you accommodating Mister Hill's request to make an old lady happy; that is not my purpose. I want you to do it because you feel that the time is right take on

something which would be of interest to your grandfather. It'll
not be easy for you. There's a great deal for you to learn about
the world, Zachary; not everyone will be as concerned about
you as your family. You won't be an employee of Mister Hill's,
but you are repaying a favor, and you may find he is a firm
taskmaster." She reached over and patted him on his knee. "But
then, you're not looking for things to be easy in your life, are
you?"

He smiled. "Believe me, Grandma Letta, I'm looking forward to this move. I think it'll be a challenge."

She smiled back. "I know you will do a good job, Zachary;
I've great confidence in you."

Before he could reply, she stood, walked to the window,
and looked out at the evening. "Gentlemen, we'll talk about this
at breakfast." She turned. "I want a few moments alone with my
memories. Please leave me for a few minutes before I go to bed.
I will see you both in the morning."

Zack stood and gave her a good-night hug. She looked at
Del and said, "I am sincerely overjoyed at the news of your
marriage. There is little in life that could have given me more
pleasure."

"Thank you, Loretta."

Del had a broad smile on his face as he and Zack left the
library and went downstairs to Zack's favorite room in the
Boynton house—the game room, with its elaborate ship mod-
els, a table for chess and backgammon, a heavy mahogany card
table, and, Zack's favorite, a massive, carved-oak billiards table.

Del went to the billiards table and began setting the balls for
play; Zack picked his favorite cue from the rack on the wall.

As he busied himself, Del said, "You grandmother's seeing
this Hill thing as important."

"She thinks your marriage is pretty damned good, too."

"Aw, hell, Zack, that's not what she's thinking about; it's
you and what you're going to be doing."

"Repaying the favor?"

"Come on, you know better than that. Your grandpa
would've had you right in the middle of Hill's doings."

"Would it have been that important to our railroad?"

"Not on your life. It would have been important because it would've moved you out into another part of the world; things are tough out there. Your grandpa'd want you to know that."

Since Zack at ten had begun shooting billiards, Del Cummins had always allowed him to go first. Without discussion, Zack leaned over and began the game. He ran three shots before missing; Del began.

They exchanged three turns before either spoke. Watching Del make a good run, Zack said, "Tell me about this Hill situation. Seems like it might be interesting."

"You're right about that. I met with him a couple of weeks ago. I'll tell you, Zack, that man is determined to build an empire out in the northern part of this country."

Zack replied, "From what I understand, he's got a pretty good start on that right now."

Zack had met James Hill once in New York, at a social reception. Zack had come away with a good impression of Hill, but nothing spectacular. Hill seemed to be like many contemporary moguls: intense, dedicated, and determined.

Del said, "There is one thing that Hill's working on full bore right now, Zack. That's what he wants you to get involved in."

"What's that?"

"He wants to bring some of the northern tier territories into statehood."

"So?"

Del took careful aim on a particularly difficult combination shot. He stroked the cue softly. "So, my friend, he is enlisting the assistance of every business he knows to help with the cause."

"That includes the Dakota and Western?"

"Exactly."

"Del, where the hell do I come in? I've never been involved with the railroad."

"No, but you're one of the owners."

"Come on; I have some shares, that's all!"

"But your grandpa did more than that. The Boynton name is a hell of a good name in Dakota, believe me."

"My name's not Boynton. The people out there can't think much of a guy named Horton."

Del made another, easier shot. "Don't sell those frontier people short, Zack. They know you're a Boynton, and the Boynton name is currency every place the Dakota and Western serves." He looked up. "And a lot of other places in the territory, too."

Zack chalked his cue. "Explain something, Del: why the hell should I care if some Wild West territories become states? How can it affect our railroad?"

Del straightened up from studying his next shot. "According to Hill, everyone doing business in the territories is hurt by the way the territorial governments are run. I've seen it myself, Zack: a lot of bums who get appointed to jobs through political connections."

"Politics. I hate politics."

"Who doesn't, except the politicians? But it's a way of life for the Dakota and Western. I was in Washington yesterday and this morning, just trying to get a small piece of right-of-way so we can make a switching yard in Ashland. Those Washington bureaucrats can make things tough for an honest businessman."

"Bribery?"

"I can't go for that, Zack. Your grandfather would do his best to play the political game, but he'd never cross the line of bribery; nor will I."

"What about Hill?"

"I don't think so. He'll use all the political influence that he can muster, but he's straight as an arrow. You may not know it, but he built his entire railroad without land grants or financial compensation from the government. He's the only railroad builder who did that; quite an accomplishment."

Zack had lost interest in the billiards. He put his cue back in the rack and sat on the edge of the table. "Del, the land grants are going to be a problem. I've heard in New York that there'll be investigations, and some people could lose their shirts."

"The investigations have started, Zack. Some of the developers have been abusing their title to land-grant property. People are getting angry, and angry voters get the attention of congressmen."

"As I said, I hate politics."

"Well, you're going to have to learn a lot about them because Hill's depending on us to pitch in just like everyone else. He's lined up one or two individuals from each of the territories. Your grandmother told you he tried to hire me away?"

Zack nodded.

Del went on. "He couldn't have done it, even if I hadn't gotten involved with Felicity. Even if he had talked your grandmother into selling, I wouldn't have worked for him. I'd probably have gone into ranching; Felicity and I kind of like the idea of running cattle."

Zack laughed. "You're a city boy."

"Not anymore; neither is she." With an exaggerated accent, he said, "We're gone western, pardner."

Zack went and picked up his cue again. Back at the table he lined up a shot.

"It's not your turn."

Zack grinned and said, "I give up, you win, I'm just practicing." As he made his shot, he said, "Are we meeting him in Dickinson?"

"Nope. First Chicago, then to Saint Paul. Hill lives in Saint Paul."

Zack looked up. He saw a worried grimace on Del's face. "Why Chicago?"

Del responded, "I'll tell you in the morning."

"Now."

After a pause, Del said, "Well, Hill wants us to meet with a gal named Leah Page . . ." Del let the rest of the sentence hang in the air.

Zack said, "And?"

Quickly, Del blurted out, "She's a nice lady, Zack, really. A nice looker, bright . . ." He searched for the next words. ". . . sure bright, you can bet on that, she's in business, too. Just like us."

"What's her involvement? Politics, too?" The "too" came out as caustically as Zack could make it.

"Sort of."

"What 'sort of'?"

Del was taking much too long to decide which ball to play. Zack's voice returned to an amiable tone. "Come on, Del, level with me."

Del pulled himself up erect. "Well, my friend, James Hill's enlisted the assistance of Leah Page to try to muster the support of women in this statehood issue."

"So? Why was it so hard for you to say that?"

"Well . . ." Del was laboring; Zack waited patiently. "Well, Zack, you see, Leah Page is pretty influential with the national suffrage movement."

The noise of Zack's pool cue hitting the table shattered the normal quiet of the game room. "Delbert Cummins, just what the hell have you gotten me into?"

Del looked sheepish. "You haven't called me 'Delbert' in a hundred years."

"Don't beg the question."

"It's just that Hill wants us all to work together. She's from Washington Territory; her family's still living out there. But he feels the suffrage people in Dakota Territory can be of help, that's all."

Zack paced around the table; he was facing too many new matters for comfort. "I can just see her: horsey face, figure like a cow, voice like a teamster. Dresses in those silly white and purple shrouds."

"I told you she was attractive and bright and . . ."

"You told me all of that. And I'm wondering if you were completely honest."

"Aw, Zack, how could you suggest I'd mislead you?"

Zack stopped pacing and perched on the table. "Del, you've

gotten me into this project. That's good, and for a good reason. I want you to have the best marriage that anyone ever had in this whole world. But I'll be hanged if I can see where you have to dump me into the muddy slime of politics, then add insult to injury by making me associate with one of those suffrage horses."

"They're not all that bad."

"The ones I've seen marching down Fifth Avenue are that bad."

"Leah Page is different. Remember, I told you she is in business; doing damned fine at it, too."

"She's not one of those jolly-hockey-stick females?"

"Would I be lying to you about something as important as this?"

"I hope not; we have always been on the square." Zack paused, looking at his friend. "She is attractive?"

"She is that. I've never seen you shy away from a good-looking woman."

"Is she going to Saint Paul?"

Del nodded. "The last I heard, Hill was sending down his private car for us to use from Chicago to Saint Paul."

Zack froze. "Hold it, Del Cummins. This all sounds a bit much for just getting us to give a little help. Hill seems to be going pretty far to hook us in."

"It just shows how serious this is to him. He's doing all he can to get what he wants; that's his style."

"And this Leah Page, where does she fit?"

"I told you. Hill thinks she can do some good with the suffrage movement."

"And she's not a horse-face?"

"You wait and see."

After a silent minute, Zack said, "Let's go see if there is anything sweet in the kitchen; cook usually leaves me something."

"You're not angry?"

"Not now," Zack answered, "but you're in serious trouble if we get out there and I have to listen to some screeching woman. Serious trouble!"

CHAPTER 2

Leah Page lifted the pendant watch and saw it was 2:17. She had about an hour before her next meeting.

The man across the table asked, "Am I keeping you, Leah?"

She smiled and shook her head. "No, Sam, never. I enjoy you too much."

Samuel Gompers grinned; he wanted people to like him. "You flatter an old man." His black walrus moustache moved as the grin turned into a smile. "But please don't stop . . . ever."

"Sam, you're not, definitely not, an old man. How old are you?"

"Thirty-eight."

"That's not old, for goodness' sake."

"Sitting at a table with a pretty young woman makes me feel old."

"Who's doing the flattering?"

He chuckled. Now it was he who looked at his watch. "Good heavens, I'd no idea. We've been here two hours!"

Their waiter came up to the table. "Would you like a fresh decanter of coffee, Miss Page?"

"Yes, Max. Thank you; that would be nice."

The waiter was a tall, skinny, gangly man, balding early; his German accent was masked slightly with an obvious effort.

Gompers knew that the waiter knew who Gompers was. Just about all workingmen knew the stocky frame and the bushy black hair of the man who was head, and one of the founders, of the American Federation of Labor. Still, the waiter was being pointedly obsequious to Leah. Gompers wondered if the waiter knew Gompers was in Chicago to meet with Bill Pomeroy from the Hotel and Restaurant Employees' Union. A good many German immigrants worked as waiters; most of them were organized into the union. Gompers had helped Pomeroy negotiate a work agreement with this hotel, the Palmer House, but now Pomeroy was mismanaging the union's affairs. One thing Gompers and the AFL did not need was problems with one of the biggest unions in one of the biggest cities in the nation.

The waiter said, again to Leah, "Chef's made some fresh petit fours for dinner this evening. Would you like some?"

Leah smiled at the waiter. "No, Max; that is very kind." She looked at Gompers. "What about you, Sam?"

"I am not a man to turn down sweets." He looked up at Max. "Please, that would be nice."

The instant of hesitation let Gompers know that the waiter would serve the treat only because of Leah Page. That was all right with Gompers; he liked the way she had earned respect. Part of his pleasure with Leah Page was that she had signed a work agreement for her small leather-goods plant in Baltimore. She was a responsible business owner and operator.

He noticed her looking out the window by their table. The view from the mezzanine Tea Room in the Palmer House was being more and more obstructed as the skyline of Chicago changed.

Leah had mixed emotions about the signs of progress. The growth was an indication that jobs were being created and that poverty might be lessened. But the construction also indicated that more and more people were coming to Chicago, already too crowded, and that influx tended to generate more poverty. Looking down at the intersection of Monroe and State streets, at the mass of humanity moving in slow waves, had a chilling effect on her; most of those in her sight had a relative who was ill or a child who was undernourished or a parent approaching despair. Immigration had its blessings, but it also had its costs.

Still gazing down at the street, she asked, "Is it good or is it bad, Sam?"

"Do you mean the people or the building?"

"I mean the flood of people. What was it last year: three . . . four hundred thousand?"

"Over half a million."

"How can it keep up?"

Gompers laughed. "I imagine that was being said when my parents brought me here. I think it'll keep up for a long time. The way industry is going, we need people."

Leah turned back to look at him. "But we're also cramming the cities. Housing is poor, food is limited, health is endangered."

He nodded. "And working conditions are obscene."

"You know that better than anyone, don't you?"

"I see some pretty awful situations, Leah."

Leah remembered back when she had first met Samuel Gompers. Two years previously, he had come to her plant near the Baltimore Harbor, where she made fine leather products for ladies' high-quality stores. A month before, she had sent for the police to expel a union agitator who had been rude to her. Then Gompers arrived: polite, gentle, understandable. On that first visit, he had pointed out some bad conditions she had allowed to develop, things such as her stock people piling crates in front of fire exits. It was not that she had planned those things. It was just that bad habits seemed to evolve into normal work patterns. On that first visit, she had agreed to permit the Boot and Shoe International Union to represent her employees, even though she made no shoes or boots—her workers did manufacture leather products. Leah had consistently paid a premium wage, and most of her employees were women; she was not about to abuse the trust her women placed in her. Besides, even with reasonable wages and an improved workshop, her profits were considerable.

"You saw a mess in my plant, Sam."

He gave a laugh, deep and sonorous, like his voice. "Leah, your plant was a palace compared to some places I've been in. Someday I'll take you into the tenement sweatshops where they roll cigars."

Gompers had made her the same offer several times in the past; he had started life as a cigar maker, and his labor foundation was in the Cigarmakers International.

He remembered. "I've said that before, haven't I?"

The waiter arrived with the new pot of coffee. He set a plate of petit fours in front of Gompers.

"Thank you, Max."

"Will there be anything else, Miss Page?"

She looked at Gompers, who was lifting one of the sweets to his mouth. He smiled. She said, "No, Max, that'll be all. Could I have the check?"

Max left the table.

Gompers chewed quickly, swallowed, and said, "This luncheon is on me, Leah."

"Not today, Sam."

"But I insist."

Leah was not going to let Gompers pay. She knew that the president of the American Federation of Labor received less than five dollars a day salary. From that, he was expected to take care of most of his necessary business expenses, and, amazingly, take care of his wife, Sophie, and their half-dozen children.

She warmed the tepid coffee in her cup and watched Gompers devour his sweets. "Sam." He looked up. "Please don't stop. You know James Hill has recruited me to do what I can to help get Washington Territory admitted as a state." He nodded and took another petit four. "Am I right in helping him? I like the man, but I so often suspect motives."

Gompers swallowed, lifted his napkin, wiped the icing

from his moustache, and picked up his cigar. "Leah, this state-hood thing is political. I've refused to let the Federation get involved. Some of our people would bury us in politics, but labor has no role in that arena."

"Mister Hill feels it's important for the eight or nine territories."

"Sure he does. The man has financial resources, he has power. He's frightened to death that the railroads'll be taken over by the government. The Grangers and the Knights of Labor are in favor of that. Hill probably can prevent such a thing if he's able to influence the congressmen and senators who'll be elected from the new states."

"Is he wrong?"

"I think the railroads should be a national property; just like the telegraphs. Those utilities are too important to be run by men like Hill."

"You don't like him?"

"I don't know the man, Leah. I understand that he's a personable chap, that he's reasonable as an employer, that he pays as well as anyone. I just don't trust anyone who controls as many lives as he does. It frightens me."

Leah laughed. "You sound like one of those Socialists."

He puffed deeply on his cigar. "Don't, my dear. Do not get me started on that issue."

"I thought all of you labor men were Socialists."

He slid his emptied plate to the side and put his elbows on the tablecloth. "Some of my early shopmates were zealous Socialists of the Marxian school. They were as high-minded a group of idealists as could be found, working hard to establish trade unions. But far outnumbering these stalwarts are the many kinds of Socialists who have tried to undermine trade unionism in order to get votes for The Party. You must know that, Leah."

She said, "I have little use for most of them."

"According to my experience, professional Socialism accompanies instability of judgment caused by an inability to recognize facts. The conspicuous Socialists have uniformly been men whose minds have been warped by a great failure, or men who found it absolutely impossible to understand the fundamentals necessary for practical plans for industrial betterment."

"But Sam, that conflicts with your wanting to have the railroads owned by the nation. Industrial development has come from men executing practical plans. Government's role has been minor."

"But now there are abuses by business."

"Sam, be realistic. There are abuses by your unions, too."

He raised his hands. "I don't mean to offend a capitalist like you."

She laughed.

"Honestly, Leah, I know you're right, just as you know I'm right. You asked me about Jim Hill; he's one of the businessmen I don't trust.

"What about the statehood issue?"

"I want to see it. That territory must be bigger than Europe. It's got to be part of the nation. Surely, the idea of local people running their own government is good."

"What about labor out there?"

He thought for a moment. "Montana, Idaho, Washington, all have strong organizations. The rest are mostly agriculture or cattle."

"Would you give me the names of some who could help?"

He gave her a wry grin. "Your father could help you in— Where is it your parents live?"

"In Olympia, you know that!"

Gompers also knew that her father, who was in the timber business, was hostile toward unions. She smiled at Gompers for toying with her. "You're wicked."

"Just ask your father."

"Stop it!" It came out with a soft hiss. "You're always teasing me."

They both laughed.

"Seriously," she said, "I need some names, or at least one name."

"For you, or for James Hill?"

"Does it make a difference?"

"It does. The price will be more for Hill."

She pursed her lips. Gompers toyed with the small tuft of hair that he grew as a beard below his lower lip. "I do enjoy teasing you."

Leah came close to withdrawing her request. The man across the table from her had found a warm spot in her heart; he was honest to a fault, and he cared about people. She suddenly was feeling guilty about using her friendship for the benefit of James Hill.

Samuel Gompers had spent his adult life dealing with people. He found joy in them, and he had become a student of human emotions. The look he saw on Leah's pretty face told him he had challenged her too hard. He traced a finger around the pattern on the linen tablecloth as he said, "There's one man I can think of who can be of help to you." He gave a mock smirk. "And to James Hill."

She opened her mouth to cut him off.

He raised a finger to stop her. "Now, Leah, let me finish. The man's name is Jim Cavanaugh. He represents the Federation in the northern part of the West. He came into labor out of the mines."

She nodded and guiltily tried to block what he was saying.

"I'll write to him," Gompers offered. "You can depend on anything he tells you."

He reached into his jacket and pulled out a small notepad, tore off a sheet, and wrote the name and address for her.

As he slid the paper across the table, she said, "Sam, I'd just as soon . . ."

"Enough of this, my friend. I know you wouldn't be in league with James Hill if you didn't have good reasons." He reached over and patted her hand. "You contact Cavanaugh; he'll help you out."

She was not yet convinced in her own mind that she would use the information. "Sam, I believe that James Hill has the interest of the West in his heart."

"I find it hard to believe that any man who's made millions of dollars has any other than selfish interests."

"You're a cynic; I never knew that about you."

He grinned. "I fear I must leave your fine company, young lady." He stood up. "I've got to go back into the cruel world of reality. This has been good for me."

She rose and offered him a hug with a peck on the cheek. "It's been good for me, too."

"I'll be in Baltimore in a couple of weeks. Will you let me repay the luncheon then?"

She responded, "If I'm there, we will have lunch at Hausner's."

His eyes widened. "Now that's an imperative. Let me know how you make out with Jim Cavanaugh."

"I'll do that."

With a courtly bow, he turned and left her alone. As Gompers exited, the waiter Max came over to her, carrying the check on a small tray. She frequently met with business associates or friends in the Tea Room; she liked the understated decor and the friendly staff. Just a month previously, she had sat at this very table for a productive private hour with Susan B. Anthony, who was trying to induce Leah to attend the National Woman Suffrage Association annual meeting in Washington. Leah had had to refuse due to the demands of her own business, but the two friends had accomplished quite a bit toward involving other businesswomen in the association.

Max asked, "Will there be anything else, Miss Page?"

"Yes, Max, please. I'd like more coffee; I'm expecting someone in . . ." She looked at her watch. ". . . in twenty minutes."

Max showed confusion and was upset with himself; he was trying so hard to master this new language.

She was sitting back down as she saw his face. "Oh, Max, I'm sorry. I only asked for the check because I was afraid Mister Gompers would try to pay. I should've told you before."

He looked relieved. "I'll clean this table and bring you a fresh pot. Thank you, miss." As he cleared away Gompers' plate and cup, she picked up her portfolio from beside her chair and began studying the facts and figures of her company.

Business was going well for her. She had been brazen to
enter a business that was so strongly controlled by men, but she
had intentionally started very small, and by the time she had
made a reputation for quality and dependability, she was too big
for her competitors to stop. Her technique had been simple. She
had targeted only one ladies'-wear shop in each big city in the
East and Midwest. After one fashion season, she had expanded
to more stores in each city. Soon word of her product reached
the department stores, and she was ready to supply the demand.
Her male competitors were unable to best her price and quality;
she was grudgingly accepted into the industry.

The accounts showed her that she could be making a great
deal more money from her concern. The fact that she hired
mostly women, and paid them a wage equal to that of the men
working for other leather-goods companies, was more of an
affront to her competitors than her success in business. But—she
smiled—their attempt at forming a boycott by her clients had
failed; her clients' customers were women. She looked out the
window again.

The crowds were still moving along the streets below. She
wished there was more she could do to make their lives easier;
maybe she'd find a way.

She brought her eyes back to the ledger sheets.

A couple of minutes had elapsed when she sensed that she
was being watched. She looked up: a tall, blond man was standing about five feet off to her right.

"Miss Page?"

She nodded. He approached and extended a hand. "I'm
Zack Horton."

As she responded with a handshake, he added, "Sorry I'm
late. The train was delayed in Gary. I don't like to be late."

She smiled. "Those things happen. Sit down and have
some coffee; or would you like tea . . . or something else?" Max
had glided back.

"Coffee's fine."

Max went off and returned with a fresh coffee cup, then
left.

She looked back toward the entrance. "I don't see Mister Cummins."

"He had to go to Pittsburgh."

She looked concerned. She asked, "Do you take cream?"

"Yes, please. And some sugar."

"One lump or two?"

"One would be fine."

"I'm disappointed. Mister Cummins promised he'd be with you."

"He promised me the same thing, but there was some last-minute trouble with rails he had ordered. He should be here this evening. He sent his apologies."

"He's a nice man. It was a pleasure to talk with him."

Leah arranged the coffee in front of Zack and busied herself for a few moments putting away her papers.

Zack looked over the rim of the cup as he drank some of the coffee. Del had been right; she was attractive. Leah Page was wearing a dark green nainsook skirt and jacket with a white ruffled broadcloth shirt. Her blond hair was neatly set in soft waves; it looked easy to maintain. Her lips were well formed, her nose was small, and her eyes were a soft, almost iridescent hazel. From what he could calculate, she seemed to have an appealing figure, not plump, but not skinny, either. He guessed she would stand over five and a half feet; she was actually five feet seven inches tall.

He could not help noticing that the papers she was organizing were ledger sheets; Del Cummins had said she was a businesswoman, the diligent and successful owner of a specialty leather-goods firm with a plant in Baltimore and one planned for Chicago. Her trade in fine gloves, fashionable belts, and dainty purses to retail outlets in several major cities had also expanded into an export trade.

She turned her attention back to Zack. "I appreciate the chance for us to meet."

Zack gave an honest grin. "I've got to tell you, Miss Page, that I am pleasantly surprised."

She looked perplexed.

He explained. "Well . . . Del had said you were involved in the suffrage movement and, candidly, I . . ."

She burst into a hearty laugh. "And you had envisioned some severe-looking woman dressed in equally severe attire?"

With a show of chagrin, he nodded.

"Well," she said, "not all of us who believe in women's right to vote are drab."

He sipped his coffee. "And not all of you are quite as attractive."

"That is rather bold of you, Mister Horton." She seemed to be fighting back a blush. "But I thank you for the flattery, even if flattery is the food of fools."

"I didn't intend to embarrass you, nor to be especially bold. Del tells me we're going to be seeing quite a bit of each other. I've a habit of saying what I think."

She studied him for a moment. "If you're being that frank, you may as well tell me how you feel about the National Woman Suffrage Association."

He had actually given no thought to the subject, other than to dismiss it. He tried to hide his lack of interest by saying, "I've not been averse to your movement, nor have I been supportive. I was raised in a household where respect for other people's beliefs was a paramount concern."

She evaluated his comment. "Then you would have no objection to saying a few good words on our behalf, if the occasion arose?"

"I'm not a very good evangelist, Miss Page. But I can promise that I'll say nothing against your cause."

She took a sip of coffee. "I can see I've some convincing to do, Mister Horton."

He shrugged his shoulders. "I'm always willing to listen, Miss Page."

Leah poured fresh coffee into each of their cups. As she added the cream and sugar, she said, "I won't plague you too awfully much on that issue. Sometimes I forget that not every-one is as concerned as I am."

He accepted the coffee. "I guess we all have things like that in our lives. Seems to be a human characteristic."

"Well, it looks like we're going to be seeing each other on some regular basis."

This woman across the table from him was about his age, and she was appealing. Maybe this venture with James Hill was going to be more than just business. "I can see where we could have some fun out of this, Miss Page."

He caught an instant of reaction. It was not a flare of anger nor resentment, but it bothered him.

She sat there trying to hide what she was feeling. The last thing she wanted out of helping James Hill was an involvement. Two important things had happened when she had started her business; she had learned she was apt at managing a company, and she had let herself fall in love with a man who had deceived her. The man was supposed to be a Dutch importer of leather goods, he was supposed to be a duke related to the royal family, and he was supposed to be single. Since that episode in her life, she had been very careful about becoming vulnerable.

"Is there anything wrong, Miss Page?"

"No, nothing is wrong, Mister Horton."

"It could be fun."

"I guess it could."

"We could try."

She was weighing how to handle the situation. Horton seemed like a nice young man, but he also came across as a charmer. She decided on distance. "Mister Horton, there probably will be some *fun*, as you call it, but this work with Mister Hill is very important. I've got my business to consider."

Zack said, "Tell me about this business of yours."

"If you're really interested, I could talk for hours. But that might bore you."

Zack laughed. "Far less bored than if you talked about the suffrage movement."

She returned his laugh. "That, Mister Horton, is not kind. You should be more tolerant."

Zack did not respond; Leah waited to make sure he had

accepted the reprimand in good nature, then said, "My business? We purchase split leather from tanneries and make it into hand-bags for ladies, delicate belts for special fashions, and gloves, lightweight gloves for dress occasions."

"There's a market for that, obviously."

"I've been in the business for about four years, and my customers keep demanding more. They also try to get me to expand my line of goods. I might do that someday, but not until I've my current items made and sold as well as possible."

Zack sat back and took out a small leather cigar case. He asked, "What about this?"

"No, thank you."

He approached a blush. "I didn't mean . . . I was just wondering if you made cigar cases."

She reached across the table, took the case, and examined it carefully before she handed it back. "No, we don't make anything like that . . . not at the present. But it's the sort of thing we could make well. I might think about it someday."

"Do you mind if I smoke?"

"Not at all."

While he was lighting his thin cigar, she said, "Mister Hill came to me just about a year after I began selling my goods to a couple of department stores in Saint Paul. It seems that Mrs. Hill had bought some and mentioned the quality to her hus-band. Our very first meeting was right here in this room." She pointed to a table across the room. "It was there, if my memory serves me, and Max—our waiter today—was quite impressed that I was meeting with the famous James Hill. That's why we are sitting at this choice table today; my bona fides were estab-lished back then."

"Does that mean Max'll give me a good table from now on?"

"That depends on how he perceives the outcome of our meeting. There are degrees of influence, but I'm sure you know that."

"So, I'm to assume the meeting with James Hill went well?"

"It did. As a matter of fact, you might be interested in that."

"I'm here to learn all I can, Miss Page."

Her face brightened with a smile. Zack liked the looks of her smile; her teeth sparkled in the frame of her sensuous lips.

"I'm listening," Zack prompted.

"James Hill wanted to talk to me because he was looking for freight to be shipped westbound over his rail lines. He was bringing timber east from Oregon, minerals from the Rocky Mountains, and a great deal of grain from the plains states. He needed something to ship back in the empty cars. He's a genius, do you know that?"

Zack grinned before he said, "I know he's successful and well respected, but it doesn't take a genius to know the value of filling empty freight cars on a railroad."

"Ah." She was enjoying herself. "But it does take a genius to send his agents to Japan to see what the Japanese could use. He found that cotton was in great demand, so he shipped cotton from Georgia all the way across to Tacoma and Portland. As it has happened, his agents also learned that Japanese women had a liking for delicate leather products. Granted, I only use three freight cars a month from the plant in Baltimore, and there'll be two from here in Chicago when we begin operations, but those are five cars that don't head west empty. Mister Hill gave me a very good shipping rate. By this time next year, I hope to double my exports, and Mister Hill expects to double his cotton shipments. That's one reason he wants statehood, so he can extend his own railroad; now he has to use other lines to complete the trip from Montana to the Pacific Coast."

"I'll keep a sharp eye on James Hill; he seems to be very unusual."

Leah chuckled. "James Hill has figuratively written a whole new book on how an industry can create a market for its goods or services. Most of his experiments have proven to be sound practices. My case is a good example. Mister Hill has done me a favor, a big favor, that's made it possible for me to pay a fair wage to my employees and still make a good profit. That is all I ever hoped for when I took the gamble of going into business."

Zack looked seriously at Leah. "If all you tell me about your business is as you say, I know several New York investors who'd be pleased to become involved in any expansion."

"I don't mean to be rude, but I'm afraid the usual investor would also expect to change the way I run my businesses."

"You sound cynical."

"With good cause." She pointed down toward the people moving along State Street. "There're a million people out there in this city and the majority make a daily wage that's barely enough to feed and house themselves. And that wage is for twelve to fourteen hours a day."

Zack looked at the flow of humanity. He had grown up watching his grandfather working similar long hours and worrying over making a success of his businesses. He opted not to reply.

Leah said, "So, James Hill has enlisted me in an effort that he feels is important to the stability of his railroad empire."

Zack tried to imagine what the territory in the West was like, and why it was worth so much effort on the part of James Hill and the others who were fighting for statehood. He said as much.

She answered, "Mister Hill says that the territorial governments are difficult to deal with; they're controlled by the Congress and the executive branch and are sometimes impossible to . . . well, how should I put it . . . sometimes impossible to manipulate."

Zack grinned. He was beginning to enjoy Leah Page's candor.

"I may," she added, "have misstated his attitude, but James Hill wants to get things done, and he doesn't enjoy having to curry favor with the lawmakers in Washington."

"I'm sure he knows how to play that game."

"No question; he's a master. I've seen him in operation. But he feels more comfortable dealing with state legislators, as in Minnesota and Wisconsin. He'd like to see his railroad running where he wants it to go, across to the West Coast. A northern tier transcontinental railroad; his own."

"I can't see any way in which I can be of value to him in that project." Zack held up his thumb and forefinger spread about a half inch apart. "I don't know that much about the issue."

"Simple, Mister Horton. It seems your railroad's highly regarded in Dakota Territory, thanks to your grandfather and Del Cummins."

A thought came to Zack. "So I'm to be used by James Hill."

"We're all used in this life, Mister Horton. It's not a very nice truth, but it's one that we should all face sooner rather than later. When I realized it, it struck me that I was defenseless against being used."

"How did you handle that?"

"I decided to make sure that I was being used in some way that would help me in my own ventures. I don't know if I am succeeding, but I don't feel abused."

The last words were said with an amused smile. Leah looked at her watch. "I'm awfully sorry, Mister Horton, but I've another appointment in just fifteen minutes." She gathered up her purse and portfolio, made a sign to the waiter, and gulped down a last swallow of coffee. Before he was aware of what was happening, Zack was standing and listening to her telling the waiter to put the charges on her account. He cut in, "I'll take care of the coffee, Miss Page." Then, to the waiter, "Could you come back after Miss Page leaves? Thank you."

As Leah began to move, Zack blurted, "Miss Page, I've a dozen things I need to ask you."

She reached out and patted him on his arm. "I'm sure you do, as do I. There's one thing I'll leave you with: You and I are the 'younguns.'"

"'Younguns'?"

"'Younguns.' Mister Hill's referring to us as the 'younguns.' I'll tell you all about it at dinner."

"Dinner?"

"Of course, tonight on the train going to Saint Paul. Didn't you know I would accompany you? Let's hope Mister Cummins arrives in time. We're to be aboard by seven."

With that, Leah whisked past him and was away. Zack plopped down in his chair. He had never met a woman who had developed a business the size and scope of Leah Page's. And he was beginning to think he had never met one quite so attractive. He looked up as the waiter came back to the table. Zack asked, "Your name's Max, isn't it? I thought I heard Miss Page call you that."

Max nodded.

"Well, Max," Zack asked, "is it possible to get a drink of bourbon in this place?"

Max gave his best smile. "It is, sir. Quite possible."

"Then, if you don't mind, let me have one, please."

As the waiter went scurrying off, Zack tried to pull the pieces together. He was anxious for Del to show up in Chicago; there were quite a few questions that needed answering.

The dinner had gone well. Del Cummins, who had arrived at the train in the nick of time, cracked a few jokes he had heard in Pittsburgh.

They were an hour and a half out of Chicago, riding in the private railway car of James Hill.

The meal had been modest: steak, roast potatoes, and fresh peas and carrots. Ice cream was the dessert, accompanied by pots of coffee and tea. No wine was served, although beer and whiskey had been offered as the train pulled out of Chicago's Grand Central Depot en route to Milwaukee, which was the first major city on the route to Saint Paul. The trip would take thirteen hours.

Zack lifted a spoon of ice cream but, before he ate it, he gave a soft laugh.

Del asked, "What's the joke?"

Zack replied, "The joke is that this is crazy. Two days ago I figured I was going make a noble gesture to help a family friend, and here I am sitting in the private car of one of the nation's biggest railroad moguls, eating ice cream and wondering what's going to happen next. It is crazy."

Leah looked at the two men. "It may be crazy, Mister Horton, but it's certainly a pleasing way to travel."

"There's no question of that, Miss Page. I guess I'm more concerned that Hill will feel as though he's put me . . . us . . . in his debt because of the courtesy."

"James Hill's not one to conjure up such devious schemes. He's merely being hospitable."

"I hope you're right, Miss Page, because—"

"Just one minute, Zack," Del Cummins cut in. "For an hour and a half, I've listened to you two going at Mister This and Miss That, and I think it's time you drop those formalities. You are Zack, and you are Leah, and that's the way it should be. Hell's sake, if you're going to be stuck together, then you'd better be more friendly."

Leah and Zack looked at each other and grinned. She said, "It's Zack, then."

He nodded. "I'll try to remember: Leah." Zack ate his spoonful of ice cream, then said, "Where was I?"

"You were in the process of making too much out of a kindness," Leah said. "James Hill's expecting you to accept his request for help, and he wants you to arrive in Saint Paul ready to work, not tired out from a long train ride. At least, that's the way I see the thing. He's really a very thoughtful person."

"Well, this private-car business seems more than just thoughtful."

She shook her head. "Some people! A person does something nice and right away he's suspect."

Zack said, "I'm looking forward to getting to know the man. We'll see if I'm right. I just feel uncomfortable."

Leah insisted, "Then relax."

He finished his ice cream. Del was lighting a cigar, and Leah drank her coffee. Zack looked around the interior. At the rear was a plaque identifying the car as *L'Etoile du Nord*. Zack asked about the name, and Leah explained that it was in honor of Hill's adopted home, Minnesota; Hill had come from Canada originally. The car was not as grand as some of those owned by the magnates of the day, but it was very comfortable. In the forward part of the car were four small sleeping rooms, two with only one bed, the others with two Pullman-type pallets each. Next came a spartan kitchen, followed by the dining section, which could accommodate eight at its cramped but comfortable table. Adjacent to the dining area was a small compartment that Hill used as his office and sleeping quarters, and then came the lounge that occupied a full one third of the car. The appointments throughout were attractive: varnished and polished Norway pine, glistening brass hardware, and dark maroon upholstery.

Unlike many owners of private railway cars, Jim Hill had only one in staff: Calvin Jones, a Pullman porter turned majordomo. Jones was slim and tall, his face could create a smile to make any guest comfortable; grey tinged the sideburns of his hair. Most private cars carried a cook, a valet, a messenger, and two porters, but Hill saw no justification for such a number of servants. If there were many guests, he would add some help for Calvin, but would have simple meals catered by depot restaurants. His guests could take care of their own clothing and baggage, as he himself did.

Calvin came out of the kitchen area and approached the table.

"Miss Page, gentlemen"—Calvin had a sonorous voice that seemed more apt for a preacher than a Pullman porter— "we will be arriving at Milwaukee shortly. If you don't mind, I would like to clear the table."

Leah rose. "That's no problem, Calvin."

Zack and Del stood up. Zack asked, "How long will we be in the station, Calvin?"

"We will be there for a full ten minutes. You all may leave the train if you wish. I'll be going to the telegraph office; I always do, because Mister Hill often has instructions. If any of you have messages you wish dispatched, I can take care of that for you." He looked for a response.

Del said, "Nothing from this quarter, Calvin." The others agreed.

The porter started putting the dishes on his tray and began what was obviously a set speech. "Milwaukee is the largest city in Wisconsin and sits 580 feet above sea level on the west shore of Lake Michigan. It was first a village in 1835 and chartered as a city in 1846. The population is about two hundred thousand, half of whom are of the German inclination. The city is a major center of commerce in grain, flour, and lumber. Pabst, Schlitz, Blatz, and several others have breweries here." He gave a sheepish grin and added, "I'll be obtaining an appropriate measure of the refreshment if any of you would care to have some later this evening." Del Cummins gave a broad smile. "Well," Calvin concluded as he straightened up with his tray, "we will arrive . . ." He looked at the Regulator clock on the wall. ". . . in just about twelve minutes." Then, with a toothy, beaming smile, he added, "We will not leave without you, I promise."

Leah led the way into the lounge part of the car. Zack carried along his unfinished coffee, and Del took his cigar. They settled in the comfortable armchairs.

Del said, "I guess we'll be in about eight in the morning. Good night to catch up on my sleep."

Leah agreed. "If Mister Hill follows the form that I've come to know, we'll be very busy."

Zack raised a finger as if demanding their concentration. "How long is this meeting with Mister Hill going to take? Do you have any ideas?"

Del shook his head. "As I see it, he wants to give us his views and set out some sort of a schedule. I've not planned for more than a day or two."

Leah said, "Not much more than that. Actually, I'll be in Saint Paul for only two days, because I know he wants me to go out to Olympia; Washington Territory is really due for statehood. I'm not too upset about having to go; I'll have a chance to see my folks. It'll be a quick trip; I'm scheduled back in Baltimore in three weeks at the most."

Zack felt a strange disappointment. How could she become involved in his own effort in Dakota Territory? That was the problem: he had no way of knowing what his effort would be, until he heard from James Hill.

The train began to slow down. Calvin came and said, "Lady and gentlemen. Remember, it is a ten-minute stop."

The Union Depot was busy even at nine o'clock at night, with four trains standing at loading platforms. Inside, in the main terminal area, Leah excused herself—she did not enjoy using the lavatories on trains—and Del invited Zack to visit the taproom of the restaurant, where Del wanted to make a serious comparison of the local beers. Zack said he would rather just walk about—he had been spending a goodly number of hours in railway cars over the previous few days.

Zack did wander for a few minutes. He saw families and individuals rushing for their trains. Many were obviously immigrants. They clustered together, children staying close to the mother. The clothing was generally new, even if a bit tested by weeks, possibly months, of travel to this new land. And there were the prized possessions. Often it was for the man a tool of some kind: a saw or hammer, an axe, or even a shovel. Zack spotted one man with a bundle of leather wrapped around long tongs and mallets: obviously a blacksmith. Back in New York and Philadelphia he saw the new arrivals blending easily into the chaotic activities of the cities. Out here these arrivals were venturing into an unknown land. In concentrated masses of population many things were organized and controlled; here the people would be scattered out on the lonely prairies, possibly miles from the nearest neighbor. They were bound for an adventure.

But then, that was what Leah Page had suggested. He decided to follow her lead and treat the days before him as an adventure. Why not? If James Hill was building an empire and being a part of history by fighting for statehood, he could be a part of that, too.

And as long as Miss Leah Page was on the scene, there might be some fun in the whole thing.

The three met by the platform gate and walked to the end of the train, where the *L'Etoile du Nord* was attached to the express to Saint Paul. Calvin Jones was signing some papers for the delivery man who had brought a case of Pabst. As they greeted him, he responded, "I'll be back in the lounge in a few minutes; there is a telegraph message for you from Mister Hill."

The train was pulling out of the station as Calvin came into the lounge, carrying a silver tray with three pilsner glasses of lager. When he had put them in place in front of the guests, he handed a yellow Western Union envelope to Leah. She opened the telegram, read it, and passed it to Del Cummins who in turn passed it to Zack.

WILL APPRECIATE YOUR ATTENDANCE AT THE FUNERAL OF AMOS PILLSBURY AT 10 AM. SOME SCHEDULE CHANGES WILL BE NECESSARY. REGARDS—HILL.

Del Cummins took a swig of beer and said, "That doesn't sound like a bunch of fun."

Leah Page asked, "Why us? For goodness' sake!"

Zack was silent. His adventure would have a sour beginning.

CHAPTER 3

SAINT PAUL—WEDNESDAY, MAY 30, 1888

"Zack, I really don't like this."

"Take it easy, Leah." He took a firmer hold on her arm and tried to give both gentlemanly assistance and moral support as they climbed the long marble stairs leading into the Saint Paul's First Presbyterian Church on Summit Avenue.

"I didn't come here for this."

"None of us did."

"Then why are we here?"

He was irritated with her. "We are here because Mister Hill wants us here."

"Damn him."

"Easy."

At the top of the stairs they were greeted by a pair of men dressed in severe black coats, trousers, and tall hats. The man on the right offered a black-bordered funeral card. Zack sensed that Leah was about to refuse. He took two cards and nodded to the ushers. Leah stepped aside, balking at entering the church.

In a whisper, Zack pleaded, "Please, Leah. It will only take an hour."

She did not respond.

More carriages were arriving and depositing mourners; Zack was anxious to avoid bringing attention to Leah and himself. "Just an hour," he repeated.

"Where is Del Cummins?"

"I told you, he's with one of Hill's people; something to do with Dakota and Western business. Rates or schedules, I don't know."

She snapped, "Oh, your business is important? I have a business, too."

Zack did not reply. After a short pause, she said, "I didn't come to Saint Paul to go to a funeral. I don't even know the poor soul they're burying."

Zack did not know why Leah was having such a strong reaction, but he would wait for her to explain. To him, attendance was a mere formality satisfying Hill's request. The dead man, Amos Pillsbury, had been a little-known cousin of Charles Pillsbury, the operator of the huge flour-processing mills, and word had come to Hill that a sizable turnout for the funeral was wanted.

When they had arrived in Saint Paul that morning, one of Hill's executives had met them and explained that it would be appreciated if they would attend the funeral with Hill and his family; after the funeral they and a large party of Hill's friends and associates were to go to Lake Minnetonka, ten miles southwest of Saint Paul. Another unexpected bit of information was that President Grover Cleveland was in Saint Paul on a private visit to bolster his renomination campaign and line up contributions. That news did not sit well with Leah Page. She had some firm, not to say violent, opinions about the president; she saw Cleveland as a lecher and an ignoble politician who was not worthy of the high office.

Zack kept glancing around at the arriving carriages and the steady flow of mourners up the stairs of the church. Fortunately, the people moved by quickly, and few took notice of Leah's attitude.

Zack said, "This will only take a short time." Then, grasping for a straw to help him along, he added, "You look quite attractive this morning."

She was wearing a dark maroon velvet skirt and jacket over a dark grey blouse, and a wide-brimmed hat made of the same maroon velvet decorated with a black ribbon. Her only jewelry was a choker of grey pearls above the high collar of her blouse. She was wearing her hair in a chignon.

Not wanting to laugh just outside a funeral, Leah raised her gloved hand to cover her mouth. In a muffled voice she said, "Zack Horton, you're really an awful person."

He gave a false look of confusion. "I'm not awful. The colors go well with your hair; the attire's not frilly or inappropriate. You do look the part of a grieving friend."

She recovered her bad temper. "In the first place, this is the only dress I brought with me that would fit the occasion. Second, I wasn't going to run out this morning and buy something gloomy just because Jim Hill was rude enough to force you and me to attend this morbid event." Zack was wincing.

"Furthermore," she softened her voice, "I barely know you. Why should you be my escort, and how dare you say things about my dress! Are you making fun of me?"

"I am not! I'm doing what our host has asked; escorting you to this ceremony is a duty." He saw her frown. "A very pleasant duty, I might add." Her look became less severe. "Now look, Leah, I don't like being here anymore than you do. It's all part of dealing with Mister Hill."

She said, "You don't even know Jim Hill, Zack."

"Del's told me enough. I am not ready to take offense until I know that the obligation could have been avoided. As I said, it'll all be over in an hour or so."

"I'll be damned if I'm going to the cemetery; I draw the line at that!"

"I agree. Apparently, Mister Hill's not going to the graveside service, either. We'll go right from here back to the train station."

"That's a promise?"

"That's a promise."

She looked skeptical. She chewed softly on her lower lip; he sensed that she was still at the point of walking away. "Look," he explained, "Del found out that Mister Hill doesn't want to be at this funeral either, but it's important to him. He even made arrangements for Mrs. Hill to be here, too."

Leah nodded. "I heard about that when I was changing clothes at the hotel. The bishop gave her a dispensation to attend a Presbyterian church."

"Right. And that was a big thing to her."

"Zack, for God's sake, don't be so innocent! Hill got permission for Mary Theresa to enter a Protestant church, and the bishop will be getting a new Catholic hospital or a new Catholic school; Hill *bought* the damned dispensation."

"That should show you how important it is to the man. All he wants from us is a little support for a friend of his."

"That friend also happens to be about the biggest customer of the railroad."

As Zack opened his mouth to continue the argument, he saw two carriages coming along Pleasant Avenue, just crossing Walnut Street a block away. Both carriages were draped in black mourning crepe. One was obviously carrying the Pillsbury family; the other was the hearse. Zack urged, "Let's get inside."

Leah turned to look and saw what was coming. "I can't, Zack. Oh, God, I just can't do it."

"Leah, we can't walk away now. Just take a deep breath and come on."

A third carriage rumbled from the opposite direction, no doubt from the armory, because there was a mounted escort of cavalry dressed in formal uniforms; that carriage would be bearing President Cleveland.

Zack grabbed Leah's arm and whispered, "We are going inside! If Grover Cleveland can spare an hour, then you and I can do the same."

Leah growled back, "Cleveland is looking for a campaign contribution. That's why he's here; he wants money from Hill, and now he can tap the Pillsbury coffers, too."

Zack began to steer her to the main entrance; she pulled her arm free. "I'll go in under my own power, thank you."

Zack grinned. As they neared the doorway, they noticed that the hearse and family carriage had stopped a half block away to allow the president to arrive first. "Look at him!" Leah hissed.

President Cleveland climbed down to the sidewalk. The man was huge. An inch under six feet, he carried 272 pounds. "Portly" and "corpulent" were two of the words used by friendly commentators.

Still in a low voice, she mumbled, "The fat lecher."

Zack was torn between scolding her and bursting out in a laugh. Instead, he said, "You are in rotten form, Miss Page."

"There's nothing to be happy about, and now I have to endure seeing that obscenity."

President Cleveland, his very young wife, and the rest of his party had collected together at the bottom of the steps and were about to start climbing.

Zack said, "I'm through arguing with you, Leah; I'm going in."

Leah was either going to have to stand there awkwardly while the president passed or get inside quickly; she saw that following Zack was the lesser of two evils. She hurried after him.

Organ music, low, rumbling, sorrowful notes, floated around the crowded church, bathing it with the sounds of grief. Large depressing arrangements of lilies put an appropriate face on the presence of death. Leah Page shuddered as she followed Zack down the center aisle. "Oh, damn," she let slip out between clenched teeth.

Zack halted abruptly, ignoring the usher who had been leading him down to the pews for James Hill's contingent, and guided Leah into a pew near the back.

As they quickly took their seats on the aisle, Leah picked up a hymnbook. She told him, "I do not often lose complete control."

Zack opened the funeral pamphlet so as to look properly part of the ceremony. "I'm seeing an interesting side of you."

Keeping her eyes on the open hymnal, she said abruptly,
"I've got to get out of here."

He put his right hand gently on her shaking hands; they
were damp and hot. Her face was very pale. "Are you going to
be all right?"

"I'm not sure. Oh God, I am sorry, Zack."

A murmur worked its way from the back of the church to
the front; President Cleveland, with Mrs. Cleveland tentatively
holding onto his arm, moved down the aisle and took his seat
right beside James Hill.

Not a full minute had elapsed before the pallbearers made
their way toward the altar area. Just as soon as the coffin had
passed, Zack whispered, "We're getting out of here."

Leah snapped a quick glance at him. She searched to see if
he was being serious; his eyes gave her the answer. "That would
be the nicest thing I can think of."

Zack took the hymnal from her hands and replaced it in the
pew rack. He calmly stood and stepped out into the aisle, and
she, after a disbelieving hesitation, followed. Behind them the
congregation's attention was focused on the placement of the
coffin. Without a word, he guided her out and down the stairs
and began walking south on Pleasant Avenue. They walked
silently for five blocks; Leah was hoping that Zack would not
suddenly change his mind and head them back to the church.

Finally, confident that he would not change his mind, she
asked, "Where are we going?"

Keeping his eyes forward and not lessening his pace, he
said, "I don't know. I do know you were in trouble back there,
and I wasn't interested in ministering to a swooning maiden."
On the next block, Zack spotted the entrance to a restaurant. He
guided Leah toward the door.

They came into a small foyer with a stone floor and dark,
highly polished oak paneling on the walls; brightly colored beer
steins rested on shelves behind the reception counter. The hostess was wearing a Bavarian dirndl, her grey hair plaited and
secured like a halo at the top of her head. "Ah, good morning,

my friends. You are very early for lunch." Her speech was heavily laced with a guttural German accent.

The woman led the way through a carved wooden arch into the dining area; there were no other customers. The dining room was large, with Alpine paintings and bric-a-brac, and the tables were dressed in checked tablecloths and wine-bottle candle holders. The hostess showed them to a table by a back window, a window that looked out into a small, neatly landscaped garden shaded by two massive maple trees. As they took their seats, the hostess said, "This is Mister James Hill's favorite table. The maple trees remind him of Canada."

Zack asked Leah, "Would you like coffee?"

She accepted.

The hostess left them. In less than a minute, she was back carrying a tray.

They declined the offer of something to eat and were left alone.

After unbuttoning her jacket, Leah reached up and pulled two six-inch-long pins from her hat, put the pins and hat on an adjacent chair, and then deftly removed the five hairpins that had been holding her chignon in place. With a shake of her head, the hair fell softly down, and she smiled as the golden frame settled more comfortably around her face. "There, that's more like it," she said.

Zack added sugar and heavy cream to his coffee. "Feel better now?"

She sipped her coffee, then said, "I should explain."

"Explain what?"

"My actions—why I acted like such a fool."

Zack raised his hands. "You need not. Don't even think about it."

She ignored his offer. "When I was very young—I'd just turned eight—my grandmother died. At the funeral, an aunt, not a favorite aunt at all, insisted on taking me up to view the body. I was terrified. My poor mother did all she could to keep me from hysterics. My aunt was roundly scolded, but the damage had been done. I quiver when I even think about a funeral." She had been studying the pattern of the tablecloth. Now she looked up. "Silly, isn't it? I'm really sorry to have burdened you with my foolishness.

"It is not silly, Leah; we all have things that upset us."

She studied him for a moment, then asked, "What upsets you? Just so I know what to expect."

He paused for thought. "Damned if I know. There must be something."

She burst into a laugh. "You condescending oaf! Any worthwhile gallant would have come up with at least three terrible things to make a woman in distress feel better."

Sheepishly, he asked, "Don't you feel better?"

"Not at all."

"What you need is to relax. Do you want something to eat?"

She declined. He kept quiet for a few moments, then he said, "Not to change the subject, but you never did tell me what you meant when you said we're the 'younguns,' remember, on the train?"

She smiled. "Mister Hill referred to you and me as 'younguns.' The man is only fifty, but it seems he is determined to look on us as mere children. I had no intention of worrying you about it; I was kidding."

"Do you feel like a 'youngun'?"

She pursed her lips, forcing a mock sternness on her face. "Sir, sometimes I feel as old as one of Hamlet's witches, sometimes I feel as young as a schoolchild."

"How do you feel right now?"

She thought. "I feel like a youngish businesswoman who should be back attending to her business."

"I'm glad you're not; I'm glad you're here."

She grinned. "Well, 'youngun,' we're stuck with this for a span of time, like it or not."

"I don't know how long I'm stuck. If I'm not keen on what Hill has on schedule, I might just head back to New York."

A flicker of anxiety showed on Leah's face. She said, "I thought you'd made a commitment."

"I did, to my grandmother. Hill asked for help, she offered me, but she made no promise. I don't want to take on something I'm not capable of doing, Leah."

"I can appreciate that, Zack, but there's nothing you can't do in this situation. Mister Hill needs the influence of your railroad to encourage people to work for statehood. Why would you want to avoid helping?"

"I didn't say I was quitting; I just said what could happen. I'm not considering myself 'stuck,' as you put it."

She finished her coffee. She was using the action to hide her feeling: dismay at the thought of this young man walking out of her life. She chided herself. She had known him for less than a day, and she had set a rule for herself that she would not get involved again. But she knew she was a normal, healthy woman, and avoiding involvement was going to be impossible and maybe even foolish. Besides, the man across the table from her had a charm that could aid in getting broad support for Hill's quest for the Northwest territories to become states.

Zack was doing some thinking of his own. He was annoyed with himself over his cavalier comments to Leah; he knew they had to have sounded pompous. That was probably why she was looking so concerned. He admitted to himself at that moment that the presence of Leah Page in this adventure was making it more attractive. Originally, he had looked forward to being around Del Cummins and venturing out into the region where his grandfather had built a successful business, a part of the family heritage. Both of those attractions could have been satisfied in fairly short order; that might not be the case with getting to know Leah Page.

Her voice was flat as she said, "There are other aspects to all of this, Zack. Not just the railroads."

"How so?"

"Well, numerous other groups stand to gain. The farming industry is very active, mining corporations are deeply involved, and then there are the politicians." She did not know why she was working so hard to interest him.

"There always seem to be politicians."

She laughed. "Yes, that's true, but when it comes to statehood it's easy to see why the politicians are concerned. There are thirty-eight states now. They provide for seventy-six members of the U.S. Senate. Six new states will have twelve new senators, and the balance of power in the Congress may easily be thrown one way or another, probably to the Republicans."

The congressional balance of power had not entered his mind. How on earth was he going to be of any value in that aspect? He knew nothing of politics. "Well," he said, "I guess I have a lot to learn." Zack looked toward the archway; this time he saw the hostess. He said to Leah, "I'm ready for more coffee." As he signaled the hostess, the front door opened and Del Cummins walked in.

"Well," Zack said, "I'll be hanged. That man can find me anyplace; always has been able to do that. Ever since I was a kid."

Del spotted the pair at the table and came across with the hostess. He ordered a beer.

Zack demanded, "Now how did you find me this time?"

Del pulled out a chair, nearly sat on Leah's hat, but settled safely in another. He said, "Accident," then gave a sheepish grin. "I figured I'd need some nourishment to carry me through the service, but maybe I'm in luck. Is the funeral over?"

"Not by a long shot, I'd guess. It turned out to be a big occasion. President Cleveland's in attendance. I'd bet it will go on for hours."

"Nope. Look at this." Del pulled out a sheet of light green foolscap from his coat pocket and handed it to Zack. The heavy paper's embossed printing announced: "In honor of the observance of Memorial Day, Mr. and Mrs. James Hill are celebrating with friends and associates at a gala to be held at the Hotel Lafayette on Lake Minnetonka." Below the announcement was a list of events and times, beginning with a reception at noon at the Hill residence on Summit Avenue.

Zack growled, "What the hell is this?"

Leah asked, "What is it, Zack?"

Zack handed the announcement across the table. While Leah read, Del said, "I just found out about it this morning. It seems that Grover Cleveland really wants Jim Hill's support. He's never had it, but Hill is a smart businessman, I've got to give him that. He really has little use for President Cleveland because of this statehood issue; Cleveland has been one of those blocking admission because he knows most of the people who will be elected will be Republicans. But Hill also knows that Cleveland might be reelected, so he agreed to invite the president to the Memorial Day gala he already had planned. You can bet that Hill will get something out of the effort."

Zack felt a surge of impatience. He had yielded to his grandmother's wishes and come to Saint Paul to help James Hill, but he had not yet met the man. He started to voice his emotion, but was checked by a memory. Years before, when Zack was first being introduced to the business world, his grandfather had told him to realize that other people had problems in life, and that sometimes Zack's own problems were going to have to wait a bit for resolution. Zack asked Del, "So when do we talk to Hill?"

Del said, "We can go to the reception at noon."

Zack thought for a moment, then stated, "That's no good; it will be a mess."

Leah agreed. "I've been to two functions at the Hill house and both times it has been chaos; people love to visit there. Hill has an impressive collection of Troyon and Corot and Delacroix paintings. I wouldn't expect you'd find a minute in that hour to talk."

Del said, "Probably the best bet is to try for time on the train ride. The cars are going to the lake via Minneapolis to pick up more guests; that would be my suggestion."

Two couples came into the dining room led by the hostess. The new arrivals were dressed somberly; they looked as if they had just left the funeral. They offered polite smiles. In a hushed voice Del said, "Looks like the ceremony is over."

Leah smiled. "Unless they slipped away just as we did. Wouldn't that be marvelous? All of the dragooned guests quietly eased out the back door and arrived here! We could have a very exciting party, sort of an Irish wake."

Del lit up a cigar, then said, "You really are a wicked woman."

Leah replied, "Yes. Yes, I am wicked and I am proud of it."

Zack looked at Leah. "President Cleveland will probably be at the Hills'. Would you like to meet him?"

Her eyes widened in disbelief. "Any woman interested in her virtue should keep as far from that man as possible."

Zack broke out in a laugh, choked slightly on a mouthful of smoke, and waved his hand to stop her from going on; Cleveland's reputation, even since he had been in the White House, was scarred with talk about his dalliances. There was rumor that Cleveland had fathered an illegitimate child before he was elected to the presidency.

After a moment to calm himself down, he said, "I pray that I never incur your wrath, young lady. You have a bitter sense of humor." She laughed.

The people at the other table, well across the room, looked as if the laughter was an intrusion. Possibly, Zack thought, they were sincere mourners who had actually known Amos Pillsbury.

Leah and Del also noticed the reaction and, by common consent, they all decided to get back to the depot. As they made ready to leave, Zack said, "I've got to get my luggage at the Ryan."

Leah told him, "I don't have to go to the hotel; my things have already been taken to the train. Why can't we just stay here? Let's forget all about going out to that silly lake and relax. The three of us."

Zack and Del looked at each other. Jokingly, Zack said, "We could stay here all day long. We could try to drink all of the beer in the cellar. Of course, Mister Hill would be done with all of us. I'm not sure he won't have something to say about us slipping out of the funeral."

"Don't be a pill."

"I am being a realist."

"They would not miss us for one moment."

"It is not a matter of being missed. It is a matter of me getting business done here, and getting on with my life."

She leaned forward, set her elbows on the table, and cradled her chin on her laced fingers. She was having some fun; he could see it in her eyes. "Please, Zack, let's not go."

Sometime in her youth, he thought, she must have spent hours in front of a mirror batting her eyes; she was a skilled performer. She looked lovely, and he was half tempted to call her bluff.

Pretending to do so, he cocked his head, smiled, and asked, "Are you serious?"

She unlaced her fingers, threw her head back, and gently shook her hair. "No, you know I'm kidding."

"I was pretty sure, but I had to ask."

Del Cummins huffed. "Let's get down to the hotel. This could turn out to be a miserable day if I don't get a bit more beer in my belly."

►◆◄

L'Etoile du Nord was waiting on a Saint Paul, Minneapolis, and Pacific siding at the Union Depot on Third Street. The locomotive, a brand-new Baldwin 2-4-2, was decorated with an abundance of red, white, and blue bunting; two large, beautiful Stars and Stripes were set on poles in brackets on each side of the glistening brass headlamp. Between the *L'Etoile du Nord* and the locomotive, four other cars had been hooked up, ready to roll. Ahead of Hill's car was President Cleveland's palace car, ahead of that was a Pullman dining car, then a shiny new passenger coach, and, right behind the locomotive and tender, a baggage car loaded with carriages, steamer trunks, and the other paraphernalia the wealthy needed to endure a three-night stay at a luxurious vacation resort. All things considered, it was an elaborate collection of railroad equipment to make the short trip from Saint Paul to Lake Minnetonka. Hill, in response to a question from a hostile newspaper reporter—one Hill always claimed was in the secret employ of the Northern Pacific Railroad—explained that the use of the top-of-the-line equipment was not at all extravagant, because the train would be traveling first to Minneapolis to hook on two other palace cars that would be carrying important personages from that city to the lake resort. The trip, Hill had argued, was not going to be a mere ten or twelve miles, but closer to thirty miles. With a wry smile, Hill then terminated the interview.

Leah, Zack, and Del had gone to the Ryan Hotel, where Zack and Del excused themselves to go to their rooms for a quick bath and a change of clothes before the ride to Lake Minnetonka. The trio had reached the Union Depot before Hill and his guests arrived from the reception. As soon at they boarded the *L'Etoile du Nord,* Leah had doffed her jacket but was still sweltering in the heat. To their surprise, Calvin Jones greeted them dressed in a business suit and tie, rather than in his porter's uniform. Del, who had quaffed two quick glasses of beer at the hotel, said, in a jovial, semiserious tone, "You should both know that our friend, Mister Calvin Jones, has been elevated from porter to manager of *L'Etoile du Nord.* I overheard that news this morning."

Calvin beamed with pride. In a polite whisper, he told Leah, "I had one of my girls set out a lighter frock for you, Miss Leah. It is in compartment D."

"You devil!" She laughed and gave him a sisterly hug. "You now have your own staff?"

Calvin explained that Hill had wanted more service for important passengers. He had replaced Calvin with a new porter and added two female staff to handle the cooking, service, and housekeeping that had formerly all been done by Calvin. Calvin was to supervise. In a few years, Calvin Jones would be responsible for all Pullman car service on the entire network of Hill's railroads. But, for the moment, the only thing Calvin Jones wanted was to see that Hill's guests were very comfortable.

Leah went to change, leaving Zack and Del with Calvin in the main salon. As soon as she was gone, Calvin announced, "I guess I had better tell you gentlemen, there will be no spirits served during the ride out to the lake."

Zack looked puzzled. "I didn't know Mister Hill is an abstainer."

"He isn't, Mister Zack. But the boss gave me firm orders."

"You're not wanting to keep us from getting tipsy, are you, Calvin?"

"Lord, no! You know I believe in everyone taking their proper share of refreshments but—just between you and me— the boss thinks some of the bunch with the big boss . . ." and he gestured toward the presidential car ahead, ". . . well . . . the *big* boss might have some people along who can't handle a social drink. If you know what I mean?"

"We can smoke?"

Calvin gave a wide grin. "Smoking is *always* a good social pastime. Mister Hill believes in that, for sure."

Zack asked, "How are we doing on time?"

Calvin pulled on the chain across his vest and extracted his railroader pocket watch. "I would say they will be arriving in ten minutes; we will pull out in twenty."

Zack nodded and walked briskly back through the dining room to the corridor giving access to the sleeping compartments. He rapped lightly on the door to compartment D, calling, "Leah?"

Leah responded, "If you come in that door we are both going to be embarrassed, Zack."

"I have no reason to come in. Just hurry up."

"Give me two minutes."

"Take one."

There was no reply.

He returned to the salon and glanced out the window at Third Street. A large crowd had gathered on the corner with Sibley Street; uniformed police were trying to keep the crowds on the sidewalks. Zack said to Calvin, "It is amazing how the word gets out."

Calvin told him, "The crew from the president's car has

been going crazy with people wanting to get a look inside. Just plain folks wanting to see something special, I guess."

"Well, Cleveland had better hope his staff is not getting people mad at him; he has a good chance of losing the reelection."

"He will get my vote."

Zack liked that in Calvin Jones. James Hill had made no secret of his resentment toward Grover Cleveland over the statehood issue. But Calvin Jones was a strong Democrat. Hill once said he kept Calvin close just so he could have a feeling for his opposition, but it was known that Hill possessed a genuine fondness for Calvin, and Calvin was extremely good at his job.

A swelling of noise came from the crowd. Zack looked out the window again. A squad of mounted cavalry came smartly down Wakouta Street and moved with precision toward the small grassy park in front of the depot. Zack called, "Leah, step it up."

Leah was already on her way out of her compartment. She called back, "Don't be in such a rush."

She moved lithely into the salon and gave a reasonable rendition of a pirouette. She had changed into a silk organza garden-party dress that sported a modest décolletage but a daringly short hemline that came a full three inches above her ankles. As she twirled around, the action displayed a flurry of white petticoats under the flowered print of her wide skirt. She was wearing white stockings and high-buttoned shoes; she carried a wide-brimmed straw hat and a small parasol that she displayed with panache. Both the hat and parasol were trimmed with the same soft pastel print that made up the design of her dress.

Zack was tempted to suggest to Leah that the dress, attractive as it was, was not the thing to be wearing when the funeral party arrived at the train, but he reminded himself that the intent of the excursion to Lake Minnetonka was a social celebration of Memorial Day. It was an occasion with solemnity, but with some joy; memorializing the men who had died in the Civil War, it was also a reminder that the nation was one because of the sacrifices of the young men who fought. "You look lovely," he said.

She came to rest in the middle of the salon and struck an elegant pose. "Now, what is the hurry? And was it worth the wait?"

"In reverse order: Yes, it was worth the wait; and the hurry is that there is to be no consumption of spirits during the ride out to the lake; that will be about two hours."

She cocked her head, gave an exaggerated pout, and asked, "And what is the solution to the dastardly dilemma?"

"I thought we could slip away and reinforce ourselves with a nip or two."

Calvin, who had been watching the scene with quiet amusement, offered, "I don't think that is a good idea, folks."

Del asked, "Why not, Calvin?"

"Mister Hill will be arriving soon and we will be leaving right after that. I would surely be feeling bad if you missed the departure, and that is a possibility."

Zack explained, "All we are going to do is slip out to the lounge of the Railway Restaurant in the depot and have a bit of refreshment." The restaurant in the Union Depot was regarded as a fine place to eat and, in this progressive community, it provided a separate lounge where women could accompany men for drinks; it was less than a hundred feet from the siding.

Calvin rubbed his chin in a manner he had picked up from James Hill when he was doing some serious contemplation. He could, if necessary, run to the lounge if worse came to worst. "You promise to be back when you hear the departure warning whistle?"

"We will not fail you, Calvin."

Del offered, "Calvin, I'll get them back on time. Will you accept our promise?"

"Yes, sir."

Zack nodded to Leah as he told Calvin, "That's settled. We will be back in time."

They stepped onto the platform, and a burst of cheering rose from the crowd across the street as the cavalry unit executed a drill that lined the horses and riders up on each side of the drive leading to the depot entrance. Up on Sibley Street, the first carriages began arriving from the Hill reception. Zack gave a quick look at who was riding in the lead carriage, saw it was not Hill, and took Leah's hand. "Let's move."

Together, they ran into a side entrance of the depot.

▶◆◀

By the time James Hill arrived at the Union Depot with his wife, their children, and the rest of his holiday party, the crowd of sightseers in front of the station had swelled to three thousand gleeful merrymakers. Hill would later remark to a biographer that half of the city's 120,000 people were on hand that day to see President Grover Cleveland. The president and his entourage had preceded Hill by a full ten minutes, and the train crew had been harried by Cleveland's protocol chief about getting moving. President James Garfield had been assassinated in a train station just seven years previously, and the memory weighed heavily on presidential security personnel. As Hill walked from his carriage along the platform to the *L'Etoile du Nord,* the stationmaster passed on the concerns and comments of Cleveland's people; Hill smiled blandly and said he would accommodate the requests within reason. James Hill was not inclined to do too much kowtowing to the Democratic president. *Kowtowing* was a word Hill had learned with great pleasure from Chinese railroad workers. Hill would extend a considerable amount of deference to the head of state out of respect for the office, but he would not allow himself to be pushed in regards to his railroad; the Saint Paul, Minneapolis, and Pacific would run according to his will.

Inside his private car, as family and guests were making themselves comfortable, Hill met with Calvin Jones in the compartment that served as Hill's office and sleeping quarters. Hill treated Calvin Jones like the management-level officer of the company he would become; Calvin received the same brisk, good-naturedly abrupt handling given any employee Hill trusted. The first five questions were answered to with five *yeses.*

Are the guests aboard? Will Mister Cleveland be coming back to Hill's car as planned? Are the iced tea and hot coffee in good supply? Did the flowers for the ladies arrive? And could Calvin get out a cooler suit and a more comfortable pair of shoes? The sixth question was answered by, "They were here earlier."

Hill looked up from the checklist on his desk. He stroked his beard, a sign always dreaded by Calvin Jones. "That's fine, Mister Jones. Now, I know where Messrs. Horton and Cummins and Miss Page were earlier. If I ask you again, I assume you will tell me where they will be later on; what I really want to know is where they are now. Calvin, I have not even met this man Horton yet, and I am considering getting him involved in some of my ventures. Now, are they on the train?"

Calvin's thought was: I knew it! But he was not a man to let anyone get into trouble if trouble could be avoided. He said, "I'll go check."

"Calvin!" Hill's voice halted the man's movement. "I have known you now for what? Twelve or thirteen years?"

"Fifteen years, sir."

"And in that time I have come to know you well, my man, very well. Now then, regarding these three people: I did not see them at the funeral; I did not see them at the reception at my home, and I do not see them on the train. From your actions I can see you know something about them, but for some misguided reason, you are reluctant to divulge the details." He raised his hand to prevent speech from Calvin's open mouth. "Don't say anything that I do not want to hear." Hill looked at the clock on his desk, then at the schedule on his desk, then back at Calvin. "This train is pulling out in exactly seven minutes. At that time, I intend to be standing on the back platform watching the departure. I expect to be able to turn to Zachary Horton and say a few words, and I expect to look back in the salon and see Leah Page with Mister Cummins sipping iced tea or hot coffee. Is that clear?"

"Yes, sir."

"Well, then. Leave me alone so I can do some paperwork."

"But you wanted me to get out a summer suit and comfortable shoes for you."

"You are right, I did want that, but I'll do it. You are free to attend to any duties which might be quite important to you and . . ." His lips curled in a friendly grin. ". . . possibly important to some other people."

Calvin was out the door before anything more could be said.

He found Leah, Del, and Zack in the lounge of the restaurant and was startled to see that Zack had been drinking a large glass of milk and Leah had a half-filled glass of iced tea in front of her; only Del Cummins was drinking beer. With some urgency, Calvin said to Zack, "We'd better go quick; himself is looking for you."

Zack nodded and stood; Leah did not argue; Del finished off his beer. As Zack was taking a couple of greenbacks out of his wallet, Calvin asked, "If you don't mind . . . I thought you all sneaked in here to have some libations."

Leah chose to answer. "We did. Mister Pure Innocence here decided he was going to have to be on his good behavior this afternoon, so he ordered milk. Milk, for God's sake!"

"Lord-ee," Calvin said. "And I thought I was going to have trouble with you."

Zack put the money on the table and asked, "Is Mister Hill worrying you about us?"

"No, not worrying me; he just said that the train was going to pull out on time, and you had better be there on the observation platform with him. He's looking forward to meeting you. That ain't worrying, Mister Zack. That's ordering."

Leah asked, "Did he mention me?" There was a slightly hurt tone to her voice.

"Yes, Miss Page, he said he is looking forward to seeing you again."

The special Memorial Day train pulled out of Union Depot exactly at 1:45.

In recent years, James Hill had developed an intense liking for military bands. He had noticed that Henry Villard, founder of the competing Northern Pacific Railroad, had made an extensive use of military bands during the ceremonies for the driving of the last spike in his transcontinental route, and the newspapers and quarterly magazines had made quite a thing of it. Now James Hill made sure that bands were present at every reasonably important function of the Saint Paul, Minneapolis, and Pacific. As the train was backed from its siding to the switching yard that would get them onto the main track, members of the Saint Paul Police Marching Band entertained the crowd. The fourteen musicians played tubas and trombones, a more than adequate number of bass drums, and two annoying accordions. Hill was not all that pleased with the Scandinavian flavor of the booming presentation because he was more inclined to British martial music. But he was satisfied with the spectacle as he stood on the observation platform, waving to the crowds. In an aside, he said to Zack, "It is nice to meet you finally, Zachary; your grandfather felt a great deal for you. I hope you are proud of his accomplishments."

Zack said, "Grandfather Boynton was the most important person in my life, sir."

Hill turned and looked directly at Zack. "And, as I remember it, your own father gave his life in fighting for the Union."

Zack nodded, then it dawned on him that he had not connected the significance of the gala to his own life.

Hill said, "So it is fitting that you be taking a part in the Memorial Day celebrations." Then, looking away, Hill added, "I tried to join up myself, but this stopped me." He raised a finger and touched his left cheek.

Hill had lost his left eye in a childhood accident, and sometimes his craggy face, complete with well-earned wrinkles and a stylish beard, looked ominous when the false eye did not match the good eye.

"We have things to discuss, young man."

"Yes, sir."

"Has Miss Page told you very much?"

Zack followed Hill's gaze as the train moved back into the switching yard. He realized that the railway owner was evaluating the performance of his train crew. Zack responded, "Miss Page mostly discussed her efforts on behalf of suffrage. I do not think she would presume to discuss any other aspect."

"Nonsense. The woman is bright; she knows what the problems are. Possibly she was merely being polite."

"I have no way of knowing that."

"What we have in front of us, young man, is a project that will require a multitude of talents. Del Cummins told me you have some talent for getting along with people. I can believe that, because it was the most notable attribute of your grandfather. If that is all you inherited, then you received a splendid legacy."

Zack said, "I hope I can do more than reflect a pleasing personality, Mister Hill. I think Grandfather Boynton gave me more than that."

Hill went back to studying the movement of the train. "We will see about that, won't we, Mister Horton?"

The train crew, which had practiced the departure four times the previous day, was moving with easy speed away from the depot proper. Hill kept his gaze fixed on the vast marshalling yard, a plain of steel rails and wooden ties that he had built into one of the leading train centers of the nation. Including the Northern Pacific yards, the center spread a full three blocks from the Steamboat Landings on the bank of the Mississippi River up to Fourth Street, and ran south for over three thousand feet, through cramped acres of track siding, switching sections, warehouses, and workshops. Hill knew the exact construction of every square foot, each water tower, coal-storage bin, and roundhouse. He was a man with a need to know all of the minutiae of any task he might undertake.

As the train moved past the thirty-foot-high switch house, he waved to the men at the levers who would open the tracks to the main line. Beaming at the energetic salutations offered in return, he spoke: "This once was a grove of trees and a swampy meadow; I remember that, Zachary. When I came to this town there were less than two thousand people. Now look at it. You are looking at the very heart of my railroad, the core and foundation needed for the building of the great empire to the west. Without all of this there would be no farms on the plains or mines in the mountains; through this center flows the life-blood of our nation's commerce. You would think that men like Cleveland, and those other politicians, would be able to see the broad horizon as I can see it, as all of the men of vision out here can see it. Greatness! Zachary, greatness."

Hill often waxed poetic when talking about the future. Zack was finding the enthusiasm of an empire builder infectious, beginning to feel that he might have his own visions of his place in the scheme of things. It dawned on Zack that he might be able to earn the feeling of accomplishment that was one of the rewards—possibly the greatest reward—for a lifetime of building a dream and seeing it come to fruition.

The train stopped backing up; it had reached the point of the switch to the main line. Trackside, levers were being thrown, heavy metal devices were set in their proper places. In the cab of the locomotive, valves were being turned and gauges set. Then all was done, and the engine began driving the wheels of the train to the north.

As the train began to pick up speed, Hill said, "I am thinking of changing the name of the Saint Paul, Minneapolis, and Pacific. Does that interest you, Mister Horton?"

"I am here to learn everything I can."

Hill laughed. "I hear a slight hint of your grandmother in that statement. I imagine she has made a reasonable effort to encourage you."

Zack joined in the laugh. "My grandmother has always had her ways of encouraging me, Mister Hill."

"I spoke with your grandmother three months ago about acquiring your railroad, Zachary. I really do intend to have the Dakota and Western as a part of my system. But I also acknowledge her wisdom in wanting to see you involved in the transaction. Del Cummins is a fine man, an outstanding manager who will do well in anything he takes on in life; but you are young, you need this type of experience. Don't expect me to be a soft negotiator or easy taskmaster, Zachary Horton, but don't expect me to do anything which would offend your grandmother. She is a fine lady. We will work all of this out to our mutual benefit."

The words were blunt, but they also sounded sincere. He was beginning to think the experience with James Hill was going to be well worth his leaving New York.

"The Great Northern," Hill was saying.

Zack looked at him questioningly.

"That is what I am going to name my railroad: the Great Northern."

Since Hill had bought the then small railroad in western Minnesota, the line had gone through several name changes. With each new section a name was added or modified. Zack assumed that Hill was about to reveal another purchase or destination, but Hill said, "This holiday I will announce that my line will be the Great Northern Railroad."

Zack understood. There would be no more commas, no more destination identifications; just this simple and grand statement of what James Hill had built; a great, *the* great northern railroad.

"Do you like it?" Hill asked.

"It is appropriate and tells the story, sir."

"You bet it is, Zachary, you bet it is. It will also make it easy for people to accept the name when I finally take over the Northern Pacific, as I will do, have no doubts on that matter. The Great Northern Railroad." Hill tasted the words as he would taste a fine brandy or perfect cigar. Then he turned back to watching the scenery pass. They were on Chicago and Milwaukee track now, heading toward Murray Hill and Ridgewood Park. Hill felt a glow of pride as the commercial and residential buildings slipped past, pride founded in the knowledge that he was a major factor in the growth of the whole area. He had even been instrumental in helping the Chicago and Milwaukee obtain their right-of-way for this track. He savored the prospects of growth. "I did not see you at the funeral. Did you get delayed in Chicago last night?"

"No, sir." Zack thought quickly, then added, "I left before the service ended. I was at the back of the church."

That Zack had left before the service began did not make his report a lie; he hoped Hill would not ask for details.

Hill asked, "What did you think of the eulogy?"

"I didn't hear that, sir. I left before the eulogy."

Hill gave a quick glance at Zack and dropped the subject.

The train was beginning to gain real speed, rolling along the north bank of the Mississippi River toward Murray Hill. The cool breeze generated by the motion was delightful. Hill moved to the left side of the rear platform and looked toward the river. They were angling away from it now. "That river gave me my start, Zachary; everything I have today began right there. I was, I guess, about ten years younger than you are. I had come from Ontario and was heading for the Orient; I was full of dreams." He paused. "God, what a wonderful time that was." He looked at Zack with a pleased expression. "I missed the last wagon train heading toward Oregon, and that was the best accident in my whole life. I had to work, so I managed to become employed at a steamboat shipper, then began business for myself as a forwarding agent. My first big customer was this very railroad, the Saint Paul and Pacific."

The locomotive engineer gave a shrill blast of the steam whistle as they passed Murray Hill; people waved; Hill waved back. He said, "There is so much we must discuss, and we will do that at the lake. First, it might be important for us to have a talk with President Cleveland. I am not sure how, but there must be some way that we can use the old Democrat to our advantage. I want you in on the talk."

Zack protested, "Mister Hill, I know nothing of what we are heading toward. I might say something wrong."

Hill let out a raucous laugh. "Hell, Zachary, do you think Grover Cleveland knows a damned thing about most of what he says? Of course not. You listen to me while we're with him. You can never make a mistake when you are listening."

Inside the car, Del Cummins had taken to his compartment, where he was making some notes regarding the meeting earlier in the day with Hill's accountants. In the lounge, Leah Page was visiting pleasantly with Mary Theresa Hill. On Leah's previous trips to Saint Paul the two women had gotten along fairly well, mainly because Leah avoided delving too deeply into Mary Theresa's beliefs regarding suffrage. Several years previously, Susan B. Anthony had attempted to enlist Mary Theresa in the cause, an attempt that had been politely—but emphatically—rejected. It was not that Hill's wife was opposed to the concept; it was simply that she was the consummate wife and mother. Their talk on the train today focused on the problems of keeping good house servants, about which Leah knew virtually nothing; and about the problems of obtaining just the right leather for ladies' gloves, about which Mary Theresa knew virtually nothing. All in all, it was a socially correct interlude.

As Hill and Zack came back into the lounge, Hill boomed, "Well, ladies, we will be expecting your serious attention when President Cleveland speaks in Minneapolis."

His wife chided, "Now, James, you hold your tongue. Suppose he heard you?"

Leah said nothing, but the thought of having to listen to a man she abhorred made her grimace. Hill spotted the look and said, "Zachary, you'd better keep an eye on this lady; she holds promise. Anyone who is wise to our presidential guest definitely holds promise."

President Cleveland's speech in Minneapolis required considerably more than the few minutes James Hill had anticipated. When the train arrived in the Chicago and Milwaukee Depot on Washington Avenue, it was greeted by Democratic Party stalwarts who, unbeknownst to anyone, had scheduled a rally at City Hall on Hennepin Avenue, four blocks away from the depot. Cleveland, not fond of excessive physical exercise, declined the offer to lead a walk over such a long distance. A cab equipped to handle the president's girth was found, and the hourly rate of one dollar was waived by the cab owner in exchange for three autographs from his notable passenger. Cleveland was able to anger interest groups from just about every segment of the political spectrum, but he did have an outstanding ability to enthrall a crowd of voters, even though his voice was high-pitched and sometimes squeaky. He spoke for a full half hour.

Hill had opted to remain at his railway car and entertained the guests who joined his party in Minneapolis. There was a considerable gathering in the dining car where refreshments were served, and people began to get into the spirit of the Memorial Day party. Hill, a recognized stickler for schedules—especially when he did the scheduling—hid his anger well.

When Cleveland arrived back at the train, and as soon as they were rolling, Calvin Jones ushered him into the salon of the *L'Etoile du Nord*. While Zack and Leah were to be a part of the meeting, they demurred when asked if they needed any refreshments. President Cleveland announced that he was interested in a tall glass of whiskey, with ice, with branch water. Calvin, respecting the man who led the nation but in the employ of James Hill, looked to Hill for permission. Hill gave a barely perceptible nod; there was no help for it.

With the drink served and Calvin gone, Hill introduced the subject. He was only two sentences into his opening statement when Cleveland interrupted with "Ah, I just want to stop you for a moment James but . . ." He pointed his cigar at Leah Page. ". . . is madam here as your scribe or something?"

Hill stared at him. Zack looked down at the floor, and Leah Page was unable to stop an angry flush from rising up to color her cheeks.

"I mean," said Cleveland, as if trying to compound his crass attitude, "if she is here to take notes or something, then someone should get her a paper and pen." He smiled at Leah. "Heaven knows she is pretty enough not to need any sort of excuse, but from what you have started to tell me, James, this sounds like a meeting of import." Then, more sternly, "Why is she here?"

Leah opened her mouth, but Hill cut in, "Mister President, Miss Page has been very active in trying to help us develop a sound policy regarding suffrage in the territories which will be coming into the Union."

"Well, little lady, why don't you just tell us what you have to say?"

Leah knew she could not talk to that man at that instant. She said, "I think Mister Hill has something more important to offer at this time, Mister President."

Hill seized the opportunity. When he began talking about Dakota Territory, he said that Zack was one of the owners of the Dakota and Western Railroad, and that they were going to be enlisting the assistance of Theodore Roosevelt, who was living in that territory. Roosevelt had been prominent in the Republican Party and had served in some minor political posts.

Cleveland could not let that pass. "Now just a moment, James. You may not know this, but I have a certain loathing for Theodore Roosevelt. The man is a pompous ass."

Leah glanced at Zack, who was glancing at her; they were both glad they had not had anything to drink. If they had, they both knew, they would have broken out in loud laughter.

Hill handled it well. "It matters little whether you like the man or not, Mister President. The fact remains that members of my staff have been working diligently to aid the territories gain admission."

Cleveland nodded. "You are right about my feelings toward Roosevelt, James. It might interest you to know that the man has, in fact, had a meeting with Auggie Garland, my attorney general, and I have received a complete report on what Roosevelt had to say about Dakota Territory and statehood. The important thing for the moment is to keep Mister Roosevelt out of all this. There are members of Congress who would relish the opportunity to hurl a few rocks at Roosevelt, and the press would pick that up with equal gusto. If that happens, then there is no way any territories will be admitted as states for a very long time."

Hill stood up and looked out the window, studying the passing countryside of gently rolling pastures for grazing milk cows. The pause dragged on for nearly a minute before President Cleveland emptied his drink and looked around impatiently. "Where the devil is that manservant of yours? I could do with another one of these."

Zack sprang up and picked up Cleveland's glass. "I'll go take care of this."

"Why don't you let the little lady do that chore, boy? Women's work, you know."

Zack did not pause, but headed toward the corridor and the kitchen. Hill continued looking out the window, and Cleveland then directed a smarmy smile at Leah.

The man was totally unattractive to her. His hairline was receding on each side of his head, leaving a clump right at the top of his forehead. His ears and nose were big, and a bushy, walrus-style moustache extended down on each side to the middle of his chin. It was his eyes that annoyed Leah the most; they were hard, cold, and piercing. The noticeable bags under his eyes did not help his appearance. She pulled her infuriated glance away from him for fear that he might misunderstand her attention. Only two years before he had married Frances Folsom, who was twenty-eight years his junior. Leah was repulsed when she remembered that the man had been Frances' guardian for eleven years before he married her; she felt very sorry for the wife, who seemed to be a charming woman.

Zack returned, setting the drink on the table in front of the president. Hill spoke while still looking out the window. He said, "I am confused, Mister President. You say that Theodore Roosevelt should be kept out of the picture, as if that could help the cause, yet, as I see your past actions, you have been opposed to new states."

Hill turned from the window. Cleveland took time to relight his cigar before he offered, "I have not been a champion of statehood, James. That is true, but I have changed my feelings on the matter. For, oh, I would say, twenty years or more, the territories have suffered innocuous desuetude, and the time has come to rectify the injustice. When I am reelected and when we have the new Congress in place, I intend to push strongly for execution of the Enabling Act. The territories are worthy of admission, and I will see that it is done. But there is great turpitude afoot in political circles to try to prevent any new states at this time. That is my reason for wanting to keep this out of the hands of political opportunists such as Roosevelt."

Hill resumed his seat across from the president. "That might not be all that easy. If plans go as scheduled, Mister Horton will be seeing Mister Roosevelt fairly soon. Roosevelt might become very involved, publicly."

Cleveland digested that unwelcome news. He announced, "Let me tell you one thing. You are obviously seriously trying to do some good for the territories of the Great Northwest. As far as Utah Territory and the Mormons are concerned, they will never be even considered for statehood so long as they hold to their belief in polygamy. Never! As far as breaking up Idaho Territory and casting the pieces hither and yon, you can forget that. Do you know Senator George Hearst? He is trying to do something along these lines. He wants to create the New Mining State out of western Montana and northern Idaho. Now that is not going to be accepted, simply because the next logical step would be to put southern Idaho in with Utah. Twenty-five percent of the people in Idaho are Mormons, and that would give these Latter-day Saints just too much land, too many resources, and a dangerous flock of people under their political control. This idea of Hearst's, gentlemen . . ." and he gave a condescending smile to Leah, ". . . and lady, is one thing that could ring the death knell for statehood."

He finished off his drink, dropped his cigar into the empty glass, and stood up. "Of course, James, my reelection will be a critical ingredient if statehood is to progress. I must say that your gracious invitation to attend this important remembrance will weigh strongly in matters which concern you. I know that you have not been one of my staunchest supporters, but I do take this gesture as a measure of your dedication to your railroad business and to the good of the Northwest."

Hill stood as well. "I surely think it was splendid of you to take the time on this, Mister President. I had no idea, when I invited you to the Memorial Day celebration, that I would be burdening you with more troubles. Thank you for your patience."

Hill extended his hand and Cleveland shook it. "That is my job, James. Now, I think I will go back and visit with my family a bit, and get ready for a very nice holiday with you, your family, and friends."

Cleveland turned to leave, but paused and looked at Leah. "Could you tell me, young lady, just what is your stake in this? Mister Hill has a vested interest in his railroad, and Mister Horton owns the Dakota and Western. I can understand their concerns, but what is your piece of this pie?"

Leah replied, "I represent the National Woman Suffrage Association. Mister Hill has been kind enough to give us moral support, and I am using his good offices to try to see that when the states are admitted to the Union, then women will have the vote and the other rights due them."

Cleveland laughed. "So," he said, "we have another suffragette. When will you women learn?"

Leah grinned. "We have learned, Mister Cleveland, and we have learned well: We will get the vote."

"Ah, Miss Page," Cleveland said. "Sensible and responsible women do not want to vote. The relative positions to be assumed by man and woman in the working out of our civilization were assigned long ago by a higher intelligence than ours."

Angry retorts flooded into her thoughts, but all she said was, "I certainly disagree with you on that, sir."

"Well, that's what makes horse races, young lady." He gave a slight bow and said, "Now, let's put all of this behind us and enjoy the hospitality offered by Mister Hill."

With that, he turned and left.

As soon as he was out of earshot, Leah Page exploded. "That pompous ass . . . that arrogant bastard . . . that mound of horse dung . . . that—"

Zack cut her off. "Hey, take it easy."

James Hill was laughing so hard he had to plop down into his chair. Through his laughter, he said, "Miss Page, the next time I go down to the engine repair workshops, I will take you along; you can interpret all the things the men say that I fail to understand."

Zack, also laughing, went to Leah and took hold of her shoulders. He said, "I think someone is going to have to wash out your mouth with soap."

"Well, it won't be that stupid buffoon."

James Hill said, "I think we could all wash out our mouths with something stronger than tea or coffee." He pushed the buzzer for Calvin. "Miss Page, will you join Zack and me?"

Leah responded, "Mister Hill, that would be wonderful." She was feeling some of the tension ease out of her, and she added, "I thought you had set a rule against any drinking on the ride out to the lake?"

With an elfin grin, Hill said, "Did Calvin tell you that?"

Both Zack and Leah nodded.

"In a moment of Puritan fervor I did set the rule. But then I am also the one who can rescind the rule." All three laughed as Calvin Jones came into the salon.

Lake Minnetonka was a magnificent gift of Nature quickly seized upon by the residents of Saint Paul and Minneapolis. Early on, as soon as people began displaying an interest in using the lake as a vacation resort, rail access was put in place. The short lines connecting the cities to the lake made money and politically impressed residents of the Twin Cities as a considerable public service.

Hill's railroad maintained a spur that ran right to the Hotel Lafayette on the north shore, and, because he was so sympathetic to the needs of the resort, the management spared no expense to give him a grand reception. The fact that the president of the United States was arriving was of minor import to the management; James Hill deserved the best on his own merit.

A spanking new barouche stood ready to transport the Hills and the Clevelands the eighty yards from the train platform to the hotel entrance. The other guests arriving with the Hill party were able to use twelve passenger carriage busses, or they could walk. Zack Horton and Leah Page opted to walk.

The Lafayette was decked out in appropriate bunting, and the festive trim portended a light, happy couple of days. Two tables were set in the lobby to handle distribution of room keys and to sort out baggage delivery; the hotel orchestra played softly from its perch on the balcony.

Each guest received a portfolio containing a handsomely printed welcome and a schedule of events, some of which were obligatory, some optional. In the obligatory category were dinner the first night in the main dining room, lunch the next day, and the following lawn reception at which there would be patriotic music and a Memorial Day speech by President Cleveland. It was also clearly stated that each of Hill's guests would attend the soirée to be held on the lawn facing the lake that would culminate in a display of fireworks. Optional activities were badminton and croquet, fishing from skiffs to be provided by the hotel, and small steamer cruises to points of interest on the fifteen-mile-long lake. The weather was beautiful. The temperature, compared to that of the cities they had just left, was fifteen degrees cooler, with the thermometer hovering right at seventy.

It was quarter past four when Zack and Del had finished signing in and receiving their room assignment; Leah was only a few moments behind them. They met by the grand staircase.

Leah asked cheerfully, "Well, what do we do now?"

Del, in a somewhat grumpy mood, said, "I've still got a whole mess of paperwork to get done." Then, in a lighter vein, he added, "I guess I'm stuck with facts and figures, and a case of beer."

Zack asked, "Is there something I can help with?"

Del shook his head. "Naw." He smiled, looking at Leah, and said, "She's pretty enough for you to spend the rest of the afternoon on."

Leah mocked shyness. "Why, Mister Cummins, ah do believe you are playing the matchmaker."

Del laughed. "I've been doing that since he came of age, madam. I don't think I will ever succeed."

Zack cut in. "You two are having great sport at my expense, but I do think there must be something we could be doing other than sitting in the room with a pile of statistics, Del. Let's find something to amuse Miss Page; how about it?"

Del looked tempted but said, "Fact is, I'm as tired as I can be. I'll probably take a snooze before the big dinner tonight."

Zack turned to Leah. "Looks like you're stuck with me."

"That's fine. I just want to get moving. I am depressed from that funeral . . ."

"You didn't even go!"

"Well, I am bothered by the thought of the funeral." She added, "And, I am annoyed by having to talk to that obscene person we have to call our president."

Del chuckled. "Zack, you'd better get her distracted from all of her problems, or else it will be hell tonight at the dinner. From what I hear, Mister Cleveland is going to make another speech."

Leah snapped, "I refuse to listen to that man again."

Zack placed a hand gently on her shoulder. "I will rescue you from that; don't worry. But, for now, I'm following my counselor's advice and inviting you to find some amusement which may lighten your mental burden."

"Fine. I'll need to change, though." She started up the stairs. "Give me a few minutes."

"Ten . . . at the most. I want to relax and enjoy myself," Zack responded.

He turned to look at her. The light from the patio windows was playing on her face, and her features were lovely. He began to entertain thoughts that had very little to do with railroads or suffrage.

She said, "Zack . . ." She paused as if to organize her decision before going on. "Are you planning to take me to the banquet tonight?"

He smiled. "I had no other plan."

"I would enjoy that."

After a quick hand flick that passed for a wave, he bounded up the stairs. Del followed.

Their rooms were adjoining on the second floor in the east wing. Del followed him in, then went through the door to his own room. Zack's bag was on the rack at the foot of the bed, and he needed only a couple of minutes to unpack and change into white trousers, a soft cotton shirt, and a light brown jacket. He felt a tie was not necessary. He was in the bathroom giving a couple of brush strokes to his hair when Del Cummins walked back in.

Zack saw Cummins in the mirror. "Hey, Del, why don't you come with us?"

"Not this time. You go have some fun with her; you seem to be getting along."

Zack continued brushing his hair. "She is a nice lady." He set the brush down and came into the room.

Cummins said, "What do you think of her?"

"As I said, nice lady."

"More than just nice, I'd say. She's one pretty woman."

Zack could not hold back a grin. "Are you promoting something, Del, or are you just making chatter?"

"I'm not promoting anything; it is just nice to see you around a woman near your own age."

Zack sat down on the edge of his bed. "Why do I feel the influential hand of my grandmother in all of this?"

"Well," Del replied, in a sheepish tone, "she did mention that you seemed to be attracted to older women, like that French lady in New York."

"So, Grandmother has been talking to you." Zack stood and walked to the window. "For your information, that 'older woman' is just a bit older than I am. I think the fact that she is married is what really bothered my grandmother. But I'm done with that interlude. I have no commitments right now. I'm just playing the field, as they say at Saratoga."

"Leah Page looks like she might be eligible for more than just 'playing the field.'"

"I'm not ready for serious things, Del. You know that."

"I'm not sure I do know that, Zack. You could be thinking about a woman in your future."

"Is this another message from Philadelphia?"

"No, it's not that. I just think you could start thinking about a family pretty soon."

Zack turned and looked at his companion. "Now that you've decided to put a wife in your future, you're trying to find a way to get me tied down. I swear, Del Cummins, you are a pistol."

"Hey, Zachary Horton, I just want you to be as happy as I am, that's all."

Zack went to Del and extended his hand. "I know you mean what you say, my friend. I think that Leah Page is a fine, attractive woman. I don't know what will come of meeting her, but I'm really not ready to take that step in my life."

"Wait until you come up against a few of those winter nights in Dakota, when the temperature gets to forty below. Those sheets in the bed are awfully cold."

Zack laughed. "Maybe that will convince me."

Del looked back into his room at the stack of papers waiting for him. He shrugged. "Aw, to hell with it. Let's go find that gal and see if I can get you interested a bit more."

"Quit matchmaking."

"I'm thinking about the cold winter nights ahead of you."

▶◆◀

They found Leah waiting in the lobby, and, at her suggestion, they moved to a table on the front veranda of the hotel. They all ordered lemonade, and while they waited for it to be served, Leah ran through a long list of possible activities. She ended by saying, "I'm voting for a canoe ride; that sounds like fun to me."

"That leaves me out," declared Del.

"Why?" she asked.

"Simply, madam, because I am a railroad man from the flat plains of Dakota Territory. I find no joy in anticipating trusting my life to some skimpy little thing some people might call a boat. I am a dry-land person."

Zack argued, "Come on, Del; be a sport."

Del delivered a lengthy insincere dissertation on the hazards of the water and canoeing. He was patently obvious in his motives; he wanted Zack and Leah to have some time alone. He was just about out of arguments when the lemonade was served.

For the next minute, they sipped, then Leah Page spoke. "Zack, I've been wondering: what did Mister Hill have to say to you on the train ride?"

"Not much of anything, Leah. Oh, he spoke quite a bit about quite a few things, but he did not make any specifics regarding his plans for us. He voiced his views on the importance of statehood, that sort of thing. I'm sure you have heard it all before."

"But nothing specific. I would really like to know what the plans are so that I could arrange my schedule."

Zack laughed. "I appreciate your concern, Leah, but the way things are going, I have given up on plans. With us being expected to take part in the funeral and this holiday, any hope of moving quickly seems impossible."

"It's not that. I've budgeted enough time to allow for distractions, but I am still in a quandary as to what is involved. I know what my task is; a lot of it can be done by letters, because I know most of the women who can influence decisions in the territories. But Mister Hill seems to have evolved a larger strategy that includes you and Del; I hope he is not planning any trips that will take a great deal of time."

Zack asked, "What makes you think anything like that?"

"Well." She hesitated an instant, then went on. "Quite candidly, your first asset to contribute is your family tie to the Dakota and Western Railroad."

Zack looked wounded.

Quickly, Leah added, "Don't let your pride be injured, Zack Horton. That is your *first* asset. Your second is that you are intelligent, friendly, and young. Remember that most of the people out on the frontier are young; most of the powerful men, like James Hill, are not young. Your traits could be useful."

"You make me sound like a commodity."

"That's the way I see it."

Del Cummins offered, "She's not that far from wrong, Zack. It is the young people, young families that are building the West."

Leah smiled at Del. "The problem is," she said to Zack, "to take advantage of that asset, you will have to go and meet people."

Zack digested that thought, then said, "I plan to meet people. As soon as this meeting with Hill is over, Del and I will be going to Dakota. That's already part of our plans."

Leah's face was serious. "I hope, Zack, that your plans meld with Mister Hill's."

Del Cummins said, "I think we should . . ." He stopped talking as Calvin Jones approached their table.

Zack said, "Well, here is the best trainman in the West."

Calvin smiled politely, then said, "Mister Hill would like to see you, all of you, up in his rooms."

They all looked at each other. Leah turned back to Calvin. "Sounds serious; is it, Calvin?"

"No, no, Miss Leah. He just told me to find you and tell you."

Zack asked, "Why are you looking so glum?"

Calvin scratched his chin. "I just found out that I've got to go back with the train to Saint Paul; bringing some more people down first thing in the morning."

Calvin had probably thought he was going to have a couple of days off, and he had probably been looking forward to the relaxation.

Del asked, "When do you have to leave?"

"We're going back in about an hour." Then, confusing the trio, he added, "But you'd better talk to Mister Hill about that. I've got to get to my work."

Before anyone could ask what he meant, Calvin gave a polite nod of his head and was gone.

►◄◄

The Hill suite was large enough to allow for a comfortable parlor as well as the bedrooms behind three closed doors. The parlor was a corner room looking over the landscaped front lawn and a spectacular view across Lake Minnetonka. James Hill was seated behind a small oak desk. He stood and extended an affable greeting as the trio arrived.

"I am sorry to interrupt your afternoon, but there are some things which need to be discussed. Here, sit down." He indicated a grouping of wing chairs set in a semicircle around a small sofa. There were bottles of spring water and glasses provided with ice; Hill offered them as refreshments.

To make casual conversation, as he was sitting down, Zack said, "The rooms are as nice as can be, Mister Hill."

Hill smiled, nodded, then said, "We will come to that in a few minutes, Zachary." Then, looking at Leah, Hill asked, "May the gentlemen smoke, Miss Page?"

"I have no problems with that, Mister Hill."

Zack passed, but Del and Hill devoted a few moments to lighting up cigars.

Leah looked around the room. It was finely decorated in a manner that was masculine, but not overpoweringly so. She spotted a John Kensett landscape that she had noticed previously on a visit to Hill's home in Saint Paul, and she guessed that it was in the Lafayette Hotel suite in an effort to make Hill's stay as comfortable as possible.

Hill took a seat on the sofa by himself. "Zachary, what I have to say pertains mainly to you, but I want Miss Page and Mister Cummins to hear what I have to say, just so there is no misunderstanding."

Zack began feeling slightly uncomfortable.

Hill looked at Zack and said, "The first thing is that I feel that you are just the man I have been looking for to give me a bit of assistance in this project of mine."

Zack wondered why he felt a sense of relief at those words; it was as if he had been looking for acceptance. Zack realized he had come to like the gruff railroad mogul, probably because he reminded Zack of his grandfather.

Hill continued. "All that I have known of you, Zachary, is what I have been told by friends and associates who were willing to offer an opinion. I knew your grandfather only slightly, but he spoke highly of you. There are men in New York whom I trust, and they told me that you have potential in the world of finance. Mister Cummins has been kind enough to share some of his opinions of your sterling character—which I feel may be a bit biased—but he helped convince me you are a man of energy; that is important for what I need to do. Even Miss Page has made her own contribution—"

Leah interrupted. "Mister Hill! I have never spoken to you about Zack."

Hill smiled. "That is true, Miss Page, but I know you would have distanced yourself from any individual who did not come up to a certain set of standards; I have not seen you disdain his company."

Leah felt a blush on her face. She took a glass and poured herself an unwanted drink of spring water; anything to avoid looking at Zachary Horton.

Hill, sympathetic to the embarrassment he had caused her, poured himself an equally unwanted measure of water before he went on. "I need, Zachary, a man who can share in what I see for this nation. There are great, great things about to happen, and I intend to be a part of them, but I am not so foolish as to think that I can do it all by myself. I can hire men to do the legal work or the financial work or the political work. What I need is a man who can talk with people, learn what they need, and learn how to gain their support. It is a dream that I have, and I hope you can have the same dream."

Zack said. "I cannot say that I have ever thought of the future as a dream, Mister Hill. I can say that I have seen immigrants coming into New York by the thousands, and I know they need work, and that work must be created by people willing to invest in the future. Those are only observations, though."

"Zachary, dreams are the manifestation of observing. You see a pretty woman and you dream of loving her; you see a better life and you dream of how to obtain it. You have to be able to see something before you can dream of it. I think you have seen the things which can inspire ambition. Ambition is only the pursuit of dreams."

Zack protested. "I am afraid, sir, that you give me more nobility of actions than I deserve. I have no major goals; I am merely learning now, so that I can set goals for myself."

"Learning is noble in its own right. You must see that. Learning is absolutely vital to any steps forward. This business of statehood is a step forward for thousands of people now living in the territories. They have learned, most of them have learned, that their lives are being ruled by the whims of powerful politicians, thousands of miles away, who have no idea of the trials inflicted by territorial rule. Our nation needs a strong central government, but we also need broad self-government. The people need to be able to face the lawmakers, and I mean face them right there, toe to toe, in the halls of the state capitols. Citizens should not have to live with only the hope that they can bring some influence to bear. Good heavens, the people in the territories cannot even vote for one of the men responsible for making national laws in the Congress.

"We in the railroad industry have brought this nation together for the first time in our history. Citizens can now travel across this great land in a matter of days, not months. It is our responsibility and duty to see that they are now brought into the era of self-government. The days of the frontier are gone; they vanished when the Golden Spike was driven into the transcontinental railroad. Do I bore you?"

Leah said, "Mister Hill, what you are saying is just what the suffrage leaders are saying."

Hill nodded. "And that is why you are here, Miss Page, and that is why I have imposed on you to neglect your own business. Don't even begin to think that I am not sympathetic to the sacrifice you are making in being away; you will not suffer, believe me when I say that."

"My business will get by without me for a little while, Mister Hill."

Hill stood and walked to the window facing the lake. He said, "On an afternoon like this, you two should be out on that lake in a canoe enjoying each other's company. But the fates that conduct our lives have brought you here to this room, to this grumpy old man who is wanting to gain control of your energies." He turned from the window. "And you, Mister Cummins, I wonder what you would be doing this minute if I was not robbing you of your time?"

Del laughed. "Probably having a nice cool beer, Mister Hill."

Concerned, Hill asked, "Would you like one right now? I can order some brought up."

"No," Del protested, "I was merely making a joke."

"I know you are a conscientious man, Mister Cummins, but, if a cool beer would enrich this moment, then you will have it."

Del declined.

Hill took his seat on the sofa again. He studied Zack for a few moments, then asked, "Do you have any idea about our industry, Zachary? I mean what our industry really is?"

Zack answered, "I know that my grandfather's entire life was devoted to the industry, and there are thousands like him."

"I wonder if your grandfather ever told you of the heritage you have wandered into?"

"I don't know that he ever sat me down and talked about it."

"Well, he should have." Hill reached for his cigar. "You may not realize it, Zachary, but this business goes back to the 1500s in Europe at a coal mine in Alsace in France. The railroad is first mentioned in England in the late 1600s, again at coal mines, in the north of the country. An intricate system of canals had been constructed to provide for water barges' efficient movement of goods and raw materials throughout the island empire. But the goods and raw materials had to be transported from their source to the canals, and therein lay a major problem. There was a great demand for coal for both domestic and industrial use. Heavy wagonloads of coal had to be moved from the mines to the canal terminals before they could reach London and Liverpool. After spring rains the wagon wheels would sink down into the mud roads. Some enterprising teamster came up with the idea of placing heavy planks on top of the mud, and that worked well, until still heavier wagons were dispatched over the roads and the planks sank down into the mud. The next step came when someone had the idea to place crosswise planks every four feet and thus disburse the load factor over a wider area. The wooden road functioned well.

"It was not long, however, before the traveling planks began to wear through under the heavy loads. A cargo shipper in Wales is credited with first protecting the planks with sheets of iron, but that innovation created wear on the wagon wheels, so the wheels were protected with iron rims. The next step in the progression came when a flange was set in place, first on the metal-protected planks, then on the iron-rimmed wheels, and railroads were born to serve the needs of industry and society."

Hill had been enjoying his lecture; his audience of three had, too. He smiled like a proud teacher as he asked, "Have you ever wondered why the rails of our railroads are set at a standard four feet eight and a half inches?"

There were no replies.

"The horse chariots of the Roman Empire had wheels set at that measure, and the British built their own wagons with that same width. When wagons became trains, the rails were set accordingly.

"It was 1820 before anyone tied the concept of speed to the movement of commerce. A horse on the ironclad railroads could pull eight times the load it could on a dirt road, and that satisfied most shippers; the quantity of weight did not come to bear on the quality of time as long as mercantile leaders saw most of their trade carried in ships which had plied the sea lanes at between five to ten knots for thousands of years. With the introduction of the sleek, fast clipper ships, speed was violently introduced into the equation of the marketplace. As the steam engine began to replace the sail in water commerce, steam was also wedded with the railroad, and the demand for faster service catapulted onto the scene.

"Once the genii of speed was unleashed, there was no stopping the ingenuity and inventiveness of man. The short single-use railroads, made, say, merely for hauling coal from the mines to the canals, began to give way to common carriers that would haul diverse cargos over comparatively long distances. In 1823 the first steam locomotion railway was established in England, and, by the 1850s, most industrialized—and many agrarian—nations in the world were being served, to some degree, by railroads.

"In the United States, steam-driven train service was initiated on Christmas Day in 1830 by the South Carolina Railroad. By 1856, railroads were functioning on both the Atlantic and Pacific coasts when the Sacramento Valley Railroad began service between San Francisco and Sacramento.

"The Civil War had both a dampening and an encouraging effect on the expansion of railway service throughout the country. Growth was dramatically inhibited, because the industry of the North was necessarily dedicated to the manufacture of materials needed to keep the huge armies equipped and on the field of battle, while financial resources and manpower were also involved in the prosecution of the war. On the other side the potential for rapid growth became evident when the railroads were used to move troops and a steady flow of equipment going to the devouring conflict that would insure the future of the Union. Another by-product of the war was the sudden wealth of investors who had benefited from selling the government products needed in the war.

"So the stage was set for the building of the American Empire. The lead parts were to go to the investors; the setting was to be the broad expanse of a continent; the plot would be the most dynamic proliferation in population and wealth of any nation in history. We are not in a business that sprouted up overnight, nor is it one which has a casual effect on our lives and economy. Railroading is the lifeblood of our nation."

As Hill paused and drank some spring water, Del Cummins

stood and walked over to the window. He looked down across the front lawn to the small hotel depot and the gleaming Baldwin locomotive at the head of the small special train that had brought Hill and his guests to the lake for a holiday. It came to his mind how far the industry had come from its origins, from those planks set down on muddy roads. Progress, from the expedient of utility to the extravagance of luxury. He said, "I had no idea about all of this, Mister Hill. I've been around this business for a good many years and I never thought about the past; my only concern was the present."

Hill joined Del at the window. "That was the way I was when I began, Mister Cummins, and that is the way it should be. The vital task is to make a business function well. Only then can one afford the indulgence of seeking the past. But now my interest is in the future." He turned and faced Zack and Leah. "The future that you two young people are being asked to help develop. I spoke for so long so as to infect you with some of my hopes. Zack, I've imposed on a long friendship with your grandparents to muster some help; help which I need desperately. This is a chance for you to join the ranks of men like Lewis and Clark, who walked across the Northwest to open the continent. Can you see your way clear to join in my effort?"

Zack had known the answer since his grandmother had first posed the proposition.

"Yes, sir. No problem."

Hill turned to Del Cummins. "And, Del, you have no problem giving some assistance?" Hill paused, then added, "Word has come to me that you are planning a marriage."

Del blushed as he replied, "I can be away from the Dakota and Western from time to time; the road is running well." Then, with pride, he said, "Besides, Felicity Patterson is an understanding woman."

James Hill looked at Del. "Is that Matt Patterson's widow?"

Del nodded.

Hill gave a warm smile. "She is a fine woman. I knew her husband well; he shipped much of his farm equipment on our line. A tragic accident. I take it that you are friends with Mrs. Patterson?"

"I am that. I hope to marry her."

Hill placed a hand on Del's shoulder. "That is good to hear. She deserves a full life, and you will be a good husband, I am sure."

Hill turned to Zack. "Will you join with me?"

"I will, sir."

"Fine." He moved over to where Leah Page was sitting and said, "You are not being excluded from this, Miss Page. I thank you for you patience. I felt it was important for you, too, to know the depth of my feelings."

Leah rose and extended her hand to Hill. "I appreciate hearing what you said because, for different reasons, we are all hopefully heading in the same direction. I cannot say that I hold as deep a passion for your industry, but I do know that what I believe in is tied to your own beliefs. I think that you"—she looked at Zack—"and Mister Horton and Mister Cummins can also advance my own hopes for the territories out west. I think I am very proud that you included me in your plans."

"That is simply splendid," Hill boomed. "Now, let us get to just what we must accomplish."

There was a knock at the door leading to the hallway.

Hill went over, opened the door, and found himself facing President Cleveland's secretary. "Well, Mister Oliver, what can I do for you?"

Christopher Oliver was a tall, gangly man whose pompous attitude was crowned with a voice that projected an annoying whine. "Good afternoon, Mister Hill. The president has instructed me to advise you that he will be able to meet with you in fifteen minutes."

Hill wanted to say *Tell the president that I am busy,* but he also wanted to keep the ear of Cleveland. "Tell the president that I will be most pleased to meet with him."

Secretary Oliver moved his upper lip and nose in a way that looked as if he was smelling something very unpleasant. "Thank you. The president has instructed me to tell you that he would like to have the meeting here in your quarters, Mister Hill."

"That's just fine with me."

Oliver continued, "The president feels his own quarters are simply too confused with visitors at this particular time, Mister Hill."

Hill grinned. "There is no need to apologize, Mister Oliver. The president is most welcome in my quarters."

The look on Oliver's face turned from disdain to anger because he realized he should not have apologized. Having bested the bumptious secretary, Hill began to close the door as he said, "I will be here when the president is ready, Mister Oliver."

After coming back to the sofa, Hill said to the trio, "I don't know why I get pleasure out of bursting those fellows' bubbles, but I do. My wife would call it a venial sin; I call it good sport."

The realization came to Zack that he was going to enjoy associating with James Hill.

Hill took his seat, indulged in a short, satisfied puff of his cigar, then said, "We must get to things quickly now that we will be exposed to a royal visit."

Del Cummins teased, "President Cleveland, being a Democrat, might take issue with your moving him up to royalty, Mister Hill. He postures as a man of the people."

"Ha!" came immediately from Hill. "That man is an imperious buffoon." Looking at Leah, he asked, "What did you call him?"

Blushing, Leah replied, "I'd rather not use that language again, Mister Hill; I lost my temper."

Hill laughed. I remember: an arrogant bastard. That is exactly what he is."

Del said, "You must have really lost your temper, Leah."

She continued to blush.

Hill took charge. "Zachary, I want you to have a meeting with Theodore Roosevelt." Turning to Del Cummins, Hill asked, "You know him, don't you?"

"Yes, sir. His ranch is near our railroad and we have done business. I like him."

Turning back to Zack, Hill continued, "Roosevelt is an easy man to like, and he has a vested interest in seeing statehood. First, he has a considerable ranching operation in Dakota, and secondly, he is a Republican, the major political inclination in all of the Northwest territories. That's why Grover Cleveland has been fighting statehood, and probably still is, no matter what he says. He'll probably lose the Congress, if not his own office of president, once statehood is established." Hill paused to sip from his glass of water. "I want you to spend some time with Roosevelt, get his views, listen to his suggestions, then talk to those he mentions as possible supporters. I think we know most of them, but you may be able to elicit new names."

Zack waited, but Hill did not continue. Zack asked Del, "Where is the Roosevelt ranch?"

"South of Williston, near the Montana Territory border. I'll show you on a map."

To Hill, Zack said, "That does not sound like an especially arduous task. I should be able to do that in a few days."

"Fine." Hill pulled himself up and walked to the window again. While looking down at the people playing croquet, he said, "When you are done with Roosevelt, I want you to go on to Montana and see Marcus Daly. I will arrange that meeting by telegraph message, just as soon as you are ready to move. And then you will be going on to Idaho and Washington territories."

Zack was stunned. Leah Page was sympathetic, and it showed on her face.

Hill turned from the window, smiling. "Miss Page, I am going to have to ask you to pay a visit to Wyoming."

Her sympathetic look gave way to surprise.

Hill added, "And, Del, there is probably going to have to be some help from you on these direct, personal visits. I do not know what the demand will be, but I anticipate calling on you."

Del was the first to respond. "Mister Hill," he said, "our own railroad is in need of management. I agreed that I could wait to break in Zack, but things need attending by someone."

Hill resumed his seat. "There is little you can tell me about the Dakota and Western, Del. One reason my own managers have been looking so diligently at your books is to see how you have been managing that road. You have done an outstanding job."

Del smiled a weak appreciation of the compliment.

"You have done so well that you have even been able to lure some of my good personnel to your company. The truth is that you have highly competent managers, your station and section people are doing a good job, and your train and maintenance crews are functioning at a high level. If I ask you to help, and thereby cause some harm, then I will assume the responsibility. I am a hard businessman, Del. I do not think I will have to back up my promise."

Leah asked, "How long will we be involved, Mister Hill?"

"I do not know."

The vagueness bothered Leah, and it showed.

"I have already promised you no damage, Miss Page. Believe me, there will be better business for you once statehood is established and I have lines all the way to the Pacific Coast. The money you will save on shipping your goods to Japan alone will more than make up for any disturbance now. I know you pride yourself on paying your employees good wages; you'll be able to pass on those profits to them in the form of raises. Your company will not suffer for your involvement in this effort." He paused for a breath, then added, "Besides, you will find the Wyoming people quite anxious to further the cause of universal suffrage. You will be pleased with what they are doing out there."

Zack asked, "Can you give us *any* rough idea of the time involved, Mister Hill?"

"The time will be determined by events. I have been working in the Northwest for twenty years and I am not done with what I want. It won't be anything like two decades, but it will take several weeks, maybe even months." While Zack absorbed that, Hill added, "One other thing, Zachary. I am now treating you as a peer. You are a fellow railroad owner and you

are joining me as a partner in this statehood effort. I will appreciate it if you will call me Jim." Turning to the other two, he said,
"That includes both of you, please."

Hill stood and went to his desk for two envelopes. Coming
back, he handed one to Leah, the other to Zack. "These are
introductions; I have preceded them with telegraph messages
advising of your coming."

The letters were sealed; Zack and Leah were beginning to
blurt a flood of questions when Hill precluded more discussion
by returning to his desk and picking up a solid gold pocket
watch. "The train will be leaving to go back to Saint Paul in just
forty-five minutes. You will be given the necessary identifica-
tion passes that will allow you to travel freely; my general manager in Saint Paul will provide you with a reasonable amount of
capital to cover your expenses."

Del was the first to find his voice. He said, "That was why
Calvin told us we should speak to you about the train's return."

Hill laughed. "Calvin is a discreet soul, isn't he?"

Zack said, "Mister Hill . . . Jim . . . you have loaded our
plates full, and very quickly. I know I have a dozen questions."

Leah agreed.

Hill nodded. "Please try and understand. The Pillsbury
funeral caused us to lose valuable time, and the presence of
President Cleveland has not made things easier. My manager
will be giving each of you complete files on this whole business.
You'll have time to study them as you travel. Your trains leave
at nine o'clock tonight."

Leah said, "This is a bit overwhelming."

Hill walked over to her and extended his hand. "It is, isn't
it? But time is the most precious possession and we must not
waste any of it. I failed to mention that I will be joining you
shortly; I would not leave you alone out there."

Zack rose, protesting, "I still have a dozen questions."

Hill shook Zack's hand. "Read the files you will be given;
then telegraph me any questions you might need answering."

Hill shook Del's hand, too, then said, "Now the three of
you had better get out of here before his eminence, Grover

Cleveland, arrives. He will have a stroke if he knows you are going to see Mister Roosevelt, Zack." He ushered them to the door. "I will be seeing all of you very soon."

There was a knock as Hill reached the knob. In a hushed voice, Hill said, "See how lucky you are! I have to indulge the president, while you are able to escape."

With a warm smile to each, he said, "Have a good trip." He opened the door. "Ah, Mister President. My friends were just leaving."

CHAPTER 4

DAKOTA TERRITORY—THURSDAY, JUNE 7, 1888

"That's just perfect, my friend. Now stay like that and don't move."

Zack Horton was about as uncomfortable as he had been in a long, long time. The grass right in front of his face was wet with dew, but it had mixed with dust, which was sticking to his face. His clothes were damp, the early morning air was chilly, and he was not feeling at all "perfect."

"Now!" It was a soft but intense whisper. "Look now!"

Zack lifted his head with effort and followed the line along which his companion was pointing.

Zack saw it just as the other man said excitedly, "That's old Ephraim; that's my very own grizzly bear. Now ain't he a feisty-looking fellow?"

The sight was impressive, even at a hundred yards. There was no way to tell the weight of the animal, but he looked as if he could run five to six hundred pounds.

A firm hand on his shoulder pressed Zack back down. "Don't let him see us."

Zack turned his head slightly to look at his host, who was

intently studying the bear. The man was a rancher-cowboy named Theodore Roosevelt, the one James Hill felt could best help Zack in the Dakota Territory. As Roosevelt admired the big, muscular bear devouring the berries off a chokecherry bush, Zack began to wonder what he was doing lying in range grass just after dawn on an ugly patch of earth called the Badlands. He had arrived at the Roosevelt ranch in the evening two days previously, and since then conversation had covered everything from wildlife to the effects of drought on the land. There had been no discussion of the issue that had brought Zack to the ranch; every time he introduced the subject, Roosevelt would divert the talk to some other, seemingly trivial matter. Zack was beginning to wonder if Hill had been so wise in his decision to make this the first stop in Dakota Territory.

Otherwise, Roosevelt had turned out to be an amiable sort of person. Zack had found out that Roosevelt was thirty years old and had gone into politics after graduating from Harvard in 1880. He had served in the New York state legislature and then on the New York City Police Board, but had failed in an attempt to be elected mayor of New York. What Zack had not found out was that Roosevelt had suffered a double tragedy when his wife and mother died on the same day, February 14, 1884. The shock of the loss had driven Roosevelt to seek solitude in Dakota Territory. After buying his ranches and getting them started, a task that required a year and a half, Roosevelt reentered the political arena back east, but he still returned to the place where he could organize his thoughts and goals.

Roosevelt's refusal to discuss the problems of interest to Zack had worn Zack's patience thin; after lunch, he decided now, they would either get down to business, or he would leave.

"Look! Look," Roosevelt whispered. "Just look at that."

Zack raised up again and looked out at the grizzly. The bear had gorged himself and was sitting on his haunches licking his hands; it was a playful and innocent scene.

Roosevelt, still in a whisper, said, "I hope the old fellow

behaves himself, because if he starts getting at my cattle then we will have to finish him."

Resigned to this sight-seeing, Zack asked, "Are the bears a problem?"

Roosevelt kept studying the bear. "Not too much; they took none of my cattle last year, and none so far this year. The grizzlies are moving out of this area, heading up into the high country of Montana and Idaho. Their worst enemy is the settler. This whole thing is going to change soon and—"

Roosevelt cut himself off. "Look, damn it! Look at him!"

It was truly a fine sight to a city dweller or even a rancher. The massive grizzly was rolling on its back, its four paws waving in the air as if bouncing an invisible ball. As he pawed to the sky, he was rocking back and forth like a child playing on a parlor floor—until he became a bit too exuberant in his motions and fell over to his left side. The tumble made him bound violently to his feet, as if something had intruded on his playtime. He stood there, cautious for a moment as he sniffed the air. Suddenly, the bear froze, his snout pointed right to the clump of range grass that was hiding the two men. Roosevelt whispered, "Don't move. He can smell better than he can see, but we don't want to take any chances. Just stay still!"

The bear moved his nose back and forth ever so slightly, trying to get a fix on the strange scent that was coming to him. Then he effortlessly rose up onto his hind feet and reached out his forepaws.

Zack began to feel some concern. Roosevelt said, "Hold your position. I don't want to shoot him."

Roosevelt had brought along a 40-90 Sharps, "a weapon for which I myself have much partiality," he had told Zack, who was carrying a borrowed .38 Marlin with long cartridges. "But it will not produce any good results on a bear" had been Roosevelt's opinion. Zack now wondered if he was going to have to use it.

Roosevelt murmured, "Easy, Ephraim . . . I don't want to shoot you. . . . Easy, boy." Zack could not take his eyes off the animal.

The grizzly was a full six feet tall, his color a black so deep that it looked blue in the dawn light. The pads of his paws were easily eight inches across, and the curved claws stuck out a full two inches. Old Ephraim's face seemed like an oversized dog's but when he opened his mouth the canine teeth glistened an inch and a half long. He was an impressive animal with a regal bearing. Regal but dangerous.

The bear moved his head slowly, sniffing the air again for a moment, then gave a rumbling roar that split the clear morning like a deadly knife.

"Good!" Roosevelt exclaimed.

"Good?" Zack demanded. "What the hell's good about that roar?"

"It means," Roosevelt explained, "that he knows we're out here but he doesn't know where we are. He'll be pulling out in a second or two."

The prediction was accurate. Gently, in a fluid motion, old Ephraim lowered back down to all fours, turned, and began to scurry away. In half a minute he was out of sight down into a gully.

The two men held their positions until they were sure the grizzly had gone; then Roosevelt rolled over onto his back and propped himself up on his elbows. "Time for a smoke. We've earned it."

He pulled out an embossed leather cigar case and extracted two short panatelas. As they lighted their cigars, Roosevelt said, "It's a shame to see those grand animals leaving, but they cannot stay. We cannot let them stay. They are simply too dangerous."

Zack had pulled himself up into a sitting position. After he took a quick puff on his cigar, he said, "That was impressive."

Roosevelt gave a chuckle. "My friend, everything out here is impressive. Just the name gives me a thrill: the Badlands! Now isn't that just a grand name for any place? Look at it; it is superb."

To Zack's eye the surrounding region was desolate, but he nodded. Roosevelt said, "The river flows easy and narrow through this valley. The cottonwoods thrive on the plentiful water, and the rest of the area is grass, perfect for grazing my cattle. And look off to the edges of the valley, where the land rises in steep high buttes. Those crests are sharp and jagged." He moved his cigar as a pointer and added, "Some of the buttes spread out into level plateaus, others form chains, and still others rise in steep isolation. Some of them are volcanic in origin and composed of masses of scoria; the others, of sandstone or clay, are worn by water into the most fantastic shapes. In color they are as bizarre as in form. Some of the buttes are overgrown with gnarled, stunted cedars or small pines, and they are cleft through in every direction by deep narrow ravines."

Roosevelt stood and dusted off the flecks of mud from his trousers. "In spite of their look of savage desolation, the Badlands make good cattle country: good grass, and the ravines provide protection in the hard winters."

Zack said, "It has a beauty of a type, but it is desolate."

Roosevelt said, "That's it; you've hit it on the head! Desolation is the thing that makes this all so great."

Zack replied, "People have come to this desolation and found homes and a way to make a living."

"By the thousands, tens of thousands, and this will make a great state."

Zack was startled. For a full day and a half he had been trying to get Roosevelt to focus on statehood, and now, just when he had been reaching the point of giving up, the man was opening up the subject with no prompting. Zack could not resist asking, "Sir, if you don't mind telling me, why the hell has it taken so long for you to be willing to talk?"

Roosevelt broke out into a hearty, bellowing laugh that echoed across the cold morning air. "That," he said, "is just my annoying habit, Mister Horton. I need to know a man before I can really share private thoughts with him."

"How did I qualify?" Zack was smiling with relief.

"To be worth his salt a man has to be able to look about him and see the splendor of this great nation. He has to be amiable on an outing." A twinkle came to his eyes as he added,

"He also should be able to put up with the rigors of roughing it in the wilderness."

Zack looked down at his clothes, soiled from the morning dew and mud. "Well, Mister Roosevelt, if getting filthy is equated with roughing it, then I guess I qualify."

"Good!" Roosevelt boomed out again. "That's very good." He gave one last look after the grizzly. "Well, let's hike back to the ranch house and see if they have some breakfast for us."

Roosevelt had led the way out from the ranch well before sunup, navigating through the darkness for twenty minutes to arrive at this spot. With daylight fully established, Zack was surprised to see they were actually within sight of the house. He said, "That bear comes close."

Roosevelt, walking at a brisk pace, replied, "That old fellow will come right up to the front porch, and that bothers me; he is getting much too familiar. I wish he would just wander off and find another home before my foreman is forced to shoot him. I would not like that at all." Roosevelt had looked back over his shoulder. Now he concentrated on the rough ground ahead of them as he said, "Keep up, now, Mister Horton. I can smell that food on the grill."

The ranch house was no primitive homestead. It was a substantial, elegant, one-story log structure containing all the amenities necessary for comfortable living and entertaining guests. The logs had been peeled clean of bark and were individually notched to provide a tight fit; no log was under ten inches in diameter. In places where the fit was loose, chinking of mud from the nearby riverbed was neatly molded into place to prevent drafts; the logs were finished off with a ship's varnish. Roosevelt's favorite spot, as Zack had found out the previous afternoon, was the twelve-foot-wide veranda on three sides of the building. A dozen homemade wooden chairs and benches provided places to sit as cool breezes blew up from the river. For three hours the evening before, Zack had enjoyed the pacific atmosphere of the veranda while Roosevelt had talked of diverse subjects; Roosevelt's mind seemed to be a storehouse of data and anecdotes.

Inside, the building balanced the feeling of a frontier cabin with an urbane character. The large front parlor was supplied with leather lounge chairs and sofas set strategically around the large rock fireplace with a mantel upon which sat a Seth Thomas eight-day clock. The wide-board floor had been finished and polished; thick bearskin rugs shared the duty with comparatively fragile Persian carpets. Stuck into available cracks were deer, elk, and antelope antlers that served as parking places for shotguns, rifles, and a dozen different types of outdoor clothing. Along the west wall, interrupted by only two small windows, rough-hewn planks had been made into sturdy shelves on which rested hundreds of books ranging from Coues' *Birds of the Northwest* to Poe's works. Roosevelt had said, "Out here in the Badlands you somehow think the place looks just exactly as Poe's tales and poems sound." There were eight bedrooms to accommodate guests, "so that one can be alone if one wishes to." A huge kitchen was well equipped and staffed to prepare substantial, stick-to-the-ribs food for a dozen dirty, hungry cowboys or a proper offering of gourmet dishes for visitors from the East dressed impeccably for a candlelit dinner.

Topics of conversation on the veranda or in the large front parlor or at the dining table were as broad as the vista from any room, from politics to poled Herefords. It was easy to end up in an argument on just about any subject when at the Roosevelt ranch.

When Zack and Roosevelt came through the parlor and entered the dining room, the sideboard was set with an abundant breakfast, customary for most large ranches: eggs, flapjacks, ham, sausage, fried potatoes, fresh-baked bread, and biscuits with a tureen full of grey gravy. There were apples and strawberries, coffee, milk, tea, and orange juice. Roosevelt mounded up a large plate containing one of each item of fare; Zack took only a couple of eggs and biscuits. Both men continued talking about the encounter with the grizzly and were lighting up cigars before Roosevelt permitted talk to focus on Zack's mission.

Not wasting time on a subject that was certain to be familiar to Roosevelt, Zack said, "Mister Hill is working very hard on this statehood matter, Mister Roosevelt."

"Ah, James Hill. I like that man. He mentioned all of that in his letter of introduction. And what does he think of the prospects?"

"Mister Hill is worried, seriously worried."

"And well he might be, Mister Horton. Forcing these territories to remain virtual colonies could seriously threaten Jim Hill's railroad operations in the whole Northwest."

Zack rose and went to the window that faced toward the south. The early morning sun was coloring the buttes and draws with every hue from pastel green, blue, and orange to bold reds and yellows. "It is all so peaceful looking," he said. "I'd hate to think of all this remaining in the limbo of territorial status; I need to know what can be done to help statehood along."

"I'd give every bit of my energy to help move this thing forward; I agree with Jim Hill."

Zack turned and looked at his host. "Is there a chance that statehood might not come? That could be bad."

"It could be worse than bad." Roosevelt pulled himself out of his chair and brought along his cup of coffee as he joined Zack. "You see that country out there; it is a tough, hard land. The Great Plains can freeze you one moment and burn you the next. And the Rocky Mountains are even harder; they allow no room for error if a man intends to survive. My point is that this land of the Northwest has created sturdy, independent, and resourceful individuals. They are good citizens who deserve the right of self-government and proper representation." He finished his coffee.

Zack turned to Roosevelt. "Mister Hill sent me here to see if you can help."

"I think I can. I have developed some influence here in the territory, and there are a few important people whom I count as friends. I will help. The most important thing in the immediate future is to push these territories into statehood; that is my own feeling."

"I concur, Mister Roosevelt."

Roosevelt returned to the table to pour himself more coffee. "I might be able to supply more than Jim Hill thought when he sent you to me. By a happy circumstance, when I was serving in the New York State Assembly, I made the friendship of men who have now come into power. One is Sam Cox, a member of the House of Representatives in Washington. He can offer some considerable assistance. Also in the Congress is Bill McKinley from Ohio. He is a good Republican, and he has his eyes on the presidency, so I am sure I can enlist him. Of course, we can't count on much from this fellow Cleveland. I had my fill of him when I served in the New York State Assembly and he was governor of New York; he's a hard man for a good Republican to stomach."

Zack resumed his seat at the table. "You seem to know your politics, Mister Roosevelt."

"Well, I've done my share of studying, but, I have only begun. I was brazen enough to try and win the mayorship of New York City, and that proved to me that one needs more than simply the desire. A fellow assemblyman in Albany told me once that all a young man had to do to win was to really want to; that's simply rubbish."

"I guess I'm doing my studying now," Zack said, "but, for me, it is a very interesting experience; James Hill doesn't seem to let boredom travel around with him."

Roosevelt laughed, a deep, chuckling laugh, then said, "James Hill is no man to let things get dull. He has millions of dollars and he could easily sit back and enjoy them. But he stays in the middle of any fight he can find."

Zack nodded. "This statehood issue can become a handsome fight."

"That's true."

"And it can be a dangerous gamble for Mister Hill."

"No question about that."

"Why do men like Hill take chances like that?"

"Mister Horton, if you stay with Jim Hill awhile you won't need to ask that question. Men who get things done in this world are men who cannot walk away from a challenge. I think you might be that kind of a man."

"I have little to lose."

Roosevelt went back to the window. He studied the broad expanse of the landscape in front of him, then said, "You have a great deal to lose, Mister Horton: you are carrying the trust of another man, and one loses more than can be measured when a trust is not kept." He turned and gave a long look at Zack. "I think you are a man who will get the job done; Jim Hill is a good judge of character."

There was a silence for a couple of moments, then Roosevelt said, "Well, enough of this dallying over breakfast; there's work to be done."

The immediate area around the Roosevelt ranch house was enclosed with a white-painted post-and-rail fence. At the back of the house, one hundred feet away, was a barn with an attached stable that opened onto a small corral. The ranch foreman was sitting on a bale of hay, waiting with two horses saddled. As they approached, Zack said, "You run a pretty efficient operation, Mister Roosevelt."

"A good ranch sort of runs itself, Mister Horton; all it needs is a few good hands to keep a sharp eye out to see what needs to be done.

"Morning, Jeb," Roosevelt called. "Got them ready?"

The foreman called back, "Manitou is raring to go, Theodore. He seems to know just when you're going to need him."

"I need him just about every day, Mister Horton. Manitou is a stout, strong horse that can lope along for miles. One of the most surefooted animals I've ever seen. Couldn't hunt or ranch without him, I'll guarantee you that. He has an easy mouth, and I can just drop the reins when I get off him and he will graze right there for me. A fine animal."

Zack had realized that riding was about to enter into his visit. "Are we going someplace, Mister Roosevelt?"

"We're going to take a little ride to a neighbor of mine. He's a man who can tell you more about the politics of this territory than I ever could think of telling."

"We're going by horse?"

"You do ride don't you, Mister Horton?"

"I've ridden some. Social riding, the kind of thing you do on an old horse through a city park."

Roosevelt stopped walking. "You can sit on a horse?"

Zack smiled. "I have a few times, but I'm no hard-riding cowboy."

Roosevelt started walking again. "You'll do just fine. Don't worry. Jeb has saddled up Arab for you, and Arab is one fine, easy-riding animal."

The previous night, Zack had been given some rough woolen trousers and a canvas work coat to wear for the early morning hike. He was wearing street shoes and no hat. The foreman, Jeb, quickly produced a pair of leather chaps, which he attached to Zack's waist and secured to his legs, a pair of soft, tough gloves, and a much-used, wide-brimmed hat that was almost clean and slightly too big.

"There!" Roosevelt boomed. "You're looking like a proper cowboy now, Mister Horton."

"Looking the part isn't being the part, Mister Roosevelt. I think I am about to make a fool out of myself."

"Nonsense. Climb onto that horse."

Zack was given a leg up by the foreman. All of Zack's previous experience on horses had involved small English saddles. As soon as he settled in the Western-style saddle, he felt a confidence that he had never experienced. He sat there getting the feel of it as the foreman adjusted the stirrup length. He held onto the pommel, moved slightly, and decided he was going to get along just fine. The horse, Arab, was not a big animal, but he shifted slightly, getting used to the new rider. Jeb looked up and said, "The word we use out here is 'Whoa!,' Mister Horton. You want him to stop or settle down, just tell him."

Thoughtfully, the foreman took a tight grip on the halter and led Arab for two full circuits of the corral. That gave both the horse and Zack a chance to settle in together. In that short time, Zack began to enjoy the feel of sitting on an honest, well-trained working horse.

As soon as the foreman was sure that Zack was at ease, he gave a nod to Roosevelt, who announced, "You're ready, Mister Horton. Let's get riding."

By the time they rode out of the corral, it was only twenty minutes after eight, but Zack was feeling as if the better part of the day had passed. The hike out to watch the bear, the substantial breakfast, the briskness of the morning air, all induced a feeling of reality that was hard to muster in city life. He liked the feeling.

They rode north at a casual pace. The sun was well into the sky to the east of them, pushing the early morning chill west. The view was beautiful in its starkness. The soft contours of the land had been molded tenderly by the winds and rains; only the abruptness of the gullies and the bold walls of the buttes gave sharpness to the scene. The muted colors were becoming more vivid under the higher sun. Even the scrub bushes were changing from soft grey and brown to richer blends that gave an illusion of Nature doing its duty to welcome man.

They had ridden in silence for ten minutes, with the loudest sounds being those of the horses' hooves softly touching the ground and the comfortable creaking of the saddles and other tack. A gentle breeze created a lulling, wispy melody as it flitted through the grass and sagebrush.

Roosevelt asked Zack if he was getting used to the Western saddle. Zack replied that he was quite enjoying himself. Then Zack asked, "How far is your neighbor's ranch?"

"Do you mean in miles or in time?"

"Either."

"About twelve miles ahead of us. It should take us just about two hours. We'll be picking up the pace as soon as you feel you can handle that pony."

"I'm feeling almost at home."

"Say, that's splendid. I'll lead the way. You just give a holler if I'm going too fast."

Roosevelt gave his horse a soft nudge with the heel of his boot. They rode at an easy canter for the next ten minutes; Zack held his seat well and found the ride a new experience. It seemed to him that the cow pony functioned as a partner with the rider; before, Zack had always felt he was in a constant battle to exert his will over the animal. It was wonderful to be on a horse that was anxious to move across the sprawling land. Up ahead, Roosevelt kept glancing back, smiling, and nodding.

At the ten-minute mark, Roosevelt yelled back, "You're doing fine. Let's try this."

This, it turned out, was a full gallop.

Roosevelt's horse lunged forward; Roosevelt leaned down with his head close to the head of his horse. It was obvious that Roosevelt was an accomplished horseman.

Unbidden, Zack's horse followed suit, and suddenly the ride turned into a tough piece of work. Zack copied Roosevelt by leaning down with his head nearly touching the horse's neck. He fought to keep his balance and pick up the rhythm of the movement as his horse seemed intent on trying to catch up to Roosevelt's. Zack begin to fear falling off, and he found himself, for the first time in his life, actually talking to a horse. "Easy, boy. Slow down, damn it!" Suddenly, desperately, he remembered the foreman's instructions and added, "Whoa, horse!" The horse did not respond.

The pair of horses were speeding along a well-defined wagon road at a smooth run, but what if his horse took it into his mind to cut out into the brush? That would be dangerous. With great reluctance, Zack yelled ahead, "Too fast! Slow down!"

For a moment Zack thought that his pleas were not reaching Roosevelt, but, just when Zack was beginning to wonder if he would survive a jump off the running horse, Roosevelt pulled up. Zack's horse, much to Zack's relief, slowed and came to an easy stop next to him.

Roosevelt was grinning. "I guess that was too fast."

"I was seriously thinking of jumping off."

"He wouldn't have let you."

"What the hell's that mean?"

"That's one of my best cutting horses. As soon as you lifted your right foot out of the stirrup, he would have dropped his rear end and skidded to a halt."

"I don't understand."

Roosevelt pulled out his cigar case and offered; Zack accepted if only to delay continuing. "I should have told you about Arab. We use cutting horses on the ranch to separate cows from the herd; he is trained to stop if the rider is going to get down. He can halt his forward motion in just a few steps; it's a very valuable skill."

Without a word, Zack gave a soft spur to his horse. As soon as Arab had moved forward a few paces, Zack lifted the weight off his right stirrup. Arab halted. Emboldened with his new-found knowledge, Zack tried it three more times, each time allowing the horse to move a bit faster along the road. Each time the trick worked.

Roosevelt had been allowing his horse to come forward slowly, watching Zack experiment and enjoying his cigar. With confidence, Zack wheeled Arab around and sped back to Roosevelt and, with élan, brought Arab smoothly to a halt. "I do like that!"

Roosevelt grinned. "You are doing well for a tenderfoot."

"I could learn to like this."

"I'd hire you in a minute to work on my ranch."

"I would have to learn more than I know now."

Slyly, Roosevelt said, "That's what you are out here for, Mister Horton."

"I don't know what I gain by learning how to ride Arab."

"It is important for you to learn all you can about this wild country. Jim Hill knows all there is to know about railroads, even to the degree of how to lay track."

"But his knowledge helps him make his railroad better."

"And your knowledge will make you able to give him a better report."

Zack smiled. "I don't know if he'll be interested in my ability to stop a horse going a hundred miles per hour."

"No," Roosevelt replied. "Riding a horse is no great information, but little things will make you more aware of the big problems. Minutia, Mister Horton, is the stuff of which import is made."

Zack reached down and patted Arab's neck. Roosevelt gave a nod of his head and spurred Manitou into another run; Zack gave Arab his head.

They rode through the morning, alternating between fast gallops and easy canters, and arrived at Ollie Svenson's ranch at ten minutes before eleven.

Ollie Svenson had immigrated from a farming community near Burgsvik on the Swedish island of Gotland in the Baltic Sea. He had been in North America for eleven years and had farmed in the Dakota Territory for five of those years; he had brought with him a wife, four children, and a five-generation family tradition of raising wheat.

Many of Svenson's friends, including Theodore Roosevelt, had thought that Svenson was wrong to attempt wheat farming so far west of the grain centers in Minnesota and Wisconsin, but Svenson had realized two things that few others had realized: that rail transportation would come to a shippable product and that there was going to be a market for the hard-shelled winter wheat that grew so well on the Great Plains. He had used every penny he was able to save and borrow to purchase these four thousand acres of wheat land. When Charles Pillsbury in Minneapolis had devised a way to cheaply process the hard-kernel winter wheat, and James Hill extended a spur of his Saint Paul, Minneapolis, and Pacific Railroad to within fifteen miles of his farm, Svenson's future had been assured. In just two years, Svenson had been able to retire all of his debt and begin rebuilding his savings.

As the two men rode up to the farm house, Zack Horton's impressions were simple: spartan and efficient.

Ollie Svenson had carved out two acres for the homesite, which was enclosed in a sturdy, whitewashed fence. There were areas allocated for a kitchen garden, a chicken coop, and even a children's playground. Rich, well-tended grass covered the ground, and a shelterbelt of tall junipers had been planted along the whole perimeter of the homesite.

Roosevelt pulled up his horse a hundred yards from the front gate. "This fellow is a very important man in this region, Mister Horton."

Zack studied the prosperous-looking farm. "How's that?"

"He is what's known as the Grand Master of the Patrons of Husbandry in Dakota Territory; that's a very powerful position."

"Is that the outfit calling themselves the Grange?"

"Exactly. The proper name is the Patrons of Husbandry. They are a force to be listened to; take my word on that. In the rural regions of this great nation, there are well over twenty-one thousand Grange Lodges, and they have the ears of many politicians."

"I've never met any Grange members. Are they dedicated?"

"Ah, now, that word is too soft. They're more than dedicated. They are militant."

"And apolitical."

"That's right. They are apolitical in the extreme. You'll find Ollie an interesting and emphatic soul."

Roosevelt led the way up to the front gate and, as the two men dismounted and hitched up their horses, two young children came bursting out of the front door of the house screaming, "Uncle Teddy . . . Uncle Teddy."

Zack smiled at the familiar singsong of the Scandinavian accent: "uncle" came out as "onkle" and "Teddy" came out as "Tee-a-dee"; it was a friendly, melodic reminder of Saint Paul. Zack was to learn later that Roosevelt loathed the moniker "Teddy" but accepted the name when issued by children. Two of the children, a boy and a girl aged seven and eight, burst out through the gate and fell into a bear hug from Roosevelt, who ended up struggling to extract a generous fistful of paper-wrapped sour balls that, once in his hand, were quickly confiscated by the children. "Now, where's your daddy?"

The in-unison replies were: "In the shed" and "Fixing the reaper."

"This is Mister Horton. I've brought him to meet your daddy."

The children respectfully acknowledged the introduction. The boy asked, "Are you here to help fix the reaper?"

Zack laughed. "I'm not good at that sort of thing."

Roosevelt said, "Let's go see what the trouble is. Maybe we can get that machine working."

The children led the way across the lawn and around the house. As they were passing the back porch, the door opened. Inga Svenson came out and offered a friendly greeting, immediately followed by an invitation to stay for lunch, which was nearly ready. Roosevelt introduced Zack, and both men accepted the invitation.

Mrs. Svenson pointed toward the barn and work shed. "Ollie's out there."

Roosevelt nodded. "Well, we'll go see if we can help with that reaper."

As they stepped into the work shed, Zack was immediately impressed with the extreme neatness of the place. Tools were hung from the walls in regimented order; scraps of wood, leather, and metal were organized into ordered stacks; and even the floor, which was hard-packed dirt, was swept clean. Ollie Svenson was on his back on the floor, half-hidden under the jacked-up frame of a large wheat thrasher. From under the machine came a baritone rumble. "Gutt demmed fecking bolt don't fid!"

"Get a bigger hammer, Ollie."

"Whoose dat wid de smart moudth?"

"Theodore . . . Theodore Roosevelt."

"Den you gotta know better den talk smart moudth wid me, Teeodoor Roosevelt. You go play wid de kids. I got work to get dun."

"You're making me look bad in front of my guest, Ollie."

"Ooops!"

Svenson wiggled his way from under the thrasher; he was covered with dust and splotches of black grease. He was a tall man, six feet two inches with a muscular frame, but, because of his height, he looked skinny. After he wiped his hands on an oily rag, he extended his right to Roosevelt. "Well, Teeodoor, why you let me make a fool of myself in front of your friend?"

"That was not my plan, Ollie. You just have a foul mouth when you battle with these gadgets."

Roosevelt indicated the parts that had been removed from the machine. Svenson said, "Dat machine don't run by itself; I gotta talk to it . . . a lot." Then, looking at Zack, he said, "Don't pay no mind to me, mister. I cuss at the dirt I plow and the plants that grow and the cow that I milk; it helps."

Zack extended his hand as he replied, "A little cussing can do wonders."

Roosevelt said, "This is Zack Horton, Ollie. Mister Horton is an associate of Jim Hill's; he is also the grandson of Clifford Boynton and is going to take over the Dakota and Western."

Svenson smiled broadly. "I liked your grandfather, Mister Horton; and your railroad is goot. Mister Hill is a fine man, too. You doing something with him, huh?"

"Proudly."

"Vell, it is good for a man to be proud of his work, I gotta say dat. But you got problems dat you should be fixing."

"I'd like to hear about them."

"Ah, you've heard dem all right. You gotta get dat Jim Hill to quit charging us too much to ship grain. Your grandpa knew the right rates, and dat Irishman, Cummins, he do goot, too. Jim Hill, he charge too much."

Zack did not reply. There was little or nothing that he could do to influence Hill's freight rates. The fact was that Hill's rates had been more fair than most railroad operators'. Zack was not sure that Svenson had a case, because the monies collected, at least on the Saint Paul, Minneapolis, and Pacific, were being poured back into expansion of routes and equipment. Another fact, and few customers were aware of it, was that James Hill took no salary from his job as president of the railroad; he was willing to make his money from the growth of his stock and payments of dividends. Zack knew that most of the other railroads were exploiting the shippers by charging whatever the traffic would bear; if the price of grain rose, then the costs of shipping rose accordingly, and generally the farmer was held to a marginal profit. James Hill had been one of the few railroad owners to battle the practice, but he had not only lost the battle each time, he had also come close to being shut out of interline business, which was an important source of revenue, generated when he moved his equipment over other railroads' tracks. In addition, it was a fact that many railroads granted financial paybacks—illegally—to both grain-storage operators and flour mills. Jim Hill was already considered a renegade in the rail industry for not joining in on the price fixing. Politely, Zack told Svenson that he would be glad to pass on any point of view that would improve the service of Hill's railroad. Svenson, a wily man, was equally polite in accepting Horton's transparently condescending offer.

Roosevelt cut in. "Let's not get all too serious about that problem, gentlemen. Mister Horton here is trying to find out about the prospects for statehood."

Svenson's smile vanished. He demanded, "Mister Horton, what side are you on?"

"I think the territories should be brought into the Union. From what I hear, it is the only thing that can be done."

Svenson still seemed a bit wary. "There is great danger listening to dem fools who is against statehood, you know dat?"

"I think the danger would be in not discussing the situation, Mister Svenson. Mister Hill wants to do everything he can to get the legislation passed."

Roosevelt asked, "How many of your people are willing to pitch in, Ollie?"

"Maybe just about all de members."

"That's a pretty good voting bloc."

"You darn right dat's a good voting bloc, and we will deliver." Svenson stroked his chin, then he went over and picked up a gear and began to study the cogs. It was a full minute before he said, "By golly, maybe you could do some good here. I've got an idea."

Roosevelt and Zack waited, but nothing came. Finally,

after what seemed to be an interminable pause, Svenson put down the gear, pulled out his pocket watch, and said, "It's not too early for us to have lunch. Let's go to the house."

With that he walked out of the shed, leaving his two guests staring at each other. A smile crept onto Roosevelt's face. "Let me tell you, Mister Horton, the most important ingredient to success is getting along with people. Let's play along with him for a bit and see what's brewing in that Swede's mysterious mind. Remember, he's a powerful man in these parts and he didn't get there without some sense of what needs to be done."

"I'm willing to wait him out."

"We won't have long to wait, if I know Ollie."

It was not that Zack did not have an appetite. The long horseback ride had made the prospect of a meal attractive, but, as with breakfast earlier and dinner the night before, the massive quantities of food set on the lunch table were overwhelming. Inga Svenson was a slight woman of medium height and slim build. Her husband was also slim, and the Svenson children showed no excess weight at all. Zack wondered how they stayed trim when faced with meals such as this one. There was a large kettle of a thick vegetable-beef soup that, along with three loaves of fresh-baked bread, could have made a meal by itself, but that was merely the beginning. A roast of beef was complemented with carrots, peas, beets, and mashed potatoes with gravy. Fortunately, service plates and bowls were passed around, so Zack was able to limit the amounts he took. He was not so lucky with dessert. Inga Svenson cut him a slice of apple pie that would have been enough for two or three servings.

There were pitchers of fresh milk, and coffee as strong as the milk was pure white. At the meal's end, Zack felt as if he could not move from the table.

As Inga and the children began clearing away the dishes, Ollie let it be known that they would now continue their discussion.

"Mister Horton, I've been thinking about how your Mister Hill could help. I've come up with an idea."

Roosevelt gave a polite burp and looked at Zack. "I told you this would be a worthwhile trip."

Zack took a sip of coffee. "Mister Svenson, I'm ready to hear anything, if my stomach will just get on with the business of digestion."

For the first time since they had met, Svenson laughed.

Roosevelt said, "Ollie, all that is needed is a push in the right direction to get all the voters working hard for statehood. We have some problems here; for instance, should we be one state or two? The territory is too big, I think. We should be split. I'll get into that later with you."

Svenson nodded. "Yes. But first, I think that we can get you some real help from our Grange organization." He looked at Zack. "You know about the Grange, Mister Horton?"

"I've heard of them, sir, but not enough to know much."

"Well, if you're going to know about the West then you'd better get yourself some knowledge. Right after the Patrons of Husbandry started, we had 3,360 lodges spread out in all the farming communities. That was in 1873. Now there are over twenty-one thousand."

Actually, there were 21,697 Grange Lodges listing a quarter of a million members. Like T. V. Powderly's seven hundred thousand Knights of Labor, the Patrons of Husbandry were organized along Masonic lines, with officers named Master and Lecturer and lower degrees of Laborer, Cultivator, Harvester, and Husbandman. Women were accepted into the order, with the only distinction being in their titles, such as Maid, Shepherdess, Gleaner, and Matron. The high-ranking women were identified as Demeter (Faith), Pomona (Hope), and Flora (Charity). Like the Knights of Labor, the Patrons of Husbandry also held secret meetings and instituted many Masonic-type rituals and customs. As with those who had joined the Knights, those who had come into the Patrons had banded together in a common interest—in the Patrons' case, agriculture. The two fraternal orders had different objectives: the Patrons were mainly interested in government assistance when crops failed, while the Knights wanted better working conditions in plants, factories, and mills. Both organizations wanted to see the government take over the American railroad system, but that common thread was not strong enough to bond the fraternities together as a political power. That was not to say either was weak; both groups wielded considerable clout with elected officials. Zack Horton was just about to find out how powerful the Patrons of Husbandry really were in the Great Plains farm belt.

Ollie said, "I don't know if Teeodoor has told you, but I hold a state office within our fraternity."

"No," Roosevelt fibbed, "I didn't tell him anything about that; I felt it was your place."

"I appreciate that, Teeodoor." Then, to Zack, "I'm Grand Master for the Dakota Territory, Mister Horton. In that position I have the attention of a large number of members . . . and a few others, too."

Roosevelt chortled; Zack could not fail to catch the import of Roosevelt's reaction. Zack listened.

"The fact is, Mister Horton, there is to be a state conclave in a couple of days. In that single gathering you would find more influential people than you could visit in weeks of traveling around the territory."

"I'd like to be able to take advantage of that, Ollie."

"That's what I'm offering."

"Then I accept."

Roosevelt gave a broad smile. "Bully! That is just splendid. Where's the meeting, Ollie?"

One of the children called from the kitchen, "There's a rider coming!" And the others began to screech, "It's Jeb! It's Jeb! It's Jeb!" Those exclamations were followed by a rush of little people pouring from the kitchen toward the front door.

Roosevelt pulled out his gold pocket watch. "We've only been here a couple of hours. Jeb must have come nearly right after us."

Ollie called back toward the kitchen, "Inga, you'd better be getting some food out here for Jeb. He must have ridden right through mealtime."

The three men rose and walked to the front door. Jeb had

already dismounted and was being swarmed over by the Svenson children. Ollie yelled, "Hey, you kids, stop that! By golly, the man has a right to get his feet onto the ground after a long ride!"

Their disciplined response was immediate. As Jeb was hitching up his horse, he called back, "Hey, Ollie, don't fuss at them. Kids are great."

Roosevelt walked down the steps and asked, "What's so important to bring you all this distance, Jeb?"

Jeb walked through the front gate into the yard, followed by the children; they had expected to receive some treat from the visitor, and they had come up empty. Their feelings were apparent on their faces.

Ollie Svenson scolded, "You kids are getting spoiled." He turned to Roosevelt. "Some of the folks that come here should be less ready to spoil, and more practical, like Jeb."

As Jeb approached the men, he reached into the inside pocket of his leather vest and pulled out an envelope. He said to Roosevelt, "This came about an hour after you left. I opened it and thought you'd be wanting to read it."

Zack Horton could see sweat stains on the envelope of good-quality paper; he could not make out the neat handwriting.

Roosevelt pulled the letter out, read it quickly, then looked off abstractly at the horizon. He gave a second glance at the message and said, "I'm glad you took the initiative, Jeb; this is important." Roosevelt turned to Zack. "Charlie Fairchild sent this to me. It seems I've got to get a move on to travel to Washington."

Horton knew that Fairchild was President Cleveland's treasury secretary, appointed to the office a year before. What Horton did not know was that Fairchild, like Roosevelt, was from New York State and the men were close friends, even though in opposite political parties. "Zack, I'm sorry, but Jeb was right to rush this to me; I've got to be hurrying back to the ranch. With luck, I can catch the train out of Williston tomor-

row afternoon. I think we'll have to break off this visit with
Ollie."

Zack was not pleased. He had just begun to see that Ollie
Svenson could be of considerable help.

Ollie Svenson also felt some annoyance, because he wanted
to cultivate Zack Horton's influence with James Hill. If he did
so successfully, it would be important to all of the Patrons. Ollie
said, "Hey, wait one minute."

Roosevelt was trying to analyze all the implications of
Fairchild's message. Because of Roosevelt's experience with the
New York City Police Department, Fairchild was asking
Roosevelt to serve on a special committee set up to study how
the Secret Service could be better used for national law enforcement. There was strong resistance to the creation of any agency
that might smack of a national police force. Roosevelt had been
an advocate of having the Secret Service take on wider duties
than protecting the president and investigating counterfeiting
schemes. Roosevelt's dream, however, would remain only a
dream until he himself became president thirteen years later. But
at that moment, standing outside Ollie Svenson's farmhouse,
Roosevelt was focusing his thoughts on broadening the duties
of the Secret Service.

"So what do you think?"

Roosevelt pulled his thoughts back to Ollie, who repeated,
"So, what do you think, Teeodoor?"

"Think about what?"

"What do you think about Zack here staying with us? I can
get him to Williston tomorrow and then take him to the conclave in Bismarck if he wants to go."

"What do you think, Zack?"

"Think? I think this is all very funny. I just came from
Bismarck a few days ago; that's where the Dakota and Western
headquarters are. I come all this way to find out that I should be
meeting in Bismarck with Ollie Svenson!" He laughed. "I'm
game, Mister Roosevelt. Does this idea conflict with your
plans?"

"Not at all, Zack. My interest with you and Mister Hill is

to get something done about statehood. You know I don't like railroads and the men who own them; I don't like the way they control so much money and run people's lives. I do think Jim Hill is a good businessman, but there is always the chance that those scoundrels back east will begin to influence him."

"Mister Hill is not like those moguls from New York, Mister Roosevelt."

"I know that, Zack. I'm counting on him not changing."

"I don't think you have to worry. I haven't known him long, but . . ."

"I always worry until the job is done, and the job at hand is to see to statehood for our territory."

"That is Mister Hill's main hope, Mister Roosevelt."

Roosevelt turned to Ollie Svenson. "That idea is a good one, Ollie. You can talk to Zack tonight, and then I'll see you in Williston. Jeb, you go take a look at Manitou and Arab and see if they're ready for a ride back to the ranch; that fellow you rode over is in no shape for a return trip. Ollie, could you bring Jeb's horse to Williston tomorrow?"

Jeb cut in, "Just leave him out to pasture, I'll pick him up in a few days."

Ollie joked, "You tell dat horse of yours to stay away from my mares; I don't need dat problem."

Roosevelt took Zack by the arm and led him past the silent children and out the front gate. "While they're busy I want to talk to you a bit, Zack." They walked along the path leading east to a small creek.

"Zack, I've known you only a couple of days, but I've come to like you. I consider myself as good a judge of men as I am a judge of horses; I think you're honest. The main thing you need to make a success of your life is getting along with your fellow man; I can see you know how to do that. But right now you have the lives of many people in your hands." They arrived at the creek.

"Zack, the people here are carving out their futures with plows and axes and shovels. Their monument is the land and the resources that God has set down for us to use. There's been big trouble with the Indians here, and a lot has been done wrong, but there's no way that this land can be set aside for a bunch of savages to use as a playground. It's too bad that the Indians have been cheated out of their lands, and it's too bad that they are going to have to change their way of living, but there is no other way for this country to succeed. Thousands of farms are going to be carved out of this wilderness, and the buffalo are going to be eliminated to make way for cattle; it's the way things will have to be."

Zack nodded and said, "Mister Hill said that the roots of the future have been planted in rocky soil, but when they take hold the growth will be strong."

Roosevelt smiled. "Zack, have you ever tried to uproot a tree that's growing in a rock outcrop? Hill is right. There's to be no stopping what this place is destined to be. You have to work as hard as you ever have in your life."

"I'll do my best."

From near the barn, Jeb yelled, "Hey, Theodore, we'd better get to riding."

Roosevelt extended his hand to Zack. "You tell Jim Hill that he can call on me if he needs any help back in New York or Washington. I'll do anything I can; you can count on me."

"I believe that."

"Well, don't slack off just because I'm going to pitch in with the work; there's still a lot to be done."

"I think I'm just beginning to realize how much there is to do. People like you and Ollie Svenson will be needed. I've got some big traveling to do."

Roosevelt grinned, "You're young, and able to handle that." He tipped a finger to the brim of his hat and walked away.

Zack stood silently watching this new acquaintance head for where Jeb was waiting with the two horses.

For the first time since leaving James Hill back in Minnesota, Zack Horton was beginning to see that his job was going to provide more than just a sense of accomplishment; he was also going to, in his own way, join in on the building of the nation.

►◆◄

Inga Svenson awakened Zack Horton half an hour before sunrise. "Ollie will be through his chores in a few minutes," she said. "You might want to wash up before breakfast."

She left the small guest room where Zack had slept. He saw that she had placed a bowl of warm water on the shelf by the window, together with a razor, a bar of soap, and a clean towel.

The Svenson house was gently quiet. Outside the open window, Zack could hear the soft noises of farm animals beginning their own day; Ollie Svenson's voice was barely audible as he coaxed the horses to take their fodder and the cows to give their milk. While he washed and shaved, Zack Horton had a fleeting image of himself working a farm, raising a family. He wiped the excess soap from his face and grinned at the thought.

In the kitchen, Inga was preparing a massive offering of eggs, sausage, and potatoes. The yeasty smell of fresh-baked bread floated teasingly around the room. Inga, looking up for only an instant, announced, "There is pie and coffee if you want to start in right now. You had better get what you can, because the children will invade us pretty soon and there is no telling what they will be grabbing."

In the center of the plank table sat a plate with wedges of apple pie left over from the supper the previous night; a white-enameled coffeepot waited invitingly on a trivet near large bowls of strawberry jam and rich, golden butter.

"I'd weigh a ton if I spent much time on your farm, Mrs. Svenson."

"You could do with some fattening up, Mister Horton. They don't seem to feed you city people very well."

Zack sat and used his fork to lift a small slab of pie onto his plate. He poured himself coffee and, feeling comfortable fitting into the farm routine, began to eat. He was chewing the first mouthful when Ollie Svenson came in carrying a pail of milk. "Morning, Zack."

Zack nodded his greeting.

"Good," Ollie said. "You are getting some of Mother's good food in you. You can use it."

Zack swallowed and said, "You all seem to worry a lot about me not eating."

"If I had you working for me, then you would be needing some meat on your bones. Dern city folks."

The melody of Ollie's Scandinavian accent came naturally to Zack's ear now, and he was understanding it with no trouble at all.

Breakfast combined the consumption of excessive amounts of food and a study of the Svenson children as they sleepily began their day. The meal was over and the children shooed away from the table before Zack realized he had heard not one conflict among the children. The Svensons were doing something right in rearing their offspring; maybe it was simply a part of living on a farm.

The sun was up just enough to give dawn to the road when they headed away from the farm toward Williston, where they were scheduled to meet with Roosevelt, then board the eastbound train on the first leg of their journey to Bismarck.

The conversation between the two men was casual as they rode in the comfortable buckboard pulled by Ollie's favorite horse, Onsdag; the seat was padded with cushioned leather and made comfortable by leaf springs. Svenson had told Zack the ride would take about six hours, which meant they would arrive just before noontime; the train was scheduled to depart at 1:50. With time to kill and conversation casual, Ollie Svenson set about educating Zack about the territory.

He was a veritable encyclopedia of information about Dakota. Each fact, each anecdote, showed how much pride Svenson had in his farm and territory. He was proud to contribute a sizable fraction of the sixty million bushels of wheat Dakota produced each year, proud to be an integral part of the economy that was making the territory ready for statehood. He remarked that one reason Dakota should be admitted to the Union soon was that the majority of people in the territory did not object to paying federal taxes. Right now the people of Dakota were paying federal taxes of ten dollars for each dollar spent by the government in the territory. They had seen to the construction of an asylum for the insane at Jamestown, a soldier's home in Lisbon, and a substantial territorial prison at Bismarck, as well as a youth reform school at Mandan. Those and other public institutions were massive structures generally built of native stone, meant to last, meant to convey the impression that the territory was ready to see to its own future.

They had just ridden through the small town of Alexander when Zack was brought back to the reality of being on the frontier.

The road was taking them north over easy, rolling terrain; they were about eighteen miles from where they could cross the Missouri River into Williston. The morning was bright, with only a few wispy clouds floating overhead. As they came around a bend in the road, approaching a small grove of dense willow trees, they saw four men sitting on a fallen tree with four horses tied to the branches of the willows.

Ollie hissed, "Oh, boy, dis could be bad trouble."

Zack did not grasp the meaning at first, because the quartet looked like some travelers resting their horses, but the men jumped up and began taking up positions across the road, blocking passage. He began to get ready for trouble. Ollie said, "You just let me handle this, Zack."

Zack was not convinced. The four were rough looking. Their clothing was dirty and rumpled, their faces were decorated with either dirt or scruffy beards, and all of them were wearing side arms.

Ollie eased Onsdag to a stop and said, "You dere is being in my way, now."

The leader looked at his companions and said, "Hear that, fellows? We is being in his way."

The other three broke out laughing.

The leader, in a singsong mocking of Ollie's accent, announced, "Dere gonna be no way for you to get by here, old man."

The opposition did not look good to Zack; the four were young, tough, and obviously ready for a confrontation.

Ollie demanded, "What's your business with me?"

"We have no business with you, Swede, and you have no business on this road. Now just turn this rig around and get the hell back where you belong."

Zack whispered to Ollie, "What the hell is going on?"

"Don't worry. I can handle these bandits. You just hang on, hear me?"

The leader of the gang reached up to grab Onsdag's harness but, before he could touch the straps, Ollie shouted, "Onsdag! *Skynda pa!" Move!*

The horse reared up, flicked out its hooves, and gave a frightening whinny. As his hooves came back to the ground, he gave a violent leap forward. At the same time, Ollie reached down and grabbed an axe handle that had been resting at his feet. The buckboard bolted forward. Ollie swung the axe handle like a club and smacked the leader of the group squarely in the middle of his head; the man fell like a stone.

One of the other assailants leaped forward on Zack's side of the buggy. Impulsively, Zack made a fist of his right hand and smacked down at the man. He aimed at the head but the buckboard jerked violently and Zack's fist connected with the man's shoulder. Zack drew back to swing again. Ollie was manipulating the reins, steering the galloping horse down the middle of the road; the attacker held on despite the buckboard's gathering speed. Ollie yelled, "Use this!" as he pushed the axe handle at Zack. Zack was able to deliver a telling blow. The man lost his grip and fell hard to the road as Ollie urged his horse on. A full five seconds passed before Zack heard the first report of a gun. He glanced at Ollie, then back to where the attack had happened. "Damn, Ollie, a rough bunch."

Ollie was concentrating on getting Onsdag under control. They sped along the road; Zack was paying attention to keeping his seat because the buckboard was jouncing unpredictably over the ruts and potholes in the road. A series of gunshots made

Zack throw another glance backward; all of the four men were shooting.

Zack looked at Ollie. He was grinning broadly.

Zack yelled, "What's funny?"

Ollie yelled back, "Dey rotten shots, by golly. Right?"

Zack laughed in warm agreement; he had a new respect for this farmer.

Ollie Svenson steered them around a sharp bend in the road and through a shallow creek. Once clear of the creek, he began working the reins to slow the horse down to an easy trot.

"Dis horse loves dis stuff. He is a good one."

Zack was impressed by the horse, but he was more impressed by the way Svenson had handled the confrontation. He asked, "Who the hell were they?"

Ollie shrugged his shoulders. "Damned if I know." He had slowed the horse to a walk. Zack kept glancing back, and Ollie said, "You don't worry. Dey is going to need a few minutes to get their horses, and even then they might not be coming after us. They don't know if we have guns or not."

"Did you expect this?"

"By golly, I'd have had myself a gun . . . and one for you, too. No, I had no idea."

After another minute of the easy walk, Ollie said, "You get a good grip, Zack. I don't like to run this horse but he doesn't mind, and we'd better be putting some distance between us and those gunmen."

With a couple of Swedish words and a flick of the reins, Ollie gave the horse his head; the horse took it.

For the next twenty minutes, Onsdag maintained a gait that Zack would not have believed possible for a horse pulling a wagon with two men over a road that was pitted with ruts. It worked; there was no sign of pursuit, and Ollie slowed the pace.

Zack asked, "Really, Ollie, what was all that about?"

"Dat's the way it is out here sometimes on the frontier, Zack. The bad ones is the ones who come into the territory looking for gold; a lot of them are no good. We have U.S.

marshals and territorial courts, but the whole place is so big that we can't protect everything from those bandits."

"They play pretty rough."

"It's a rough country."

"Then I'd start carrying a gun."

"Then I might get shot, or get you shot, or my wife and kids."

"You almost *did* get shot . . . and me, too."

Ollie gave a glance at Zack. The farmer's eyes were hard. "But we didn't, by golly."

▶◆◀

The train station on the edge of Williston was crowded with travelers waiting for the trains that would be carrying them either east or west. The westbound had pulled in on schedule at 1:30; the eastbound was due at 1:50. At the far end of the platform, which was the least crowded, Theodore Roosevelt was scribbling furiously in his small pocket notebook.

"What did the fourth one look like?" Roosevelt asked without looking up. Ollie described the fourth assailant. Roosevelt wrote as he said, "I'll have my boys go looking for those rascals; we can't have our citizens accosted on the road."

"Don't you go worrying about that now, Teeodoor. Nothing happened, and those bad eggs came away with a couple of cracked heads."

Roosevelt laughed. Turning to Zack, he said, "You got in a couple of licks then, too?"

Zack had resolved to treat the incident with the same light attitude displayed by Ollie Svenson. "I merely popped the man on the head with Ollie's axe handle. All a part of life in the country, I guess."

Roosevelt gave another boisterous laugh. "You are learning quickly, Zack. You'll become a frontiersman yet."

"If I hang around you two long enough. You take me out to challenge a damned bear, and Ollie gets me into a fracas with highwaymen! One tends to learn quickly in those situations."

Turning back to Ollie, Roosevelt said, "It is serious,

though." Placing a friendly hand on Ollie's shoulder, he added, "There are too few people like you in this territory, and we cannot afford to lose you. That would be a disaster for the rest of us."

Ollie pointed at Zack and said, "This man could do a lot to make things better out here. We need Mister James Hill to be more fair with his freight charges; then we will be able to concentrate on statehood instead of worrying about making a living."

Roosevelt stroked his walrus moustache. "You are being politicked, Zack. Do you know that?"

Zack grinned. "I don't know the dollars and cents of the railroad business yet, but I do know that my grandfather would have set a fair policy and that Del Cummins would still follow a fair policy." Zack looked at Svenson and said, "I also am learning that Ollie Svenson could be good at politicking. He is damned good at swinging an axe handle and driving a buckboard."

"Well," Roosevelt said, "you just don't let Ollie begin swinging his verbal axe handles at you, because then you will know the full sting of him. You should convey his feelings to Jim Hill, though. The grain farmers out here do need a break on shipping to the mills."

"I will convey that message."

Ollie cut in. "Oh, now, by golly, Hill is better than the others, but that is not really saying much. You look at his profits, and you'll see what I mean."

Roosevelt said, "I might talk to some of those fellows in Congress about getting more lawmen out here so we can stop incidents such as confronted you, Ollie."

Ollie's reply was prevented by the wail of the arriving eastbound train. On the station platform anticipation gave way to excitement. Children began chattering, parents began gathering their brood away from the edge, and families began their leave-takings with relatives.

The train chugged to a halt, and the three men quickly found their way into the dining-room car, which, for the three hours until dinner would be served, would act as a club room for businessmen and the well-to-do who used the car for quiet talk, moderate drinking, and comfortable cigars. The dining car's majordomo had been alerted that two important passengers would be boarding at Williston, and he had set aside the choice table nearest the middle of the car; fresh flowers, a box of cigars, and a decanter of bourbon waited to accommodate the trio. They would travel together as far as Minot; there Ollie and Zack would change for the Bismarck run.

"This," Roosevelt noted as he took his place next to the window, "will be a splendid interlude."

►◆◄

Zack was cornered, trapped, by Louis Church, territorial governor of Dakota. They were in the reading room of the Sheridan Hotel, the main residence for major officers attending the Patrons of Husbandry convention. It was a reasonably large hotel built right beside the railroad tracks, so it also functioned as the train depot. The facilities were far above those of most hotels in the Northwest, with luxury fittings in each room and a dining room that set a table equaling anything to be found in the more urbane Northeast. And, at two dollars a day, the Sheridan was within the budgets of most delegates to the territorial convention. It was owned by the Northern Pacific, James Hill's major competitor in the region.

Knowing that Zack was one of the owners of the Dakota and Western, and that Zack was working with James Hill on the prospects for statehood, Governor Church had spent most of the day trying to gain a few private moments with him. For five minutes the governor had extolled the scope of farming in the territory with lines such as "and sixty million—that is, young man, millions—of bushels of wheat and another twenty million bushels of corn."

Patiently, Zack nodded.

Governor Church placed a hand on Zack's shoulder. "Think of it, boy! This territory contains 150,000 square miles, more land than all of New England with New York, New

Jersey, and Maryland thrown in. We have four thousand miles of railroads serving seven hundred thousand people. Do you realize that only one state had half that population when it was admitted to the Union? That was West Virginia. Hell, Mister Horton, we are ready for statehood! Now!"

Zack smiled. "Governor, you'll get no argument from me."

"Will Jim Hill give us some more help?"

"What can he do, Governor Church? The Minnesota delegates to Congress are on your side; Mister Hill has encouraged them."

"We need more. We need Hill to bring those congressmen out here, use that damned railroad of his to help us lobby."

Zack tried to compose a noncommittal response. "I'll pass along your views. Mister Hill has his own policies, sir. I can speak for the Dakota and Western, and we will do everything possible; Del Cummins is strongly committed to statehood, and so am I."

"To hell with the policies, young man. The time is nearly past for action. We satisfy every standard for admission and we, by God, deserve to be entered into the Union."

"I couldn't agree more."

"Then get Hill down here. Get him to take a look around."

Zack himself began looking around, hoping to find Ollie Svenson or Del Cummins to rescue him from this interrogation. The room was crowded with small groups of conventioneers discussing their various interests; there was no sign of Svenson or Cummins. Zack was staying in Del's small house on Clark Street, and Zack was sorely tempted to escape there. But he knew his obligations demanded he put up with people like Governor Church.

"I don't mean to press," the governor was saying, "but you have to get Hill and his people to put more pressure on the Congress; it is vital."

Zack looked at the man. Church was not the old stereotype of territorial governor. For dozens of years the posts had been given to political hacks and presidential cronies, frequently men who had never been near the territory. But since the territories had been allowed to have their own legislatures, a new breed of administrator had been put into the office, homebred community leaders. Church was one of the new ones, a man who believed in the future of the territory. Zack said, "I promise to pass along your words, governor."

Church smiled and extended his hand. "You get Jim Hill to come and visit us here; we will show him it is worth his efforts."

Zack was loath to tell Governor Church just how much James Hill knew about Dakota Territory. Zack had been studying Hill's reference file and knew that Hill had been spending a great deal of money to smooth the way to statehood for Dakota.

The governor was pumping Zack's hand as he added, "Why don't you come over to my office tomorrow morning? I can give you a much better picture of the whole thing." Zack eased his hand free. "I can show you just how well we have made ourselves ready for statehood, Mister Horton. You come visit me and I'll give you some information you can take back with you. Did you know that we have provided all of the necessary elements for the territory to be divided into two states? We've put an insane asylum in Yankton, down south, and we have a similar facility in Jamestown up north. There is a penitentiary down in Sioux Falls and a fine, big hoosegow right here in Bismarck; maybe you'd like to pay it a visit."

Zack grinned. "I think I can do without seeing your penitentiary, sir."

Church gave a good-natured laugh. "You're right. But I'm just wanting to impress you with what we have done. Our colleges are situated to serve two states, and even the pope in Rome has authorized a diocese for Jamestown to share the faithful with the bishop who handles the south of the territory." He puffed out his chest. "We have done our work, believe me."

"I do, sir. I am impressed."

"Then you'll come by my office in the morning?"

Zack said he would try.

The governor realized he had been pressing pretty hard, and he switched to a less strident tone as he said, "I would hope we could talk more this evening. Maybe we could impose on Mrs. Church to provide us with some vittles."

"I'd like that, but Ollie has me scheduled to meet with some of the other Grange officials for dinner."

Church gave a quick nod and an "Oh, yes." Zack sensed that the governor was feeling slighted about not being invited, but that was Ollie Svenson's problem.

Zack spotted Ollie Svenson entering the room, but any hope of a quick rescue was shattered when people began flocking around their leader. Svenson was obviously enjoying the clamor. He wore a huge red, white, and blue rosette with two foot-long streamers identifying him as a platform officer. Svenson bobbed his head in Zack's direction, indicating that Zack was to come over; Zack did not know how to avoid taking an abrupt leave of the governor.

Church had seen Ollie's gesture. He said, "I think he wants us to go over to him." Then, with a patronizing chortle, he added, "I think we're expected to rescue him from that mob."

Zack did not reply; he was beginning to wonder if he would ever be shed of the insistent chief executive.

When Governor Church and Zack reached Ollie, they received dark looks from the men who were lobbying Ollie about the next morning's session. Politicians and strangers were not received well by the delegates. "Boys," Ollie said to them, "I've got to do a bit of business with Governor Church."

Moving as deftly as any crafty politician, Ollie ushered Zack out of the room, the governor in their wake. The lobby of the hotel was more packed than the reading room, and Ollie had a difficult time plowing through. At last he steered his way into the station waiting room, which was, by previous agreement, off limits for convention delegates. Fortunately, a train was not due for another two hours, so the room was empty. "Now!" Ollie whewed. "Maybe we can have some privacy."

The governor offered, "Why don't we walk over to my office in the capitol? That will be private."

"That's all right, Governor Church, there's nothing really private to discuss. I just want a moment away from the press of the conventioneers."

"You'll have to come to the national nominating convention this summer, Ollie; the crowds here are nothing compared to the mobs at a political convention."

"No, thank you, governor; this is too much for me." Turning to Zack, Ollie asked, "Will you be going to either of the conventions this summer?"

Zack shook his head. "I've got the foreseeable future pretty well committed to learning about the Dakota and Western. I don't think I will be able to afford the luxury of attending political conventions."

Ollie said, "Governor," and placed a gentle hand on the governor's shoulder. "A couple of my close friends are going to be having dinner tonight over in Mandan. We have a few things to discuss with Zack, and I'd invite you to come along, but I know that you must have a press of appointments keeping you busy."

The attempt at politeness did not work on Governor Church. "Nonsense, Ollie, I'd love to come to dinner."

Zack could tell by Ollie's face that he regretted trying to be tactful. Ollie pressed, "I don't think you'd like to sit around and listen to a bunch of us complaining to Zack about the freight rates on the railroads."

Pompously, Church said, "I am always interested in the commerce of my state, Ollie; you know that."

Ollie nodded. "I guess you are, governor." Then he asked, "You would really like to come to our dinner, even if we just do a lot of gabbing?"

Church chuckled. "As a confirmed politician I am most interested in gabbing; that is my stock-in-trade."

Ollie laughed. "Then you are most welcome, my friend."

Zack was finding a perverse amusement in Ollie Svenson's predicament; but he was also irritated that he would again be saddled with the loquacious governor. At that moment, he spied Del Cummins passing the door of the waiting room and quickly excused himself. As he darted away, Ollie called, "You get back here in time for dinner. By golly, you do that, Zack."

Zack waved his acknowledgment and passed out the door into the hotel lobby, just in time to see Del leaving by the front. Zack bumped into a couple of conventioneers in his rush; he made it to the entrance just as Del was climbing into a hired buggy.

"Hey, Del!"

Del turned and threw up his hands. "Where the hell you been? Climb in."

Zack ran to the buggy.

As the driver moved down the driveway, Zack explained he had been "listening to Governor Church."

Del laughed. "He is a good soul. He just talks too much."

Zack asked, "Where are we going?"

With joy in his voice, Del announced, "Felicity is back!"

"That's great," Zack said. "Now I will finally meet her."

When Zack and Del had first come to Bismarck from Saint Paul, Felicity Patterson had been out of town. She had left a letter for Del that explained her absence. It turned out that her husband, just before his death, had bought two hundred prime farm acres on the Big Sioux River. She had gone there to sell the land and would be back as soon as possible. Del had telegraphed her to come home; but Felicity Patterson was a single-minded woman, and her telegraph back, even though it closed with "love," made it clear that she was going to complete her task.

The Patterson home was on Oak Avenue, set on a large lot with young trees on each side. It was a small, two-story house, like most of the houses in that part of town: painted white, with two chimneys, and a front porch. As the buggy came to a halt, Del asked Zack to wait for a moment. Zack teased, "You afraid I might see you kiss her?"

Del blushed and ran up the front steps. In less than a

minute, he was back at the front door with his arm around his fiancée's shoulders.

Zack was not ready for Felicity Patterson. Del had mentioned that her hair was red; he had not said it was a flaming, brilliant auburn, cut short in a style that could have been called mannish if it had not been so extremely feminine. Del had said Felicity was slight; he had not said she was a perfectly proportioned petite, just one inch over five feet. Del had said she was pretty; he had not said her face looked like an artist's image of a perfect women—perfect save for the barely discernible presence of a few freckles that accented her green eyes. She was dressed in a long grey skirt and white cotton blouse with a small cameo at the throat. Zack recognized the cameo as one Del had shown him years before; it had belonged to Del's mother.

Zack was elated that his friend had captured the heart of this woman.

As he climbed up onto the porch, Felicity greeted him. "Zack." Her voice carried an inflection that said, I know you, I like you, and I am happy to see you, finally.

Brusquely, Del asked, "Well, what do you think of her?"

Zack accepted Felicity's hand as he replied, "I think she is too good for you."

To Felicity, Del said, "I told you; he has always been rude to me."

"Come in, Zack," she said. "Let's visit."

The interior of the house was as neat as a pin; not one item seemed to be out of place. The furniture in the parlor was modest but comfortable; the hardwood floors were polished under spotless area rugs. The windows had lace curtains; the sofa arms had doilies. Zack said, "Felicity, I have seen where Del lives. Are you sure you want him to bring his innate messiness into your life?"

Del repeated, "I told you."

She laughed, told the men to sit down, and went to the kitchen to get refreshments.

As soon as she was out of earshot, Zack said, "She is lovely."

"I was lucky."

Zack paused for a moment, then said seriously, "She is lucky, too, Del. I am happy for both of you."

"Thanks Zack. I hate to mess up your life, but I have to respect her wanting to get out of here. She does not like the town at all."

"From the looks of what she has done to this house, it doesn't appear she is all that unhappy."

Del looked around. "I guess you're right about that. Lord knows what our next home will look like if she's happy there."

Felicity came back with a tray containing cups, a coffeepot, and a decanter with three small glasses. She said, "I don't think you two will be getting much in the way of spirits at the Patrons' convention, so we might as well have our celebration drinks right here and now."

She poured coffee for them, and a measure of whiskey into each glass. With those distributed, Zack stood. "I feel an urge to offer a toast to my old friend and my new friend. But if I did, I would be the only one drinking, so I offer a toast to this day. It is a day on which Del is happy because you are back, I am happy that you two are going to be married, and, Felicity, I hope there are some things which bring you happiness on this day."

She smiled. "That was sweet, Zack. I do have a great deal to be happy about." For the next twenty minutes they talked about those matters that are important to new acquaintances, then Felicity announced, "You men are going to have to entertain yourselves; I have shopping I must do for dinner."

Del said, "Don't worry about us; we have to go to a meeting with the Patrons' big shots."

She stated, "Delbert Cummins, Zack might *have* to go to a meeting, but you, sir, are going to spend the evening having dinner with me. Right here. I hope that is agreeable."

Del chuckled. "Do I have a choice?"

She smiled sweetly. "You do. You go to dinner with Zack and do not bother to come back here . . . ever. Or, and this is what I would like, stay with me."

Zack raised both of his hands, jokingly, as if he was trying to stop two combatants. "There's no need for discussion on this, Del is staying. I've seen too much of him the past week or so, anyway."

Felicity said, "Good. That's settled." As she headed toward the front hall, she said over her shoulder, "I'll be back in a few minutes."

As the door closed behind her, Del said, "I do love that woman, Zack."

"You had better love her; she is not going to accept anything less, from what I have seen of her."

Del poured them each a second glass of whiskey. "There's one thing that I had better get you ready for, Zack."

"What's that?"

"Tonight, when you're with these fellows, keep the conversation on the statehood issue. Let them know that the Dakota and Western is going to do everything it can to support them."

"That won't be hard, Del; that's the truth."

"Yeah, but there is one matter that's bound to come up, unless you work hard to keep away from it."

Zack put down his glass. Del's tone of voice was more serious than he had heard for some time. Del continued, "The Patrons of Husbandry are committed to having the federal government take over the ownership of all of the railroads in the nation."

"You mean Ollie Svenson and his people?"

"Exactly."

"They haven't said one word about that to me. What's the idea?"

"The idea is that the Patrons of Husbandry, and the Knights of Labor, and a whole mass of other organizations are determined to have the railroads out of private hands. They're throwing in the telegraph business, too."

"Why?"

"They say both of those services are too much a public service to be in the hands of business leaders who run a monopoly."

"That's crazy! There's plenty of competition in the railroads."

"No question," Del agreed. "But there have been a lot of bad feelings over rate fixing and land grants. I, personally, feel they have some good arguments; so did your grandfather."

"The government would ruin the railroads."

"That's the truth, and that's why your grandfather and I agreed to fight it. But the movement is there, and Ollie Svenson is dedicated to the cause."

"Why hasn't he mentioned it?"

"I don't know; I guess that he wants to get you on his side first. Just keep your guard up if they start getting into it."

Zack sat back in his chair. He did not like to think of a man like Ollie Svenson being devious. He realized he was going to have to be alert to the subtleties of politics.

He looked at his friend. "I hope Felicity gets back soon. It's nice to be in company you can trust."

►◆◄

The dinner party arrived at the Inter-Ocean Hotel in Mandan shortly after seven that evening. The Inter-Ocean was another of the many hotels built and operated by the Northern Pacific Railroad. While some were purely utilitarian, many bordered on being extravagant; the Mandan Inter-Ocean was one of the latter.

The group had crossed the Missouri River on the Northern Pacific bridge in a small palace railway car pulled by a yard engine. At the Mandan station they were met by a carriage from the hotel; the manager was on hand to greet them as they pulled up to the front entrance of the three-story building. The entrance was not all that elegant, only a small porte cochere, but, once in the lobby, it was easy to see that the Northern Pacific had a special feeling about the future of Mandan.

The walls were paneled with dark-stained oak, and the ceiling was decorated with the ornamental tin squares that were the latest rage in public buildings. A massive rock fireplace sat unlighted, waiting for the chill of an evening. Two photographic enlargements, three by four feet, held the place of honor over the mantel. The one on the left showed the Fifth Infantry Band at the Last Spike Pavilion near Garrison, Montana Territory, and the other showed Main Street, Bismarck, with a huge evergreen arch in place welcoming the dignitaries who had traveled across the continent to celebrate the driving of the spike. Both pictures had been taken by Jay Haynes.

Governor Church spoke almost reverently as Zack studied the photos. "That was a moment to remember, and a fabulous trip to enjoy, Mister Horton; a proud instant in the history of this territory."

"Did you go on the trip?"

"Ah, yes, I was fortunate enough to be a part of it. President Grant was there, or did you know that?"

Zack said, "I don't think I have done much studying about the Northern Pacific, governor." Then he added, "But I'm learning."

Governor Church nodded.

James Hill had been the only railroad builder to move slowly and insure that his railroad used as few steep grades as possible. Hill's philosophy was that his approach would cost more during construction but that lower operating costs would quickly recover the investment.

"You know," the governor noted, "the Northern Pacific had to break up the dignitary train to pull the cars up over Mullan Pass to the ceremony; the grade was too steep for the locomotives to do their job. It was quite embarrassing to Mister Villard."

Henry Villard was the creator of the Northern Pacific, and the nemesis of James Hill. Everyone knew that Villard had constructed the Northern Pacific Railroad over steep grades and had built expensive bridges over rivers and gorges in his drive to complete the first northern tier transcontinental railroad. Villard's technique did indeed lead to high operating costs, and would eventually bring the Northern Pacific into bankruptcy.

Zack did not take up the opportunity to criticize the Northern Pacific. Governor Church let the matter drop, and they joined with the others as they were greeted profusely by the Inter-Ocean Hotel manager. There was a large table set up at the west end of the lobby with delicate pastries and liquid refreshments. There were no alcoholic beverages because the Patrons of Husbandry had taken a prohibition stance, and was trying to ensure that the state would be alcohol free when it was admitted to the Union. The hardworking farming class in the north of the territory was solidly behind prohibition. But the similarly hardworking cowboys of the open ranges, and the miners working in the south, were determined to have their liquid refreshments contain alcohol. In two weeks, when the mine unions would be holding their state federation convention in Mandan, the lobby table in the Inter-Ocean Hotel would bear a burden of liquor.

Talk among the party was easy but serious, as the conventioneers caught up on what had happened in one anothers' lives since they had met the previous year. There was much good cheer about the blessings soon to issue from the heavy spring rains in the region; none could guess that they were only one year away from the beginning of a drought that would ruin many farmers. Ollie Svenson, the proper host, drifted back and forth among the guests, but he showed his concern to keep Zack from being too bothered by Governor Church. Zack finally told Ollie not to worry. "He's a good man."

Ollie smiled. "He is a long talker, that one, by golly."

After twenty minutes, the party was led into a small, private dining room that had a splendid view of Bismarck. When all were seated, service of the meal began. Conversation continued on many subjects.

The fare was unpretentious but elegant. The soup was a thick potato gruel followed by a serving of brook trout, and then venison roast presented with a variety of vegetables. Dessert was a selection of chocolate cake, apple pie, and a rich pudding. Through the entire meal there was a constant supply of hot coffee and freshly cooked breads, both dark and light.

As Zack was finishing his second slice of pie—he had never in his life eaten so much as he had over the previous few days—Governor Church took it on himself to continue his professional role. "Did you know, Mister Horton, that you are sitting in a place that claims some of the oldest history on this continent?"

Zack sipped some coffee, then responded, "Here, in this dining room?"

There was general laughter from the diners. Ollie said, "No, Zack, we all know what the governor is talking about. You might be interested."

Church continued. "The Mandan Indians made this place along the Missouri their final home."

"Oh," Zack said. "I remember that Lewis and Clark spent time with the Mandan."

Church continued. "Do you remember reading that Captain Lewis referred to the Mandan as the *Welsh* Indians?"

"Welsh Indians, as in Wales?"

"Exactly."

"No," Zack admitted. "I don't remember that."

"Captain Lewis was referring to the legend that the Mandan are derived from a mixture of Welsh and Indian blood. Many of the Mandan had red hair, and some had soft blue eyes. There are, in fact, three hundred words used by the Mandan that sound the same as Welsh words and mean the same thing. The Welsh word for bread is *bara;* in Mandan it is *bara.* The words for cow are the same; *buch* in Welsh and *buwch* in Mandan. And so on. That is one way to trace their history back to a Welsh prince named Madoc, the Prince of America."

Zack looked around at his dinner companions, hoping to see some sign that Governor Church was telling a joke; all of the faces were serious.

"Back around 1170, the prince called Madoc was caught up in a family power struggle. His father had died, and his five brothers were battling to see who would become king. Madoc was a pacific soul, and he hated being in the middle of the conflict; two of his brothers had been killed. Because he was the youngest and so mild mannered, there was little likelihood he would be elevated to the throne, so he turned to his real love in life—the sea. Madoc had been sent by his father on a couple of commercial trips into the Mediterranean; Madoc knew boats. He collected three small vessels and crews totaling forty-six men. They crossed the Atlantic and ended up in the Gulf of Mexico, at a place now known as Mobile, Alabama."

Zack gave a shallow laugh and said, "Hey, now you are kidding me, governor."

The governor rubbed his hand across his chin, took time to light a cigar, then sipped some coffee before he stated, "You find this interesting, don't you?"

"With all due respect, sir, I find it unbelievable."

Ollie cut in. "You can believe it, Zack; the governor is telling you one of our most interesting bits of folklore. By golly, you haven't heard the best part."

Governor Church dipped the tip of his cigar in his coffee and took a puff, then said, "Madoc could not know where he was, but he knew the place was spectacular. The weather was blissful compared to Wales, there were wild fruits and limitless supplies of fish, and fresh, sweet water was bountiful. He decided to colonize the place. He left one of his ships and thirty men, then sailed back to Wales. The conflict between his brothers had graduated into a minor war, and Dafydd, his eldest brother, was quite willing to see the end of Madoc and, at the same time, get rid of a few troublemakers, so a colonizing expedition was launched with a dozen ships and three hundred settlers. The actual history is vague, because there is no written record, but the Welshmen under Madoc settled along the coast. When the warlike Indian tribes of Georgia and north Florida caused problems, the Welsh migrated north. They moved up into Tennessee, near Chattanooga, and did well until forced out again by hostile natives; they traveled northwest. They encountered Seneca tribes who were friendly, and this is where the Welshmen differed from most other colonizers; they integrated into the Seneca through marriage. The Welshman, through history, has been known as a fierce warrior, as fierce as the North American Indian, but a lovely twist of fate brought two peace-loving nonconformist groups together. The Mandan tribe was the result."

Zack said, "It is an interesting myth."

"No myth, Mister Horton, believe me. The Mandan displayed not just similarities in language to the Welsh. Their farming techniques are not found native to any other tribes, and they used boats identical to the Welsh coracles, a wooden frame covered with animal hides. Identical, I tell you."

"That is amazing."

"Amazing, and absolutely true." Governor Church looked around the table accepting the nods of the diners. "One more thing," the governor added. "The Mandan tribes always settled on knolls, near water, and dug defensive moats surrounding their villages. How is that for amazing?"

Zack said, "I have never heard a more amazing story, Governor Church; that was three hundred years ahead of Columbus."

Ollie put in, "And don't forget Leif Eriksson. He was a hundred years ahead of Madoc."

During the governor's story, the diners had finished eating. With quiet efficiency, the waiters had cleared the table, leaving only cigars and coffee, and had disappeared. Ollie saw Zack's observation and explained, "I made arrangements with the head waiter to leave us alone for our business talks once we were through eating."

Zack nodded. To Church, he said, "Thanks for an interesting tale, governor. There should be some research done on that; it is an impressive dimension to the history of Dakota Territory."

"Oh, there has been extensive research, Mister Horton. Back in 1797, a Welshman named John Evans came over and did a considerable amount of work. He even lived right here in Mandan with the tribes."

"Then you should publicize it. It's a fascinating bit of history."

The governor laughed. "There's good reason to keep the whole thing just an interesting slice of history. We don't need any publicity on this. The real reason John Evans came over here was to try and prove that Wales had a legitimate claim on this territory. We don't need that."

Zack joined in on the general laugh. "I see what you mean."

Ollie said, "I have not had a chance to tell you, governor, but Zack and I left Teeodoor Roosevelt just yesterday. He told us he was going to set a bug in the right ears in the nation's capitol."

Zack expanded. "We visited with Mister Roosevelt at his ranch and traveled with him from Williston to Minot; he is determined to help the cause of statehood in the nation's capital."

Zack looked around at the group. They were honest people, hardworking individuals who were building the nation. He was feeling a glow of accomplishment at being a party to the making of history.

During dinner Zack had listened as the diners spoke, touching on the many problems of forging a civilized, structured society. He picked up phrases about crops, and about harvesting, and about equipment, but mostly about families. This society was oriented to families.

Zack thought about Del Cummins and Felicity Patterson, about to launch their own family. They were a handsome couple and would make a fine marriage; Zack was pleased for Del. For no reason, Zack's mind wandered into reflections on Leah Page. It was a strange phenomenon for Zack to have memories of a woman intrude into his daily routine, but it had been happening with his recollections of Leah. Suddenly the way she said a word or moved her head would be in front of him, almost visually. It was confusing. She had been a part of his life for only a few days. He wondered what she was doing at the moment. There had been no communication. Telegraphs from James Hill gave no indication of Leah Page's progress, and Zack felt offended by the lack of news. He knew he had no right to know about her, but still he wished he would hear something.

CHAPTER 5

BALTIMORE—FRIDAY, JULY 6, 1888

Leah Page crumpled up the yellow telegraph message and tossed it impatiently into the wire-mesh wastebasket by her desk. She picked up the square-foot sample of leather, dyed light grey, from her blotter, rubbed the fingers of her right hand strongly over the smooth leather, then brought it up close to her nose and took in a deep breath.

"Clarence!" she called. Clarence Martin, her secretary, was in through the door even before the echo had died. "Did you smell this?"

He nodded, looking a little guilty. "Miss Page, I did not know whether the odor was too strong or not. I was going to tell you."

She raised both hands in apology, then said, "I'm sorry, Clarence. I should not have spoken so harshly." She moved her shoulders, regaining her composure, then said, "The odor is too strong. I want you to send the sample back to the tannery, with a letter stating the complaint. Tell them that I want a fresh sample . . ." She looked at the large calendar on the wall off to the right. ". . . by Monday afternoon. That should give them enough time to solve the problem."

"Yes, Miss Page." Clarence paused, then said, "They will have to work on Sunday to get it on such a tight schedule."

"We're already two days late, Clarence. We'll be working a few Sundays before this order is filled." She added, "I want you to return that sample with the letter personally. Wait for their reply."

He smiled; it was not the first time Leah Page had sent him on similar tasks.

She pursed her lips, then said, "Do not threaten them, but you can let them know that I've been approached by another supplier."

"I didn't know that."

She laughed. "Of course not, you silly man, because we haven't had any such approach. But you can *imply* such a thing, can't you?"

Clarence gave a throaty laugh in response. He especially enjoyed working for Leah Page when she was entering business battles.

"You do that right now, this morning. I want a positive response from them by lunchtime."

He turned to leave, stopped, and asked, "What about the telegraph message from Mister Hill?"

"I don't know." Impatience was back in her voice.

"It is the second one this week. Should I compose a reply?"

She slowly swiveled her chair around and looked down onto the traffic on Pratt Street. A block away, she could see ships being loaded, carrying products out of the Port of Baltimore. "I don't know, Clarence." Then, swinging back to face her desk, she said, "I'll tell you this afternoon."

"Thank you, Miss Page." He left her alone.

In her travels, Leah Page had been given an egg-shaped rock, polished smooth by eons on a river bottom. The present had come from a friendly buyer for a chain of stores in Georgia and Alabama. She had forgotten the buyer's name, but the present had become her constant office companion, especially when troubled with a problem. During those times, when she was sure she was alone, she would spin the rock-egg on the polished oak of her desk and simply watch it spend its energy and come to rest.

She began spinning the rock. She was having a problem with James Hill's demands.

After leaving Saint Paul, she had dutifully journeyed out to Wyoming Territory, where she had accomplished a great deal for both statehood and for woman suffrage. Even the staid James Hill had been verbose in his compliments. She had made new contacts with a dozen influential man and women who had previously been noncommittal about the issues, and she had reinspired some of the suffrage supporters who had lost interest. One reason for Leah's considerable success had been the coincidental appearance of Abigail Scott Duniway in Laramie. Abigail Duniway was a prominent suffrage leader along the northwest Pacific Coast, dreaded by legislators in Oregon State and Washington Territory. She was the owner and publisher of the *Northwest News,* a newspaper that enjoyed wide readership. Together, the two women had dazzled Laramie, then Cheyenne, and finally Casper. Despite Leah repeatedly directing credit for their success toward Abigail Duniway, James Hill had insisted that the achievement was all Leah's.

Now, through a letter ten days ago, and yesterday and today through telegraph messages, Hill was insisting that Leah make another trip to Wyoming Territory. Leah did not want to go.

She was telling herself that she needed to stay in Baltimore and ensure that the fall leather goods were shipped on time. That position was acceptable for public consumption, but she knew that there was a deeper reason. She did not care to make this expedition for Mister Hill because she knew that Zack Horton was not going to be involved. Zack's letter had arrived two days previously. He had explained that he was working very hard to learn what Del Cummins knew about running the Dakota and Western, that he was enjoying the people who were the railroad's customers, that he hoped to be back east soon and would like very much to meet Leah in either Chicago or Baltimore, whichever would suit her schedule. That had pleased her very much—but then he added that he had reluctantly agreed to go farther west, "to Idaho Territory for a few weeks," at the request of James Hill. With that, Leah began feeling almost angry at both James Hill and Zack Horton.

It was not as if she was besotted by Zack Horton, but she had found him to be attractive and interesting. It was not as if she was pining for the man; her business kept her too busy to long for any man. But she would not mind getting to know Zack Horton a little better. Was that so unreasonable?

The rock came to a stop.

She reached down and retrieved the crumpled telegraph message from the wastebasket. With the heel of her hand she smoothed out the message.

PLEASE RESPOND IMMEDIATELY. URGENTLY REQUEST YOU TO JOIN MY PARTY IN SAINT LOUIS FOR VITALLY IMPORTANT MISSION TO WYOMING. NO QUESTION WOMAN SUFFRAGE MOVEMENT WILL BENEFIT GREATLY FROM THIS DEVELOPMENT. WILL BE LEAVING SAINT LOUIS MONDAY EVENING SIX PM JULY NINE. AGAIN REQUEST YOU RESPOND IMMEDIATELY. SIGNED JAMES HILL.

Leah accused herself of procrastinating. She felt no pressing compulsion to help James Hill, but she did feel an obligation to do what she could for the cause of suffrage. And she found she was hoping—maybe against hope—that Zack Horton might be included in Hill's "mission."

She had checked the train service from Baltimore to Saint Louis; she would have to catch the four o'clock Baltimore and Ohio train if she was to reach Saint Louis in time.

Aloud, she said, "I have time to decide. I can wait until after lunch before making up my mind." In the secret enclave of her mind where she kept her fervent wishes, she had already decided: She would go.

Sir George Roberts had received his knighthood from Queen Victoria in 1884 as a direct result of the American Civil War. Cattle herds in the United States had been depleted by the troops' demand for beef. Because England supported the Confederacy, shipment of new breeding stock to the Union was forbidden while the war was going on. In 1866, George Roberts had left his Lucky Hill Farm near Harlech, Wales, and gone to Madison, Wisconsin, where he had negotiated the sale of five of his prized Ayrshire bulls at the startling price per bull of £1,250, in those days, about $6,552.50. He was quite pleased with his turn of profit and the next year, 1867, due to the magnificent performance of his bulls and their progeny, he sold an additional ten bulls and twenty breeding heifers. That year's sale was at a considerable premium over 1866. His export business to the cattle-hungry ranchers and dairy farmers of the United States was off and running. Roberts used some of his expanding wealth to endowed a children's hospital in Caernarvon, and, in 1884, farmer George became Sir George in a ceremony that confirmed to Freda Roberts—Lady Roberts by virtue of the investiture—that Queen Victoria was a splendid monarch, even though she was not Welsh.

Sir George had now cut back on his business operations in an effort to enjoy the fruits of his labors, although he still dabbled in cattle ventures simply to keep his hand in. One of his dabbles was an eleven-thousand-acre cattle ranch north of Casper in Wyoming Territory. He was atypical of the British investor who owned land in Wyoming; two or three times a year he would actually visit his holdings. He was well liked and respected by those who came to know him, but to most in the territory, Sir George seemed the same as all the rest: an arrogant, rich foreigner exploiting the land for his own gain. Sir George accepted the former reaction with warmth and aplomb and ignored the latter. He operated a good ranch, paid fair wages to his hired hands, and reinvested some of his considerable profits for ranch improvements.

Sir George and Lady Roberts had come to Wyoming that July of 1888 to oversee the arrival of a shipment of Herefords he had sold to a neighboring rancher. They had spent three weeks in the insufferable dry heat and had been making final preparations for the journey back to Wales when the request came from James Hill for a meeting. Sir George had met Hill socially two years previously at a reception in Chicago, and Hill's status as a leading railway mogul was not lost on Sir George, who relied on rail transportation for his cattle. An exchange of telegraph messages resolved that they would meet in Yellowstone National Park in the northwest corner of Wyoming Territory. The site had been suggested by Sir George; he and Lady Roberts had never visited the park. James Hill was motivated to agree—he wanted a favor.

Sir George was standing on the veranda of the Mammoth Hot Springs Hotel with Major Marvin Carver, who was the commander of the U.S. Cavalry detachment responsible to the Department of the Interior for the management of Yellowstone. Major Carver enjoyed the work. His troops were easy to manage, because Yellowstone duty was a plum for both officers and enlisted men, and the private contractors who operated the hotels and restaurants and provided guide services and stagecoaches for visitors shared a sense of pride in their stewardship of a truly unique natural phenomenon. No other place in the world offered such a concentration of thermal activity, from the bubbling mud pots to the dramatic geysers erupting boiling water into the sky.

Looking out from the veranda, Sir George was studying the Mammoth Hot Spring Terraces across from the hotel. "Fascinating," he said to Major Carver. "Simply fascinating."

The major smiled. "Yes, Sir George, it never fails to grip one with a sense of awe."

It was awesome. Here the calcareous deposits of seventy active springs covered two hundred acres, which were ribboned into more than a dozen terraces in which 160-degree water churned, then overflowed down the lower terraces, all the time depositing calcium carbonate, which solidified and built new dams, adding to the spectacle. The colors captured in the minerals ranged from soft pastels to stark reds and greens; the water was deep azure.

Pulling his attention away from the sight, Sir George pulled out his pocket watch. It was 2:30. "It seems the coach is running late."

Major Carver stroked his bushy moustache. "It will be here shortly. They left Cinnabar right on time; I had a message to that effect. He is traveling by private coach."

"Good."

"You seem anxious to leave our park, Sir George."

"Not at all. Lady Roberts and I have enjoyed every moment, and especially the fine hospitality extended by you and Mrs. Carver."

Sir George had been at the park for three days, and he and his wife had made all the side trips they could. They had seen the 310-foot Great Falls of the Yellowstone, but they were going to have to wait until after the Hill meeting to make the long trip down to the geyser basins and Yellowstone Lake. The major's wife had offered to accompany the Robertses on that journey; she took advantage of every chance to visit Old Faithful, which performed its 150-foot-tall display every sixty-five minutes. At dinner the night before she had said, not for the first time, "I could go there every day of the week and not be bored."

Major Carver bowed. "It has been our pleasure. It's not often a lowly major in the U.S. Cavalry gets to entertain royalty."

Sir George chuckled. "Don't confuse me with royalty, major. I'm nothing more than a farmer with a piece of paper from Queen Victoria. I made a lot of money."

"There has to be more to it than that."

"There is: political connections."

Both men laughed. The major cut off as he saw a coach coming toward the hotel. "Here's your man now."

Sir George watched as the coach rounded the curve of the driveway. The rig was pulled by a four-horse team and seemed a bit ostentatious for the seven-mile trip from Cinnabar, but then he realized that Hill was a man with money and obviously in a hurry; besides, the last part of the road to Mammoth Hot Springs was steep. Before the coach had eased to a stop, Hill was out the door and moving quickly up the front stairs. Sir George saw there another passenger getting out of the coach more slowly; it was a woman.

Hill gave a broad smile and extended his hand. "Sir George! Good to see you."

"And you, Hill. You are looking well."

"Feeling fine. Just busier that I want to be."

"Isn't that the case in all our lives." There was a slight pause. "I'd like you to meet Major Marvin Carver, commandant of this outstanding facility."

Hill shook hands with the major. "I saw some of your troops on the road into the park; fine-looking unit."

"They are good men."

"Spotless uniforms, horses groomed well, good discipline."

"They work hard."

"It shows."

During the exchange, Sir George glanced back down at the stagecoach. The woman who had climbed out was standing, waiting. She was young, young and attractive. It can't be his wife, Sir George thought. Ah, a daughter.

"Mister Hill, your daughter is waiting."

Hill looked down from the steps. "Oh, she's not a daughter." Then he called, "Leah, do come up here."

Good heavens, Sir George thought, has he brought some chippy along? What will Freda say? Oh, my!

Leah Page came gracefully up the stairs. Major Carver noted she was dressed sensibly for travel in the park: a skirt, blouse, and jacket of light weight. Her shoes looked sturdy. Smart woman.

Hill introduced her, adding, ". . . an associate representing an organization in Chicago that's working very hard with my railroad. A special project."

Sir George shuddered; she had to be some sort of a paramour. Why else such a convoluted introduction? "Pleased to meet you, Miss Page." He could not hide his reservations. She offered him her hand. My God! A paramour with no decorum; Freda will be furious.

Major Carver was entertaining no unseemly thoughts. He did not question the motives of men of James Hill's rank. He said, "Pleased to meet you, Miss Page." Turning to Hill, he said, "Mrs. Carver and I would be pleased to entertain you and Miss Page at dinner this evening, Mister Hill. I could have you picked up at . . . say seven o'clock."

Hill smiled. "Thank you for the offer, major, but I must decline. We'll be returning to the train in a couple of hours."

Cheeky! Sir George thought. He was not used to devoting three days to waiting for two hours of conversation. He barely heard Major Carver say, "Well, Sir George, you and Lady Roberts will be coming to dinner?"

"Certainly," Sir George agreed. "We'll see you this evening."

The major gave a fingertip salute and walked down the stairs.

Sir George collected his thoughts, then said, "My goodness, Hill. I thought we were going to have a good visit, certainly dinner this evening."

"I had hoped so, too, Sir George. That's why I asked Miss Page to come along, to visit with Lady Roberts while you and I talked."

Freda Roberts was not a woman to be pushed into a corner with some older man's young lady. Hill caught the drift of Sir George's thoughts and explained, "I had intended to bring along Mrs. Hill, but she came down with an indisposition that forced her to stay home."

Leah Page smiled. Mary Theresa Hill had refused to come and meet with anyone called "Sir" anything. The Archbishop of Canterbury had, earlier that summer, made a rather rude pronouncement about Pope Leo's encyclical on mixed marriages. As Mary Theresa had said, "Anyone with a 'sir' before his name has to be a toady of the queen, and she is the Church of England. I will not talk to any of those devils." Mary Theresa took her Roman Catholicism seriously, especially since she and James Hill were a mixed marriage.

Hill added, "Let me assure you that Miss Page is not . . . that is . . . she is surely—"

Leah cut in. "Sir George, rest assured that Mister Hill and I are absolutely only business associates. There is nothing more than that."

Sir George saw that he had blundered. "I didn't mean to insult either one of you."

Leah continued. "No insult is taken. I have a great deal of respect for the Hills, and he has been kind enough to give considerable assistance to my organization. When he asked me to stand in for his wife, I was very proud."

"Please, please, let's stop this. I had no intention of starting off on a bad footing."

Hill laughed. "You think I'm young enough to be a roué, Sir George?"

Flustered, Sir George protested, "By no means! That is . . ." Desperate, he turned to Leah and asked, "What is your organization?"

Leah replied, "The National Woman Suffrage Association."

Relief surged through Sir George. He said, "Hill, you rascal, you did your research on me, didn't you?"

Hill smiled. Hill had indeed found out that Lady Roberts was a stalwart officer of the Welsh Suffrage Movement.

Leah Page, who had not been given that bit of intelligence, asked, "What are you two talking about?"

They explained. She blushed, half in amusement, half in anger. She said, "Mister Hill, you always find some way to amaze the people around you."

"I didn't plan this, Miss Page. It is all a coincidence."

Sir George said, "I am wondering about you and your

coincidence, James. I think I'll keep my guard up during our meeting."

"No need. I'm here in both of our interests."

"Well," Sir George said, "let's get to it, then." He turned to Leah. "Come along, young lady. We have work to do."

There were three hundred rooms in the Mammoth Hot Springs Hotel, but only five suites. Because of his title and his position as a substantial Wyoming rancher, Sir George had been able to get the choice suite on the second floor looking onto the beautiful terraces.

When he led James Hill and Leah Page into the parlor, Lady Roberts was sitting on a sofa, metal-rimmed glasses perched on the bridge of her nose, working diligently on a small piece of needlepoint.

She looked up and set her work neatly on a side table. "Well, George, I see we have guests; what a pleasant surprise."

Freda Roberts was not at all surprised. If Sir George had walked in with an elephant, he would have warned her, discussed it with her, and made sure just how the visit was to be handled. Lady Roberts ran an efficient life for her husband. If any surprise had been possible, it would have been that a beautiful woman was part of the scene, but Lady Roberts gave no indication that she was pushed off balance even one smidgen. After a cursory salutation to James Hill, she said to Leah, "Child, do come here and talk with me."

Freda Roberts had a way of making people feel welcome.

Sir George and Hill stood for a moment while the ladies settled on the sofa and began to talk, then Sir George asked Hill if he would like some refreshment. Hill accepted and was led into another, much smaller sitting room fitted out as a smoking-room-cum-office. There were two morris chairs separated by a low table on which rested a tray holding the makings for drinks; a cigar humidor offered a selection of Havanas. Both men soon were nursing glasses of whiskey and water. Sir George asked, "Now, what can I do for you?"

Hill began talking.

Back in the parlor of the suite, Lady Roberts was saying to Leah, ". . . and we are Methodists, but still George does like to have his little nip now and then." She gave a sympathetic smile. "I reckon it is proper for the men to sneak off every now and then."

Leah was tempted to say, "I wouldn't mind joining them," but she had committed herself to the role of keeping Lady Roberts busy while Hill did his business.

Lady Roberts delicately probed into why Mrs. Hill had not made the trip. Leah, just as delicately, gave an adequate, but not fully honest, answer. Lady Roberts observed, "So you were kind enough to come along and entertain me while the men did business."

Leah felt a flush come to her face. She was grasping for some new subject when Lady Roberts added, "Men are truly difficult, don't you think?"

Leah smiled, not knowing how to respond. Lady Roberts patted Leah's knee. "Child, you don't have to answer that. I just think it a shame that men feel we have no place in their business world."

Leah offered, "Oh, Mister Hill is not like that. I guess I neglected to mention it, Lady Roberts, but I am in business." Leah explained about her leather business.

"My dear, that is simply splendid. Oh, I would so love to do something like that. We women must exert ourselves when we feel compelled by our beliefs."

"I totally agree, Lady Roberts. I also am very involved in the women's suffrage movement."

Lady Roberts was taken aback. "Well . . . now . . ." She collected her thoughts, then said, "I am quite pleased."

Leah grinned. "I am afraid that my presence here is something of a ruse on Mister Hill's part; he knew you were involved in suffrage, too."

Lady Roberts lifted her right hand up to her mouth. "And you knew this?"

"I had no idea. I found out a few minutes ago when we arrived."

Lady Roberts lowered her hand. "That explains why Sir George was in such a fine mood when he came in. He had been quite pensive about the meeting with your Mister Hill, but I know that news pleased George; it certainly pleases me."

"Why is that?"

"Well, because it is obvious that Mister Hill put a great deal of thought into this meeting."

"But it is bordering on deviousness."

"True, but, child, it also shows a determined man."

"He is determined; no question there. He has helped our organization, but only to the extent that we help his own interests."

"Do not, Miss Page, ever look askance at anyone who can help the cause. There are too many people who are against us. Take help, in any degree, where you find it, and be thankful."

Lady Roberts led the conversation into child labor and adequate schooling, which led them into a discussion of women moving into areas of employment other than teaching and nursing. The talk moved back to suffrage, and Lady Roberts bragged that the Wyoming Territorial Legislature had passed into law the right for women to vote; she added that she had had no part of that, because "for a foreigner to meddle was out of the question; don't you agree?"

Leah was not sure she did agree. Lady Roberts was a clear thinker who was eloquent in her speech; she could bolster any cause.

They then gossiped about the movement's leadership, which led naturally to Susan B. Anthony. Lady Roberts complained that she had never been able to attend any of the Anthony lectures in London; "George is always running me one way when I want to go another."

"He doesn't approve of the movement?"

"My lands! Did I give that impression? George is most supportive. But our schedules always seem to conflict, and no matter how deeply I believe in anything, I will not let it disrupt our family life."

Leah related a short biography of Abigail Scott Duniway, who had never come to Lady Roberts' attention. "Isn't that simply splendid?" said Lady Roberts. "These western regions seem to have their share of dedicated women."

Then Leah Page mentioned the name of Victoria Woodhull.

"Oh, child, now you have come to one I know of and have met. Miss Woodhull has been quite scandalous in England; do you know that?"

Leah laughed. Some of Victoria Woodhull's escapades—as well of those of her sister, Tennessee Chaflin—had been the subject of sensationalized newspaper accounts and traumatic discussions within the suffrage movement. Victoria Woodhull's pronouncements on free love had infuriated suffragettes trying to distance themselves from such radical opinions. Lady Roberts said she had been at the famous meeting where Victoria sneaked into the hall in disguise because the police were trying to serve her with a summons. At the proper moment, she had shed her disguise, jumped to the speaker's podium, and spoken for five minutes before the police in the hall realized what was happening. As the police began to hurry toward her, she ran out the side of the stage and escaped through a back-alley door. "It was really quite exciting for all of us. I think half the audience wished it had the courage of Miss Woodhull."

Lady Roberts did add that there were some shameful aspects of Woodhull's life. "Of course, George has made it extremely clear that he would not think it wise for me to be at many more such meetings." She laughed fondly. "He is so protective."

In the half hour they had been talking, they had realized they had much in common and much more they would like to discuss. Lady Roberts looked at the watch on her necklace. "Well, let's save something to discuss later. I want to take you across to the terraces for a look at the springs; it is a sight which will live with you forever."

"I'm afraid we had better wait here; Mister Hill wants to return to the train as quickly as possible."

"Why is he staying on the train? George can obtain splendid accommodations right here in the hotel."

Leah smiled. "I wasn't clear; we are leaving today."

"Child, do stop talking foolishness. He can't be planning that."

"I'm afraid he is. As soon as he is finished with Sir George."

Lady Roberts stood and adjusted the collar of her blouse, then smoothed out her skirt and primped her hair. With a sly grin she said, "That's utter nonsense. You come with me."

Lady Roberts led the way and entered her husband's office without knocking. The men were deeply involved in a dialogue as she announced, "I think we must speak, gentlemen."

Both men rose, and Sir George offered a warm smile. "Well, now, ladies, this is as nice an interruption as we could have."

James Hill was just barely able to twist a glare of annoyance into a feeble smile; the interruption came at a most inauspicious time. He had been just about to accomplish his purpose.

Lady Roberts said, "George, Miss Page has just this minute informed me that Mister Hill is reluctant to impose on your hospitality, that he feels they must leave after just arriving."

"I know that, Freda, my pet. Mister Hill has the press of important business calling him away."

Lady Roberts folded her arms and tilted her head just slightly. "I know he probably told you that. However, I know that he is merely being polite, because he is such a fine gentleman." Then, with a tone and emphasis that left no question as to what she wanted, she stated, "So, George, it is incumbent on you to insist that they stay over for at least a couple of days."

Leah was hard put to avoid bursting out into a laugh; Hill was stroking his beard furiously. He knew he was being manipulated, and he saw that Lady Roberts might be skillful enough to prevail. He pleaded, "We really must be leaving, Lady Roberts. I have a long trip ahead of me."

She offered a delicate laugh. "You are such a gentleman, Mister Hill. I think George can convince you that you will be most welcome to stay. Besides, Miss Page and I have a great deal to discuss."

Hill was irritated. His ploy of using Leah's affiliation with the suffrage movement had backfired on him. Crossly, he wanted to accuse Leah Page of causing the situation, but he knew the ultimate fault had been his own. He looked at his host; Hill knew at that instant he had lost the battle. Sir George, after thirty years of marriage, was able to read his wife and she, for whatever reason, had conveyed her wants. He looked at Hill and said, "The fact is, old man, that it might be well for us to extend our talks, do some sleeping on the ideas."

Hill knew how to fight and win but also how to lose. Sir George had been right on the verge of agreeing to Hill's request, but the deal had not been struck. Hill had been through dozens of business negotiations in his life, and he knew he could win this one, but not if he had to combat Lady Roberts. Could he take Leah Page aside and have her use her considerable wiles to change Lady Roberts' mind? No, that would be impolitic. He flicked a small ash from his cigar into the spittoon. He needed Sir George's aid. He could get it with the investment of a bit more time. He would simply have to work harder to catch up after he left. He put on a smile. He said, "You are right, Lady Roberts. I did not want to impose on your holiday here in the park."

All of them knew Hill was lying, but he was doing so gracefully.

Lady Roberts beamed. "I say, that is splendid, Mister Hill." Grasping Leah Page's arm, she announced, "I'm going to take my new friend for a walk over to the terraces."

Sir George asked, "My dear, would you please have someone tell the manager I would like to see him up here so we can arrange rooms for our guests?"

"I would be delighted."

"And have the front desk send a message to Major Carver

that Mister Hill and Miss Page will also be joining him for dinner."

She nodded.

Hill said, "I want to thank you for your kindness, Lady Roberts." She acknowledged with a slight curtsy. "And, Miss Page, would you please send the stage back down to the train and tell them to have Calvin pack us some clothing? What we'll need for another . . ."

Lady Roberts grabbed at the pause and inserted, "Two days."

Hill nodded. "Another two days. Let Calvin know I want him up here. I'll find him a room." He turned to Sir George. "Calvin is my number one on the train."

Sir George smiled. "By all means."

With that out of the way, Lady Roberts waited a couple of moments, then said, "Well, we are off on our jaunt. We will return in an hour or so."

► ◆ ◄

Fort Yellowstone was one of the more attractive and well-maintained facilities in the army, and the officer named to command the fort always considered himself lucky, not least because he was constantly required to entertain personages who might be able to help a career along. The fact that the Department of the Interior provided a special fund for entertaining visiting dignitaries made the assignment painless. For the evening with the Robertses, Major and Mrs. Carver had planned an outdoor feast under a tent canopy erected over their back lawn. The weather seemed to promise no rain, and their guests could enjoy the extravagant scenery. The major had gone on, "It will be a sort of outing for them. Roughing it, so to speak."

"Roughing it?" Spode china, Waterford crystal, and Gorham sterling flatware lay on an Irish-linen tablecloth. The meal of buffalo steaks, fresh carrots, peas, tomatoes, and lettuce was topped off with strawberries from Mrs. Carver's own garden. A commendable burgundy was served with dinner, champagne with dessert, and Madeira with coffee and cigars. Attire for the evening was casual. Hill and Sir George wore serge trousers and cotton shirts; Hill had also chosen to put on a sweater against the possibility of a night chill. Major Carver was in dress mess and looked very handsome; he also looked uncomfortably warm, even in the shade of the canopy. Casual dress to Lady Roberts meant boldly allowing the top button to be open on her shirt-waist dress, a large silk scarf over her shoulders. Lucy Carver managed to look comfortable, proper, and even elegant in her neatly designed—although obviously homemade—calico print. Leah Page was the most casually attired in a dark brown corduroy riding skirt with matching leather boots and a white blouse sporting a simple lace collar.

James Hill complained that he had eaten much too much, just as Sir George politely asked if there were, perhaps, any more strawberries. The answer was a regretful "no." While the ladies cleared the table and took the dishes into the house, where two orderlies would wash up, the men retired to the veranda.

High cirrus clouds highlighted a sparse collection of cumulonimbus clouds off to the west; the sky was splashed with the soft colors of a late mountain evening. Rays of light were still touching the tips of the surrounding mountains; to the east, Mount Evarts' grey rock formations shone and to the south Bunsen Peak gleamed white with snow near its 8,775-foot crown.

During the meal, Major Carver had given his guests his customary recounting of the park's history. He told of the early trappers and mountain men such as John Colter and Jim Bridger who had come into the region alone and who came out with extravagant claims of fantastic natural phenomena; their stories were discounted as impossibilities. It was not until 1870 that a formal survey was made by Henry Washburne, the surveyor general of Montana Territory, Samuel Hauser, who was to become the first state governor of Montana, and Nathaniel Langford, who eventually would be named the park's first superintendent. President U.S. Grant signed the law creating the park in 1872 after Congress passed the act, so simple in its words, but so lasting in effect: "The tract of land in the territories of

Montana and Wyoming, lying near the headwaters of the Yellowstone River . . . is hereby reserved and withdrawn from settlement, and dedicated and set apart as a public park or pleasureing-ground for the benefit and enjoyment of the people." Major Carver had actually felt tears come to his eyes as he repeated the memorized words. It was not an affectation; anyone who came to know the park as he did could easily display similar emotions.

The park's development had not come quickly. Military engineers and civilian construction crews built roads and bridges and wooden walkways over the years, but even now there was much more to be done: more hotels to be built, roads to be cut through the mountains, and observation points to be refined. "But we will do our work. It is a noble cause."

"Indeed, it is," Sir George had said.

"You are to be commended," James Hill offered.

The major was pleased.

As they watched the day finish off in grand fashion, Hill said, "You really should think about bringing the railroad up to the hotel. That climb from Gardiner is steep."

The major replied, "I do not think so, sir. A rail bed would damage too much of the terrain; we are mandated to retain all that is possible."

Hill did not argue. After all, the Northern Pacific or the Union Pacific would be the one to benefit most from a rail link into the park. "That is probably the best policy."

Hill sipped from his glass of Madeira and let his eyes travel over the scenery. He was resigned to waiting for the proper moment to reopen his negotiations with Sir George. He knew the moment would come. He also knew that Sir George was playing his own game and had shown no willingness to reopen the subject.

"Sir George," the major was saying, "I am considering some sort of fodder for the buffalo this winter. My sources in Montana are adequate, but I was wondering if you knew of any Wyoming suppliers who might be available."

"We grow our own," Sir George replied. "I am fortunate

to have a considerable water supply right on the Powder River. We could possibly assist you if you are in need."

The major smiled; he had hoped for that answer. It was a way to make a park guest feel involved. "That is nice of you, sir. Maybe we could talk about that in the morning."

Hill, not interested in fodder, decided to amuse himself by setting a fox among the chickens. "Major Carver, you spend good money to feed those annoying bovines? The bison is such an unnecessary animal."

The major sensed a trap, but he also felt that Hill was setting him up for a good-natured tease. "Mister Hill, we do feed the poor brutes." He puffed his cigar, then asked, "As a railroad man you have little use for the bison, is that right?"

"To me," Hill admitted, "the bison is a prehistoric residue. It is only a burden. You said you were mandated to retain the natural aspects of this park. Yet, if you feed those beasts, you are thwarting the design of Nature, because they do not belong here."

Major Carver grinned. The fraternity of railroad owners, to a man, had long wanted to eliminate the bison on the open plains. The migrating herd had been estimated at over eighty million animals, but it was facing extinction now due in part to the efforts of the railroads. Bison crossing railroad tracks were a threat to trains traveling at fifty miles per hour, and the grazing bison consumed millions of tons of fodder that instead could feed grazing cattle. Gently, the major pointed out, "The bison is just about gone, sir. A few thousand have drifted into the park and have found it a reasonable home."

"But you violate your own standards; it does not belong here."

"Sorry, Mister Hill, but the bison has been here as far back as we have reports by man. Mister Osborne Russell said so in his *Journal of a Trapper,* back in 1830."

"Be that as it may," Hill countered, "by your actions you are propagating a species unnaturally."

"We are also charged with protecting the wildlife of the

park. I take that to include seeing they do not starve if the winter is severe.''

Hill gave a soft laugh. The skirmish had been satisfying. "A point well made, major. Without reservation, I can say that you are doing an outstanding job with a very delicate national treasure.''

The men settled back to watch the decay of twilight as night eased across the sky; faint stars began to glimmer in the sky to the southeast. Soon it would be dark.

The large front room of the Carvers' residence was warm and comfortable. Leah felt it was a bit too tidy; not one thing was out of place, and all seemed to have the imprint of military discipline. The walls were the varnished insides of the huge logs used to build most of the structures in the fort. Even the chinking between the logs showed attention: it glistened. There were area rugs on the wide planks of the wooden floor, and white organdy curtains framed the four large windows. The furniture seemed to be locally made, from pine stained to look like oak, but the cushions of dark red velvet had the mark of professional upholstery. Simply framed pen-and-ink sketches of the park hung on the walls. The only violation of regimented order was the wooden frame on a stand set next to the stone fireplace. It contained a sampler that measured three by four feet. Lucy Carver said, "Please, let me get us some light.''

She went to the lamp table in the corner of the room, removed the chimney from a kerosene lantern, and struck a match to the wick. After replacing the chimney and deftly trimming the wick so that it was as bright as possible without causing smoke, she returned to the work in the wooden frame, which Lady Roberts and Leah Page were examining.

They had brought the dishes into the kitchen, then had sat in the formal dining room to enjoy their own cups of coffee, "away from all of that talk men insist on" was the way Mrs. Carver had put it. After the customary compliments on the meal, the lovely home, and her husband's excellent work, the talk turned to the suffrage movement. Lady Roberts had introduced the subject by asking Mrs. Carver if she had ever met

Abigail Scott Duniway. Mrs. Carver had never heard the name.

Leah Page was quick to see that Lucy Carver was not a likely candidate for an evening's chat on suffrage. But Lady Roberts, assuming that all women of the West were strong individualists, continued, "Well, dear Lucy, we must arrange for that some time soon. This Duniway woman sounds like a most dedicated person."

Lucy Carver gave a tepid smile and a not-too-earnest nod. Trying to lead the conversation onto another course, Leah asked, "Have you and the major been on the frontier for a long time?"

"Lands, no." Lucy was anxious to leave any talk of suffrage, but she was hostess and did not want to injure her guests' feelings. Lucy Carver had absolutely no use for suffragettes. "I was from Highland Falls, New York"—she saw that Lady Roberts did not know the town and added—"near West Point"—still no recognition—"about forty miles north of New York City." That worked. "Like so many girls in Highland Falls, I met my husband at West Point . . ." The look of puzzlement came back to Lady Roberts. "West Point is the United States Military Academy."

"Oh, certainly. Like Sandhurst?"

"Exactly."

"How romantic."

"It was, really it was."

"That is lovely."

Leah was close to giving a hug to Lady Roberts; she saw the woman as pure, healthy innocence. Then she remembered how Lady Roberts had manipulated James Hill earlier in the day, and she questioned her own judgment about innocence; she would not like to tangle with Lady Roberts on anything.

Lucy Carver gave a quick chronology of her married life and the travels involved in military life, then cut herself off because she did not want to bore them. "It has been fun, and it has given us an interesting life."

"Dear Lucy," Lady Roberts said. "You have been living with history."

"I have learned a great deal." They had drunk two cups of coffee each, and Lucy felt that was adequate. She stood. "I'd like to show you something. Please come."

They followed her into living room.

As she set the lamp in place, Lady Roberts exclaimed over the sampler, "Child, that is magnificent! Such detail!"

Leah Page, who had never had a bent for fine needlework or other "womanly endeavors," was also impressed with the work. "It's beautiful."

Lucy said, "It is the Oregon Trail."

The sampler depicted the United States from the Mississippi River west to the Pacific Ocean and from Arkansas north to the Canadian border. It was predominantly hues of green, with emerald for the flat plains and jade for the mountains. Rivers, lakes, and the Pacific Ocean were light blue, and the Oregon Trail itself was yellow.

"Good heavens," Lady Roberts cried. "This is more a tapestry than a sampler." She turned. "You are most talented."

Lucy blushed, pride in her eyes. She knew she had created a piece of fine historical art. "The route was two thousand miles from Missouri to Oregon. It was really the thing that allowed for travel to the West. Earlier, before the trail was opened, the only way to the Pacific Coast was by ship; most people could not afford the trip, and many were reluctant to endure its dangers. But three hundred thousand people crossed the continent by the Oregon Trail."

Lady Roberts exclaimed, "I had no idea!"

Lucy nodded. "Most of them walked, because their wagons were loaded with possessions. Thousands died along the way. It was a hard journey."

"Pour souls." Lady Roberts leaned down to study the sampler more closely.

Shyly, Lucy said, "I'll share a secret with you."

"Child, I'm not allowed to have secrets. George and I have secrets, but not me alone."

Leah laughed and said, "I doubt if Lucy's secret is of major consequence, Lady Roberts."

Lucy confirmed, "It is not. You can tell Sir George, but I don't want Marvin to know; he might be angry."

Leah chuckled at Lucy's coyness. Then Lucy instructed, "Look very close, right there where the trail follows the Platte River bending to the southwest."

While Leah followed the directions, Lady Roberts pulled her eyeglasses from her skirt pocket. Adjusting them, she said, "Show me."

Lucy pointed. "See there, right where there are two different shades of green?"

Leah was the first to spot it. She asked, "Is it an elephant?"

"Exactly."

"Where? I do not see the devil!"

Lucy used her finger again and showed the outline of a lighter green elephant, about an inch across and three quarters of an inch high. "Oh, my! Would you look at that. I'd never have seen that. It is quite well hidden."

Lucy said, "I don't want Marvin to know about it because he feels that it is a vulgar expression, and he is very strict about my using vulgar expressions."

Leah asked, "What does it mean?"

Lucy blushed again. "There are several off-color meanings, but those were made up after the major traffic on the Oregon Trail had ceased. 'Seeing the elephant' was the way the pioneers described that moment when they could go no farther; they had reached their limit of endurance. Some turned back, some settled where they were, some simply up and died."

Lady Roberts murmured, "The poor, blessed souls. What a sad thing."

Lucy said, "I don't see it as sad; it shows how determined the people were to open this country. There were brave pioneers who traveled that trail, and they made this land what it is today."

Still studying the details of the sampler, Lady Roberts said, "It is a proud thing, what they accomplished."

From behind them came "Well, ladies!"

"Oops!" came from Leah.

"Good gracious!" came from Lady Roberts.

"Oh, my!" came from Lucy.

All three were startled by the resonant voice of Major Carver; flustered, they all moved quickly away from the sampler.

The major was accompanied by Sir George and James Hill. All three were amused by the fluttering women. The major asked, "What in heaven's name is wrong?"

"Nothing" came in a sort of harmony from the three; the more they tried, the more guilty they looked.

Lady Roberts was the first to recover. She crossed the room to her husband and said, "Well, George, is it a nice evening outside?"

Sir George grinned at her.

Major Carver suggested a game of whist and the Robertses agreed. Hill allowed that he was tired and would walk back to the hotel. Leah offered to walk with him. Hill, always conscious of public appearances, declined so strongly that his words bordered on being a command. Not wanting to annoy him further, Leah said she would return with the Robertses after the game.

After polite thanks, Hill departed for the hotel; Leah was left in the uncomfortable position of being the fifth for a game requiring four. However, Major Carver insisted that she sit in for him while he made the rounds of the post. Leah had an enjoyable time as Lucy Carver's partner, but the Robertses were excellent whist players and capped off their evening by winning the game.

Leah and the Robertses reached the hotel before ten o'clock. Leah enjoyed her bath in the hot spring water piped into the hotel bathrooms.

Meanwhile, Lady Roberts was attempting to explain to Sir George the mystery of "seeing the elephant."

►◆◄

James Hill arrived in the hotel dining room at twenty minutes past six the next morning; Sir George was already there, halfway through his breakfast.

After morning salutations, Hill joined Sir George at his table and ordered his own meal of eggs, ham, toast, and coffee. The waiter's surprising offer of freshly squeezed orange juice was gratefully accepted.

The two men spoke of the previous evening and of the Carvers' fine hospitality until Hill's food was set in front of him. As he began to eat, Hill said, "I hope we can settle this issue this morning, Sir George."

Sir George grinned as he spread butter on his toast in advance of applying huckleberry jam. He said, "We'll resolve that at this table, James. Rest assured."

What Hill wanted from Sir George was a commitment to spread money around—with quiet discretion—in aid of the cause of statehood for Wyoming Territory. The amount of money proposed was ten thousand dollars. Hill would gladly provide the capital, he had said, but it was critical that he not be known to be involved. Hill was meddling in the affairs of a territory that was Union Pacific country, and if word ever reached the ears of his opposition, Hill could be in trouble. The rail barons looked on trespassing by a competitor as sacrilege.

Sir George's only hesitation was that he, himself, might be considered an interloper. He said, "James, this territorial legislature has passed laws prohibiting ownership of land by foreigners; the feelings against us are that strong."

Hill was chewing a piece of ham, but nodded.

Sir George continued, "I have no objection to doing anything that can help these people, but I do have to step cautiously, you understand."

Hill swallowed the ham, drank some orange juice, then said, "In the first place, I appreciate your delicate position, but I know that you don't hide from fights. In the second place, I am asking you to use your influence in Washington, not here in the territory."

That caught Sir George off guard. To gain time, he gazed out the window. Stagecoaches were being readied to take visitors on to the geyser basins or to Yellowstone Lake. Later in the day, he and Lady Roberts would continue their own sightseeing in a private coach. He did not mind that he and his wife had delayed their journey back to England for the meeting with Hill, but what Hill was suggesting would obviously demand still another delay, one that could become lengthy.

Hill, as if he sensed Sir George's mood, said, "I am talking about three or four days . . . a week at the most . . . in the District of Columbia."

With some reluctance, Sir George asked, "What is your plan?"

"What we need are some social events: luncheons, dinners, theatre parties, receptions. That is where the money will be spent. I will have no part of outright passing of money to elected representatives, but I do believe in the use of friendly gatherings to gain an ear that might be receptive in a relaxed atmosphere."

"Surely, there are men enough in your circles who could do this."

"Not men of substance who have a large interest in the territory."

"But what about the Union Pacific people? They must—"

"I do not work with them, not on this!"

"Oh, yes. I forgot about all of that competition you Americans hold so dear."

Hill smiled and countered, "The Union Pacific people might well be working on just such a project, and probably other wealthy ranchers in the territory are doing the same; I cannot deal in conjectures. I want to see the statehood issue being pressed forward as hard as possible."

"But Wyoming is not even being considered."

"Believe me, Sir George, it's not in the current bill, but Wyoming is being considered. Statehood is close for this territory, and I want to see it come to pass."

"An admirable posture for you to assume . . ."

"From which I will not bend, Sir George, I shall not bend."

Hill's chair was angled so that he could enjoy the view of the terraces but could also see the entrance to the dining room. He spotted Leah Page about to enter. At the same moment, she saw that he was sitting with Sir George and began to retreat. He gave a vigorous wave for her to come and join them.

At the table, both men rose with "good morning"'s and an added comment from Sir George: "You look lovely this morning, Miss Page."

Leah gave an appreciative nod and accepted the chair that Hill had pulled out. He asked if she would like to order, but she only wanted coffee. Hill motioned to the waiter, who presented her cup before she had her napkin in place.

Hill said, "I've been trying to enlist Sir George in our efforts, Miss Page."

Leah responded, "I think you could help, Sir George. Wyoming, from my point of view, should come in with the other states." She sipped her coffee, then added, "You know that this territory has already granted suffrage to women?"

"Yes. Freda was delighted."

"Miss Page will be in Washington on this project, Sir George."

Leah was taking a second sip of coffee, and she sputtered, nearly spilling some down her dress. "I will be where, when, Mister Hill?"

Nonchalantly, Hill said, "I have initiated a program that we hope will be effective enough to influence Congress."

"And I am expected to go to Washington, too? Is that your plan, Mister Hill?" Hill was fumbling for words. Leah, back under control, looked at Sir George. "You will find, sir, that Mister Hill is capable of many surprises." She offered an honest smile.

Hill finally said, "Sir George, you will have to try to understand me. There are times when I forget that Miss Page is not in my employ. All she does, she does for her own beliefs and her own cause. I am frequently careless when I am deeply involved in a project; good people like Miss Page endure much from me."

Sir George understood. "I can remember when I was building my cattle business, James. I would not like to face all of those poor individuals who were subjected to my bludgeoning ways." Turning to Leah, he added, "You must forgive men like us, Miss Page. We tend to step over bounds too easily."

Leah laughed. "I have trod on a number of toes in my own career; I understand." She did not want to dwell on the subject. "Will Lady Roberts be in Washington with you?"

He laughed. "I have not yet agreed to go, myself." There was the slightest twinkle in Leah's eyes. He quickly said, "Now you hear me, young lady, there will be no business of you enlisting Freda's aid in this." To Hill he said, "When women begin to work their wiles, there is no safety."

Hill chuckled. "Maybe I should have asked Miss Page to discuss this with Lady Roberts; all would have been settled."

Sir George said, "Seriously now, I can see the merit in what you propose, James. Let me think on this for a bit and consider all of the ramifications."

Hill could only acquiesce.

Sir George flashed a glance at Leah. "And there will be no deviousness on your part, madam. Not one word of this to Freda."

Even though she smiled at him, he was not really sure she would obey. He had best go to his wife immediately, get the first word in. "Give me an hour, James." He signed his check, stood, then added, "I will meet you back here."

When Sir George was out of earshot, Hill told Leah, "We will be leaving in two hours. I've told Calvin to have our coach ready."

"Isn't that taking a gamble, Mister Hill? Sir George could insist that we spend a couple of more days."

There was a confident look on Hill's face. "The man is sold on the idea. He will agree."

"Lady Roberts seems to like our company; she might force him to make our staying a condition of his acceptance."

Hill grinned. "Lady Roberts enjoys *your* company, Leah. If he lays down that condition, then *you* will have no option other than to comply."

She glared at him, trying to read his thoughts. "If you are serious, Mister Hill, then you will find more trouble from me than any opponent you have ever faced. I hate it when I know I am being used."

He reached across the table and patted her hand. "I am teasing you; don't be so touchy. The man will do as I asked."

Hill turned out to be right. Within an hour, Sir George was back, promising his assistance; it was agreed they would meet in the nation's capital in a month's time.

◀◆◆◆◆◆▶

CHAPTER 6

*BOISE CITY, IDAHO TERRITORY—THURSDAY,
JULY 26, 1888*

Fredrick T. Dubois sat in a heavy swivel chair, his boots propped up on a scarred oak-topped desk. The boots were calf high with pointed toes and two-inch heels; twill trousers were tucked into the tops of the boots. His jacket, a black wool cutaway, hung on a rack behind the desk; his flat-topped, wide-brimmed fedora hung on the same hook. He wore a maroon and gold brocaded vest over a white cotton shirt; his tie was a long black string held at the throat by a clump of gold nuggets.

"Of course not," Dubois replied to Del Cummins. "On the floor of the Congress I wear a plain brown lounge suit, but for social functions I dress like this; people sort of expect it of me."

Zack Horton chuckled. He could imagine the reaction in the nation's capital when Dubois showed up in his Western mufti. Even though they had only been meeting for ten minutes, Zack and Del had taken a liking to Dubois.

Though Dubois was the nonvoting territorial delegate to Congress from Idaho, he had kept in close contact with Ezra Baird, the man who was currently marshal and who had loaned them his office for the meeting. The office was in the court-house of Boise City, in the same block as the territorial legislature building. Dubois turned the question around, "Do you always dress like that?"

Cummins broke into a laugh; his suit was a rumpled mess, the front of his shirt bore food stains, and his shoes were scuffed and dirty. His reply was "Only when I am meeting important politicians."

Both Zack and Cummins were travel worn. They had spent over two and a half days getting to Boise City from Bismarck. Their trip had been fine as far as Butte, Montana Territory, because they had ridden first class—that had cost them $72 each—and had indulged in the luxury of Pullman sleeping cars for an additional $21.50 each. But from Butte to Boise City in Idaho Territory, they had traveled over short legs, through Dillon, Montana, over the seven thousand feet of the Monida Pass, to Pocatello in Idaho, where they had changed trains again for the run to Boise. They had arrived at six in the evening and been met by Fred Dubois, who had received a telegraph request from Theodore Roosevelt. Dubois, a fellow Republican, was pleased to accommodate a man who was a rising star in their party. But, politics aside, Dubois felt his territory was so evenly divided along party lines that he was bound to represent both factions.

James Hill's mandate to Zack and Del was to meet with the people in Idaho who had the power, and in the southern part of the territory that meant the Mormons. Making contact with the Mormons meant going through Fred Dubois, who had, as U.S. marshal, dealt with the Mormons during his entire tenure.

Sending Zack and Del into Idaho Territory had been an idea that grew out of a meeting between Hill and Roosevelt in Saint Paul. Initially, Hill had indicated he would be joining them, but he later withdrew, explaining that he had been away in Wyoming for so long that business demanded his presence in Saint Paul.

Del had been a bit miffed, because he was making a concerted effort to train Zack for the job of running the Dakota and

Western, a task that was obviously going to take another couple of months. But the annoyance over having to go to Idaho was softened for Del by Felicity Patterson's absence; she had gone back to Philadelphia for a two-week visit with her family. Del had given her strict instructions to call on Grandmother Boynton, who would soon be the same as family.

Zack's reaction to Hill's request was ambivalent. He was enjoying the challenge of the Dakota and Western, but he had also received a long letter from Leah Page in which she described her trip to Wyoming Territory. He thought—hopefully—that Hill might also dispatch her to Idaho Territory. His hopes proved to be false.

The meeting at the train station had been amiable, and they had walked to the courthouse for, as Dubois explained, "some privacy and hot coffee."

The sun was still high over the mountains to the west of the city, and it was easy to see that Boise City was going through rapid building. Some streets were still just smoothed dirt—"You should be here during spring runoff; it's a mess"—and the sidewalks were still planks set on railroad ties—"Watch you don't get your foot caught on those warped boards"—and, even at that time of day, there was the noise of hammering and sawing—"It'll be light till ten o'clock, so they work." The small talk had given Zack time to take a measure of Fred Dubois, and Zack liked what he saw.

Dubois finished off his cup of coffee, lowered his feet off the desk, and went to the stove to refill. "I've put you into the Overland Hotel; three silver dollars a night. No greenbacks."

Cummins asked, "Why no greenbacks? That's all I've got."

"It's a throwback to the War Between the States. This territory tried to secede with the Confederacy; it didn't but the folks still rebelled by refusing eastern money—greenbacks."

"Hold it," Zack said. "Back up a minute. They tried to secede?"

"You bet they did. It was a tough and independent bunch that pioneered this region. They nearly pulled it off."

Zack got up from his bench and went to refill his cup. "Let's get to business."

"Fine with me." Dubois sat assumed his boots-on-desk position.

Zack said, "Mister Hill has received information from Mister Roosevelt that the Mormons may be a problem, that they may cause a fuss if they are not granted a state of their own."

"There's no question about that; I've had many discussions with them on that very subject."

Zack sat down. "Then I guess we came to the right man."

"I don't know about that, but I do know the people involved. The Saints—the Church of Jesus Christ of Latter-day Saints—are having a whole bunch of problems with the federal government. You can't really blame them for grasping at statehood."

"You've worked with them?"

"I don't know if you could call it 'working with them,' I have spent just about all of my time enforcing the law on them."

Zack was confused. "Look, Fred, maybe we're putting you in a bad position. All I'm trying to do is gather information; it's up to others to do the battling."

"No, I think I can help. The Mormons are a good enemy. They're honest to the point of hurting themselves and you never wonder where they stand. I meet with them all the time."

"But you said you battled them."

"Exactly." Dubois stood and turned to a territorial map mounted on the wall behind the desk. His hand drifted slowly over the southern third of the territory as he said, "This whole section as good as belongs to the Mormons. About twenty-five thousand of them. That's out of about eighty-five thousand total population. It is a matter of responsibility on my part; I represent them in Congress. On their side, it's a matter of facing the facts; they have to use me. We get along just fine."

"Tough on both of you."

"Not really. What was tough was when I was marshal; hell, I arrested hundreds of them. Threw them in jail."

"Why?"

"They broke the law and they violated the oath."

"I don't know about the oath."

Dubois sat down. "Back in 1884 we'd really gotten fed up with the Mormons. They had all these crazy ideas about religion, and they worked so damned hard that they were buying up all the land. And there was the matter of polygamy."

Del Cummins put in, "I heard about that. They let a guy have a whole bunch of wives."

Dubois laughed. "That's about it. But it is against the law. Plus we instituted the oath. We made them swear they were not polygamists or they could not vote or serve on juries. Here, I've got a copy of it somewhere." He rummaged in his desk, then handed a paper to Zack.

Zack read it:

You do solemnly swear, or affirm, that you are a male citizen of the United States over the age of twenty-one years; that you have actually resided in this territory for four months last past, and in this county thirty days; that you are not a bigamist or polygamist; that you are not a member of any order, organization, or association which teaches, advises, counsels, or encourages its members, devotees, or any other persons, to commit the crime of bigamy or polygamy, or any other crime defined by law as a duty arising or resulting from membership in such order, organization, or association, or which practices bigamy or polygamy, or plural or celestial marriage, as a doctrine rite of such organization; that you do not, either publicly or privately, or in any manner whatever, teach, advise, or encourage any person to commit the crime of bigamy or polygamy, or any other crime defined by law, either as a religious duty or otherwise; that you regard the Constitution of the United States and the laws thereof and of this Territory, as interpreted by the courts, as the Supreme Law of the Land, the teaching of any order, organization, or association to the contrary notwithstanding; and that you have not previously voted at this election; so help you God.

Zack looked up, incredulous. "And you get along with them?"

"Just fine. They know where I stand and I know them. As a matter of fact, when I got the telegraph message the other day, I began setting up a meeting with them for you; it was easy to figure why you were coming. The meeting's set for tomorrow."

Zack said, "That's good. We could do with a night's sleep in a normal bed."

"Ain't that the truth," Cummins put in. "I'm ready for a good bath, too."

Dubois said, "There's one other thing. The meeting isn't here in Boise City; we'll have to travel a bit."

Zack and Del looked at each other. Zack asked, "How far?"

"I'll tell you about that tomorrow."

"Who are we meeting?"

"That can wait until we are on our way."

Zack stated, "It all sounds kind of mysterious."

Dubois stood and drained his cup of coffee. "There are things going on that are fairly delicate right now. I had to meet certain conditions before they would agree to the meeting; one was secrecy."

"Any other conditions I should know about?"

Dubois nodded. "I won't put us in any tight situation. You'll get the information you are looking for."

Zack was the last to stand as he said, "That's what we are here for."

Dubois said, "Let's go get you two something to eat."

Boise City was a mining town, with the usual wide open, hell-bent-for-leather nighttime activity. Not too far from the center of territorial government, near Crane Creek, was one of the collections of bawdy houses, gambling dens, and saloons that invariably appeared within days of a confirmed gold strike. The first strike near Boise City was made in August 1862 in Grimes Creek; by the spring of 1863, twenty thousand souls were

beginning their panning and quartz mining. The region was one
of the few absolute bonanzas in the mining West; wages were
running to eighteen dollars a day (compared to four or five
dollars a day in other regions) and one pan of gravel and dirt
from Grimes Creek could easily produce eighty dollars in nuggets and color, which was what the prospectors called the residue, almost as fine as flour, remaining after washing water over
the diggings. Early on the businesses that catered to the prospectors were housed in tents or hastily constructed log buildings,
but over the twenty-five years that the region had been producing riches, most proprietors had invested in substantial establishments. Saloons frequently were decorated with crystal lamps,
mahogany bars, and risque paintings to go along with good
whiskey and reasonably talented entertainers. Gambling rooms
had come to be almost elegant, with flocked walls, polished
furniture, and gaming tables at which faro, poker, and fan-tan
were run by professionals who, in that age, were considered
respectable. Nearly all operated kitchens from which came good
meals.

Fred Dubois took Zack and Del to the Doe and the Fawn,
which was one of the more respectable poker parlors/restaurants,
patronized not only by prospectors who had struck it rich but
also by territorial legislators, bureaucrats, and lawmen. The place
was run by an astute, innovative proprietor named Lillian Mack,
who took no nonsense from her patrons and who delivered fair
gambling and good food. Dubois had known her from her first
days in Boise City, when she had been struggling to make her
way without entering into corruption and vice.

She greeted them at the door. She knew they were not
there for gambling, because Fred Dubois had other ways to
waste his money, so she led them into one of the three small
rooms devoted solely to dining. Lil Mack employed the tradi-
tional male waiters decked out in black trousers, white shirts,
and black bow ties, but she also broke with tradition by having
attractive females, dressed in satin and lace gowns, who saw to
the delivery of beverages from the bar. There had been a time,
in her first years of operation, when Lil had provided accommo-

dations on the upper floor for bawd trade, but she gave that up when she had to spend as much time breaking up fistfights as she did in the more lucrative business of gambling. She did not forbid her girls from striking private deals after hours but during working hours, especially in the dining rooms, the girls provided only prompt and friendly service.

Del Cummins spotted one particularly comely attendant standing by the door to the kitchen. As the trio sat down and Lil left, Cummins asked, "Tell me, Fred, what's the purpose of the ladies?"

Dubois laughed and explained they were there only for visual benefits; Zack also laughed and asked, "Del, I thought you were exhausted; was I wrong?"

As he set his napkin in place, Del shrugged his shoulders. "Exhausted might be a heavy word when you talk about a looker like that; she is beautiful." Then, seeing the accusation on Zack's face, he added, "It is no sin to be simply looking at a pretty lady."

Zack laughed. "You'll soon be a married man, Del; don't let guilt start grabbing hold of you now."

They were presented with menus. The dishes were both diverse and expensive. Zack mentioned that to Dubois, who explained that Lil Mack worked hard at getting good food— which included deep-sea salmon and Oregon oysters—and that there was enough money in the region to support the prices. Zack and Dubois ordered fish; Del ordered elk steak.

As the waiter left for the kitchen, Zack said that Dubois' comment about money seemed valid: the room was richly decorated, and the tables bore linen tablecloths, silver dinnerware, and crystal goblets.

Dubois said, "There's been a bundle of money here since the beginning." He reached into his coat pocket and pulled out the makings for a cigarette. He offered them to Zack, who clumsily rolled one for himself, then passed the pouch and papers back to Dubois. Del was working on a cigar. As Dubois swiftly rolled his cigarette, he said, "There's one hell of a story about the beginning of this town, just to give you an idea. This

man's name was Sherlock Bristol. He arrived in December of
'62. He and some friends spent the first days erecting log cabins,
then made snowshoes and began prospecting the area. Bristol
and his friends contracted with a man to dig a well so they
wouldn't have to haul water from Moore Creek, which was a
couple of hundred yards away. One day, when he was out
prospecting, the well digger spotted some flecks of gold in the
dirt about twenty feet down. The find panned out at $2.75 for
the first couple of shovels. As he told me, 'When I returned that
night I could not have bought the claim on which my house was
built for ten thousand dollars.' His property eventually earned
him three hundred thousand dollars."

"Damn!" came from Del Cummins. "Maybe we should
get out of railroading and come out here to try our luck."

Dubois shook his head. "Save yourself the trouble, Del.
The territory is producing lead, silver, and a lot of gold still, but
it takes big money now. Equipment, wages, shipping costs:
millions of dollars are required now to begin making any real
money. There are still a few diehard small prospectors making
a living, but the money is in something like this"—he gestured
around the room—"where you make money off the workers.
It's always been that way."

Del did not look too downhearted. Dubois said, "But
don't let that stop you from coming out here; we need people.
We're all interested in being admitted to the Union, and the
more people the better our chances. This territory is eighty-four
thousand square miles and we have eighty-five thousand people;
that scares a Congress where men come from states that have
hundreds of people per square mile."

The waiter arrived with their plates just as one of the
serving girls came up with champagne in an ice bucket and three
glasses. As the waiter set the food on the table, the girl said,
"Miss Lil sends this with her regards."

Dubois acknowledged with a smile and nod; Del was awed
by the slab of elk meat placed in front of him. The waiter
delivered hot rolls and butter, along with bowls of mashed

potatoes, carrots, and lima beans. Del said, "Lots of food for a fancy restaurant."

Zack chuckled. "Del has a problem with some of the serving sizes in the eating establishments back east."

Dubois nodded. "They drive me crazy in Washington. Some of those meals I have back there just barely fill a tooth cavity."

As they ate, conversation was limited to requests for salt, pepper, or butter. Lil came by a couple of times to insure that her friend was well attended, and she sent a second bottle of champagne; Del Cummins had a thirst. At the end of the meal they were served Boise-wrapped cigars—each mining town was quick to support local cigar makers—and snifters of a respectable brandy.

Zack asked, "Come on, Fred, tell us about the meeting tomorrow."

Dubois raised his hand. "Tomorrow. Trust me."

Zack asked, "What about the division of the territory; is Mister Hill right to be concerned?"

Without hesitation Dubois came back, "A smart man is always concerned where politics is involved, but I think it's close to being a dead issue. The whole thing goes back to the days when mining was first developing in the panhandle. The Salmon River comes just about due west across the territory from the Bitterroot Mountains. It dumps into the Snake River right at the northeastern corner of Oregon. Now the Salmon is a rough river, and it made a natural border for the panhandle because it was just about impossible to cross. The natural inclination was for the mining people to look for easier access. As a result they felt a closer tie with Spokane, Ellensburg, and Yakima than they did with Lewiston or Boise City, and surely they had no affinity for the Mormon communities in the southeast; that area was so foreign as to seem like another country. Annexation to Washington was, at one time, a possibility, but it is so slim now that I'd say it isn't possible. The railroads changed all of that. They bridged the rivers and made it possible for people in the north to travel to the rest of the territory with ease. Your Mister Hill and the other railroad men just about tied the place together."

"Is it worth me going up there to meet with the miners?"

"I'd say so. I can't go with you because we are getting ready for the political conventions, but I've sent a couple of telegraph messages and we should have an answer tomorrow. I do know that George Hearst is up there; he is still trying to pull off a major realignment."

"I heard about the New Mining State."

"Right. The most damned fool thing I ever heard of in all my years out here. Senator Hearst is set on trying to lump the western Montana mines with the northern Idaho mines. But the Congress would never let so much of one industry be controlled by one state. That bastard Hearst has financial interests in the mines, too; did you know that?"

Zack nodded.

"Well, it is wrong for a man to try and pull off a deal just so he can make more money; Hearst has more money than God, as it is."

"Could I meet with him?"

"I'll put you in touch with one of his friends. That should be no trouble." He then folded his napkin and set it on the table as he stood. "Right now, I think it is time for me to call it a day. I used to be able to go until dawn, but now I get tired before sunset."

As the other two stood, Del asked, "Zack, you wouldn't want to hang around here for a while, would you? Maybe play a little faro?"

"Del, I don't know the first thing about faro."

"Couldn't do any harm."

Zack smiled. "You'll have to go it alone. I'm going for a bath and bed. You stay here if you want."

Del shook his head. "Not on your life. You'd probably fall in the tub and break a leg. Then your grandmother would give me hell."

Dubois was grinning. He offered, "Then you could come out and prospect, Del."

"No." Del's voice was disappointed. "I'll go for the bath and bed, too. Just as well, because I'd have spent a lot of money."

Zack paid the bill over Dubois' protest, and they walked to the Overland Hotel. As they parted in the lobby, Dubois said, "I'll be by around 6:30 in the morning. We have to catch the seven o'clock train."

"Damn" came from Zack. "Do we have to go by train? I'm starting to see timetables in my sleep."

"Sorry. That's the only way."

They ate breakfast on the Union Pacific train the next morning. Because the coffee was tasty and the chairs comfortable, they rode in the dining car for the entire three hours to Shoshone, about 110 miles southeast of Boise City. Once they were settled comfortably after their breakfast, Dubois revealed that they were going to see a man named Wilford Woodruff. The name meant nothing to either Zack or Del; their expressions showed that. Dubois asked, "Know the name John Taylor?"

Still no response.

"What about Brigham Young?" Both men nodded, and Dubois explained, "John Taylor, like Brigham Young, was the president of the Church of Jesus Christ of Latter-day Saints. John Taylor died just about a year ago; Wilford Woodruff is going to be the next president unless something awfully strange happens. I do not expect anything strange to happen. But in any event Woodruff is a powerful man in the church, and he has agreed to meet with you."

Zack gave a polite smile. "But why all of the secrecy?"

"Things are not going well for the Mormons; they are being harassed pretty strongly by the federal government . . ." Dubois paused. "The fact is, the man is hiding out."

Del bristled. "Are there warrants out on him?'

Dubois used his hand to suggest Del lower his voice; there were a few other people lingering over their coffee in the dining car. In a hushed voice, he said, "No, but Woodruff does not want to talk to any of the federal people, and they want to talk to him."

"Hell, Fred, you're federal people," Del challenged.

"I'm not a lawman anymore."

"But you're a congressman. That should count for something."

Zack gave a quick glance at Del, a glance that suggested, Let it drop. He did.

There was a short stop in Glenn's Ferry, and all three men went out onto the station platform to stretch their legs. The terrain was rolling hills with bluffs off in the distance. Only a few people were arriving or departing. Del Cummins studied the scenery for a few moments before he said, "Ain't much to look at."

Dubois said, "Not much now, Del, but give me a little time. I'm going to show you something that will stay in your memory for all of your life."

Zack asked, "Pretty country ahead of us?"

Dubois replied, "Awesome, beautiful country. There is so much out here! The people back east have no idea. Someday I hope we can share it with them."

The whistle toot announced the departure, and they made their way back to the dining car. Their table had been reset during their absence, with a new cloth, silverware, and china. As soon as they sat down, the dining-car waiter arrived with fresh coffee. As the train started up again, almost as if to avoid any return to the subject of the Mormons, Dubois began talking about the accomplishments of the people living in the territory: the state prison, the insane asylum, the orphanages, miles of railways, and millions of dollars in industry. Zack listened patiently, but Del felt himself nodding off to sleep and began to consider excusing himself to go back and have a catnap in the passenger coach. At last, though, Dubois seemed to have run to the end of his catalogue of pride.

Zack said, "Back in Bismarck, I met with Governor Church; he ran through a similar list."

"I know the governor." Dubois waited to see Zack's point.

"Well, it just seems to me that there is some sort of required list that you territorial people have to follow."

"We have a pride in these things."

"But it's as if there is some primer for you to go by."

Dubois gave a sheepish grin. "We have our schools, too. Did I miss that?"

Zack laughed. "You know what I mean."

"I know exactly, Zack. And there is sort of a primer. It's the Northwest Ordinance of 1787."

Del had pulled himself partially out of his lethargy. He asked, "About the Northwest territories?"

"Not the ones we know today. Back then the western frontier was Ohio, Tennessee, and Kentucky. That's what they called the Northwest territories."

"Damn." Del grinned. "It's hard to think of those states being the frontier."

Zack agreed, "And just over a hundred years ago."

Dubois said, "A lot has happened in those hundred years, but back then was the beginning of adding states. In addition to a few minor details, the ordinance required that a territory have at least sixty thousand residents and be free from slaves; it promised that all admitted territories would come in as full partners in the Union."

The headwaiter came to their table, gave a friendly smile, and asked, "Anything you need, Mister Dubois?"

"No, Glenn, everything is just fine."

The headwaiter asked, "Going on to Pocatello?"

"No, we're heading up to Ketchum for a look around; these men are in the mining-equipment business. From back east."

The man smiled. "You're going into rough country, gentlemen; good thing you've got Mister Dubois with you. He knows how to smooth rough things out." He left them alone.

As soon as he was away from the table, Dubois chuckled. "That, as you might have guessed, was interesting."

Del said, "I caught it; it was kind of hard to miss. Any

dining-car waiter who didn't know your destination wouldn't be in his job long, not on our railroad."

"Exactly," said Dubois. "Glenn was fishing around. I doubt if I fooled him, but he's mollified; he was able to let his waiters see he was a friend. That's important."

Zack observed, "You're a good politician."

"Out here, there are only good politicians; any other kind is either a federal appointee or dead."

"That's a real problem—the federal appointees."

"Oh, it is. I was one myself, but it didn't take me long to find out that I had better earn my keep or these people would serve me my head. That same ordinance we were talking about, it sets out all of the rules for running territories, and the whole thing is structured badly. Article four of the Constitution deals with new states, and it also allows for Congress to set up the regulations; the Congress did a rotten job. The people in the territories are mostly at the mercy of political appointees, and a great many of them are nothing more than crooks; most of the rest are incompetent."

"But you started as a political appointee."

"I was lucky." Dubois looked out the window at the passing scenery. He brought his attention back to the table and occupied himself with rolling a cigarette. Del drank his coffee; Zack waited.

Dubois said, "I was lucky because I got here after the bad times, really bad times, when the Vigilantes were running. Those were tough times. The territory was so big and the budget so small that it was impossible for the marshals to cover all the area, and the miners in the camps decided to—probably had to—set themselves up as the enforcers of the law. Due process became a quick encounter with a rope around the neck. I'm glad I came after that."

Del said, "But you had to go arresting all those bigamists."

Dubois nodded. "I guess that wasn't any easier. I never enjoyed arresting anyone, but I enjoyed enforcing the law. Does that make any sense?"

"It does to me," said Del.

Zack asked, "The Northwest Ordinance, it still is in effect, after a hundred years?"

"As I said, it's been modified, and that's why you always hear us talking about prisons and schools and the territorial constitutions which the ordinance now requires. The population minimum has been boosted now, to conform to the states' allocation of congressmen; we're looking for at least one hundred thousand people, the more the better."

"Dakota is way over that," Zack pointed out.

Dubois nodded. "There'll be no problem with splitting up that territory; they'll just have more congressmen. Idaho will be lucky to get one."

"You feel Idaho will be admitted?"

"If not right now, it will be soon. The big thing is to get something moving through Congress. Then a whole batch of territories can come in."

Zack raised an eyebrow. "Even Utah?"

Dubois shook his head. "That's another problem."

The forward door of the dining car let in a gush of air as the conductor entered to announce, "Shoshone next stop . . . Stopping at Shoshone."

Zack reached into his pocket and dropped two cartwheels—Morgan silver dollars—on the linen tablecloth. Dubois looked with a scolding eye, as if to say, Too much, you'll spoil them.

Zack said, "They kept us in coffee, and I don't want them to think their congressman is traveling with pikers."

Dubois stood and adjusted his coat neatly. "All those waiters will think is that I'm traveling with some easterner who has too much money to spend."

The conductor came back through the car and said, "The train up to Ketchum is running a half hour late, Fred."

Dubois clapped the conductor on his shoulder. "Now how the hell did you find out I was going to Ketchum, Frank?"

With a wry smile, the conductor responded, "We have our ways."

On the platform of the Shoshone station, as the train pulled out toward Pocatello, Dubois said to Zack, "Do you see why I wanted to keep things quiet? There's a bush telegraph out here that works better than anything Western Union can offer us."

Zack laughed and took off his coat. It was only a little past ten o'clock, but the summer sun was heating up the air; no breeze blew to cool things off. Del Cummins, as he doffed his jacket, too, asked, "What do we do till we catch the train?"

"We're not catching a train," Dubois answered.

Questions formed in the others' eyes.

"We'll just wait here a couple of more minutes, until the eastbound gets out of sight. I'll guarantee you that conductor is in the rear car, watching."

The eastbound finally swung to the south heading for its next stop at Dietrich. Dubois then said, "Come on with me."

Several people standing on the platform called, "Howdy, Fred." In almost each case, Dubois was able to respond with a first-name salutation. Dubois led Zack and Del down the steep stairs over to a freight-storage area where a four-horse stagecoach was parked in the shade of a huge oak tree. As Dubois came closer, the stage driver stepped out from where he had been leaning against the trunk. "Howdy, Fred."

"Howdy, Charlie." Dubois stopped and turned to his companions. "This is our ride to the meeting."

The driver joined the three men. Dubois asked, "Any problems?"

"Nope. I got Clem riding shotgun; Billy and Walt'll be covering our tracks riding tailgate." Then, with a casual abruptness, the driver said, "Let's get going. It's gonna be a hot one."

They loaded up and, before Zack had pulled the door of the passenger compartment closed, a whip cracked and the horses lurched forward.

The stagecoach had well-padded seats and substantial springs, and the speed they were moving caused a flow of air that cooled the men quickly. Dubois said, "We're looking at a couple of hours in this contraption. We pick up fresh horses when we cross the river on the ferry. You might as well sit back and enjoy the view."

Zack looked at their guide and said, "You have a lot of people involved for a secret meeting."

Dubois continued looking out the window. "Just a few of my friends who're willing to lend me a hand."

Del Cummins was craning around, looking out the back window. "Those friends of yours are packing some pretty good iron. I'd guess they were more for protection than just friendly help."

Zack asked, "Do we need protection, Fred?"

Dubois shrugged. "Out here, you want your friends around if you need help. And in this country, if you need help, you generally need it in a hurry."

Zack asked, "Are these Mormons dangerous?"

Dubois shook his head. "No more dangerous than any other men trying to stay alive."

►◆◄

The route south from Shoshone took them through some lava-rock formations that were a startling sight. Eons before, a black, porous rock had been pushed up to the surface by a long-gone volcano chain. The geological event had covered much of the Northwest. In other places wind, rain, and erosion had converted the rock into fertile soil; in one small segment of southern Idaho, the elements had conspired to leave the rocks visible.

The creaking of the coach's springs, the air being blown in at twelve miles an hour, and the constant swaying motion of the seats were enough to inhibit conversation. Every now and then Dubois would pull his gaze away from the scenery and give a grin, as if to say, Ain't this some sight? Zack indulged in sightseeing while wondering about the meeting: What the hell was he getting into? Del Cummins dozed, comfortable in the knowledge that the driver and the man beside him had Winchesters, and the two outriders keeping pace behind the stage carried holstered Colts.

When they arrived at their destination, the scenery was spectacular. The Snake River had cut a 1,200-foot-deep ravine, creating the Great Shoshone Falls. The river was 950 feet wide and dramatically dropped down 210 feet. The spectacle was enough to distract Zack from the meeting, but his mind returned to his mission as they entered the parking area of the small Shoshone Falls Hotel.

It was only the sign over the entrance that let Zack know it was a hotel; at first, he thought it something like a feed store or, at best, a boarding house. Off to the west of the hotel, a couple of dozen men were milling around in a small grove of trees. At the center of the grove a table and chairs had been set on the ground; fifty yards away horses stood in a temporary corral near three covered wagons.

As the stagecoach came to a noisy halt, Dubois said, "Well, Zack, they were good to their word. You've got your meeting."

Dubois was the first one out. As Zack and Del climbed down, Dubois said, "Wait here a few minutes. Let me go and talk with them."

Obediently, Zack and Del stayed in the shadow of the stagecoach and made a quick study of the Mormons.

Almost all wore beards, some of them long. Their clothing was, to a man, neat, generally black trousers and coats. Most were wearing hats. Tensions seemed to emanate from the men around the table; they kept glancing around, some watching close by, some studying the horizon. None of them seemed comfortable.

Charlie, the stage driver, climbed down and stood beside Zack. He said, "That bunch there . . . all but a couple of them are bodyguards. Them damned Mormons are the most body-guarding people I've ever seen."

Zack asked, "You don't like them?"

"I ain't got much use for them, mister. But Fred gets along with them, and I guess that's important. They're a standoffish pack of bastards. I never saw one really give a good hard laugh; I don't trust men who can't laugh."

Dubois had moved comfortably through the waiting Mormons, exchanging brief greetings with several of them as he went to the table. The crowd parted and Zack saw that at the table, sitting on a simple wooden chair, was a white-headed man who rose as Dubois approached. They exchanged handshakes, and Dubois took one of the chairs. One of the Mormons poured a tall glass of water and set it on the table in front of him. For the next several minutes, Dubois sat in serious discussion with the man who had to be Wilford Woodruff, destined to be the next Prophet of the Church of Jesus Christ of Latter-day Saints.

After what seemed too long a time, as Zack was starting to get impatient, Dubois left the table and came toward the stage.

Dubois said, "Del, how about you and Charlie and the boys going into the hotel and grabbing some lunch? How about that?"

There was no question that the suggestion was an emphatic order. Del gave a sideways glance at Zack, who nodded.

When Del, Charlie, and the others had headed toward the hotel, Dubois said, "Woodruff is ready to meet with you. Don't be afraid to ask him anything you want, Zack. Believe me, there's nothing you could ask that he hasn't been asked a dozen times before." Zack nodded. "Okay, let's go see what the old guy has to say."

Woodruff extended a reserved welcome to Zack. After cursory platitudes were exchanged, Woodruff indicated they should sit "and enjoy the comfort of the shade."

As they took seats, Zack was provided with a glass of water. Woodruff's hand made a barely noticeable movement, and within a few seconds his contingent had moved away, drawing back a full forty feet; Woodruff was politely providing privacy for the meeting.

Woodruff's face bore the faintest trace of a smile. The man wore a heavy, wool jacket and a wide, white tie at the collar of his shirt. He sported a beard that was not as trim as a Vandyke, but not full or bushy. His hair, eyebrows, and beard were chalk white, but it was the eyes that riveted Zack's attention; they were soft blue and seemed as if they could penetrate to the core of any thought. His voice, as he opened the conversation, was soft, a gentle voice; not at all the kind of sound Zack had anticipated from a man who was the leader of tens of thousands of followers and in his eighty-first year of life. Woodruff said, "I am interested to know why you felt compelled to speak to me, Mister Horton." He emitted an aura of confidence, a presence of strength.

Zack smiled as he replied, "I would like to say that this was all Fred Dubois' idea, but that would not be accurate. An associate and friend of mine, James Hill, was told that it was important that your church members not be openly opposed to statehood for Idaho. His source was a man named Theodore Roosevelt. Mister Hill asked me to come out to Idaho to find if there is any such opposition, and any truth to the suspicion that Utah might want to secede from the United States. That information is important to Mister Hill."

Woodruff nodded. "Let me save you some time. I know about your Mister Hill, and I know what his interests are, so there is no need for you to explain them. I appreciate that you have gone to a great deal of trouble to attend this meeting, and I hope I may be able to give you something to take away with you."

Zack raised a hand politely. "I have no intention of trying to pry into the affairs of your church, sir."

"I understand." Woodruff sipped some water, then wiped his brow with a handkerchief that was already damp from use.

Zack said, "I'm sorry to have put you to so much trouble." He gestured toward the entourage. "I seem to have caused trouble for quite a few of your followers."

Woodruff gave a quiet laugh. He explained, "The presence of these brothers is not your doing. I am quite uncomfortable with the attention. I do not resent their presence; they are part of my flock and I love them dearly. My discomfort comes from causing them to be with me rather than their families, and from the fact that they could be in danger if someone were to try and kill me."

"Fred told me you were sought by the authorities, but he did not mention a threat to your life!"

Woodruff looked at Dubois. "Fred, did you bring this man here without telling him the situation?"

Dubois gave a sheepish grin and slight nod.

Zack interjected, "Fred did nothing wrong, Mister Woodruff. He was very careful to keep the place of this meeting secret . . . even from me."

Woodruff inclined his head. "Over the past couple of years, I have been forced to remain away from our church in Salt Lake City. I have had to do my work at our stakes in Nevada and Arizona, a fugitive except among the faithful. I was in that distasteful exile when President Taylor died; I could not even attend his funeral. I have only been here in Idaho for the past few months. It is propitious that I am at hand when I may possibly do some good for our people."

Zack asked, "Is it possible that the members of your church would be bold enough to try and leave the Union?"

Woodruff raised both hands. "Waste no time on that, my friend. We know our future lies with the nation as a whole. As President Lincoln said, 'A nation divided against itself cannot stand.' Our concern is to gain statehood, not to divorce ourselves from the United States. We would not place any scar on our church that would mark us as fools and traitors."

Zack digested that pronouncement. It was a quite satisfactory position, so long as Wilford Woodruff was speaking with authority as strong as Fred Dubois said it was. Zack said, "We also have heard about the possibility of dividing Idaho Territory, that your church could be involved in such a tactic. Could you share your thoughts on that matter?"

Woodruff sat back in his chair and wiped his brow again, contemplating his answer. "That has been discussed by the Saints. Quite simply, there is no agreement now among our leadership; opinion is split. My own feeling is that any such move would be divisive in the extreme, especially in regards to our church. While the population of the southern segment is predominantly of our faith, there is a substantial number of Gentiles, and we must consider them." Woodruff asked, "You know what I mean by Gentiles?"

Zack replied, "I always took that to mean Christians as opposed to Jews."

"To our faith, everyone not a properly designated Saint is a Gentile."

Zack nodded.

"Then you have not heard that Utah is the only place in the world where a Jew can be a Gentile?"

"No, sir."

His mouth curled into a broad grin; he enjoyed his own joke. After a moment, the elder said, "I am sorry that I cannot reply in a definite manner. If I were to give you conjecture it would be that any splitting of Idaho Territory would not come through the efforts of our church."

"I can't ask for anything more than that."

Dubois had remained silent during the exchange, but there was one thing he wanted to get established. He said, "Wilford, it might be good if you gave Zack some of your feelings about Utah statehood. Mister Hill might be able to help out someday."

Zack shot a questioning look at Dubois.

Woodruff said, "Mister Horton, Fred is right. Give me another minute or two."

"Please, sir, know that I am here at your pleasure. The time imposed on is yours. I'm grateful for all you have given. It is just that I don't know what Fred is driving at."

Woodruff said, "Plural marriage, Mister Horton, that is what Fred is getting at: polygamy."

Zack looked back at Dubois. Was getting into this really wise? Zack did not think so, but he held his peace.

Woodruff began to explain. "By the doctrine of our church plural marriage is not only not adultery—as some in your society like to claim—but also a necessary obligation for the fullness of our lives in our religion. In fact, the Doctrine and Covenants 132:61, 62 state: '(61) And again, as pertaining to the law of the priesthood—if any man espouse a virgin, and desire to espouse another, and the first give her consent, and if he espouse the second, and they are virgins, and have vowed to no other man, then he is justified; he cannot commit adultery for they are given unto him; for he cannot commit adultery with that that belongeth unto him and to no one else. (62) And if he have ten virgins given unto him by this law, he cannot commit adultery, for they belong to him, and they are given unto him; therefore he is justified.' "

Zack nodded to show he heard, even if he did not understand. Woodruff went on, "To us, the admonishments of our Doctrine and Covenants are as holy as those of the Bible and of the Koran or any other inspired word of God. But we also have another tenet: respect of man's law. Just as the Bible notes that one should 'Render unto Caesar . . .' we also believe in necessary civil law. The United States has taken such a virulently hostile attitude toward our position on plural marriage that we will, in the very near future, relieve ourselves of being branded as criminals and outlaws for practicing our faith."

Zack protested, "Mister Woodruff, I didn't want to get into this."

Woodruff smiled. "No, nor did I. But I do want you to take back with you the knowledge that we are not intransigent. Relay to Mister Hill what I have just told you, as a favor to me."

Zack smiled. "You are the one who has done the favor by allowing this meeting. I imagine you are an extremely busy man. You have been most generous with your time and your information."

Woodruff stood and extended his hand. "I will tell you, Mister Horton, I have spent most of my adult life in the service of my church. It is not a matter of generosity. It is a matter of stewardship. Fred conveyed to me that our cause might benefit by this meeting, and I have known him long enough to trust his judgment."

Zack gripped Woodruff's hand a bit longer than he would normally; Woodruff had about him the demeanor of a genial grandfather, and Zack had always loved his own grandfather. Zack said, "It has been a pleasure meeting you, Mister Woodruff. Thank you."

Woodruff looked at Zack as if he were memorizing the face or trying to put a final value on the meeting. Finally, he nodded. Dubois turned to Zack and said, "Why don't you scoot on over to the hotel and gather up Del and the others? We'll be heading back."

Zack saw that the two men wanted a bit of time for private talk; he walked off toward the hotel. Woodruff's huge bodyguards began to drift back into the proximity of their charge.

Dubois also noted the return of the bodyguards and said to Woodruff, "Your boys still don't trust me."

"Fred, for goodness' sake, can you blame them? You probably arrested the fathers or brothers of half of them."

They both chuckled. Dubois asked, "Were you pleased with the meeting?"

Woodruff said, "If it does some good, then I will be pleased. We will see."

Dubois asked, "Were you serious about a change in church policy on plural marriage?"

Woodruff responded, "I don't know when it will happen, but I feel I will be called to the presidency. When that day comes, my first effort will be to reconcile the problem."

"Then you'll do away with the practice?"

Woodruff showed that famous cunning grin. He repeated, "We will reconcile the problem."

They were shaking hands as the bodyguards finally closed the protective circle around Woodruff again. Fred Dubois took a quick leave.

During the stagecoach ride back to the train station in Shoshone, Zack briefed Del Cummins on the meeting. Dubois then spent quite a bit of time giving Zack what he needed to know about getting around in the northern part of the territory. "I'm sorry," Dubois said, "that I can't make the trip with you, but I'm heading back east; it's convention time. Party politics matter, even for those of us who are only territorial delegates."

Zack asked, "Will the Democrats renominate Cleveland?"

Dubois answered, "Oh, he'll get that, but I'm not too sure he can win the presidency again. The man has a genius for angering folks on both sides of an issue."

During the train ride back to Boise City, the trio again spent the whole trip in the dining car, but the coffee was replaced with bourbon and branch water. Dubois penned two notes to northern contacts who might be of assistance to Zack.

As they pulled into Boise City, the day was fading into twilight. There were roiling cumulus clouds gathering over the tips of the mountains, and the setting sun painted the clouds with a combination of colors that only Nature could tolerate. Zack said, "Fred, I need to find some way to thank you for your efforts. You invested a whole day in this project of mine. What can I do?"

Dubois gave an honest laugh. "You have to learn about politicians, Zack—and I have become the consummate politician—because I am doing what I want to do. This matter of statehood is a great battle being fought on several fields; we need the support of men like James Hill, and the other railroad people like Del and you, and the bankers and businessmen you might be able to talk into lending their support. The investment you referred to was just that; I'm hoping for a return."

Del Cummins put in, "I don't envy you, Fred; politics is a rotten business from what I've seen. I'm glad I work for the railroad."

Fred said, "Del, you'd be good for politics. You might not like it, but you're a big man. Maybe you could apply some muscle to those weak-minded folks in Congress."

Del beamed. "Now that might make politics interesting. Knocking a few heads could get a lot more done."

They parted at the train station. Dubois had two meetings to attend before his day would be over; Zack and Del set about making arrangements for their trip to the northern part of the territory.

▶◆◀

The wedge of land called the Panhandle of Idaho, about thirty-eight miles wide at the topmost section, extends from the Canadian border down to Lewiston, near the point where Washington, Oregon, and Idaho meet. In that wedge, Nature deposited one of the richest and most diverse collections of metal ores in the world. Gold was the powerful magnet that originally attracted mining exploration; silver, tin, and lead were soon discovered in abundance. The Panhandle of Idaho was mining country.

The rugged terrain was at the same time a blessing and curse for the men who sought to pluck riches from the earth. A blessing, because the formation of granite mountains had eased the metals up, comparatively near the surface; a curse, because of the steep grades and jagged canyons. Mine owners were constantly faced with the high risk of equipment damage and costly shutdowns; miners went down the shafts with injury and death as ominous companions.

Zack Horton and Del Cummins had needed two days to travel from Boise City to Coeur d'Alene because heavy rains, unusual for July, had washed out some track south of Spokane. By the time they arrived, Senator George Hearst had left Coeur d'Alene for Burke, another mining town fifty miles to the east. One of Fred Dubois' contacts advised Zack to wait for a couple of days in Coeur d'Alene, because the heavy rains were creating travel problems. Zack, more than pleased with his trip to the south, was anxious to press on so that he and Del could get back to Bismarck. Against good advice, they left for Burke.

Just a short distance out of Coeur d'Alene, Zack began to regret his decision. As he had been warned, travel was hindered by railroad washouts and roads rutted deep in mud. A trip that should have taken a few hours turned out to require another two days, a delay that practically insured missing Hearst.

Zack and Del stepped off the train in Burke to find that the railroad ran smack down the middle of Burke's Main Street. The Northern Pacific had set timbers lengthwise over the track ties so pedestrians were less likely to become bogged down in mud while crossing the street.

Zack's contact in Burke was the publisher and editor of the Burke *Bulletin,* a newspaperman named Gene Miller. Zack asked directions to the newspaper office and found he and Del had only to walk fifty feet up the wooden sidewalk to the building set between the restaurant and the barber shop. The printer in the press room said that Miller was out for a few minutes and offered them chairs and coffee. Cups of coffee and the warmth of the potbellied stove were unusual offerings in the middle of July, but the rains had dropped temperatures and raised humidity until a sweater was needed for comfort. Del gulped down his coffee and announced he was going to get a shave at the barber shop next door; Zack was willing to just sit and organize his thoughts.

It was twenty minutes before Miller burst into his office, grousing about the inclement weather and growling about something called Ogopogo. Zack was able to only pick up the epithets hurled at the falling rain; Miller's other words were lost as they tumbled out on top of each other.

"Who are you?"

The demand came as Miller was pulling off his oilskin slicker; the tone was impatient.

Zack stayed a sarcastic retort. He looked at Miller, who was tall and very thin. His dress was what could be termed business-like, and the tortoiseshell eyeglasses gave an impression of studiousness. Miller pulled off his suit jacket, then slid two sleeve garters in place before setting a green eyeshade neatly onto his head. With that done, he snapped, "Mister, I asked who you are. I'm busy."

"My name is Zack Horton."

"That supposed to mean something to me?"

"There was supposed to be a telegraph message sent to you from Coeur d'Alene."

Miller looked at the clutter on his desk, then yelled to the back room, "Clyde, you get any telegraphs today?"

The reply came, "A couple . . . sitting on the typing machine."

Miller darted the six feet to the metal table holding the shiny Underwood typewriter, muttering, "Now why in the hell would he put them there?"

He ripped open the first envelope, glanced at the contents, and said, "Nope, ain't about you."

When he opened the second, he read it, sat down, read the

message again, and then busied himself rearranging the muddle of papers on his blotter.

Zack felt an urge to leave, collect Del Cummins, and head out. What, he thought, what the devil am I going to learn from this rude fellow that I don't know already? He looked around the room. He had been in a few newspaper offices in his business travels, and they all seemed to fit a mold. There was the pungent odor of printer's ink and the noise of a rotary press being cranked in the back room. The office was cluttered with bundles of papers tied with string and wooden cases packed with set type. The walls bore pasted-up samples of type and memorable pages. The one that caught Zack's eye broadcast in a three-inch tall headline: CHIEF JOSEPH CAUGHT! It was dated October 6, 1877.

Zack had a vague memory of the story: Chief Joseph had led his Nez Percé tribe in a confrontation with the U.S. Cavalry. To get Miller's attention, Zack said, "That must have been some war . . . the Nez Percé one, I mean."

Miller looked up from his desk. "War! What the hell you talking about, mister? Those poor bastards were hounded like dogs, and they still as good as whipped the whole United States Army. Huh! War!"

"I didn't know. I was in college at the time."

Miller looked up at the yellowing front page stuck on the wall. He said, "That ain't the nicest thing I ever had to put into the newspaper. Damned shame, that was."

"All I can remember was that there was some sort of killing and the cavalry captured the Indians."

"Any killing that went on can be put at the feet of the damned army. Chief Joseph just wanted to live in peace. But, no, the stupid politicians and greedy farmers were determined to run them out of their lands. Fifteen hundred miles the army chased them. Old Joseph fooled them or outfought them the whole way, and all he had were three hundred warriors burdened down with their squaws and kids. Yep, Joseph nearly whipped their asses, he did. And you know what he says when they caught him?"

"I don't remember."

"Well, General Miles finally got the Nez Percé rounded up in the eastern part of Montana and made a big thing of the surrender. So the old chief is there and his braves have done a hell of a job and Joseph says, 'I will fight no more, forever.' Ain't that beautiful? Them damned troops—and there were forty companies of them—must have felt good to hear that. Believe me, if Joseph really set his mind to it, he would have whipped them just the same way Custer got whipped. All he wanted to do was to get the hell away; headed to Canada, he was."

Miller studied the page on the wall for another moment, then turned back to the papers on his desk.

The friendly approach had accomplished nothing. Zack stood and said, "I'll come back some other time. When you're not so busy."

Miller looked up, eased back in his chair, and pulled his eyeglasses from their perch. As he cleaned the lenses on the end of his necktie, he said, "So you're needing to talk with George Hearst. Right?"

"That's why I'm here, and if you can't help me, then that's all right. I'll help myself."

"Kind of think you're important, don't you?"

"No, sir, I'm just trying to get something done."

"Who you working for?"

"Is that any of your damned business?"

Miller held his glasses up to the grey light that was coming in the window. As he replaced the eyeglasses, he said, "I guess it ain't my business. Just asked."

"Look here, Mister Miller, Fred Dubois sent me to Coeur d'Alene to meet Senator Hearst but I was delayed because of the storm and I missed him. Now, my contact in Coeur d'Alene said he would telegraph you so that you could help. If you can't, that's fine with me. You might have time to sit at your desk and act precious, but I don't have time to waste."

Miller gave a casual wave of his hand, as if to dismiss the past few minutes. "Come on, lad, sit down. Now, what's your need?"

"Simple: meet with George Hearst."

"You've missed him . . . again."

Zack stood there staring at Miller. Then, after a resigned shrug, he sat back down.

"Hearst will be back," Miller went on. "Later tonight or first thing in the morning. That depends on the weather. He's gone to look at a mine over near Wallace."

Zack chewed on his lower lip. Should he leave right away or wait—maybe waste—another day? Miller said, "I know how you feel. It's the damned weather, that's what it is. Never rained like this since I been in the mountains." Then, hoping to put a friendly touch into the meeting, he said, "That's why I wasn't here when you arrived, and that's what has me distracted." He studied Zack to see if he was making any progress. "Mind if I call you Zack? Folks around here tend to like to use first names."

Zack nodded. "No problem."

"I'm Gene," and he extended a hand to be shaken; Zack took it. Miller added, "But if you call me Pica, people around here will know who you're talking about. The miners are great ones for giving nicknames, and they don't know a pica from a pencil, but one of them heard the word and the moniker stuck."

Miller was turning out to be a reasonable man. Zack said, "Could I go to Wallace and find Hearst?"

Miller shook his head. "It'd be a waste of time, if you're asking me. Like I said: the weather. The damned fool stuff keeps pouring down. A couple of miners I know who worked the late shift last night came and told me the Ogopogo was flooding. I went up and looked at it this morning, and the water is sluicing down the side of the hill like a river; it's running right into the mine entrance."

Zack was not interested, but in an effort to be polite, he asked, "Dangerous?"

"Damned right it's dangerous. I went to the shaft manager and asked him what he was going to do, and he just about threw me out of the place."

"He didn't care?"

"Not a bit." Miller reached over to a pigeonhole in his

desk and pulled out a packet of chewing tobacco. He pinched a cheekful and offered some to Zack, who shook his head and took out one of his cigars. While Zack was lighting up and Miller was working his chew into a comfortable consistency, the wind outside whipped up a gale and rain splattered against window over Miller's desk.

"Problem is"—Miller paused an instant to settle the tobacco against his cheek—"problem is the stupid mine operators just don't have a care in hell about what goes on down in those shafts; all they want is production. Those dumb miners are busting their buttocks on three shifts; they're tired and that makes them careless. The managers keep driving them."

"What's the rain got to do with all of that?"

"Simple. As the water works its way down the shafts, it can loosen the shoring. God knows there're few enough shoring timbers used."

"Wait a minute. There's plenty of wood out here. Over the past two days, I've been traveling through dense forest, miles and miles of tall trees."

Miller nodded. "Sure you have. But did you look around this place when you got off the train?"

"I did, but I couldn't see much. It was raining too hard."

"Well, there ain't a decent tree left three miles up or down this gully; every bit of it was cut off early. The Ogopogo's three miles east of town; the mine owners don't like paying to ship in shoring timbers. They buy them, sure, but not enough. We're headed for a cave-in, that's what I'm betting."

"What about laws? There should be mine inspectors; they have them in the coal mines back east."

Miller let out a raucous laugh. "That's a good one. No, Zack, things just ain't that civilized out here yet." He looked out the window. It was getting darker. Even though there were a full five or six hours of daylight left, the sky was so packed with rain clouds that everything was dark grey, as if the day had come to the edge of twilight. Miller shook his head. "This is bad; real bad. I don't like this at all."

Zack was following Miller's line of sight when there was a

sudden blur swishing past the window. In the next second, the front door of the newspaper office flew open and Del Cummins lunged inside.

Del expelled, "Gawd-damned stinking weather they got in this part of the country!"

Zack made the introductions, then stared at Del. "What the hell happened to your hair?"

Del reached up and patted the top of his head. "Pomade." The answer was laced with considerable pride.

Del's hair was slicked down, plastered against his scalp, and dramatically parted right in the middle. Along the line where a hat would fit, there were short tufts of hair curled up in sort of a shiny halo.

Del crossed to where Zack was sitting. He bent over and set the top of his head right in front of Zack's face. "Smell it," Del demanded. "Smell the damned stuff."

Zack pulled his head back, trying to escape both the strong smell and the threat of getting grease on his face. "Very nice, Del," Zack lied. "I've smelled enough. Very nice."

Miller looked amused. He said, "So you met Terrance. He's a good barber but he gets some of the damnedest notions about what a man should look like. I always give him an extra two bits to insure that he won't try any of that stuff on me."

Del stood up and asked Miller, "You don't like this pomade?"

Miller raised his hands. "I didn't say that. It's just not for me; a lot of the miners use it, though. They like the smell."

Del looked at Zack. "Really, Zack, is it bad?"

Zack mimicked Miller's gesture of protest. "Del, you look just fine. It is . . . different . . . that's all."

Del looked around for a mirror, but there was nothing available that would serve the purpose. He turned back to Zack and asked, "What's up? What's the schedule?" He craned his neck to look back into the composing room, perhaps still searching for a mirror.

Zack gave the news about Senator Hearst, then said, "We'd better find a place to settle down and wait."

Miller announced, "You won't have any luck with that; there ain't a bed in this town, Zack." He grinned. "Seems like you're having a run of bad luck; don't get into a poker game."

Del furrowed his brow. "What's that mean, no beds in town? The barber told me there's four boarding houses."

"Sure there are. They're full of miners. And there are three hotels, but they're full of traveling men who've left the trains until the rain lets up; there's bridges and track getting washed out east and west of here. You've got to be crazy to travel in this weather."

Zack and Del looked at each other.

The newspaperman offered, "I might have just the ticket for you."

Del urged, "Dammit, man, what do you have?"

"Senator Hearst went to Wallace by wagon and left his railway car here. It's not really his car, just one he borrowed from the Union Pacific, but it's here, and he told me I could use it if needed. I think you have a need."

Zack said, "We'd know when he gets back; that would be an advantage."

"It has some disadvantage, because it's parked up near the Ogopogo on a freight siding and there's no staff; Hearst didn't bring staff. He likes to move fast."

"Del and I have been spending the past few days catching up with him. I know he moves fast."

"Settled," Miller said as he stood. "You two have anything like rain gear in those bags of yours?"

Both men shook their heads.

Miller advised, "Well, across the street is a general and hardware store; go get gum boots and slickers, and rubber hats would be a good idea."

Del snapped, "There's no rubber hat going on my new haircut."

Miller and Zack looked at each other and laughed. "The rain'll ruin your pomade if you don't get one," Miller said.

The hike to the Hearst railway car took a full forty-five minutes because the dirt road had turned to gummy muck. Zack had tried to discourage Gene Miller from walking out to the siding, but Miller said he was interested in going on up to the Ogopogo Mine to see if the rains had done any more damage.

From the outside, the car looked like any other Union Pacific Pullman car, yellow with bright red trim, but inside the similarity ended. Miller said that the car was not for the top Union Pacific executives, but for working managers when not loaned out to valued customers, as in the case of Senator Hearst. Zack saw that it did not have the elegance of James Hill's private car, but it was nice. It was seventy feet long, with the first thirty feet taken up by a lounge, the remainder divided into baggage compartments, a kitchen, and roomettes that could sleep eight. Two of the rooms were obviously being occupied because the beds were rumpled and unmade; clothing was carelessly draped over hooks and racks. Del and Zack deposited their own bags in two empty compartments and joined Miller in the lounge. The lounge was warm. A stove was radiating enough heat to displace the damp chill. Del asked, "Who tends the fire? You said there was no staff."

Miller said, "Hearst elected me to that job; suppose you two take it on and sort of pay your rent?"

Zack laughed. "I thought there was some reason for you to be so anxious."

Miller grinned. "So," he said as he moved toward the door, "I'm going on up to the mine. You want to come along and see a disaster in the making?"

Del was quick to say, "I have no interest in disasters. Besides, I'm going to take a chance to get some sleep. From what the barber said, there's some pretty good doings in town after dark, and I thought I might go check it out."

Miller cautioned him, "Don't let his advice steer you to any of our houses of ill repute; you run more chance of a fight than romance. This is not a town for outsiders."

Del grinned. "Thanks for the warning. I'd just like to relax a bit; we've been moving pretty good."

Zack said, "I'll come with you, Gene . . . Pica. I wouldn't mind seeing one of these mines of yours."

"Not much to see, but I'd enjoy the company."

From the railroad siding to the Ogopogo Mine, it was uphill and treacherous due to the mud. The rain was coming down harder than at any time during the day; the sky was very dark. The road to the mine had been cut into a bank of dirt, and rivulets were coursing down the road, cutting deep ruts. They stopped about two-thirds of the way to the mine office and entrance. Miller raised his voice to make himself heard over the rain. "If you look real hard you can see another problem!" He pointed upward; Zack looked. Through the pelting rain all Zack could see was the first few yards of the barren hill face.

He yelled back that he could not see much.

"That's what I mean! They cut all the trees off the hill to make shoring for the shafts and stopes. Erosion! If this rain keeps up the whole damned thing could slide down into the town! Come on!" Zack followed.

They slogged through ankle-deep mud for another few minutes before the ground leveled off. The rain eased back slightly, and Zack now saw the steepness of the hill and its complete lack of vegetation. The mine office was a hundred yards away across a work yard that had been cut and filled from the south side of the upward slope. Zack saw three men moving about. Two were pushing a large, wheeled bucket loaded with ore over long sheets of inch-thick steel. He could see they were heading for a dump site where they would empty the ore down to the crusher fifty feet below. The other man was standing under a slanting roof covering an opening that Zack guessed was the actual entrance to the mine shaft.

"Bastards!" Miller hissed out, loud enough for Zack to hear. The man under the lean-to only heard a noise, and he turned toward Zack and Miller. The man made an angry gesture for them to go back, to leave. "Bullshit!" Miller growled, then began striding toward the mine shaft. Zack hurried to catch up.

His words made harsh by his clenched teeth, Miller said to Zack, "They must be about ready for the midshift blasting. The men will be coming up for their lunch, and I want to talk to them."

Zack lost his balance as his rubber boots stuck in the mud, and his left foot came almost all the way out of its boot. He stopped to get reorganized, and it was then that he saw what had triggered Miller's anger: a wedge of mud thirty yards wide and fifty feet high had broken away from the main part of the hill. Water soaking the dirt had turned the mound into a slowly creeping mound of ooze that seemed headed for the mine entrance. The rain had regained its vehemence and was joined by a howling wind. Walking gingerly to avoid another mishap, Zack made it to the entrance. Miller and the man were screaming at each other over the noisy wrath of Nature, Miller demanding that the miners be brought up to the surface, the shaft closed; the man told Miller to mind his own business and get off the property. Zack expected to see fists flying at any moment. Instead, Miller stormed off toward the mine office; Zack followed, yelling, "Slow up!"

Miller halted, waited for Zack, then, wordlessly, continued toward the mine office. He bounded up the four steps to the porch and, without knocking, burst through the front door, booming, "Ludlow, you are a lousy son of a bitch!" Zack scrambled inside after him.

The burly man so addressed was sitting behind a high desk. The man was bald and could only be described as ugly. His eyes were flaring with anger. "Miller! Get out!"

The man leaped up from his stool and started across the room. He was big. Zack had a sudden wish that Del Cummins had come along.

Ludlow came to a stop a foot from Miller, both of them yelling. After a couple of seconds, Miller took two easy steps backward and, in a gesture he had used on Zack, raised both hands to quiet the scene. Ludlow was not going to be quieted. He yelled, "You get out of my office or you're in jail for trespassing . . . again!"

Miller, obviously trying to bring himself under control, gave Zack a weak smile. "Ludlow likes to put me in jail. Twice before." He turned back to Ludlow and said, "I need to talk to you."

Ludlow snarled, "You don't want to talk, you never have! All you want is to butt into my business. I will not have it!"

Zack held back. This was no battle of his, and he did not understand what was going on between the two men.

Miller took two deep breaths, calming himself. A note of determination came to Miller's voice as he said, "Look, Ludlow, I told you this morning and I'm telling you now: You are risking men's lives. I don't care that you pay them below scale, I don't even care if you work them too long hours. I do care if you knowingly let men die; that is criminal."

Ludlow cocked his head as if trying to hear better. "You serious about not given me problems on wages and hours . . . Really?"

Miller gritted his teeth. "You know what I mean. The thing right now, right at this moment, is to get those men up out of the shafts. The morning shift told me there was flooding in the east stope. The whole thing could collapse and bury a dozen men."

Ludlow's eyes were flaring with hatred. "Miller, I catch any of my workers talking to you and they're done. I'll see they never work a mine again."

"They'd be better off not working than working for you."

Ludlow rounded on Zack. He demanded, "Who the hell are you?"

"Nobody to you, mister. I just came along with Mister Miller."

"Well, I want your ass out of here, too."

Zack had had enough of the man's brass. He snapped back, "I'd rather be anyplace than right here right now, but I am here, and I think you ought to listen to Mister Miller. About half of your mountain out there has started crumbling."

Ludlow's eyes flicked back and forth between Zack and Miller, then demanded, "What's he talking about, Miller?"

"Just what I've been trying to tell you. You're headed for a cave-in."

Ludlow moved quickly to the door, pulled it open, and squinted out into the dim late afternoon. Zack heard him cry,

"Gawd damn!" He spun around and shouted, "Miller, get the hell out of here!"

"Will you bring up the men?"

"That's my business. Get out!"

Gene Miller was probably half the size of Ludlow, but he had double the purpose. Miller stalked across the room, grabbed Ludlow's shirt, and said, "You get those men out or I'll have you arrested for murder. Do you understand me?"

Ludlow seemed to be contemplating hitting Miller in the face, swatting him like a fly; Zack moved closer. Ludlow's voice was suddenly calm as he said, "Miller, you and your friend get off my property. I'm bringing the men up, but I don't want you around. Clear?"

"Is that a promise?"

Ludlow nodded. "The longer you stay here arguing, the longer before I can get to work. Now leave."

Miller studied his opponent. Finally, with an apparent reluctance, he let go of Ludlow's shirt. "I'm leaving, but I'd better see those men in town soon or I'm going for the sheriff."

Ludlow swung around and moved out the door at a run.

Miller and Zack left the office and began walking back toward town. The rain was even heavier than before, but Zack could see Ludlow running, waving to the man at the mine entrance. Miller said, "He'll run the elevator cage down with the foreman. I think he'll be good to his word."

The two men hunched against the rain and the wind during the walk, quiet until they arrived near the alley that would take Zack back to the Hearst private car. "Zack, do you want to go have a drink?"

Zack nodded. "I could do with that, and I could handle a bite to eat."

"What about your fellow Del?"

"I think Del would just as soon get some rest, build up a reserve of energy for going out tonight."

Miller laughed, then suggested, "Let's get someplace warm. We can come back and get Del later."

They continued their struggle against the wind and rain as

they made their way down to the center of the town. Half a block above Miller's newspaper office, they ducked into Petit-clerc's Bakery. As Miller closed the door behind them, he said "This is the best place I know to get warm."

A smell of yeast rising and bread baking assailed Zack so strongly that he began to feel dizzy; he had not eaten in seven hours. The place was empty except for the baker, Petitclerc, who was kneading a ball of dough as big as a washtub. Miller was stripping off his rain slicker as he called, "Denne, we are in dire need of something hot . . . and strong. Strong, I tell you!"

"Mon Dieu, Pica," the baker called back. "What are you doing out in this awful weather?"

Miller growled, "Denne, hot and strong. Don't stand there yapping!"

Zack peeled off his rain gear and found that his shirt was soaked; shivering was added to the pangs of hunger. He sat across the table from Miller and noticed that the newspaperman was shaking, not just shivering. "Are you all right?"

Miller was rubbing his hands together either to induce circulation or quiet the shake. "I must have been crazy," he said. "That damned gorilla could have killed me."

"You mean Ludlow?"

"Yes, Ludlow. I've seen the lunatic beat two men nearly to death before we could stop him; I've heard he has handled three or four in a fight. I don't know what came over me."

The baker arrived with a small tray holding two cups of steaming coffee, a silver flask, and a plate of buttered bread. As he set the tray on the table, he scolded, "Pica, you should either be home in bed or sitting by a fire. Why are you shaking?"

Miller did not answer. He had unscrewed the cap of the flask and was pouring brandy liberally into his coffee.

Zack poured his own sizable share as the baker threw up his hands in annoyance. "You will not answer me! I have bread to bake." He scurried back to his work area flapping his arms as he delivered a flood of French invectives.

Zack grabbed at a slice of bread. The butter had melted, and the taste, blended with the brandy-laced coffee, was extraordinarily satisfying. Miller finished his cup and jumped up to go to the stove for a refill. While he was pouring from a blue-enameled pot, he talked to the baker. Zack could not hear their conversation, but he assumed it was about the incident at the Ogopogo Mine. He was able to devour two slices of bread before Miller returned. Miller was starting to calm down.

Zack took a good swallow of coffee and told Miller, "I wish we had taken Del with us; he could handle that Ludlow."

Miller took a drink from his cup. "Let's drop it, Zack. I was just out of control." He looked down at his hands: they were steady. In an obvious effort to change the subject, he asked, "Who is Del Cummins? I mean, what does he do for the railroad?"

Zack explained about Del, the Dakota and Western, and himself.

Just as they finished the brandy with yet more coffee, the front door of the bakery opened and eight miners poured in, accompanied by gusts of chill wind and rain.

Each was after coffee and something to eat; the baker was hard-pressed to serve them all. The arrivals gathered around Miller's table and told him that they had been sent home early. There was some grousing about losing pay, but most were relieved to be out of the shafts and stopes. "We were working in water up to our boot tops. How the hell can you run for your life when you're in water that deep?"

Zack studied the men who made their living deep in the bowels of the earth. Their appearances were as varied as one would find anywhere men were earning a living, and they were no more dirty than men who spent ten to twelve hours a day at hard manual labor. There was an enigmatic look in their eyes that Zack found hard to decipher. He finally guessed it was a mixture of fear and pride; fear from a daily atmosphere of danger, and pride founded in the same source. They were a tough bunch. Miller did not introduce Zack to any of the miners, who accepted his presence simply because he was with a man respected in the community. One of the miners, whom they all called Elden and who seemed to be a leader of sorts,

asked Miller if he had been up to the mine. Miller nodded, and
Elden said, "I was thinking that, you know. That bastard Ludlow told us we'd better not be caught talking to you." He gave
a smirk. "That's why we're talking to you."

They all had a hearty laugh over that. Zack was impressed
that Miller had taken no credit for prompting Ludlow to shut
down and had not even mentioned talking to Ludlow. The
modesty was attractive.

Talk drifted to conditions in the mine, which, Zack gathered, were deplorable at the best of times. Miners worked in a
fetid atmosphere where toilet facilities were anyplace one felt
the urge and where the air was laced with the choking dust left
after dynamiting. As many as thirty holes would be drilled into
the face of a stope, and the lingering gasses after an explosion left
little oxygen in the air. Accident rates for hard-rock miners were
the highest of any trade in the nation, and the death rates from
accidents and industrial illness were double those in other jobs.
Mine owners, like those operating the Ogopogo Mine, added to
the problems when they skimped on basic safety measures such
as shoring. The recent rains had compounded the problems.
The nasty air was made worse by the raised humidity, and water
was eroding out the supports for the shorings. Elden declared,
"We were going to come out on our own if Ludlow hadn't
called us out; that mine is ready to give way."

Miller said, "Maybe they'll have to shut down completely."

Elden reminded Miller, "We got to have a place to work."

It bordered on the pathetic for Zack; the men really had
little choice if they were to make a living.

Another man was starting to tell about how a case of
dynamite sticks had fallen off a ledge into the water and was
floating around, dropping sticks as it moved. He asked, "Any-
body know what's going to happen to that stuff when it starts
drying out?" He gave a bitter laugh.

The question was never answered.

The front door flew open, and the mine manager, Ludlow,
came running in, screaming, "I need help!"

"Get the hell out!" . . . "Go help yourself!" . . . "I'll help you drown yourself if that's what you need!"

Only Gene Miller rose quickly and took two steps toward Ludlow. "What's the matter, Ludlow? What's wrong?"

Ludlow was soaked. He wore no rain garments, his shirt was stuck to his skin, and his trousers and shoes were covered with mud. The man was breathing deeply, trying to muster enough strength to reply. Gasping, he told Miller, "The hill broke loose . . . the whole north side is sliding." The man was terrified.

Miller went to Ludlow and grabbed his shoulder. "Get hold of yourself. What's happening and what can be done?"

Still laboring to breathe, Ludlow said, "The hill is soaked through. . . . It slid down and buried the office and entrance. . . . It's coming down toward town. . . ." He cut himself off, unable to continue.

Elden and a couple of the others were on their feet and at Miller's side. Elden's voice was harsh when he asked, "Where's it coming?"

"Down the road . . . It's at the old tailings dump."

Zack had joined the group clustering around Ludlow.

Elden almost whispered, "God Almighty, it'll take the track and the freight siding."

Miller flicked a glance at Zack, who did not comprehend what was being said. Miller told Zack, "The mine filled most of the gully with tailings; they made it into a freight-car siding."

The realization hit Zack like a hammer. "Del!"

Zack lunged forward, bouncing off two miners as he ran for the bakery door.

The rain had not let up, and daylight had finally yielded to the arrival of night. It was barely possible to see where he was running, but Zack knew the general direction, and he moved.

Behind him he could hear the others' yells, but they were not going as fast as he. Some light bled out from inside the buildings along the street, but Zack missed a rise in the wooden planks of the sidewalk and fell hard. He rolled off into the mud of the street and was scrambling to his feet when strong hands grabbed his arms and pulled him upright.

One set of hands belonged to Gene Miller, the other to Elden. The crowd of off-duty miners had grown to a dozen, several carrying lanterns; there was no sign of Ludlow. Miller ordered, "Quit fighting!"

Zack had not realized he was struggling to get free. "That doesn't mean I can't run."

"That's right."

Elden promised, "We'll run with you."

A hundred yards past the edge of town, they came to the mass of mud. Without saying so, Elden estimated that it was moving forward about a foot a second. He clamped a strong hand on Zack's arm to stop him and said, "Gene, we can't make it to the siding."

Miller was looking forward, then back toward the town.

Zack was trying to break Elden's grip. "I'm going after Del!"

Miller said, "Elden, take nine of these men and begin tearing up the sidewalk to make a barrier, a dam across the street to direct the mud down into the gully. Send the other three to warn the town. Get men, get tools. Maybe we can ditch this stuff down into the gully."

Elden said, "If that damned hill breaks completely loose, we could have five or ten feet of mud here in the next little while. You know that?"

"I know that," Miller agreed, "but if there's that much, then the town's lost, no matter what."

Elden asked, "What about him?"

"I'm going with him."

"You're crazy."

Zack could not hold back. "I'm going. Now!"

Miller said, "I'm with you."

Elden shook his head, then turned to tell the other men what had to be done.

Zack stepped forward. The first step put his foot into four inches of mud, the second into six inches.

Miller, beside Zack, observed, "This is going to be tough."
Zack kept moving.

Neither man had taken the time to grab his weather gear, but they did not seem to notice; they plodded forward. By the time Zack had taken twelve steps, he had lost one of his rubber boots; the other one was gone in the next three steps. There was no use wasting energy in talking; every bit of concentration went into the battle against the mud. It was up as high as their hips when they were nearly struck down by a tangled bundle of bushes riding on top of the mud; Miller yelled, "Zack, we'd better quit!"

Even though Miller was only five feet away, Zack had to yell. "I can't. I'm going on."

Miller was holding his lantern high. "I can't get my bearings. I don't know where we are!"

"As long as we move up, we're going toward the train. Come on!" Zack renewed the effort to inch forward. Reluctantly, Miller followed.

For the next eight minutes they forged ahead. Then the depth of the mud slacked off slightly, and Miller figured that they were approaching a point where the river of mud was separating. Zack was the first who heard it: a strange, eerie noise. Miller squished up beside him, asking, "What is it?"

"I don't know."

The sound was being masked by the roar of the wind and the pounding rain. Zack squinted, hoping to see something through the black mist that had engulfed them. "There!" He began to veer off to the right. In less than a minute, the two men saw the source of the noise: a plume of steam puffing, hissing up through the mud. It was a couple of seconds before Miller realized he was looking at the bottom of the Hearst railway car. The six wheel trucks were three feet above the level of mud that was cascading down over the bank into the gully. They could see some twisted sections of rail and a scattering of ties starting to float away.

Miller cried, "My God! It fell into the gully."

Zack was moving before Miller could grab him. "No, Zack! It's in the gully."

Zack did not listen.

He was only calf deep and realized the level was down because the mud was spilling into the gully. Cautiously, resisting the urge to plunge ahead, Zack felt his way one probing foot at a time. He finally felt the solid earth drop away and stopped to study what lay ahead. Miller was suddenly beside him.

"What are you going to do?"

"I don't know, Gene. I can't just stand here."

Miller ordered, "Don't do anything. I'm going to get some men and ropes. Give me ten minutes."

Zack did not answer. Miller gave Zack his lantern and began to struggle back the way they had come.

The car was clearly visible in spite of the sheets of rain, but it was difficult to figure out what he was seeing; he had never looked at the bottom of a railway car before. He was able to identify the stairs leading up to the rear observation platform, but he could not explain the long, structural stress bar angled between the front and rear trucks. Not knowing how strong the bar was, but knowing he had to do something, he began inching forward, reaching out as he began to brave the eight-foot distance to the bottom of the car.

He felt his foot slipping just a fraction of a second before he lost his balance. He was falling forward.

As he splashed down into the mud, he threw his arms out to try to reach the stress bar. He missed by only five inches and slid downward, under the surface, completely engulfed in the tide of mud trying to carry him away from a handhold. He worked his head free just as the mud pushed him against the bottom of the car. His hands searched frantically and made purchase on the stress bar. He could not open his eyes, and the mud slipped into his mouth as he gasped for air. He spat angrily and was able to get a quick breath. He wiped his free hand on the wooden underside of the car, then scraped the mud from his eyes. Anchored for the moment and able to see a little although it was very dark, he began to move hand over hand along the stress bar, heading for the rear. It was trouble working around the wheels, but quite quickly he was at the underside of the observation platform.

He rested, gathering his strength, then pulled himself laboriously around the iron railings. He had to stop to get his bearings again. As he looked around, he saw that the car was nearly completely on its side and half-buried by the mud. At the front end of the car, a cataract was roaring along the roof line and stirring in with the mud. Where the hell is that coming from? he wondered; no one said anything about a stream or creek. He realized the steam plume from the wood stove had stopped. That scared him. Was there water inside the car as well?

The rear door of the car was three quarters immersed in the mud and water. If he opened it, he might let the flood pour into the car, but the only other option was to break the rear window, and that might do just as much harm. He reached out into the water to wash away the goo, then cleared a little of it off his face so his eyes would stop stinging.

He moved his hand down below the mud line and grasped the handle of the door. As soon as he gave it a turn, the pressure of the mud surged inward, and he was pulled along with it.

It was pitch black inside. He tried to orient himself: he was standing on what would be the right side of the lounge.

"Del! Del, where are you?"

Silence.

He called again, and again. No response.

He had to search. He moved a foot forward with great care; there might be broken glass, and with no shoes, only socks, he could end up being the one in need of help. The car was big enough that the mud was spreading out in a shallow sheet, and he was beyond it after only ten steps, but he was having to work his way around furniture that had ended up in a jumbled tangle on the side of the car.

At the end of the lounge, he paused. How was he going to navigate down the hallway to Del's sleeping room? When the car had been erect, the three-foot-wide corridor had been comfortable; now it was a three-foot-high tunnel that he'd have to crawl on his belly. He called again, and there was no reply.

Using his hands as his eyes, he lifted himself up onto the right wall of the corridor, then eased forward a few inches at a time. He had passed over the first door—the one to the kitchen—safely and was just about to cross the second door when the car gave a violent lurch. The mud outside was pushing it farther into the gully.

He was shocked to hear his own yell, "No! Not yet!"

He shook his head, slid his hand forward to check his route, and a second, harder lurch came; the car tilted at a new, precarious angle. "Oh, shit!" he yelled, louder. He had leaned forward to continue his crawl when he was frozen by a soft, pained moan. Maybe it was metal or wood bending under the force of the mud.

"Shit!"

That was not his voice.

"Del!"

"Shit!"

"I'm coming!"

The next surge of mud might send the car tumbling farther down into the gully. Zack abandoned caution and scrambled forward to the fourth door, the one to the sleeping room Del had taken. It was closed.

Zack ran his fingers around the door and found the brass handle. He gave a turn, and the door fell inward three inches. Blinded by the darkness, he reached down to see how far it had opened; he heard the sound of water, rushing fast.

"Del! Where are you?"

"Zack! Get me out!"

The words came from above; Zack had confused the sides of the car, and now he had to work upward. But he was thankful that Del had not been in the other compartment; he might have drowned.

"I'm here. Give me a minute." He located the handle but had to reposition himself in order to get a grip. "I'm opening the door more."

"Hurry, dammit!"

Once in position, he gripped the handle and pushed; it would not move.

"Del, the door's stuck."

"What the hell do I know!"

"Give me a hand. Pull on the door."

"Zack, I'm buried under a whole bunch of something; I think my leg is broken."

"Can you reach the door?"

"I can't reach my ass. I'm buried, man, buried!"

Zack thought desperately. He could wait until Gene Miller returned with help; they could break the window into the compartment and lift Del out that way. He could also try and . . .

The car slid again, the angle increasing dangerously. Zack could almost feel it getting ready to tumble.

In a rapid hand search, Zack established the geography of the space, then eased himself up to straddle the open space leading into the other compartment. His feet slipped because his socks were still slimy and wet, but he gained enough purchase to hold himself in place while he used his back to force the door open.

It moved only an inch; there was too much weight for him to lift. He paused, then called, "Del, are you lying on the door?"

"No! I'm jammed in the corner."

"What's on the door?"

"I don't know! It's black as hell in here. Hold it. Let me try and feel around." Then: "Aw, shit! That hurts."

"Don't hurt yourself, Del."

"Great advice from you, Zack. How'd I get in this damned mess?" Zack could hear some scraping and a couple of groans. "I got it, Zack. A slab of wood. It must have broken loose from something. Try it now."

Zack reorganized his position and pressed his back upward again. The door resisted at first, but then moved slightly. Then with a bang the door flew free.

In the next moment, Zack was able to climb into the compartment, still faced with total blackness.

"Where are you?"

"Over here in the corner."

Zack reached in the direction of the voice and touched something.

"Goddammit! That's my face," came from Del.

"Where are your legs?"

"Just below my ass!"

Zack snapped, "Look, I need your help. Quit the joking."

As if to confirm their predicament, the car gave still another slide and increased its pitch in the gully. Both men were silent for an instant, then Del offered, "There's something lying on my leg. A plank or board or something. I can't move it."

Zack felt around and found a plank jammed diagonally across the corner of the compartment. The wood felt smooth, with a highly polished surface, so it might not be heavy; it was possibly just stuck. Zack twisted, pulled, and pushed with no success. He set himself in another position where he could get a better grip, rubbed his hands to get rid of some of the slippery mess, grabbed the board, and yanked. Del exhaled a pained "Yo-oo!" just as the board snapped loose. "If you're looking to break it again . . . aw, damn . . . I think you did."

Zack reached in carefully, and gently felt along Del's legs. From the strange angle of the left leg Zack could tell that it was probably broken below the knee. "We have to move you, Del."

"Don't say that."

"It is either move or be buried in this train."

There was a pause, then Del asked, "How do we do it?"

Zack admitted, "I haven't thought that one out." Gene Miller should be back soon with help, but how much could the other men do with Del down in the car? Zack reached up and inventoried what was now their ceiling. He thought for only a second before he announced, "Here's what we do. You cover your face, and I'm going to knock out the window. Maybe we can lift you out that way."

"You can't lift me, Zack."

"We'll worry about that later. Right now, cover your face."

"Do you think it'll work?"

"All I know is that when I break that window we'll either be looking up into the sky or about half of Idaho will pour down in on us. Here goes."

Zack took the plank that he had pulled away from Del's leg and shoved it upward. There was the sound of glass cracking and a shower of particles rained down. Zack slammed the plank back and forth, cleaning out the pieces around the edge.

"It worked!" Del said.

"How do you know? You can't see any more that I can."

"Maybe not, but I can sure feel the rain."

Zack had missed that; the rain was pouring in. He propped his feet on a ledge he found and hoisted himself up; he could see the glow of lights in the town. He could also see a cluster of lights moving through the rain toward the car. He yelled, "Hey! Over here!"

Gene Miller's voice shouted back, "We're coming!"

Mining towns all had hospitals. As soon as a mineral strike proved out, somebody built one—a railroad company or a mine owner or a church or a town government—but somebody always did.

Del Cummins had been in the Burke hospital fifty-five minutes before the Hearst railway car tumbled sixty feet down into the gully. The rescuers had cut it close, but then it had been a tricky and dangerous job, although they all had experience with mine disasters and had the skills involved in extricating men trapped in difficult places.

The first thing they had done was to string safety ropes across the flowing mud, five men acting as anchors. Next they moved Zack Horton out of the way so they could work without worrying about amateurs. They admitted that he had done a skillful job in reaching Del, but they all knew that any man would have gone through that effort to save a friend. But getting an injured man to safety, quickly and without compounding the injury, that took skill.

Working with speed in the poor light of kerosene lanterns, they had splinted the leg with two pieces of wood they found in the compartment. They then manhandled him out through the window. They were planning to send him across from the car with a jury-rigged bosun's chair, but when the mud pushed against the car again, they feared it would go at any moment. Two of the men grabbed Del and plunged into the mud, dragging him behind. Del hurt, and he was caked with mud, but they made it to safety and then transported him rapidly to the hospital, where his leg was set in a cast. He was scrubbed clean by a nurse who patiently endured his complaints, and then he was put to bed.

The attending doctor assured Zack that Del would spend the night sleeping off the painkiller he'd been given, so Zack went to help the miners and other residents keep the mud from washing away the town. The first five buildings, the ones nearest the mine, had taken a foot of mud, but the workers had been able to steer the bulk of the slide down toward the gully. Eight hours after Zack began helping, the town was saved.

At six o'clock the next morning, when Zack returned to the hospital, Del launched an angry tirade in an attempt to convince Zack to "get me the hell out of here!"

"There's no place to go. The hotels are packed, and the trains are still not running."

Breakfast was served, a hearty meal of good food, and Del subsided to minor fussing. His morning nurse arrived at seven o'clock.

All of their belongings had been lost when the Hearst car went into the gully. Zack teased, "Everybody in town is caked with mud. You'll fit right in."

"Not with my stuff; it stinks." Del turned to the nurse and asked, "Did you ever know how bad mud stinks?"

She was beginning her reply as Zack slipped out.

The rain was still coming down but with less intensity, and a corps of workers up at the far end of town was reinforcing the barricade; the mud flow had lessened and the threat seemed to have passed. Zack headed for Miller's newspaper office, where he found Miller busy at the typewriter. Miller looked up as Zack came through the door. "You look like hell. Coffee?"

Zack accepted the offer of coffee. "You don't look too well yourself."

Neither man had slept during the night. When they were able to leave the barricade, Zack had gone to the hospital, while Miller had begun to write up his story for the Spokane *Review* and for his own special edition of the *Bulletin,* which he planned to have on the streets by noontime.

"I'll make it." Miller grinned, then added, "Hearst is back."

Zack was surprised. "How'd he get here?"

"Arrived about twenty minutes ago by wagon." Miller broke into a laugh, "He drove through the night, planning to get back to his fancy railway car. The senator is quite put out with Nature. He's over at Petitclerc's Bakery if you want to talk to him."

Zack asked, "What about you?"

"Nope, too much work to do. You go see him; I told him you were here."

At the bakery Zack found Senator Hearst sitting with a cadre of supporters and staff. Zack was too tired to worry about finesse, so he simply walked up and introduced himself. Hearst urged, "Well, Mister Horton, sit down."

That invitation was a hint for one of the crowd to back off and to give up a seat; one man did.

George Hearst was a colorful man: sometimes boisterous, sometimes rowdy, always dapper and eager. He had started his adult life as a wage-earning miner and had wandered the western mountains prospecting. He had hit it lucky on a gold strike in Nevada, and had parlayed his findings into other mines, often grubstaking other prospectors and taking a fair share of their claims. He prospered so well that, eventually, the Hearst name would be connected with the world's richest gold mine (the Homestake in Dakota), silver mine (the Comstock in Nevada), and copper mine (the Anaconda in Montana). His ultimate dream was to sit in the United States Senate, and he had achieved it, once wealth had made it possible for him to exert his influence in California.

"Gene Miller tells me you own the Dakota and Western."

"Part owner. It's a family business."

"And you're doing something with Jim Hill."

Zack nodded.

"What is Jim's interest now? He's already a power in our national railway industry."

"Statehood."

"Ah, statehood. That's a worrisome problem right now."

Zack accepted a cup of coffee from Petitclerc. "Mister Hill has heard that you want to divide Idaho, senator. He asked me to discuss that with you."

Hearst nodded. "Jim heard right, Mister Horton, but he heard too late. I've given up on that idea."

Zack looked confused. He'd thought Hearst was aggressively working on the division.

Hearst added, "Many reasons influenced my decision, but the most important one is that Idaho is a great territory; it should stand alone." He looked around at the locals, who were listening with eager attention, then added, "I'm going to do all that I can to get this territory turned into a state as soon as possible."

The crowd around him burst into cheers and applause. Hearst savored the response for a moment, then said, "Soon, I tell you, soon!" More cheering. "And I will fight for Idaho!" The cheering continued.

Zack sipped his coffee. He had found out what he needed, and he was in no mood for a blatant political demonstration. Hearst was obviously a man cut from politician's cloth; Zack found it hard to imagine him squatting on his haunches washing gravel as he looked for nuggets of gold. Hearst was now panning for votes. If his gold prospecting had been comparable, it was easy to see how the man had done so well.

Zack spent another ten minutes with Senator Hearst as they talked about James Hill and the Great Northern ("Ah, he changed the name, did he?"). Hearst asked about Zack's experience in the mud slide and then asked, "How is your friend doing?"

"Just fine. He is fighting to get out of the hospital."

Hearst laughed. "That's a good sign. Can't stand hospitals, myself. Hate them." Then, seriously, "I'm sorry I can't offer you any help in getting out of here; the car is a total loss." He added, "Good it was only a railway car and some track; thank God no one was hurt."

Zack agreed, then took his leave of the senator.

Back in Gene Miller's office, Zack heard the best news of the day. Miller announced, "They're sending a train over from Coeur d'Alene; should be here about noontime."

"That's wonderful," Zack responded, "I need to find Del's doctor and see if we can get him out of the hospital."

Miller gave a sly look. "We'll get him out; we took him in, so we can take him out. Trouble is, the train is heading back to Coeur d'Alene; eastbound tracks are washed out. If I were you, I'd take him there, then on to Spokane. The hospital in Spokane is good; that leg was busted nasty. I don't think he'll be heading home for a bit."

Zack nodded. "We've been moving so damned much that I'm beginning to wonder where home is."

Miller stood, yanked the page out of his typewriter, and said, "Come with me to the telegraph office. I'll send this off, then help you rescue old Del Cummins . . . again!"

▶◆◆◆◆◆◀

CHAPTER 7

SPOKANE, WASHINGTON TERRITORY—MONDAY,
AUGUST 6, 1888

The considerable gathering of Del Cummins' friends in the Workingman's Hospital in Spokane was the fault of an overzealous rewrite man for the Chicago *Daily News*. In journalistic enthusiasm, he had added the word *tragic* to the story telegraphed by Gene Miller about the disaster in Burke, Idaho. When additional creativity had been added by editors in Saint Paul, Baltimore, and Philadelphia, the impression was given that Del Cummins had been exposed to—and possibly was on the threshold of—death "out in the untamed frontiers on the edge of civilization."

A furious exchange of telegraph messages brought Felicity Patterson and Loretta Boynton from Philadelphia and Leah Page from Baltimore, to join with James Hill in Saint Paul for a hurried trip out to Spokane. Belatedly, Zack had sent his own series of telegrams stating that Del was out of physical danger, and that they would both be able to head back east in a few days. His words did not carry the weight of the real "truth" printed in the newspapers; his words had fallen on deaf ears.

Once all concerned individuals were on the scene and had

established for themselves that Del was reasonably fit, James Hill took command of the situation.

Loretta Boynton, because age granted wisdom, was given the chore of supervising Del's return to Bismarck, with the valuable assistance of Felicity Patterson, who had her own ideas about how to comfort Del, but who yielded to seniority. Furthermore, Hill put Calvin Jones and the *L'Etoile du Nord* at their disposal, telling Calvin that no effort was to be spared to make Del as comfortable as possible. Del was beginning to enjoy the attention, and he relaxed.

As for Leah Page and Zack Horton, that was another matter.

In the head nursing sister's office, which had been commandeered by Hill upon his arrival, Hill told Leah, "Now that you are out here, I think you can do us some good, Miss Page. I've been able to arrange a meeting with Abigail Duniway and some of her close supporters and friends."

"Mister Hill," she protested, "I saw Abigail a short while back in Wyoming."

"Did you see her close supporters and friends?"

Leah knew she was beaten. She decided against arguing that she was needed back in Baltimore. After all, the fall orders were just about complete—and she was pleased to be seeing Zack Horton again.

She listened as Hill turned to Zack.

"I have it on good medical authority that Del will be up and about, although on crutches, by the time he arrives back in Bismarck, so there is no need for you to worry over your railroad. He can take care of that very well without you."

Zack made no pretext of protest. He had already decided that he was going to go the same path Leah Page was traveling. "The best option, Jim, because I do have a great deal to report on what Del and I learned before the accident."

Leah Page noted that the response was a bit too glib and a bit too quick to have come spontaneously. She was flattered and interested that Zack was also inclined to spend some time together.

With Zack and Leah in agreement, Hill set plans for the three of them to leave that day for the West; the others would be heading east.

A faint mist of light was drifting in through the delicate lace window curtains, and the room was taking on an amber glow as the rich, dark mahogany furniture and wood trim were illuminated. Zack Horton saw his trousers and shirt on the floor where he'd dropped them, but noticed that he had managed to hang his waistcoat and jacket somewhat neatly on the polished wooden valet next to the wash stand. He'd been near exhaustion when he finally fell into bed here in the Tacoma Hotel at three o'clock in the morning. It had been a long trip from Spokane. He shrugged and climbed out of the bed. He was used to early mornings, and he had come to like them, but today he felt sluggish. Then he remembered the hours on the train the day before, hours spent in conversation with Leah Page. Both of them were tired, but both of them wanted to share their thoughts. The encounter had not been romantic, in the sense normally applied to relationships, but it had been another step toward what could be considered romance. He began to hurry in anticipation of seeing her.

The water in his pitcher was cold, and the lather that he stirred up with his brush was inadequate, but his razor was sharp enough to compensate. Two minutes later he was pulling on his clothing.

As he entered the dining room he saw that Leah was already there. She and Hill were the only customers, and the help did not seem pleased to see another early riser. As Zack took his seat across the table from Hill, Hill offered a quick morning greeting and gave an impatient motion for a waiter to produce a cup of coffee.

Hill asked, "Did you get enough sleep?"

Zack gave a chuckle. "I could have used a bit more, but I'll make it with no trouble."

Hill nodded. "I know you will; that's the beneficence of youth, my lad."

Hill went back to his ham and eggs while Zack placed his order for juice and a stack of pancakes and a serving of fried salmon.

Leah offered a sleepy smile and drank her coffee.

The dining room of the Tacoma Hotel took great advantage of the sights up toward Seattle and still gave a fine view of Mount Rainier, which was called Mount Tacoma by the local people. Early sunlight was painting the snowcapped peaks of the Cascades and the forests to the east with soft hues of orange, pink, and yellow. Out on the water to the north of the hotel, boats were moving toward the docks while others were making sail to catch the morning tide out into the Pacific. Zack was startled by the suddenness with which this young community had become a center for commerce. Tacoma seemed to be as active as Boston, despite the fact that a couple of hundred years separated them in age.

Hill decorated his last bit of toast with a huge dollop of strawberry jam and held the morsel poised, ready to eat. He studied it as he said, "We've an interesting day in front of us."

Leah didn't take the bait; she sipped her coffee.

Zack's coffee had arrived, and he took a sip, then said, "Most days have been interesting lately, Mister Hill."

Hill smiled. "Ah, but today you will be in the presence of power, the quintessence of power."

Leah faced the fact that she was going to have to join in. "Are we meeting with one of the Chinese overlords?"

Hill paused to stroke his beard, a ploy he used while deciding if someone was making a joke. He did not think this one merited a laugh. "I see you've been doing your homework, Miss Page. There is a large ethnic problem out here." He leaned forward to continue, but, just as he opened his mouth, the waiter arrived with Zack's breakfast. Hill leaned back and ate his toast and jam.

Once they were alone, Hill glanced around in a conspiratorial manner to make sure he could not be overheard. He leaned forward again, whispering, "We're going to be meeting a man named Adam Cooper."

Zack had never heard the name and, as he began to eat, shrugged his shoulders. Hill responded to the gesture with, "Of course, that's quite understandable. Few people know the man or the power he wields in this region."

Zack swallowed his first bite and washed it down with a swig of coffee. "Are we meeting him here at the hotel? Is that why we're up a bit early?"

Hill gave a loud chortle, then lowered his voice to explain, "We're taking a boat trip this morning. Miss Page, you should know about boats, being from Baltimore." He did not wait for a response, but reached into his vest pocket and pulled out his watch. "We must be at the dock in twenty-five minutes."

When the trio came out of the lobby, a carriage was waiting for them. It was a landau; the hotel manager had engaged it for them. Its roof was up to protect against the morning dew.

The ride down the steep grade of Pacific Avenue took them past the terminus headquarters building of the Northern Pacific Railroad, softly lighted by the dawn sunrise. Zack saw an unfamiliar look of envy come onto Hill's face as they drove past.

By the time they arrived at the Tacoma dock area, the business day was in full motion. There was the importing of goods from the Orient, such as silk and tea, as well as commodities from other sources all over the world. Outbound freight carried flour, grain, timber, and coal. Tacoma also had flourishing sawmills, smelter plants, and iron and stove works, as well as businesses functioning to satisfy local needs, such as bakeries, breweries, and meat-packing houses. In the previous ten years, the city had grown tenfold, and there was no sign of the growth diminishing. There was little land down by the water's edge, so new businesses were popping up on top of the plateau above the harbor. The construction of a steam-powered tramway would be an important part of the city that was going to learn to live on two levels.

Men and equipment moved about the docks in apparent

chaos, and the carriage was having difficulty making headway toward their destination. Hill was beginning to get angry.

To Zack's mind, the whole thing seemed too confused to manage efficiently. Offices and warehouses were jammed nearly to the water's edge, and on the other side of the carriage, ships were tied up three abreast, which meant goods had to be double or triple handled both going in and coming out of the vessels' holds. Longshoremen were bumping into each other; wagons were locked wheel to wheel.

There was a sudden jolt of the carriage as the horse halted. At the same moment, the driver called out, "Trouble! Stay put!"

Zack Horton was not one to stay put no matter who was passing out the orders; he jumped out the door—into a mass of humanity flowing out from between the tightly spaced warehouses; a roar was beginning to build. The men did look as if they were forming into a mob. The flow seemed to be heading down the dock area in front of the carriage. Zack moved to the front of the carriage; the driver was having some difficulty keeping his horse from bolting. Zack went to the horse's head and took strong hold on the halter.

Hill called, "What's up, Zack?"

Zack looked up at the driver, who was working the reins with all of his skill; the horse was settling, either from the driver's handling or from Zack's hold on the halter. From inside the landau, Hill demanded, "What the devil is going on, Zack?"

Zack called back, "I don't know! Hold on."

The horse might be coming back under control, but the crowd was growing. Zack began being shoved against the horse; people were bumping into each other, and some were falling to the ground. Zack looked at the driver again and called, "You figured it out?"

The driver yelled, "Damned if I can see. There's something. We'd better get the hell out of here."

Zack could not argue with that. The problem was, how?

There were, at that time, just over twelve hundred men working on the Tacoma docks, moving goods to and from the warehouses and loading and unloading the holds of the ships. In addition, at any given moment, there would be one or two hundred teamsters driving their heavy wagons along the docks and onto the piers. At that moment, a large majority of them all were heading toward trouble. Unfortunately for the Hill party, the trouble was just 150 feet ahead, and the mob began to eddy back around the carriage after it had compressed against the flash point. There was no way to tell what was happening.

Now Zack was jammed against the flanks of the horse, which was beginning to act nervous again.

The driver yelled down, "I can't hold this nag much longer!"

Zack let go of the horse and fought his way to the cab door. Behind him was an agonizing scream of pain, and he looked back: one of the mob had taken a hoof to the shoulder.

If the horse went completely out of control, Leah and Hill could be trapped inside the landau and maybe injured. He opened the door and took Leah's hand, guiding her to the ground. She stayed close, very close to him while he turned to see to Hill. Just as Hill was halfway out of the carriage door, the horse lunged forward. Zack yanked Hill free. The horse broke into a panicked run, and the carriage lurched ahead.

Zack made sure that Leah and Hill were safe before he looked around to see what was happening to the carriage. It was not in sight.

The empty space created when the carriage had forged ahead had been filled in about twenty feet ahead. The remaining open space held only the trio—and four men standing shoulder to shoulder, facing them, looking ugly. One of the men shouted, "You got no right here."

Zack challenged, "No right to *what*? What's going on?"

"If you don't know, you've no right here. Get out!"

Hill said, "We'll get out when we please, young man. Now give a civil answer: What's going on?"

Hill's stern voice seemed to have a quieting effect on the mob ringing the space. In the momentary lull, Hill, in a near whisper, said, "Zack, go see if the carriage driver is okay."

Zack took Leah's hand and began to lead her in the direction the carriage had gone.

One of the bullies yelled, "Stay put, mister!"

Zack had had enough of the confrontation. He dropped Leah's hand and crossed the eight feet separating him from the man who had challenged him, stopping only inches from the man's face. Zack said, "Move your ass, mister, because I'm coming through."

His opponent's eyes flared red with anger, but he was so enraged that he was unable to find any words; spittle clung to the corners of his mouth like drops of venom from the fangs of a snake. Over the man's shoulder, another tough snarled, "You're one of them. I know it!"

A man beside him voiced, "Sure he is . . . just look at him."

The crowd was beginning to creep forward. The man Zack was facing was pushed so close that Zack could smell the rancid odors of garlic and fermented alcohol coming out of the man's mouth. Zack stepped back, but he bumped into Hill. Leah was beside him. The area that had been open was now shrinking; the trio was about to be closed in.

The man with the bad breath, looking at Hill, spat out, "He looks like one who'd hire Chinks."

One of his cohorts chimed in. "Yea, he looks like a heathen lover!"

"Let's get 'em!" came from far back in the crowd.

Hill, in a loud voice, demanded, "Is that what this is about? About Chinese labor?"

There was no answer.

A loud roar erupted from farther down the dock, an eerie mixture of screams, yells, and the guttural sounds of hate.

The men around Hill, Leah, and Zack began looking back over their shoulders, to see the men in the rear ranks begin to break away from the confrontation and run down the docks toward the real action. Hill grabbed the shirtfront of the man who had accosted Zack. "Now what is this silliness?"

Hill's demeanor was stinging. Cowed slightly, the man answered, "You ain't with them Chinks?"

Hill tightened his grip. "We're visitors. What's going on!"
The man snapped back, "Damned Sands Cargo is using
Chink labor. You ain't with them?"

"No!" Without taking a breath, Hill said, "You've no
right to attack people. You know that!"

One of the other ruffians snarled, "Them heathen Chinks
ain't got no right taking our jobs."

A chorus of agreements came from the men who had not
left. Zack looked at the dock workers and said, "You're not
doing yourselves any good acting like a bunch of animals."

Hill relaxed his grip on the man's shirt. "You should go
back to your jobs."

"We ain't going to have jobs if them Chinee workers get
a hand into the docks."

Zack snapped, "That's no concern of ours. We're here on
honest business. Someone could have gotten hurt."

The man gave a hard look at Zack. "You got no business
on our docks. Get out."

Zack took a step forward. "You want to see what I can do?
Anytime you're ready, so am I."

Hill cut in, "Zack, be quiet!" He turned loose of the man
and said, "Be reasonable, son. Go on back to your work."

The dockworker was torn three ways. He did not want to
back down from doing battle with these fancy-dressed businessmen; he did not want to go back to work in the warehouse; and
he wanted to attack the Chinese workers farther up the dock.
Trying to look as rough as he could, he said, "I'm telling you
to get off this dock. Now!"

He turned and looked at the remaining handful of men.
"Come on, boys. Let's get at the Chinks."

They gave a shout of approval, and all began running
toward the riot.

Hill held his hand out to stop Zack from following. "Take
it easy. I see the carriage now. We need to see what damage
happened there."

The carriage was a hundred feet away, lying turned onto its
side, but the driver and the horse were not in sight. Hill ordered,

"Now, we will walk there slowly. There's no reason to get that mob looking at us again."

As they walked toward the wreck, they could see that the heart of the riot was moving away from them, flowing out onto one of the piers about halfway along the waterfront.

As they came on the carriage, they saw, on the ground on the far side, the unconscious driver; there was no sign of the horse. They were at him in an instant; he was alive and breathing well. Leah said, "Looks like he just bumped his head."

Hill left Leah and Zack trying to wake the driver and went to inspect the carriage. In a minute he was back and announced, "The carriage seems in good form. I'd guess the horse broke the traces and fled."

A moan came from the driver.

Leah was holding the man's head off the ground. A small amount of blood ran from a slight gash in his forehead. Zack asked the man, "Can you hear us?"

There was a slight flicker of the eyelids, then, weakly, the driver said, "Where's my horse?"

The three looked at each other and laughed; the tension had broken.

Hill leaned down. "The horse is gone, man. Nowhere in sight."

The driver's eyes popped open and he made to rise, but he fell back immediately into Leah's arms. The driver said, "I must get up."

Leah said, "Take it easy. I've seen worse bumps on a log; you'll live."

Zack said, "And so will your horse. Rest a minute."

The man shook his head impatiently. "No! That damned nag is heading back to the barn and the gate is closed. She'll sure bust it down."

He made another move to get up and managed to reach a sitting position. Leah asked, "Are you okay?"

The man nodded, and was helped to his feet by Hill and Zack. He said, "Look at my damned carriage."

Hill said, "Don't worry about the carriage. I'll make good for any damage, but there seems to be little."

The driver put his hand to his forehead and felt the blood. "You're a good man, Mister Hill, but I'll stand my losses; all part of the business."

"Nonsense. You get on out of here and see to the horse. Later you can arrange to recover your carriage, but the horse comes first."

The man stood there confused; he looked about as if trying to decide what to do.

Hill said, "Driver, you don't worry about the carriage. You get back to your stable and see to your horse. Then you can do something about the carriage. I will see to any of the expenses; do not worry about that." Hill turned to Leah. "You wait here. Zack and I are going to see what the trouble is on the dock, and then we'll find Adam Cooper and his boat."

"Not on your life; you're not leaving me alone in this mess."

Hill said, "I appreciate that, but I don't want you hurt."

She smiled. "Let me worry about that, Mister Hill."

Hill seemed to bounce as they started covering the three hundred feet to the pier. As they walked, Hill said, "I've had my share of street fights, Zack."

Zack laughed. "I've seen some of that this morning."

"There are a few who have tried to best me, but I've seldom been beaten."

Leah grinned. "Someday I would like to hear about those seldom times, Mister Hill."

From far off behind them came the sound of a bell clanging; the police were on their way.

Hill prodded, "Let's hurry, Zack, before the police get here."

The mob had compressed at the entrance to the pier, and the logjam of bodies was like a wall, but Hill pushed his way roughly through. Zack was keeping Leah between himself and Hill. Both men were strong and able to move bodies, and both men were firmly ordering, "Move aside! Out of the way! Make room!" Their voices were forceful enough to carry over the shouts of the crowd and command a reaction. Both Zack and Leah were enjoying the excitement of being in a tight situation with James Hill. That novelty would soon disappear.

The pier was long. It jutted out into Commencement Bay a full 150 feet, and four sailing ships were tied up there, two on each side of the pier. Midway out, the mob had surrounded eight Chinese who were huddled down on the wooden planking of the pier; a rough-looking man in a well-worn suit was standing by the Chinese, arguing with the mob.

Hill and Zack paused one rank back from the circle. The hostile murmur from the surrounding mob could not block out the exchange between one of the mob leaders and the man in the tattered suit, who, it turned out, was the captain of one of the docked ships. He was shouting, ". . . And I'll be damned if y're be telling me how to run my ship."

His antagonist, who turned out to be one of the longshoremen's union bosses, shouted back, "You run your ship . . . we run our docks."

"I'll be the one who decides who loads my ship!"

"You'll decide to take those Chinks back on board and let my men do the loading."

Hill leaned close to Zack and said, "I hate to side with a union man, but he has a point."

Looking around, Zack whispered, "He also has the captain outnumbered."

The captain raised his fist. "The law will see who is right in this! I'll not budge me or my men."

The longshoreman stepped forward. "Don't you be waving yer fist at me!"

From back in the crowd, one of the hostile longshoremen threw a rock the size of a grapefruit; it hit squarely on the head of one of the Chinese sailors. The sailor toppled forward, blood gushing from the wound on his forehead.

At the sight of the blood, one of the Chinese sailors jumped up, yanked a foot-long knife out of his belt, and ran, screaming, at the union boss. As soon as the Chinaman moved, the boat captain pulled a pistol out of his coat pocket and fired, point-blank, at the union man.

The roar that ensued was deafening.

Unable to speak or be heard, Hill grabbed Zack's arm and forced him forward; it was obvious they were going to pitch in on the side of the underdog. But Zack was also worried about Leah. Keeping her huddled under one arm, he followed Hill, who crossed the distance to the group of Chinese in just three leaps.

Despite the quickness of the move, each of the Chinamen was being pummeled by three or four longshoremen with fists, belaying pins, and clubs. Blood was beginning to speckle the fighters as noses were smashed; then blood spurted as knives and cargo hooks suddenly appeared.

Hill muscled his way between two men who were holding one of the sailors and a third who was hitting the sailor in the stomach. Hill took out the puncher with a solid whack of his right hand, and with his left tried to pull the Chinaman free. With Leah still huddled under his left arm, Zack threw a right that connected with the left ear of one of the men holding the sailor and at the same time took a hard blow to the stomach. Hill reeled slightly; he had been hit in the head by a flying rock.

The two men managed a quick exchange of elated grins at being in the midst of a real brawl. At that moment the gunfire broke out.

Zack realized that they were involved in something absolutely dangerous. Leah! He had to get Leah out of this. Holding onto her tightly, he gave one powerful, determined thrust, slammed into Hill's back, and carried the three of them to the planks of the dock. They were down, but safer than if they had been standing. They lay next to the Chinese sailor who had been hit with the first rock.

Hill struggled furiously, not knowing he was under Zack. For the first time since he had met Hill, Zack heard profane language coming from the man, who was known to take a dim view of such words.

All around them was a cacophony of violent sounds: men

shouting out their feelings of hate and anger, sickening dull thuds as strong wooden clubs struck fragile heads, and gunshots. The fusillade grew with each second.

Hill was able to twist around and saw it was Zack holding him down. He tried to yell over the noise but all Zack could hear was ". . . off my damned back and . . . Want to help them to . . . Need protection . . ."

Leah was also squirming to get free, but Zack was able to hold onto her, too. He yelled, "Stay down! Do you want to get shot?!"

She retorted, "Do I have an option?"

He nearly burst out laughing, and Hill nodded his understanding, but continued his wriggling attempt to stand up, until a small group of fighting longshoremen and Chinese sailors fell right on top of the trio. They were then in danger of being smothered.

The few moments under the flailing battlers seemed interminable—the smell of unwashed bodies, the drips of sweat mixed with blood, and the threat to life all seemed to make seconds drag on for hours. Each moment, Zack wondered when the police would arrive, and whether they would arrive in time.

In fact, the police had arrived at the dock area very quickly, but the way was blocked by a force much greater than the four-man squad could handle. They had sent an urgent call for help from a U.S. Army detachment bivouacked next to the train terminal up on Pacific Avenue.

The police reports that followed the incident reported that 326 longshoremen and warehousemen battled forty-nine Chinese sailors and stevedores. The help of thirty army troops had been needed to quell the riot.

The violence began to subside before Zack knew for sure that help had arrived. The shooting stopped, the bodies above him lessened in their struggle, and he finally heard voices shouting orders to stop the fighting. He told Leah and Hill, "I think it's over."

Hill, pinned against the oily, dirty surface of the dock, was angry for letting himself get trapped, but he was also slightly piqued at Zack for trying to be so protective; Hill felt he was a man who could take care of himself. He said, "We'll talk about this when you let me stand on my own two feet!"

Zack felt bodies on top of him get up; then powerful hands yanked him roughly to his feet; he faced a policeman and five uniformed soldiers. In the next instant, Hill was pulled unceremoniously to his feet. The policeman demanded, "What the hell are you people doing on the bottom of this mess? You don't look like dockworkers to me."

Leah, dusting off her skirt, said, "Thank you for your observation, officer. You are right; we do not work here."

Then, grinning boldly, Zack added, "And we're not Chinese sailors, either!"

The policeman charged, "Don't give me any smart mouth, mister."

Hill was not used to hearing public servants talk in such a way, but the reason for short tempers was clear. All around them, over the whole dock area, was carnage.

The police and army troops were in the process of isolating groups of rioters to prevent more violence; the wounded and dead lay where they had fallen. In the end, the toll was six Chinese sailors killed and fourteen wounded, with one longshoreman dead and thirty-eight wounded. Two of the wounded would soon die from their injuries.

Zack stepped over to the policeman. "We are businessmen, officer. We tried to help save the Chinamen."

The policeman sneered; he had no use for the Chinese, but he was there to represent the law. "You're not a part of this?"

Hill snapped, "He told you, young man, that all we did was try to help."

The policeman's eyes flared angrily. From behind him, a firm voice asked, "What's going on here, officer?"

The voice carried authority.

The policeman raised two fingers to the bill of his cap in a sort of salute. "Hello, Mister Cooper. We've a bit of trouble."

Adam Cooper was a large man at six feet even, and he carried his medium weight well for his sixty years of age. He had a flowing white mane of hair and wore small, square Ben Franklin eyeglasses. He moved forward and said, "Jim, how'd you get into the middle of this mess?"

The policeman interjected, "You know this bunch, Mister Cooper? They say they're here on business."

Cooper burst out in a laugh. "Officer, this is Jim Hill. I guess he is *the* businessman in this part of the country."

The policeman was confused. Adam Cooper was one of the leading citizens of the Washington Territory, and there were dozens of important people who were known to the community; the policeman had never heard of Jim Hill.

Cooper walked over to Hill, "Are you hurt? Do you need a doctor?"

Hill shook his head. "I think some of these poor souls can do with assistance." He gestured to the bodies scattered around the pier.

Cooper said, "The authorities will see to that. Let's get you out of here." He looked at Leah and Zack. "What about you young folks; do you need any help?"

Leah said, "It would help if I could understand what just happened."

The policeman started to speak. "I think we had—"

Cooper cut in. "I think Mister Hill has had enough. If you need to talk to him, you can contact my office later."

The policeman nodded respectfully.

Cooper led the way back toward the foot of the pier. As they picked their way around the bodies and groups of rioters, Cooper asked, "Is this the Mister Horton you've been bragging about, Jim?"

"It is, Adam. And, I must say, he comported himself very well over the past few minutes." Hill smiled. "Even if he did treat Miss Page and me in a fairly rough manner."

Cooper looked at Leah. "You are Miss Page?"

Hill made the introductions as they walked.

They came to the end of the pier, where Cooper said, "This is all I could find to get here."

He indicated a long, flatbed wagon with a four-horse team.

He explained, "My boat is way at the far end of the docks, but I saw the riot and I knew you would be coming through. I just didn't get here in time."

The four of them climbed up onto the wagon, and it began moving slowly through the litter of bodies and rubble around the area. The ride was rough, and they held onto stakes to keep their balance. Cooper shook his head as he said, "It's a damned shame, Jim. All this violence is awful."

Hill observed, "It's getting worse, isn't it?"

"You bet it is. What's been going on is hurting our chances for statehood, too."

Riots over the Chinese issue were gaining notoriety in the national newspapers. Tens of thousands of Chinese had been brought into the country to work as cheap labor constructing the transcontinental railways, but, once construction was completed, the Chinese were dumped into society. They were an industrious lot, willing to work for lower wages just to stay alive, and that led to resentment from other workers in the West, especially in the mining camps and farming areas. Such riots were an outgrowth of the conflict, and hundreds of people had been killed. The newspaper reports published back in the states had not given the general public a very accurate impression of what was going on, even though they had created a feeling that too many Chinese had been allowed to immigrate. The trade-labor unions were supporting an Alien Exclusion Act, but possible future legislation did not relieve the strain of the moment. In Washington Territory there had been nasty incidents when Chinese were hired to help harvest the hop fields and by some of the timber operations that were manufacturing lumber for the nation and for the Orient. The situation was like a keg of dynamite ready to be ignited.

Cooper added, "I have a feeling that I know who might be behind these riots. We have had quite a few recently."

Zack asked, "What do they have to gain?"

"If the public back east thinks we are a bunch of rioters out here, then there's little chance we can ever think of becoming a state. They call themselves the Olympia Movement."

The broad avenue between the warehouses and the docks narrowed as they approached the end. Cooper called to the driver, "Jack, we'll get off here."

After the wagon came to a halt, Zack gave Leah a hand climbing down. As her feet touched the ground, he held onto her a bit longer than was necessary; the action did not seem to offend her. After her thanks, he said, "Sorry about the rough treatment a few minutes ago."

"No need to apologize. You did what you thought best; but I could have been given a little warning before you flung me to the ground."

Zack looked at her to see if there was something more being said. She sensed his reaction and said, "If there are any suggestions, Zack, you won't have to wonder about them."

He laughed. "That sounds fair to me."

Hill and Cooper had walked on; Leah and Zack followed to the end of the furthermost warehouse, turned the corner, and came to a short pier where Adam Cooper's yacht was waiting.

The vessel was only fifty feet long, not anything compared to the hundred-plus-feet lengths of the Vanderbilt or Gould yachts, but Cooper's was breathtaking. It was a perfect miniature of the steam-powered side-wheelers used in river and coastal cargo commerce, a showpiece of highly polished wood and brass. It looked as if it should be serenely sitting in a pond rather than on the murky, choppy waters of Commencement Bay.

James Hill stopped in his tracks and exclaimed, "My goodness, isn't that a magnificent sight!"

Cooper's boat had been built with a master boat builder's craft. There were only the natural colors of wood, except for the hull at the waterline, which was copperplated; the morning sun glistened on the high-luster varnish and the generous, highly polished brightwork at every reasonable point. Even the coal-black smokestack rising above the wheelhouse shone, wisps of grey smoke floating upward softly from the steam engine below the deck. Horton noticed that even the mooring lines were meticulously maintained and neatly coiled. The crew was attired in royal-blue-and-snow-white uniforms that made them look fit to serve a monarch.

Cooper responded, "Isn't she lovely? Let's get aboard. That mess on the docks has made us late."

They walked up the gangplank and were greeted by the first officer, who led them to a salon aft. Cooper gave his approval to the request to cast off.

A steward in sailor's livery offered refreshments. Cooper added, "There's any liquor you might want."

The salon was large, twelve feet wide and eighteen feet long. Five windows, one on each side and three across the back, provided a panoramic view out over the stern. All of the woodwork was varnished and showed not one speck of dust. On the forward bulkhead of the salon was a marble-faced fireplace bracketed by two floor-to-ceiling bookcases, each stocked with leather-bound works of contemporary and classical authors. The furniture was darkly stained mahogany, the tabletops looking like glass, and the leather-covered chairs looked warm and welcoming. There were cut-glass vases set in place on every reasonable surface, and a colorful arrangement of fresh-cut flowers in each vase. A small bar offered liquor and the fixings for coffee or tea. The salon was comfortable and elegant.

Both Hill and Zack accepted coffee; Leah opted for tea. Zack did not refuse a dram of brandy as flavoring. Cooper was indulging, and it seemed the proper social thing to do.

The richly carpeted floor of the salon vibrated just slightly as the engine built up steam. While the men were taking their first sips of coffee, the sounds of water churned by the paddle-wheels came softly into the cabin. Zack was beginning to relax and was beginning to feel some aches and pains from blows he had received during the battle on the dock.

Hill's overcoat and jacket showed signs of the scuffle. Cooper offered, "Let my steward take those and fix them up for you, Jim. It'd be no trouble and done in a few minutes."

Hill laughed and asked, "You have a laundry on board?"

"Matter of fact, there is that service available. I often use the ship for business trips along the coast—to San Francisco,

Portland, and I've even taken her up along the coast of Canada to meet with timber suppliers."

Hill, with the steward helping, extracted himself from his coat and jacket. As the steward was leaving the salon, Hill looked at the forward bulkhead and said, "My gracious! Would you look at that."

Hanging over the marble-faced fireplace was a large Millet canvas. Hill also owned two Millet canvases.

Cooper asked, "You like it?"

Hill replied, "Splendid." After a moment of study, he said, "How can you trust such a treasure to a boat; suppose the darned thing sinks?"

Cooper went to refill his coffee at the bar on the port side of the cabin. As he poured himself a modest dollop of brandy, he said, "If that sinks, then so do I, because it's only on board when I am here. The rest of the time it rests safely in my offices on Pacific Avenue."

"Wise man." With obvious reluctance, Hill pulled himself away from the painting. "Well, you didn't invite us here to discuss art, even though that would please me greatly. There are matters we should be getting to."

As Hill took a chair at the large, polished table in the middle of the salon, Cooper said, "There's no rush to begin talking; we have a three-hour trip ahead of us."

Hill sipped his coffee before he said, "I've got to learn to relax more and enjoy the moments of enforced inactivity; I go insane if I can't be at my work."

Cooper said, "When you are as old as I am, you'll slow down. That's why I love the boat so much; I'm stuck out here on the water and there is nothing I can do until I arrive at my destination."

Hill nodded. "But it is not fair for me to impose my behavior on young people like Leah and Zack, here. I demand a great deal of their time."

Cooper studied the pair for a moment. "They look as if they're living through it all. How about it, Miss Page: Is Hill's pace too hectic?"

Hill held up his hand. "I'll not be having you set up a trap for either of them, Adam. They're both in business themselves; they're doing well. Don't try and set the fox among the chickens. I've often said that the key to success is work, then hard work, then more work, and I think they have the stuff to make a success of life, because they don't complain about long hours. I'd not have anyone around me who was not the kind of person they are, believe me."

"Oh, I believe you, Jim," Cooper said. "I'm not trying to trap them into anything. I'm glad they're wise enough to make this investment of their time for their own futures."

To change the subject, Hill said, "You seem to have dug pretty deeply to find the man who could build a boat like this; it's exceptional."

Cooper puffed up his chest slightly. "I built this devil all by myself."

Zack said, "It's quite an accomplishment, Mister Cooper."

"I saw to this baby from the very beginning. I drew rough plans and had a marine architect do the structural work. Then, when we knew what we would need, I went out into the forests to find the woods I would need. I'm a timberman, you know, but it was not always that way in my family. My grandfather and all the men before him had been tailors; my father was the one who broke the mold and went into the lumber business. From the time I was a little tyke, I was taught about wood, so when I decided to build my own vessel I knew what I was looking for. I searched all over for the best and I found it. The keel and ribs come from magnificent broadleaf oak I found on the Olympic Peninsula, the planking is cedar from right here in the Northwest, and the decking, which is knot-free fir, was cut on my own acreage up north of here. I stayed while the trees were cut, I saw them brought to my mills and made into timbers, and I supervised the finishing of each piece of wood. It was a real joy to me."

When Cooper had finished, Hill said, "I know there are things I like about you, Adam Cooper. The way you did this boat is the way a man must perform if he's to do a job well."

Cooper said, "From what I hear, you're much the same with your railroads, Jim. Word has it that you're all the time sending memos to your supervisors about neatness in the yards and unneeded goods around stations and, this is just rumor, of course, I hear that a man will find himself in deep trouble if he does any job slovenly."

Hill did not like his reputation for being a hard taskmaster. In a brittle voice he said, "I don't worry about the men who work on my railroad, Adam, but I do fret over lazy louts and irresponsible oafs who take their wages and do not perform."

Cooper said, "You mean labor-union types?"

Hill stood up. "Not at all! I couldn't run one train a day if it was not for the trade-labor unions. They have an outstanding apprenticeship procedure, they see that their members are qualified, and they make sure the work gets done according to instructions."

"And . . . they start strikes!"

Hill shook his head. "None since I've had the line."

Cooper asked, "How so?"

"Because I know how to deal with the union bosses. They're working men, too, and, at least on our line, the men who make the decisions are willing to sit down and listen to reason."

Cooper bristled. "They don't listen; they make demands."

Hill nodded. "Sure they make demands, that's their job. But when I meet with them and after they have stated their positions, I tell them what we can afford." Hill paused for a moment, then said, "I think the big thing is that I do not, I will not, lie to my workers. If they ask for a raise or change in working conditions, then, if we can afford it, they get it."

Cooper said, "And pretty soon they'll be owning your company."

Hill said, "The trade-labor movement is with us, Adam, and I recognize that. But I'll guarantee you that they will never own my railroad: they couldn't afford it."

Cooper pressed his laugh a bit more than was warranted. "Well, let's have some more coffee."

The three men moved to the bar and each poured what he wanted.

Leah sat watching the panorama of Tacoma slip away behind them. She asked, "When will we be back at the dock?"

Cooper replied, "You'll be back in Tacoma in time for an early dinner; I'm taking the boat on up to Vancouver."

Hill and Zack glanced at each other. Then Hill said, "Where are we going right now?"

Cooper walked across the salon and took a seat next to Leah, saying, "We're going to discuss the matter of critical mutual interest. Then we'll be docking in Seattle."

Hill, impatience audible in his voice, asked, "Is it really necessary to spend that long out on the water?"

Cooper grinned. "As I was saying, Jim: Learn to relax."

Hill sounded annoyed as he said, "I don't like to use an old saw, Adam, but time is money."

"Ah," Cooper replied, "when you get to my age you learn that you must relax, too."

Hill snapped, "When I get to your age, I will. Right now there are too many things I must do in life. Lolling about on your yacht is not doing much for me."

Cooper said, "Look, Jim, I'm sorry I didn't tell you in advance, but this time will be spent well, believe me." He turned to Leah. "I know you will find the time well spent, Miss Page; we're meeting Abigail Duniway in Seattle.

Hill was still irritated. He said, "We could have met Mrs. Duniway in Tacoma. As a matter of fact, I was planning to see her when I go down to Portland in the next day or so."

By this time, Hill and Zack had moved to the large table in the middle of the room.

Cooper leaned forward on his elbows. "Jim, Abigail Duniway is critical to our efforts to gain statehood. She has her paper and she has a following; she's a very influential person."

Hill said, "That doesn't answer my question: Why does it have to be in Seattle?"

Cooper gave a hearty laugh. "Because she's there, and because I'm going there."

Zack glanced back and forth between the men. James Hill was not the type of man who could be toyed with, but Zack was surprised.

"Well," Hill said, "I guess there's nothing that can be done about it now."

"Good," Cooper was already saying. "Let's get down to it."

Hill held up a hand. "Just one thing, Adam: Don't ever do something like this to me again. I don't enjoy surprises."

Cooper nodded as he reached to the side of the bar and picked up a folder jammed full of papers. He came to the table and was joined by Leah as he arranged the material on the table and said, "We've got a lot to cover."

With Cooper's boat moving at eleven knots, the trip from Tacoma required ten minutes less than three hours. Heading north out of Commencement Bay, they traveled the East Passage around Robinson Point on Maury Island, then up into Puget Sound where they passed Alki Point and turned south into Elliott Bay. During the comfortable voyage, Cooper explained the problems facing the territories of the Great Northwest in gaining admission to the Union.

Washington Territory shared one major obstacle with all of the other territories vying for statehood: lethargy on the part of the voters. The basic problem was that the federal government in the nation's capital was footing the bill for a great many services normally provided by state governments. Law enforcement was supplemented by the presence of army troops in the territories, judges and marshals were maintained at federal cost, and the federal government also appointed and paid the salaries of territorial governors, who put hundreds of administrators in place to satisfy the needs of the people. Roads were constructed with federal money, so were waterways, and many welfare functions were paid for out of federal coffers. The people reasoned: Why should we become a state and have to pay for all of those things with our own money?

The foremost argument against was corruption. Beginning just after the Civil War, appointees to federal positions in the western territories began to return to the spoils system. While many of the men sent out to administer the territories were excellent, an equally large number were incompetent or corrupt; the men who served well received little recognition, but the ones who were scoundrels made headlines. It gave a strong motivation for statehood.

Still, the electorate hesitated.

In Washington Territory one other stumbling block had been the very explosive growth of industry. Manufacturers and businessmen benefited from laws that allowed some loopholes in payments of taxes, but it was not the corporate factions that balked, because they were making handsome profits; it was, again, the average man, who knew that higher taxes on businesses would surely mean higher prices on goods in the shops and stores.

Then there the was problem of the Olympia Movement, that renegade force. Cooper explained, "They developed this stupid idea of seceding from the Union."

Hill scoffed, "That's sheer nonsense."

"Might be," Cooper said, "but they're active, and they've enlisted some powerful people in the region."

Leah asked, "What's involved, Mister Cooper?"

Cooper pulled out a map of the Great Northwest that showed an area shaded pink. Included were Washington, Oregon, Idaho, Montana, Utah, and, to the shock of the others, British Columbia, Alberta, and Saskatchewan.

Hill, a Canadian native, blustered, "This is obscene, Adam. What utter stupidity to think that either of our governments would accept such a thing."

Zack cut in, "Just a few years ago, the United States fought a bloody war to prevent secession." He paused for an instant and added, "My father died in that war."

Leah looked at Zack. He said, "Sorry for the interruption."

After an hour of intense discussion about the problems ahead of them, Adam Cooper offered an early lunch on the same table in the salon.

Leah was asked to sit as hostess. "That's a flattering offer, Mister Cooper."

He laughed. "Any chance I have to see a beautiful woman sitting at the head of my table, I take it, Miss Page."

She gave him a warm smile. There was not a hint of lechery in his proposition; the man was a charming gentleman.

They were served poached salmon, creamed asparagus tips on toast, and boiled potatoes. There were breads and biscuits with butter and jam; the beverages were coffee, tea, and champagne. The table was set with fine bone china and cut crystal; cigars were smoked with the after-meal coffee, which was laced with a well-aged cognac. Hill had declined the champagne but had accepted cognac in his coffee; Cooper and Zack had done justice to the champagne.

Adam Cooper came back to his charges against the Olympia Movement. At one point, Cooper held that their actions were treason, and he went so far as to suggest that the best solution would be to "go on back to the times when we had our Vigilance Committees to solve those problems; that's the way to handle it."

In the short time that Zack had spent in the West, he had learned of that early period preceding organized government when the settlers had taken the law into their own hands. It was a time that everyone seemed to want to forget, and it was surprising to hear a man of considerable means, a man like Adam Cooper who was intent on introducing more government into his life, talking about vigilante action.

Hill said, "I feel, Adam, that this problem that seems to possess you so strongly is a mere whim on the part of some malcontents. If I were you, I would give it no more credence than you would to the childish prank of an errant schoolboy."

"Damn it, Jim, I hope you're right. I've been fighting too long to see my hopes for statehood dashed."

Hill smiled. "If Zack learns anything of relevance to this situation, he will communicate it to you immediately." Hill looked at Zack. "Won't you?"

"Of course." Zack reached for the silver pot containing the

coffee and, as he poured, he added, "There are a great many people I plan to see before this is over, Mister Cooper. If I come across anything, you'll be the first to know."

There was a noticeable change in the sound of the engine. Cooper pulled out his pocket watch. "Well, damn, it looks like we're about there. Let's go out and catch the sights."

It was just before noon, and Cooper's captain was heading the yacht south across Elliott Bay. Cooper led his guests out of the salon and along the port gangway to a large open area on the bow. Coming toward Seattle they had a fine view of the city. Billowy cumulus clouds were forming over the Cascade Mountains in the distance, and it was as if the city were wearing a white halo. Even the busy commerce of ships moving to and from the docks did not intrude on the grandeur of the city rising boldly from the waterfront. The businesses and homes constructed on various levels of terraces pushed up quickly toward the backdrop of the Cascade Mountains. Looking inland, past the essence of the city, the scene was painted with the deep green of dense forests, crowned by glistening snow above the timberline. Dozens of freighters and barges were at the docks or under way; tons of coal were being loaded in one place, while crates were being unloaded in others. Seattle at that time was handling a thousand vessels a year, exporting coal, hops, timber, and fish to the value of $9.2 million annually.

Cooper said, "I am always impressed when we pull into this port. Each time the commerce seems to have doubled, and so has the number of buildings."

Hill, almost wistfully, observed, "I plan to have my railroad coming here. I plan for that soon."

Cooper said, "You'd better hurry, Jim. There's forty-two thousand souls in that city right now, and there ain't much room left for more."

Hill rubbed his beard. "Adam, there's room for more people, and there's room for my railroad. You wait and see."

Cooper said, "Well, I'll keep cutting down the trees to make way for you to come through."

Hill responded, "You'd better, because I'll be here."

Cooper pointed off to the starboard. "Those docks over there are mine."

Cooper's company had two long wharves jutting out from the land; three-sail cargo ships were taking on loads of lumber. Cooper said, "We'll be docking at the Pacific Coast Steamship passenger terminal because that's a better place for Mrs. Duniway to come. I sure don't want her to have to be around those roughnecks who work my docks."

The Pacific Coast *Queen* was taking on passengers for the six-day journey to Sitka in Alaska. With the three-thousand-ton ship at dock, there was little room left for Cooper's boat to pull in to the mooring, but the captain eased in skillfully.

Hill said, "If that captain of yours ever wants a job running a locomotive, let me know; I'd take him on."

Cooper laughed. "He wouldn't be caught dead more than a mile inland, Jim."

As the crew quickly set the lines to the cleats on the wooden wharf, three women came walking briskly out of the terminal building. Cooper said, "Here comes Mrs. Duniway, Jim. Just like always, she's right on time." Then he took Hill's arm and ordered, "You go meet them!" Without another word, he began trotting back along the port gangway.

Hill looked at Zack in confusion. "What the devil is all of this?"

Zack replied with a shrug.

The three women were striding toward the gangplank.

Hill was flustered. He looked at Zack and said, "Do something!" And, with that, Hill spun around and, just as quickly, nearly at a run, followed the route taken by Adam Cooper.

Leah and Zack looked at each other and burst into laughter.

"Why," Leah asked, "aren't you running for cover like the other big, strong men? Doesn't Abigail Duniway strike fear into all males?"

The arriving ladies were being greeted by the boat's captain. Leah led Zack to meet Abigail Scott Duniway. On the way, she said, "Abigail Duniway bears the mantle of leader well. It was her efforts that brought Susan B. Anthony to the Northwest in 1871 for a lecture tour promoting the concept of woman's suffrage. It was a very important moment for all of us, and Miss Anthony has a strong affection for the work that is being done in the Northwest. We can count on Abigail's help."

The women were dressed in long, dark dresses, each with some kind of a shawl, and two of them were wearing wide-brimmed hats. The one hatless was wearing her hair parted in the middle, cut short, and pulled back severely along the sides of her head; she was obviously not inclined toward making herself attractive. She extended her hand to Leah and said, "It is so very nice to see you, Leah. What has happened to the gruff Mister Cooper?"

Leah admitted, "I don't really know, Abigail." She then introduced Zack.

The woman's grip was strong and confident. From the first contact, Zack began to like her.

Abigail turned to look at her companions. "This is Lucy Carr, and this is Babette Gatzert."

Zack had been mumbling his greetings and trying to file the names of the women. He started to speak, but Abigail cut him off. "Where is Mister Hill? We have a tight schedule."

Leah said, "Again, Abigail, I don't know. Let's try the main salon; that's where we had our lunch."

In the salon, Cooper was at the bar pouring a cup of coffee, and Hill was standing by the aft window smoking a cigar and studying the scenery. Both men looked as guilty as children caught in some prohibited act.

"Well, ladies" came from Cooper, doing a poor job of acting surprised.

Mrs. Duniway crossed to Cooper and extended her hand. "You know Lucy and Babs, don't you?"

Cooper smiled broadly as he went to each of the other women and shook their hands. Quickly, too quickly, to cover his discomfort, he introduced Hill to the women. Hill told Mrs. Duniway, "I've been looking forward to meeting you, madam."

Mrs. Duniway returned the salutation politely.

She was not a tall woman, but she was imposing due to her girth; she carried a few more pounds than necessary. Her face was not at all dainty or delicate, but she had a beauty that was accented whenever she was in a confrontation.

She was not above tangling with someone she had just met. When Hill made the error of reminding Mrs. Duniway that he had written to her a month before, offering free train passes to any women working for the suffrage cause, she declared, "I pay my own way on railroads, Mister Hill. I am quite violently against the pass system."

The use of railroad passes by businessmen, journalists, and, most especially, politicians had become an issue in the region. Railroads bestowed the passes as a kind of bribe to gain benefits from other businessmen, to have complimentary stories written in the newspapers, and to capture the votes of public office-holders. The practice would eventually become a major political issue and partially led to the creation of the Interstate Commerce Commission. But in 1888 free passes were still in common use. Immediately Hill saw that Abigail Duniway was not a woman whose favor could be gained by gifts.

Hill burst out in a loud laugh. "Mrs. Duniway, I do like the way you think. I am going to enjoy knowing you."

Adam Cooper offered the ladies refreshments. It was then that it dawned on Zack why Adam Cooper had run back to the salon: all of the whiskey bottles had disappeared.

Mrs. Duniway said, "I can smell your breath all the way over here, Adam, so don't think you can fool us by offering coffee and tea. I'd think a man of your wisdom would be willing to forego the evils of liquor and lead a proper life."

Weakly, Cooper responded, "I was merely providing some light libations for my guests. I couldn't let them drink alone, now, could I?"

Mrs. Duniway mocked a frown and said, "Well, I think it time for us to get to business. I have a difficult schedule this afternoon."

Cooper said, "Let's all just sit down and we can talk it over."

As the ladies made themselves comfortable, Cooper asked, "Abigail, are you pleased that Mister Hill came all this way to meet with you?"

"Well, Mister Cooper, I am satisfied. Incidentally, Sarah Yesler was supposed to be at this meeting; she said she had promised you in a letter." Sarah Yesler was one of the leading suffragettes in Seattle.

Cooper acknowledged, "She did say something to that effect, Abby."

Duniway said "She is indisposed with a spring cold. She sends her regrets." With a sharp look around, she added, "Let us then get on with the business at hand."

The business at hand had possessed Abigail Scott Duniway for the previous twenty years: woman's suffrage. She had come to Oregon as a girl, married, and began raising a family. But the duties of hearth and home were not enough to satisfy her energy, and, with financial and moral backing from her husband, she started a newspaper, the *Northwest News*. Early in her publishing career she began to champion the cause of women's right to vote. Her crusade was quick to find wide support in the region. While the suffrage movement back east had been derided by the majority of citizens there, the mood in the West was considerably different. Women in the East were expected to bear and raise children, attend to housekeeping, and be supportive helpmates to working husbands. Women in the West had generally participated in the long, dangerous journey across the Great Plains and rugged Rocky Mountains, and then, by choice and necessity, helped to clear fields, build homes, and do a multitude of chores formerly reserved to the man in the family. In this social environment, not only were the rights of women accepted but the male electorate worked hard to ensure that women had a say in the way government was run. There were dissenters, powerful dissenters who were mainly reacting to political forces in the East and in the Congress. Congress stoutly resisted moves to enfranchise womanhood partly because of economic pressures from businesses frightened of the women's vote and partly because of the influence of religious leaders, who insisted women must have a servile role if the structure of society was to be maintained. It was toward these dissenters that Abigail Duniway directed her attack.

Mrs. Duniway turned her attention to Jim Hill. "We are expecting some considerable assistance from you, sir."

Hill had been studying the woman as they settled in for the conference, and deemed her a bad adversary but a good ally. Hill said, "Zachary Horton is traveling around the region, running a quiet campaign for the acceptance of statehood."

Mrs. Duniway challenged, "And how will that help our cause?"

Hill said, "I think that statehood will naturally lead to an acknowledgment of the right of women to vote. Zack's efforts should bear fruit for you and your cause."

"I think, Mister Hill," her voice was emphatic, "that you are being a bit too optimistic. We fought for years before we finally forced the Washington Territory legislature to include such a provision in the new constitution in 1883. And then the territorial supreme court, just last year, ruled that the provision was unconstitutional."

Hill came back. "That buttresses my position, Mrs. Duniway: Gain statehood, and those corrupt judges will be removed from office."

Babette Gatzert said, "Judges who are elected can just as easily be corrupt, Mister Hill. The thing that must be done is to amend the federal Constitution, so that our local judges cannot use it to thwart our hopes."

Hill nodded. "I am in complete accord with you. We do need such an amendment to the Constitution."

For the next twenty minutes, the group talked about the strategies the women wanted to see employed. Abigail Duniway, having fought the battle for twenty years, was well versed in who was politically strong in each territory involved in the statehood issue. She had compiled a list of those who would be of assistance.

Lucy Carr and Babette Gatzert both contributed ideas with which Hill agreed.

As the meeting was drawing to a close, and the gentlemen stood up, Mrs. Duniway asked, "Mister Hill, will you see that Miss Page gets all the help she needs? You know the woman is trying to run a business in a world dominated by males. Please do not let me hear that you are asking too much from Leah."

James Hill had some strict personal guidelines, and one of them was to follow hunches, especially hunches that came after serious thought. He had a hunch that Abigail Duniway was not the strident ogre she made a point of seeming to be. He said, "I will do my part, Mrs. Duniway. Just make sure that Miss Page has all that she needs from *you.*"

Mrs. Duniway tried to appear miffed. "You darned men take it on yourselves to be our protectors, and you never give us a chance to stand on our own two feet."

Adam Cooper corrected her. "Now, Abby, that ain't any such thing that Jim is saying. He's just letting you know that we're all on the same side."

Mrs. Duniway would have continued to argue, but she did not want to offend James Hill. He was doing as much as any man and doing it as well as any. She smiled, rose, and went over to Hill. "James Hill, I thank you for your efforts." Then, quietly, in a voice so low that only he could hear, she added, "And thank you for treating Leah so well. I was just acting for the benefit of the other ladies."

Hill inhibited his laugh. He whispered back, "I knew that all along, Mrs. Duniway."

With the ladies seen off the boat, Hill was anxious to take his leave of Adam Cooper. The three men were standing on the forward deck, watching the departees make their way into the passenger terminal building, when Hill said, "Adam, this visit has been informative and productive. I appreciate you taking the time to share your knowledge with us."

Cooper placed a friendly hand on Hill's shoulder as he responded, "Let me tell you one thing, Jim. It is a pleasure to meet a railroad man who has some interests other than skimming off money or watering down stock. I've talked to most of your peers: Collis Huntington, Jay Gould, and even young Billy Vanderbilt. They're all men who'll do anything to squeeze two dollars where there should be only one. I think Henry Villard is probably the worst of the bunch, but, and I'm ashamed to say this, I do business with the man . . . I have to do business with him. I've tried to justify it all, but I know I'm helping him and his damned railroad make money off farmers and other shippers."

Hill looked out over the bay and the activity that was making Seattle and the whole Northwest a frontier that would soon come into its own as a center of commerce. "It pains me," he began, "to see all of this so tightly under Villard's control. But if we're able to gain statehood, we'll be able to break the stranglehold the Northern Pacific has here, and the competition will make life better for all of us."

"Ah!" Cooper said. "That's the essence of the whole thing, Jim: Competition! When we have that there'll be no stopping what we can do."

Cooper then turned to look Zack squarely in the eyes. "And you, my boy, pay attention to James Hill; you can learn a lot from a man like him."

Zack nodded.

Cooper than addressed Leah. "Young lady, I thank you for coming on board. I surely hope we will be seeing more of you in the future."

Leah grinned. "I hope so, too, Mister Cooper." She gave him a quick buss on the cheek.

Cooper smiled and extended his hand to Hill. "I've got to get this old scow sailing up to Vancouver. Unless there is anything else, I think we'd better be casting off."

Hill said, "One thing, Adam."

"What's that?"

"Don't ever tie me up on a boat again. I need to be able to move when I want to, and I never learned how to swim."

▶◆◀

Adam Cooper had made arrangements for them to be taken to the train station, where they spent the forty-one-mile ride back to Tacoma in Cooper's palace railway car. It was more spectacular than Hill's own, but Hill paid little heed to the appointments; his mind was on more important matters.

During the ride south along the rocky, jagged coast, Leah and Zack had chosen comfortable chairs on the observation platform of the car and reviewed the events of the day. Zack had been impressed with Abigail Duniway; he shared with Leah the impression that the suffrage leader was similar to his Grandmother Boynton. "Those two would get along famously," he said. "Abigail would probably enlist Grandma Letta in the movement."

"I only met your grandmother for a short time in Spokane, but I think they're both so dynamic that there would be a conflict." She thought for a moment, then added, "Despite the public view, Susan Anthony and Abigail really do not get along well in private; it's the same situation of two strong personalities."

"What did you think of her, my grandmother?"

Leah gave a snicker. "I think your grandmother is concerned that you are ignoring your personal life too much, that you are . . ." She pondered her next words. "How can I put this?"

Zack looked mildly irritated. "That I am ignoring starting a family?"

Leah shook her head. "Not that extreme."

"She thinks I should be seriously considering getting married."

"I wouldn't say that, Zack."

"I would," he countered. "If you knew how she delivered an impressive list of your attributes, you would be sitting there blushing. To render you on canvas would take a Rembrandt, and in verse would take a Shakespeare."

"Now I am blushing."

"No need to; those thoughts have been expressed about you before."

"By whom?"

"By Del Cummins . . . by Calvin Jones, and . . ." He gave her an amused smile. ". . . by James Hill."

"You're joking with me!"

"I am not!" He showed a mock indignation. "It seems everyone thinks you are a very special lady."

She said, "Let's get off this subject."

"Why?"

"Because it's embarrassing."

They arrived in Tacoma an hour and a half later.

James Hill had made a decision.

He had asked the station manager of the Northern Pacific terminal in Tacoma for the use of a private office; the manager offered his own. The offer was made with some trepidation, because if word slipped out that the owner of the competing Great Northern Railroad was doing business out of Northern Pacific Railroad facilities, the manager's job might be in jeopardy. Hill had assured the man that the use would be strictly personal.

For the first few minutes that Leah, Zack, and Hill were in the office, Hill walked around, looking at route maps and schedules; he was not spying, merely organizing the topic to be addressed.

Finally, he said, "The train for Portland leaves in just over an hour. I was impressed by what Abigail Duniway had to say this afternoon, and I feel it is imperative that we use her experienced wisdom to our benefit."

Zack squirmed; he felt bad news coming.

Hill continued, "Leah, I know that you interrupted your business operations to come to see Del Cummins, and you added to your time away by coming here to Tacoma for me. But I now feel you must accompany me to Portland to talk with some of the people mentioned by Mrs. Duniway. Oregon is a state that has influence in the Congress; you should be able to learn from their politicians."

Leah argued, "I can talk to them in the Congress, Mister Hill. It's an easy trip from Baltimore."

"Congress is in recess. We should get what we need right at the source. We are close, and it will be invaluable."

Zack was thinking that Portland would be as good a place as any to spend time with Leah.

Hill said, "And, Zack, I found a name on Mrs. Duniway's list: Joseph Toole, in Montana. He's the territorial delegate. Looks like a good prospect for support." Hill pulled out his watch. "The train to Montana leaves in thirty minutes."

James Hill was no insensitive person; he saw the injured glances exchanged by the two young people. He had not given any thought to a romantic involvement; maybe none existed. But they were young, and they were full of vitality, so that possibility was not to be denied. But Hill had made major, and sometimes grievous, personal sacrifices when he had been their age, and he knew they would find a way to survive. Still, he did not want to seem the monster they might be envisioning.

He said, "I know I frequently initiate activities which seem impetuous, too urgent, but I don't launch anything without serious consideration. I can guess that you both would like to be shut of your commitment to this blustery old man, but I know that you both strongly believe in what we're doing. So, here's my promise. After this, I will not call on either of you for help for a full month. I do not make promises lightly, even . . ." He paused to get them ready for the joke. ". . . even to my wife."

There were no laughs.

Hill said to Zack, "You'd better get down and pick up your ticket. I'm sure there are Pullman facilities available on that train. And Leah, I think you could go with Zack and see him off. I'll meet you at the restaurant after he leaves."

Leah and Zack sat for a moment, stunned. In later years, they were to remember that their leave-taking in the Tacoma train station was magnificently depressing.

CHAPTER 8

WASHINGTON, D.C.—WINTER 1888–1889

James Hill's scheme to lobby Congress in the matter of state-hood was such a success that he came to regret having had the idea in the first place. As a result of the project, he found himself bound to Sir George and Lady Roberts in a way he had not anticipated; they abandoned their home in Wales and their ranch in Wyoming and ensconced themselves in a Georgetown house that became Hill's de facto headquarters each time he was in the capital.

In addition, his wife, Mary Theresa, was so enthralled by the glamor of the nation's capital that she forced Hill to spend much of his time on the scene. He reminded Mary Theresa that she had, just a few months previously, vigorously declined even to meet with Sir George and Lady Roberts. Mary Theresa coyly told him he was exaggerating; her position was solely against the Archbishop of Canterbury, "and certainly not that lovely Lady Roberts." So the Hills were firmly integrated into the social activities that are a vital part of successful lobbying.

Since Leah's leather-manufacturing plant in Baltimore was a short train ride from the District of Columbia, Leah had become a critical ingredient in the lobbying effort; her charm was an effective camouflage for her ruthless ability to convey the threat of political reprisal from women once universal suffrage became a reality.

And Zack Horton had become a consummate walker of the halls of Congress. Zack had come to know—and be liked by—a substantial number of influential national legislators. Whenever a bill was introduced that concerned agriculture, mining, or railroads, Zack showed up to present points that would further the cause of statehood.

James Hill found a quiet satisfaction in what he considered his most substantial contribution to the issue: the recruiting of Leah and Zack.

It was a well-ordered group that met with Hill in the nation's capital on November 12 of 1888, and it was Leah Page who had organized the tight schedule. She had used the political and legislative knowledge of the National Woman Suffrage Association office; Susan B. Anthony had contributed a full afternoon to Leah and had set down the events that would most effectively reach the legislative elite. It was not Leah Page's fault that James Hill's statehood bandwagon got bogged down in political mud when Grover Cleveland managed to get himself whipped in the presidential election; that was Cleveland's fault.

Cleveland's administration had accomplished a reasonable goal for the nation by seeing the Indians effectively quieted and hidden on reservations. He had not permitted the introduction of the eight-hour workday that all sensible businessmen knew would destroy the economy. Cleveland's failing came in probably being too honest; he frequently piqued the anger of his own party members in the Senate and House of Representatives. When the election tally was finally completed after November 6, it was a startled president who found that although he had collected 5.5 million votes to Benjamin Harrison's 5.4 million votes, he had lost the presidency in electoral votes of 168 to 233. Cleveland had failed to carry the state of New York, where he had once served as governor and where he had received an overwhelming favorite-son vote in 1884; he had also failed to

carry the state of Indiana, whence came his vice president,
Thomas Hendricks. Not even the Mugwumps, a renegade collection of powerful Republicans who had supported Cleveland
in 1884, were able to protect the electoral-college vote, so James
Hill was having to do some quick backfilling to cover his having
given Grover Cleveland a platform the previous Memorial Day
in Minnesota.

It was Zack Horton who had seen the way to salvage Hill's
grand plan. Zack had pointed out that it would not be wise to
blatantly curry favor with Benjamin Harrison while the political
corpse of Grover Cleveland was still warm and in the White
House, but quick telegraph exchanges with Fred Dubois and
Montanan Joe Toole led Zack to Philadelphian John Wanamaker, who was rumored to be named as Harrison's postmaster
general. Dubois also suggested that Zack lead Senator James
Blaine into Hill's fold; Blaine had run a clumsy campaign for
president against Cleveland but was being tagged by President-
Elect Harrison as secretary of state. With the inclusion of Theodore Roosevelt in the cadre of notables, Hill's first social foray
was a success. It was a quiet affair: an afternoon tea at the Fussell
on New York Avenue, on the pretext of introducing Sir George
and Lady Roberts to Washington. Talk had quickly switched
from the appetizing watercress sandwiches to the topic of statehood and, by the end of the afternoon, Wanamaker and Blaine
had committed to the prospect. Over the next three days, eight
similar small socials took place at different locations, all with
similar results.

At the end of November, while political chaos seemed to
be prevailing in the District of Columbia, Zack drew up for Hill
a balance sheet of prospects for the statehood project. The
incoming Republican president would be bolstered in the fif-
tieth Congress by a thirty-nine to thirty-seven majority in the
Senate, even though the Democrats held a 170 to 151 majority
in the House of Representatives. There seemed little doubt that
the statehood issue would be attended to in a prompt fashion.
Hill, however, was not of a mind to leave any room for chance
or to let assumption of victory lessen the final drive. In anticipa-

tion of the Congress convening its session on the first Monday in December, Hill advised Zack to find living quarters in the capital; Zack would be directing Hill's efforts until March 4, when the Congress would recess. Hill also met with the leadership of the National Woman Suffrage Association and pleaded with them to convince Leah Page to establish a base in the District of Columbia for the same period. They agreed, and convinced Leah of the merits of the suggestion. But, Leah refused when the leaders insisted she take up residence in La Fetra's Temperance Hotel on G Street. Hill intervened and said he would rent quarters in the Shoreham, where Zack was also to stay. Leah accepted, but a few suffrage eyebrows rose at the prospect of a single woman residing in a splendid hotel in that sinful city. Leah pointed out that the suffrage movement needed to abandon Puritanical strictures if women were to reach any level of equality. Further, she pointed out, the year previously, four women residing in La Fetra's had been sent packing due to unexplained pregnancies.

At a considerable expense, Hill rented a one-bedroom suite for Leah and had three rooms in the Shoreham modified into an apartment for Zack that would provide two bedrooms and a comfortable parlor. The second bedroom was reserved for Del Cummins, who would be in the capital frequently to confer with Zack on the operations of the Dakota and Western. Hill's family physician, Dr. William James Mayo, of Rochester, Minnesota, said Del's leg had fully recovered from the surgery he had performed to correct the damage inflicted in the Idaho mud slide. For Del, travel was not a problem. His major concern was the planning of his wedding, scheduled for just after Easter.

Hill was not really sure he was pleased when Sir George and Lady Roberts announced that after going to Wales for Christmas, they would leave on Boxing Day to return to the capital. That return had not been planned or expected; Hill never liked being presented with a fait accompli.

Their decision had been reached for two reasons, one public and the other personal. A delegation of Wyoming ranchers on their own lobbying excursion implored Sir George to continue working for Wyoming's statehood, and he accepted. The personal element had to do with the Smithsonian Institution. It had been endowed by a fellow Welshman, James Smithson, in 1829. Smithson had never visited the United States, but he had been so impressed with the country's democratic principles that he wanted to do something "for the increase and diffusion of knowledge among men." He had bequeathed $535,000 for the establishment of the institution. Lady Roberts had been invited to be an advisor to the institution, and felt obligated to her countryman to see his gift to the republic appropriately handled.

They went home as planned, then returned. The trip back was an adventure. The Robertses made the crossing on the Cunard Line's *City of Paris,* a dazzling, steam-powered ship with an impressive twenty-knot speed. They arrived back in the United States on January 12, 1889.

The Roberts residence was on Stoddard Street in Georgetown, just a few minutes' carriage ride from the British Embassy near Dupont Circle on N Street NW.

On their return, Lady Roberts immediately launched herself into the frantic pace of events. She had spent some of her eight days on the *City of Paris* working out the social schedule. On Thursday night, the fourteenth, she hosted a dinner for the group she was beginning to think of as "my colonial family"—a well-taken sentiment on her part—the Hills, Leah, Zack, and Del Cummins. After that dinner, they had a strategy meeting. Zack announced that the session of the House of Representatives the next day might turn out to be pivotal; the statehood issue was scheduled for debate.

James Hill was concerned that Zack had waited until the dinner to break the news; Hill and Mary Theresa had arrived only that afternoon. Zack explained that the debate schedule had only been announced at adjournment that day. Leah read off the list of scheduled speakers, and Zack reported on the inclinations of critical congressmen and how they would probably vote.

Sir George reported that he had lunched at the Hancock

restaurant on Pennsylvania Avenue with Ambassador Morton Hobart and Senators George Hearst and Derrick Daniels. The senators predicted that the statehood issue would not be resolved in the current sitting of Congress. Hill groused that the elected politicians seemed to "take their own good time" in addressing the nation's problems. Sir George said he had invited Hearst and Daniels to a supper party planned for Saturday night at the Roberts residence; Hill would have an opportunity at that time to go into action.

Hill broke the evening off early, and Leah, Zack, and Del left to go back to the Shoreham shortly after eight. The next morning, Friday the fifteenth, Leah and Zack were at breakfast by 7:30; Del had left early on an errand for Lady Roberts.

Leah could not inhibit a giggle as she noted, "Zack, your Irishman has found kindred Celtic spirits in the Robertses. I imagine he will be insisting that Felicity go to Mount Snowdon on her honeymoon."

Zack grinned. "That man is really putting a lot into all this. Even with his game leg, he's moving around the Dakota and Western route. And the trips back here to brief me have to be demanding."

Leah noted, "He has a deep affection for you; the pair of you really are like brothers."

Zack was savoring a cup of the Shoreham's hot chocolate, and he replied with a warm smile. Leah went back to eating her eggs and studying the list of speakers. She did not lift her eyes as she asked, "What about Cox?"

Zack concentrated on buttering a slice of toast. "Cox is going to do a good job."

"I think I know that," Leah challenged. "Will he swing many votes?"

Zack smiled at her. "Samuel Cox has been in Congress as a representative from Ohio once and from New York twice! The man has chits out that he can pick up from all over the House."

"Will he use them for this?"

"I've promised him a meeting with Mister Hill tonight;

that might be enough to give Congressman Cox the proper motivation. I think he'd like to see Mister Hill do something about the rates for shipping grain to Buffalo."

Leah scoffed, "James Hill won't do that."

Zack shrugged. "All I can do is bring them together. Cox is a hell of a talker."

Leah laughed. "You are wicked, Zack Horton."

He offered another shrug.

Leah and Zack had developed a sound business relationship. Leah concentrated on any aspect of social import, the ramifications of child labor, education, and women's suffrage, and the congressmen who would react to such issues. Zack aimed specifically at those openly declared legislators who could help accelerate the schedule for voting. That had been Hill's primary goal: "Get the vote quickly."

Only once during the months of working together had their association led them into anything more than business dealings. On New Year's Eve they had agreed to celebrate together at the Shoreham's gala. They had finished dinner by 8:30, they danced and enjoyed champagne.

They made a handsome couple on the dance floor, but at ten minutes to eleven all came to a halt. A hotel bellboy approached their table and whispered to Zack that he was needed in the lobby. Zack and Leah followed the bellboy out and found Del about two drinks past his limit, in a lounge chair, unable to get to his feet; his bad leg had given out on him. Leah and Zack spent the remainder of their evening with Del at the Georgetown University Clinic in the care of the Shoreham's physician. By the time Del could again walk, it was 2:30 in the morning, and the earlier mood had been washed away by the antiseptic atmosphere of the clinic. Leah and Zack were not of a disposition to do anything more than head for their own rooms.

That memory came back to Zack as he looked across the table at Leah.

Leah said, "I have an appointment at the Pension Building this morning; one of the supervisors there has a list showing the voting records of each senator and congressmen on the various pension bills. We might be able to use that." Congressional pensions granted to citizens in dire need were the precursor of the Social Security program, which was beginning to evolve in the minds of national legislators.

Zack nodded. He had learned that any collection of data on voting patterns was useful; he had spent weeks organizing similar information that Fred Dubois had provided. Zack was, in fact, scheduled to meet Dubois later that morning to pick up records pertaining to railroads that had just been made available by the Department of Commerce. He told her his plans, then, impulsively, he reached across the table and set his hand down on hers.

It was a platonic gesture, one of friendship, a moment of contact with a fellow worker. He said, "I know what Sir George said last night about this going on longer, but I think we're near the end of our road, Leah."

She offered him a warm smile. "You're right, Zack. I know you're right."

"It might be over today."

"I think so, too."

They spent a long moment looking at each other; they both felt a pang of regret that their time together might be coming to a close. Zack brought his hand back and stood up. As he folded his napkin, he said, "Try and be there by eleven o'clock. Things should be rolling by then."

She was gathering her purse and cloak. "Save me a seat?"

"I sure will."

◀◆◆◆◆◆◀

CHAPTER 9

The bell of the sergeant at arms began to have an insistent sound, as if its vigor would hurry the tardy members to their seats. James Hill was still wearing his overcoat, although Zack had left his earlier in Fred Dubois' office. Hill was stroking his beard, studying Dubois as they walked, wondering if this modest-looking man in the simple brown suit was strong enough to go into that chamber and do battle for the sake of tens of thousands of people. Earlier, in Dubois' office, Dubois had told Hill that the debate would be decisive; this would be the big confrontation. As they walked to the cloakroom near the entrance to the chamber, Hill regretted not having done more. He voiced that feeling, and Fred Dubois observed that no man could have done more than Hill. But the words had not quieted Hill's apprehension; a historic moment was upon the United States.

"I'd better go," Dubois said as the bell continued to ring. "I'll see you later."

With that, Hill and Zack were alone. "Dammit, Zack, I hope we've won."

Zack said, "I talked with Joe Toole earlier and he is ready."

"I want to meet that man. I should have done so much earlier than this. Will you see to that, Zack? Marc Daly told me the people of Montana Territory put great trust in Joe Toole."

Zack replied, "We'll dine with him at Sir George's tonight. Fred Dubois is coming, too."

"Well, let's get where we can watch this." Hill started taking off his coat as Zack led the way to the west staircase up to the viewing gallery. They had taken only two steps up when Hill came to a halt, staring up ahead. Over the first landing hung a gigantic oil painting. Hill said, "Good Lord, Zack, that's Leutze's *Westward Ho*. It is certainly some sort of an omen."

Zack smiled and continued the climb. Hill paused, studying the painting, wondering if he should commission a copy for his private collection. The bell ringing stopped. He hurried after Zack.

The Hall of Representatives was large: 139 feet long and 93 feet wide, with a ceiling 36 feet high inset with glass panels that provided most of the light for the room. By the time Zack and Hill reached their seats, the mace—a throwback to Congress' parliamentary ancestry—had been set in place to the right of the Speaker, and the prayer was in progress.

Waiting in the front row of the gallery were the Robertses with Mrs. Hill. Leah had not yet arrived. The gallery was sparsely occupied. Less than a hundred of the twenty-five hundred seats were in use.

As soon as the "Amen" was pronounced, Hill moved to his seat between Sir George and Mary Theresa. Zack left a seat open between his own and Lady Roberts'. "For Leah," he whispered.

"Of course," Lady Roberts acknowledged.

Hill leaned over and said in a normal voice, "No sense whispering. They couldn't hear you if they had to."

He was right. Down on the floor of the hall, before the chaplain had even left his podium, a din rose as the members began the legislative day. There was talking, arguing, shouting, all at the same time—and the Speaker had not even begun his duties. There were 325 seats for members and another 8 seats for nonvoting delegates from the territories. The members were divided by a center aisle: Democrats on one side, Republicans on the other. The four delegates deeming themselves Mugwumps or Independents were seated at the rear of the hall, split equally at the far sides.

James Hill patted Mary Theresa's hand. "My dear, we are watching history being made."

His wife smiled. "James, I have prayed that things go well for you on this matter."

"Thank you, my dear."

"You've worked hard."

"We've all worked. Now the die is cast, and we'll see what comes."

What came first was an immediate battle over how the debate was going to be conducted. The procedural arguments raged with what seemed to be an underlying current of good-nature, but Hill was not pleased. He leaned in Zack's direction. "Good God, does this happen all the time?"

Zack answered, "I try to spend as little time here as possible but each time I've been here, it's been much the same."

"It's a sin," Hill said, and Sir George had the decided impression that Hill was referring to the mortal category of sin.

Sir George commented, "James, if it will make you feel any better, Parliament in London is much worse."

Hill scowled. "No wonder we get bad laws to rule our lives."

Finally, Samuel Cox, the gentleman from New York, was acknowledged by a casual nod from the Speaker. Cox moved to the podium and, after preliminary remarks about the lengthy argument, he began.

"Congress has been derelict with respect to the admission of these Territories. For reasons which can not be given within the hour, but reasons which appeal to the discretion of gentlemen, I ask that these Territories be admitted. There is a sort of glamour and fascination about the admission of States into our imperial federation. I am subject to the influences of a romantic character. In the dim outline the ancient seers saw, through the mists of western seas, our hemisphere as the home of a race which rejoiced in a 'golden age.' These dreams take hold upon the imagination. They give an illusion to our 'discretion' on bills like these looking to future empire."

Zack was analyzing James Hill's reaction; Hill seemed to be listening with rapt attention.

Cox turned from his speech and reached down for a glass of water waiting on the table behind him. Hill glanced at Zack and gave a slight nod of appreciation. Zack agreed; Cox was an orator of the first order.

Cox went into some of the legal technicalities surrounding admission of states. He referred to the fourth article of the Constitution—"New states may be admitted by the Congress into this Union"—and the 1787 Enabling Act. He was greeted by cheers when he quoted the sixty-thousand-inhabitant figure and added that all of the territories being considered had satisfied that stipulation. He quoted a British writer who had stated, "If it were possible under the Federal Constitution to admit Territorial residents to active citizenship—that is to say, to Federal suffrage—admitted they would be. But the Union is a union of States. . . . The only means of granting Federal suffrage to citizens in a Territory would be to turn the Territory into a State. . . . But it would do still more. It would entitle this possibly small and rude community to send two Senators to the Federal Senate who would there have as much weight as the two Senators from New York, with its 6,000,000 of people."

Cox used that quote to lead into the Congress' duty to face up to the dilution of power. "But after all, sir, whatever may be said or done in the last resort on this question of statehood, the admission of States depends upon the wise discretion of Congress." He pleaded that party bias be laid to rest and that his colleagues not make one admission contingent upon another simply because they had opposing party identifications. For the next half hour he recited facts and figures to establish the eligibility of the territories being considered for admission. Then he pleaded, "The spirit of this people of the Northwest is that of unbounded push and energy. These are the men who have tunneled our mountains, who have delved our mines, who have bridged our rivers, who have brought every part of our empire within the reach of foreign and home markets."

Cox lightened up for the next few minutes and provoked several outbreaks of laughter. Then he paused for an emphatic moment and related the impressions of a writer who had looked at the western part of the nation: "What Europe is to Asia, what England is to the rest of Europe, that the Western States and Territories are to the Atlantic States. The heat and pressure and hurry of life, always growing, is that following the path of the sun."

He was awarded with robust applause.

James Hill was smiling, and Sir George said, "That was rather impassioned."

Hill said, "He made the point, too. By God, he made the point."

Zack leaned over. "Wait until you hear Joe Toole."

Hill looked up at the large clock over the Speaker's chair and asked, "When will he speak?"

Zack pulled out the schedule Fred Dubois had supplied. "The Dakota presentation is next; it could take an hour."

Hill said, "I want to get out of here for a bit; does anyone want to come?"

Sir George said, "Not me; I'm fascinated." Lady Roberts and Hill's wife agreed that they wanted to remain. Hill nodded, Zack led the way, and Hill was lighting a cigar even before he reached the stairs.

At the base of the stairs, they met Leah Page running in, panting. "Have I missed it all?"

Hill told her, "No, Miss Page, you did miss a splendid speech by a man named Cox, but there is more to come."

She explained that she had been delayed at the Pension Building. Zack accepted the envelopes she offered and said they were going to try to see Dubois. "Do you want to come?"

Leah shook her head. "I want to go listen; this has been too long in coming to miss."

Hill smiled. "Any reward you get, Miss Page, is coming to

you well earned." She thanked him, gave a wink to Zack, and bounded up the stairs.

Hill watched her depart, then said, "Zack, my boy, you ought to think about marrying that woman. She will make a fine wife."

"Sir, there is nothing further from my mind right now; there is too much to do."

Hill hesitated and ran Zack's words through again; Hill hated a toady and wondered if Zack had suddenly become one. He finally decided that Zack had been revealing his honest feelings; there had been a time in Hill's own life when he had felt that way. He gave a fatherly pat to Zack's shoulder and said, "Let's find some coffee before we look for Dubois."

Zack said he knew a restaurant down in the basement.

Once in the basement they walked along the corridors, past meeting rooms of the Committee on Indian Affairs and the Committee on Waterways and Canals and a half-dozen other groups that seemed to have been relegated to the basement in political as well as physical ways. It was not as if that area was unattractive; there were frescoes on the walls depicting various national resources, and they were "quite well done," according to Hill's artistic eye.

The restaurant they chose happened to be one of the less elaborately decorated, although that white-walled, wooden-floored room was enhanced with framed oil paintings on the walls. A large canvas by Powell depicted Perry's victory on Lake Erie, and there were two smaller portraits, one of Jefferson by d'Angers and one of Hamilton by Stone. While the restaurant did not have the extravagant style one might expect, Zack noted, "It must have something. There's Senator Hearst."

Hill and Zack paused a moment for the waiter to come and show them to a table. Hearst called, "You, there. Horton, isn't it?"

Zack was momentarily flattered by the recognition, and then he realized he was standing with James Hill of railroad fame; a politician such as Hearst would remember Zack's association with Hill. Hearst made a sign that they were to come and join him, alone at the table situated just below the booming cannon of Admiral Perry.

As they sat, Hearst was profuse in his expression of pleasure at seeing Hill. He then turned to Zack. "Well, Horton, I haven't seen you since we were all covered in mud." He burst out into a throaty laugh.

Zack forced a smile; Hearst had been nowhere near when the mud slide happened, but Zack guessed being a party to a disaster might help the public image of a politician.

The waiter came and quickly produced cups of coffee; the conversation moved naturally to the matter being debated upstairs. Hearst repeated his opinion that the issue of statehood was going to languish for quite a while in the legislature. "We add amendments and send it back to the House, then they change it and send it to us; it's like a very slow game of lawn tennis." Again, the booming laugh.

Zack would normally have deferred to James Hill, but Zack had paid his dues on this project. He demanded, "Senator, what amendments? This issue has been in legislation for eleven years."

Hearst presented his reply to Hill, almost as if to put Zack in his proper place. "Things keep coming up, Jim. Some items are political and some are legal; this big a piece of lawmaking is not a simple matter."

James Hill caught Hearst's slight of Zack. He looked away from the senator as he said, "Zack, it seems our politicians are playing new games."

Zack said to Hearst, "Senator, forget what Mister Hill has been doing to help this cause; forget the efforts of the people who believe in statehood. But remember nearly two million Americans who are disenfranchised, who live under the rule of outsiders, who have broken their backs to build a great addition to this nation. What about them when you allow frivolous distractions to delay admission?"

Hearst was not used to being challenged by ordinary citizens. Even if they were associated with James Hill of the Great Northern Railroad. Hearst saw he had better change his tack.

"Horton, you're right; the Congress has been messing around. I'm working to change that. I don't see how I can do much good, but I'm trying."

Hill then asked, "What can we do to hurry this thing along, senator?"

Hearst went into a long-winded monologue on the intricacies of national politics. In his recitation, he complimented Zack's efforts and methods. When Hearst paused to collect new thoughts, Hill jumped in. "We must be getting back upstairs. I don't want to forget why we're here."

Hearst rose with them and offered his hand. "I will do anything I can, Jim. Trust me."

Hill smiled unwillingly. On the way back up to the gallery, Hill said, "Zack, I am sorry that I've put you in with this pack of oral jackals; these past few months must have been hell for you."

Zack did not respond. Indeed, it had been a misery to try to communicate in a language translated into crafty rhetoric.

When they arrived back at their seats, Joe Toole was already speaking.

Zack took his place next to Leah Page. "Did we miss much?"

Leah did not take her eyes away from the spectacle below. "He is marvelous. A great speaker." Then, with annoyance in her voice, "But look at them!"

Down on the floor, there was little attention being directed to Toole as he delivered his speech. Clusters of members stood around the chamber; talk was incessant. Some individuals were reading newspapers, and others were lounging against the walls near the exit doors.

Leah told Zack, "He presented a beautiful litany of wrongs that have been done to the territories; he's not speaking for Montana, he's pleading for the whole Northwest. Zack, he's wonderful!"

Toole's voice boomed across the floor: "We are twenty-four years old, out of debt, of sound integrity, and good citizens. We are a Republic of States and not of Territories and yet we are fringed by despotism. Professions of sympathy no longer assuage us, and no amount of insincerity will hereafter put us aside."

The mob of legislators began to quiet, to listen.

"We remember that 'sending hither a swarm of officials,' et cetera, was one of the causes which led to our Declaration of Independence. From that day to this carpetbaggers have always been odious, and their presence amongst us is and ever will be as poisonous and destructive to good government as the insidious growth of communism."

There was a ripple of applause and laughter from the audience.

"Tradition informs us that the wise men all came from the East; and so our Republican friends, unwilling to depart from the teaching of the past, determined that history should repeat itself, and proceeded to treat us in their own good time to a fine assortment of imported political dudes."

Those congressmen who had been waiting near the exits now began to drift back to their seats. Talk had nearly ceased; people were paying attention to Joe Toole.

"But under the Democratic supremacy we find that quite an invasion has been made upon what was supposed to be an inflexible fact. Instead of the wise men coming from the East, we now learn that they come from the South. Kentucky furnished us a governor; Tennessee a chief justice; Louisiana an associate justice and surveyor general; Texas an associate justice, and Mississippi, Maryland, and Tennessee each an Indian agent. If there is a warm spot in my heart, it beats for the generous and courageous South. I never knew one of her sons who could not be touched by the recital of a wrong, or who would not respond promptly to the call of duty."

There was a wave of warm applause. Then Toole pointed out that Montana had its own men to fill important civic positions, that outsiders were not needed. The applause and cheers were growing; the entire house was emotionally moving to Toole's side.

"These are briefly some of the wrongs and hardships im-

posed upon us by the provisional government established in the
Territories. . . . Obviously there is but one remedy—place in the
galaxy of States; a star on the flag; a vote and voice in both
branches of Congress. Without it there is nothing but political
insomnia and internal unrest."

Toole enumerated the accomplishments of Montana Territory. Then he added, "I want to go on record as a warm
advocate of the section of this bill which provides for the admission of other Territories whenever they shall have reached a
population sufficient to entitle them to a Representative in
Congress. . . . In this connection, there come crowding into my
memory these oft repeated and much appreciated lines:

"What constitutes a State?
"Not high-raised battlements or labored mound,
"Thick wall or moated gate,
"Not cities proud with spires and turrets crowned,
"Not bays and broad-armed ports,
"Where laughing at the storm rich navies ride;
"Not starred and spangled courts,
"Where low-browed baseness wafts perfume to pride;
"No! Men, high-minded men,
"With powers as far above dull brutes endured,
"In forest, brake or glen,
"As beasts excel cold rocks and brambles rude;
"Men who know their duties know,
"But know their rights; and knowing dare maintain.

"Upon this important question I beg of you to make no
mistake. Do not dam up the river of progress. Do not obstruct
the march of American manhood towards the destiny contem-
plated by the Constitution . . . rest assured that the wisdom and
patriotism of our course will be vindicated by the deliberate
judgment of mankind."

As Toole stepped away from the podium, the reaction was
immediate and loud: applause and cheers. The members were
now giving Joe Toole their best accolade: their respect.

In the gallery hugs and laughter were the order of reaction; Zack spotted a couple of tears working their way down Lady Roberts' face as he tried to keep Leah Page from toppling over the railing.

Leah was near tears. "Zack, this is it, isn't it? He really did it!"

"I think so."

Suddenly Zack's right hand was grabbed by Sir George, who said, "Fine job, young man! You have done a lot to bring us to this moment."

James Hill had compromised his normally staid behavior by a public embrace with Mary Theresa, but then he also went to Zack. The firmness of his handshake and his gaze of appreciation said it all. Zack was suddenly yanked away from the Hill handshake by Leah Page, who took Zack's face gently with her two hands and delivered a kiss to his mouth.

Shaken, Zack scolded, "Hey, remember where we are."

"What better place?" came from James Hill.

Leah said, "I cannot think of a single one, Mister Hill; Zack has done an excellent job."

"No question."

Zack, embarrassed, said, "It's not a law yet!"

Sir George offered, "I've seen politicians at work, Zack, and those men down there are announcing their intentions. The victory is won."

Hill placed an arm around Sir George's shoulder. "It seems you'll be able to head back to Wales."

Sir George shook his head. "Only part of the battle is won, James; Wyoming is not part of the bill. I intend to stay and see that accomplished."

Hill asked, "Zack, will you be here to help?"

Then Hill waited for a reply. There was a moment, just a hair of a moment when Zack felt a radical change in Hill's attitude. While not acknowledging Zack as a full peer, Hill had elevated him a few steps up the ladder of acceptance on the grand scale. Hill said, "Zack, do you want to stay and see it through?"

Zack began to give his agreement, but he knew that Hill was expecting a considered response. He said, "I'd like to think about that, Mister Hill."

Hill was pleased. He said, "We'll talk about that at dinner."

Sir George added, "And a grand dinner it will be. In celebration, Freda will do something very special."

▶◆◆◆◆◆◀

CHAPTER 10

The Robertses' brownstone house on Stoddard Street was a
narrow building three stories tall. The property ran through to
West Street, which allowed for a small garden at the back of the
house. The dining room faced the garden and, on a clear day,
offered a view of the Potomac River and beyond it the rising
knoll at Arlington National Cemetery.

The meal presented by Lady Roberts was indeed special:
Chesapeake Bay oysters, beef Wellington, and for dessert a rich,
elaborate trifle. Fred Dubois and Joe Toole had, naturally, been
the focus of attention and, because the table conversation had
centered on the events of the day, there was a break with custom
and the ladies stayed at table for coffee after dessert.

Dubois supplied some insight to the comments he had
overheard on the floor while Toole was delivering his speech;
Toole, after much prompting, repeated some of his more dramatic passages.

When Sir George made the pointed observation that while
the wine and champagne had been excellent with dinner, he was
becoming anxious over the delay in service of the port, Lady

Roberts said, "As much as I enjoy the company of our gentlemen, I am afraid I really cannot ignore all rules of etiquette; we ladies will retire to the parlor while you men may adjourn to George's library."

Zack was looking forward to a relaxed half hour with the men, the cigars, and Sir George's port. Across the table, Del Cummins was staring at Zack; the look carried a hint that Del would like something harder to drink. Zack asked, "Sir George, were you able to bring any of that Welsh potheen with you?"

Sir George gave a sly look around the table. "I say, potheen is quite illegal; all of you know that."

Zack grinned. "But Del would probably enjoy some."

"Ah." Del gave a serious look. "I would be taking a nip of that, Sir George."

Sir George smiled. "I may have some for medicinal purposes; would that do, Del?"

Del beamed.

Leah had been enjoying the companionship and conversation, and the fact that she had had both wine and champagne was not hurting her mood. She stood and tapped a spoon on the water goblet in front of her. "I have a toast."

She lifted her champagne glass, which was still half full.

Sir George forced amazement to his voice. "Good heavens, Miss Page, toasting is not a woman's role."

Leah's lips spread in a wide, happy smile. "Sir George, I do not think a woman's role is to be subjected to the insults and verbal abuse of a man like Grover Cleveland, either. But I was subjected to that. I've earned the right to violate some other norms."

Lady Roberts clapped her hands lightly. "Splendid, my dear, splendid!"

Leah paused, then asked, "Where is old walrus-face Cleveland lately?"

Fred Dubois said, "Our illustrious president is making himself scarce. He has to pass the mantle of power in a couple of weeks, and I wouldn't be surprised if he does not show up for Harrison's inauguration."

Joe Toole said. "The man is really bitter about winning the vote but losing the election."

Leah quipped, "Well . . . he deserved what he got!"

Everyone was smiling at her vehemence. She lifted her glass again and said, "Enough about that lout; I have a more important matter." She looked around the table at the guests and sensed what Lady Roberts had meant when she referred to them as a family; there was that sort of a bond. She turned to look at Zack. "To Zachary Horton, a hard worker and a man who gets things done."

"Excellent!" came from James Hill, who rose with the other men; Dubois and Toole parroted Sir George's "Hear! hear!" Del Cummins looked across the table with a fraternal smile as he raised his glass to Zack.

Zack, for his part, felt a blush rising up his neck. He was mildly upset with Leah, but he was also pleased; she had sounded sincere.

Lady Roberts said, "That was very nice, my dear, but"— she rose from her chair—"we simply must leave the gentlemen to their port and cigars."

Leah stated, "I want some."

They all looked at her. She explained, "I want some port; I love port."

Lady Roberts broke into a laugh. "Child, you are breaking the mold this evening, aren't you?"

"I've earned it."

A smile came to Lady Roberts' face. "You certainly have. You shall have your glass of port."

Fred Dubois said, "I think I should tell you that we're due for a surprise in about . . ." He looked at the clock on the mantel over the dining-room fireplace. ". . . twenty minutes. I just thought I'd tell you."

Lady Roberts offered, "Mister Dubois, surprises are becoming the custom in my home. There is little left that will shock me."

Dubois did not respond. The men chatted as they moved toward the library, and Lady Roberts began guiding Mary

Theresa into the parlor. Leah Page took Zack's arm and said, "Get us some port. I want to go outside."

Zack looked at her in confusion. She was dressed in a green velvet gown decorated with soft pink flowers along the bodice and down to the waist. Her shoulders were bare, her hair was brushed loose and full, and her face radiated contentment. She had always been attractive to him, but as he looked at her, her eyes were showing a dimension deeper than beauty; she was proud.

Zack shared her pride; she had been through more than had been expected. He also felt a twinge of guilt, because there had been times when he had been short and gruff with her. He said, "You'll freeze."

She replied, "I'll get a wrap, but I am going outside . . . with you!"

Obediently, he bowed and said, "I shall get us some port."

It had begun snowing earlier that day, about halfway through Joe Toole's speech. It was a light snow, but it had continued for several hours, and now the garden behind the Robertses' house showed an inch and a half of white blanket. The bushes wore a lacy canopy, and the birdbath sat like a chalky mushroom out of season.

The sky was clear, but the air was cold, even though there was no wind. Zack waited with the two glasses of port for a couple of minutes before Leah arrived. As she came down the three steps to the garden, she said, "I had the worst time convincing Lady Roberts that I'd be safe."

Zack replied, "You might freeze to death, but you'll die quite safe, Miss Page."

She crossed the short distance to where he waited. He extended a glass to her, but she ignored the offer and leaned forward to kiss him on the mouth. It was no sibling or friendly buss; it was a long, involved, serious delivery. Zack became flustered by the handicap of holding two glasses of port and was just about to drop them to the snowy ground when she abruptly broke free.

He charged, "You inhibited me with these glasses."

"I'm no fool, Mister Horton. I guess that you probably would have tried to maul and fondle me."

"You are probably right in your probably guess."

"I'll have my drink now, please."

"What's all this about?"

"I felt like doing it and I did. Anything wrong with that?"

"This seems to be your night to flout all the rules."

"Not all of them."

He handed her the port, and she sipped it delicately, then asked, "Did you bring the cigars?"

"Come on, Leah." He chuckled. "You're going too far."

"Do you have the cigars?"

He reached into his pocket and pulled out his leather cigar case. She asked him to light one for her, "because I'm not good at getting them started." She looked at his leather cigar case. "I remember," she said, "when I first saw that case. It was, let's see . . . about a hundred years ago, wasn't it, Zack?"

"At least that long."

She held his glass of port while he lighted a pair of small cigars. When he had handed one to her, she took a deep puff and blew the smoke into the night air.

He observed, "I've never kissed anyone who had just smoked a cigar."

She cocked her head and said, "You might continue that record."

"That means there will be no more kisses?"

"We'll see."

A silence came between them. Without a conscious decision, they strolled to the back of the garden, where an iron fence edged the sidewalk of P Street. There was a soft haze above the ground; streetlights and light coming from house windows gave the snow a luminous hue.

"It's been a special day, Zack."

"We did a good job, Leah. It's been fun."

"Are you staying here in Washington?"

"I think I will, just to see it through."

"I talked with Mrs. Anthony today; she wants me to take

on another project. Some problems in headquarters. But I simply cannot stay away from my business any longer. We're filling the spring orders now."

"Baltimore is not that far from here."

"Will you come there if you have the chance?"

"Would you like that?"

Her eyes and smile gave her reply.

"I'll be there when I can," he said.

She turned to him, and he leaned forward and kissed her. She came against him softly; he was still encumbered with his own glass of port, but he held her tightly with his other arm. Her free hand came up to his neck, and her soft fingers touched his chin and cheek; somehow the fingers were still warm. He was just about to toss the glass away when a call came, "Hey, Zack!"

It was Del Cummins, standing at the rear door of the house.

They broke their embrace. Del called again, "Zack . . . Leah."

She whispered, "He can't see us; don't call back."

"I see you back there. You've got to come in."

"Damn."

"Dammit."

"Hurry," Del ordered.

Leah looked at Zack. "I guess we've been caught out."

He smiled. "Let's go see what the urgency is."

"They probably want you to go off to Africa or some other place."

They started back to the house. He said, "I think they're not going to send me anywhere. I've come up with some of my own goals; new goals."

"Do those goals include one about me?"

"You bet there's one; more than just one."

Del saw them approaching. He called, "It's cold as hell out here, isn't it?"

Under her breath, Leah said, "I'm not at all cold."

Zack laughed.

When they made their way to the parlor, all of the dinner

guests were there—and so was President-Elect Benjamin Harrison.

Zack said to Leah, "So this was Dubois' surprise."

"I'd say so."

Harrison was standing in the middle of the parlor, listening to James Hill. Leah studied the president-elect. If Grover Cleveland is a walrus, she thought, Benjamin Harrison is a penguin. He stood only five feet six inches tall and was wearing white tie and tails. But, she thought, he's a nicer-looking man than Cleveland; at least Harrison's eyes look warmer, more understanding.

"Ah, Zack, come over here." James Hill made an impatient gesture.

Harrison's hair was greying blond, early for a man of fifty-five; his beard was neatly trimmed. As Zack approached, he wished he had not tossed his cigar into the snow, for Harrison was handling a large Havana. With introductions out of the way, Harrison, in his deep, mellow voice, said, "Everyone is telling me you played a major role in this statehood matter, Mister Horton; congratulations are in order."

"I did little more than help the others put some pieces together, Mister Harrison."

Hill offered, "But important pieces. I'm quite proud of Zack."

Harrison was paying strict attention to each word; he was a politician. He said, "I, for one, want to extend my thanks to you, Mister Horton. I can guarantee you that as soon as I am put in office, I will see that the statehood issue is resolved rapidly."

"That'll be appreciated by a great many people, sir."

Harrison laughed, then said, "They'll be served in this matter. I'll see to that."

Zack said, "All of the others worked just as hard. Sir George and Lady Roberts were quite instrumental. And Del Cummins as well."

The Robertses were standing beside Harrison. Lady Roberts said, "Now, Zack, you stop that silliness. We did very little."

Sir George inserted, "But it was bashing good fun."

Zack turned and motioned Leah forward. "And Miss Page did more than any of us."

Hill said, "Quite so. Leah, come over here."

As she started across the room, Harrison said quietly, "This would be the suffrage woman."

Hill nodded. "Right."

Harrison offered, "She might not think too much of me."

Leah arrived and was introduced. "Young lady, I hear the nation owes you a vote of thanks."

Leah smiled and extended her hand; Harrison was tickled to see she was half hiding a cigar in her left hand. Zack wondered how she had managed to hold on to it during their kissing session.

"Let me offer you this, Miss Page. After the inauguration, if you want to talk, please know that I am obligated to you. I know Miss Anthony well, and I have extended the same invitation to her."

Leah offered her thanks, and he turned back to talk to the others. It occurred to her that the man was not popular enough to get a majority of votes, but was politically astute enough to carry the electoral college and become president. Maybe there was more to him that she had imagined. He was, she knew, the grandson of President William Harrison; maybe suffrage would do well in his administration.

Harrison was asking Sir George about Wyoming. Sir George said, "Well, Mister Harrison, Miss Page was out there; she saw the general mood."

Harrison asked her about the territorial legislature's law forbidding foreign ownership of large ranches. Leah replied, "Yes, sir, they did do that; it was an emotional reaction to very large sums of money coming into their territory. But they also did give women the vote. That was not emotional. That was simply the right thing to do."

Harrison gave a deep laugh. "Yes, Miss Page, I am aware of that."

Lady Robert interrupted, "Mister Harrison, would you like some coffee?"

He accepted.

As Harrison walked toward the sideboard with Lady Roberts, Leah nudged Zack unobtrusively. When he looked at her, she gave a minuscule nod as if to say, Let's go back outside.

He thought: We do have some unfinished business.

James Hill caught the subtle exchange and said, "Zack, I think that's all we need right now. If you and Leah want to get some fresh air again, I can see no reason to stop you."

Harrison was coming back, juggling a cup and saucer along with his cigar. Zack gave Hill a quick nod and eased away, with Leah following.

They stopped in the dining room while Zack went into the library to refill their glasses with port.

Zack came smoothly into the dining room, miming the actions of a proficient waiter. "Madam," he said, affecting an awful French accent, "the evening awaits you."

She presented a mock curtsy and said, *"Monsieur, avec grand plaisir!"*

He halted. "Unfair!"

"Why?"

"I don't know French."

"Then don't play those games with me."

He gave her a look that said, I want to play *some* games. She told him, "I said to you: 'With great pleasure.'"

He tried to avoid a lustful look, but he failed. "As Lady Roberts would observe: Child, do try to behave yourself."

"Why?"

He said, "Let's get to the garden."

She led the way to the door and was holding it open when Del Cummins came in from the the kitchen. He was wiping his mouth with his handkerchief. Sheepishly, he admitted, "Just finishing off some of that dessert."

Zack was propped against the door; Leah had moved down to the first step. Zack said, "We're going outside."

"I can see that."

"Want to join us?"

There was a barely audible whimper from Leah. Del responded, "I know when I'm not wanted."

"Smart man." Zack started to move out into the garden.

Del stopped him. "There's one thing I think we should talk about, Zack."

Zack suggested, "Surely it can wait until tomorrow, Del."

"I'm beginning to freeze," Leah said.

Del came to the door and said, "Leah, could you come back in? Just for a couple of minutes. I really do have to talk to Zack."

She complied.

Del looked awkwardly at Zack for a few moments, then blurted out, "I'm going to Wales."

"Oh?"

"Tomorrow," Del added.

"What's this all about, Del?"

"I've talked it over with your grandmother, I've made arrangements with Sir George, and Felicity is all for it."

"What are you talking about?"

Del hurried on, "The decision not to tell you was your grandmother's. She felt you were doing so well that you shouldn't be distracted."

"Dammit!" Zack snapped. "I'm being treated like a child!"

Leah cut in. "Zack, that's silly. I'd bet that your grandmother was just trying to make it easier for you."

Zack felt anger building. "For your information, Leah, I can handle more than one important thing at a time."

Leah snapped, "Don't you get brittle with me, Zack Horton."

Del ordered, "Both of you, quiet!"

They looked at him. There was a pause, then he said, "Actually, Zack, Leah is right; it was to keep from distracting you from this statehood thing."

Zack calmed. He asked, "Del, what's going on?"

"It's pretty simple: Sir George has asked me to take over managing his cattle operation in Wyoming. The trip to Wales

is just for me to get to know that side of Sir George's operation—and to meet some other British investors."

"But why you?" Zack asked.

"You both know about the Wyoming law against foreign
ownership." They nodded. "Well, Sir George and those other
British investors are taking me on so that their public image will
be better." Del continued, "Felicity and I are being given our
own operation; ten thousand acres with stock. That will become
sort of a holding company; I'll also become sort of an agent for
the other British ranch operations."

Zack began to laugh softly. "You devil, you've really
worked all of this out." He paused for a moment, then asked,
"What about our railroad?

"It looks like that will be yours to run."

Leah presented Del with a strong, emphatic hug as she said,
"Well, I don't know about Zack, but I am as happy as I can be
for you."

Zack grabbed Del's hand. "I am happy, too, Del. This is
great news. I guess I'll have to start learning about the Dakota
and Western hands on, now."

Del nodded. "You've learned a lot. You'll do fine."

"Hold it," Zack said. "That means I've got to go back with
you."

"I think so," Del agreed.

Zack looked at Leah. There went the plans of visiting her
in Baltimore while he stayed in the capital to help finish the
statehood matter; there went the plans that might have led to a
great many things.

The implications came just as quickly to Leah; both of
them were silent.

Del said, "I guess I'd better leave you two alone. You were
going to the garden, weren't you?"

They nodded.

Del moved away toward the parlor as he said, "We can talk
more later, Zack."

Zack gave another nod. With Del gone, Leah said, "That
kind of puts a damper on tonight, Zack."

Zack was recovering. "Not completely. Let's go on outside."

Leah was reaching for the doorknob when Lady Roberts appeared in the other doorway and said, "They sent me to get you two."

Zack and Leah looked at each other and burst out laughing; Lady Roberts, always ready to enjoy any situation, joined them, then asked, "Why are we laughing?"

Leah said, "It seems, Lady Roberts, that everyone is determined to see that we do not catch pneumonia."

Lady Roberts mulled over that reply. "Oh, my, you were going to the garden." Then she said, "I'll tell them I could not find you!"

Leah said, "No, that would make you an accomplice. We can't have that."

The trio went back into the parlor. Hill was now sitting on a sofa with Benjamin Harrison. Leah walked over to where Fred Dubois was talking with Joe Toole; she was close enough to hear what Hill said.

"Zack," Hill opened, "Mister Harrison wants you to give him some background on the Mormons in southern Idaho."

"Gladly."

The president-elect stood, extending his hand to Hill, who had also risen. Harrison then turned to Zack. "It won't take more than an hour or two. I want you to brief some of my people."

Zack protested, "I don't know all that much, Mister Harrison."

Hill interjected, "Zack, you know more than a lot of people; you've met one of their most important leaders."

Harrison explained, "It will do a great deal of good, Mister Horton."

That was when it dawned on Leah Page: Zack was leaving with Harrison. She hissed, "Damn!"

Lady Roberts heard her but only remarked, "Child, you do look upset."

"I guess I am."

Zack turned and walked to Leah. "Will I see you later?"

Her eyes were flaring; her anger was easy to see. After too long a time, she said, "Maybe . . . that is . . . if your wealth of knowledge isn't needed to . . ." She cut herself off and spun around, then, practically at a run, headed out through the dining room.

Lady Roberts said, "Zack, my dear Zack, you have some fence mending at hand."

Harrison called, "Let's go, Horton."

Zack looked at Lady Roberts, then at James Hill. In the end, he said, "Coming, sir."

On Friday, February 22, 1889, the Congress of the United States passed the Enabling Act that provided for statehood for North Dakota, South Dakota, Montana, and Washington. A similar act was passed the next year admitting Idaho and Wyoming to the Union.